A PLUME BOOK

THE WEDDING QUILT

Steven Garfinkel

JENNIFER CHIAVERINI is the author of the *New York Times* bestselling Elm Creek Quilts series, as well as five collections of quilt projects inspired by the novels. A graduate of the University of Notre Dame and the University of Chicago, she lives with her husband and sons in Madison, Wisconsin.

ALSO BY JENNIFER CHIAVERINI

The Union Quilters

The Aloha Quilt

A Quilter's Holiday

The Lost Quilter

The Quilter's Kitchen

The Winding Ways Quilt

The New Year's Quilt

The Quilter's Homecoming

Circle of Quilters

The Christmas Quilt

The Sugar Camp Quilt

The Master Quilter

The Quilter's Legacy

The Runaway Quilt

The Cross-Country Quilters

Round Robin

The Quilter's Apprentice

· *Elm Creek Quilts* ·

Quilt Projects Inspired by the Elm Creek Quilt Novels

· *Return to Elm Creek* ·

More Quilt Projects Inspired by the Elm Creek Quilt Novels

· *More Elm Creek Quilts* ·

Inspired by the Elm Creek Quilt Novels

· *Sylvia's Bridal Sampler from Elm Creek Quilts* ·

Traditions from Elm Creek Quilts

The Wedding Quilt

• AN ELM CREEK QUILTS NOVEL •

JENNIFER CHIAVERINI

A PLUME BOOK

PLUME
Published by the Penguin Group
Penguin Group (USA) Inc., 375 Hudson Street, New York, New York 10014, U.S.A. • Penguin Group (Canada), 90 Eglinton Avenue East, Suite 700, Toronto, Ontario, Canada M4P 2Y3 (a division of Pearson Penguin Canada Inc.) • Penguin Books Ltd., 80 Strand, London WC2R 0RL, England • Penguin Ireland, 25 St. Stephen's Green, Dublin 2, Ireland (a division of Penguin Books Ltd.) • Penguin Group (Australia), 250 Camberwell Road, Camberwell, Victoria 3124, Australia (a division of Pearson Australia Group Pty. Ltd.) • Penguin Books India Pvt. Ltd., 11 Community Centre, Panchsheel Park, New Delhi – 110 017, India • Penguin Group (NZ), 67 Apollo Drive, Rosedale, Auckland 0632, New Zealand (a division of Pearson New Zealand Ltd.) • Penguin Books (South Africa) (Pty.) Ltd., 24 Sturdee Avenue, Rosebank, Johannesburg 2196, South Africa

Penguin Books Ltd., Registered Offices: 80 Strand, London WC2R 0RL, England

Published by Plume, a member of Penguin Group (USA) Inc.
Previously published in a Dutton edition.

First Plume Printing, November 2012
3 5 7 9 10 8 6 4

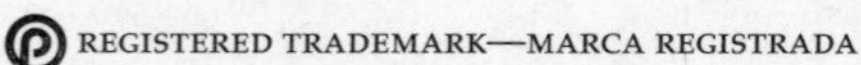

CIP data is available.

978-0-525-95242-8 (hc.)
978-0-452-29849-1 (pbk.)

Printed in the United States of America
Original hardcover design by Elke Sigal

PUBLISHER'S NOTE
This is a work of fiction. Names, characters, places, and incidents are either the product of the author's imagination or are used fictitiously, and any resemblance to actual persons, living or dead, business establishments, events, or locales is entirely coincidental.

In loving memory of my grandmother,
Virginia Kraemer Riechman

The Wedding Quilt

Mr. and Mrs. Matthew McClure

request the honor of your presence

at the marriage of their daughter

Caroline Sylvia

to

Leonardo Joseph Fiore

son of Mr. and Mrs. Anthony Fiore

Saturday, the twenty-third of September

Two thousand twenty-eight

At three o'clock in the afternoon

Elm Creek Manor

Waterford, Pennsylvania

· Chapter One ·

The tinkling of silverware on china and the murmur of conversation filled the elegant theater of Union Hall, where Sarah sat on the stage at the head table, discreetly reviewing her speech on the computer pad resting on her lap. More than one hundred members of the Waterford Historical Society and their guests had gathered to enjoy a delicious luncheon of cranberry-stuffed chicken breast, sautéed green and wax beans, and whipped butternut squash to celebrate the dedication of the Agnes Bergstrom Emberly Quilt Gallery. The food smelled wonderful, but Sarah had taken only a few bites. She had been invited to deliver the keynote address for the event, and even though she had given hundreds of speeches and lectures throughout her career as an Elm Creek Quilter, her appetite still fled before each and every engagement.

"You should eat something," said James quietly, seated at her right. He smiled encouragingly, and she had to smile back. He was such a handsome young man. He'd had his hair cut earlier that day in preparation for the wedding, his reddish-brown locks trimmed so short that they nearly stood straight up. Out of respect for the occasion he wore a blazer over his plain white T-shirt, which hugged his slender but muscular frame, and his indigo blue jeans were rolled into wide cuffs at the ankle. He and his friends seemed to believe they had invented the style and met their elders' comparisons to the fashions of the 1950s with bemused, indulgent silence.

"I'll ask them to wrap mine to go," said Sarah. "Maybe I can nibble some dessert while I'm signing books."

"I wouldn't count on it. I doubt you'll have time to set down your pen."

Considering the number of guests in attendance, she had to admit he had a point. She let her gaze travel from table to table, and occasionally someone looked up to the stage, caught her eye, and smiled. Tickets for the event had sold out within a week, delighting the president of the Waterford Historical Society, and the booksellers were doing a brisk business at the table between the theater doors. From the moment Sarah had arrived, people had been coming up to introduce themselves, sometimes sharing their memories of Agnes or of Elm Creek Quilt Camp, sometimes thanking her profusely for acquiring so many invaluable, irreplaceable quilts for the society's collection, now proudly on display in the upstairs gallery named for her old friend. So why, even though she knew her audience was friendly and receptive, did Sarah feel so nervous?

"You'll be fine once you get started," James reassured her, reading her mind. "You always are. But you'll feel better if you have something to eat."

"Yes, sir," she told him wanly, picking up her fork and sampling the roast chicken. The cranberry stuffing gave it a savory, tangy flavor, and under different circumstances she would have cleaned the plate and requested the recipe for Anna Del Maso, the chef at Elm Creek Manor. She took another bite and glanced down the table just in time to see the president of the Waterford Historical Society check her watch and push back her chair. It was time. Her mouth suddenly dry, Sarah washed down the chicken with a gulp of water. James touched her on the back as he rose and went to confer briefly with the president. Conversation faded as he took the podium—without a pad or notes of any kind, Sarah noted with rueful admiration—and adjusted the microphone.

"Good afternoon," he greeted them, his voice confident and cheerful. "Thank you for joining us today as we dedicate Union Hall's newest permanent exhibit, the Agnes Bergstrom Emberly Quilt Gallery." A smattering of applause went up from his listeners. "Some of you had the pleasure of knowing Agnes during her many years as an active member of the Waterford Historical Society, including a two-year stint as president, a post she assumed soon after she launched the campaign to save this very building. Although Mrs. Emberly was not born in the Elm Creek Valley, as a longtime resident, she cared deeply about the history of our community and was equally passionate about preserving and documenting historically significant but long-forgotten quilts discovered in storage rooms, attics, and boxes underneath beds. It was she who founded the Waterford Historical Society's extensive collection of quilts, a mission that she passed on to our keynote speaker." He spared a proud smile for Sarah. "Although I was just a kid when I knew Mrs. Emberly, I know she would be very pleased with how the collection has grown under Sarah McClure's stewardship."

Sarah felt herself flush with pride as applause rang out again, but then her heart thumped and she checked her pad to be sure she had not accidentally deleted her speech.

"I'm sure Sarah McClure is well-known to all of you as the president and founder of Elm Creek Quilts," James continued, "the world's most respected and renowned quilters' retreat. There she introduced countless thousands of aspiring quilters to the art, and inspired innumerable experienced quilters to more fully develop their creative gifts. Her contributions to the study of quilts and other textiles, including her three-volume series on the history of quilting from the medieval era through the early twenty-first century, have rightly earned her awards and accolades. Her latest book, *The Quilts of Pennsylvania*, is the most thoroughly researched and detailed state quilt documentation project ever undertaken, ten years in the making and well worth the wait. And I'm not saying that just because my name appears in the acknowledgments."

A ripple of laughter went up from the audience.

"This afternoon our speaker will tell you more about Agnes Bergstrom Emberly, whom she was proud to call a friend and colleague, and in whose memory the Waterford Historical Society has dedicated their newly refurbished east gallery. When, afterward, you view this magnificent collection of antique quilts, displayed for the first time in its entirety, I hope you'll keep in mind that the collection would not exist if not for the foresight of Mrs. Emberly and the wisdom, tenacity, and generosity of our speaker. Ladies and gentlemen, it is my great privilege to introduce to you my mother, Sarah Mallory McClure."

Sarah smiled as she rose and took the podium to thunderous applause.

"You paused after saying 'my mother' for dramatic effect," she teased James afterward, as they strolled through the gallery admiring the collection. "You always do."

"I had to," said James, feigning innocence. "But not for dramatic effect. Their reaction would have drowned out your name. One hundred sixty people simultaneously saying 'Awww' can get kind of loud."

"One hundred sixty?"

James nodded. "I counted."

"You always remember." No wonder her hand was sore. She had signed books for nearly an hour after her speech, about half of them pen upon paper, the other half stylus to pad. A traditionalist where books were concerned, she preferred the look and smell and feel of paper, but she appreciated the convenience and frugality of electronic books, as well as the ability to enlarge the quilt photos so that every exquisite detail could be seen and admired.

Sarah paused in front of one of her favorite quilts, an Album quilt fashioned from green, Prussian blue, and Turkey red calicoes, the muslin center of each block signed by authors and politicians from the mid-nineteenth century. The ink had faded away long ago and, in some places, had deteriorated the muslin fabric, but the black embroidery over each signature remained. From her research for *The Quilts of Pennsylvania,* Sarah knew that in 1860, local women had sewn and raffled off the quilt to raise money to build the first library in the Elm Creek

Valley, and that it had been displayed on the wall behind the circulation desk until the 1950s, when a new, larger, modern library was built a few blocks away. The quilt had been one of the first Agnes had acquired for the collection, a gift from University Realty, a local real estate rental and development company that had somehow obtained it when the original library was razed. At the time, Agnes and Sarah had privately agreed that the new CEO had donated the quilt not out of any particular love for quilts or local history, but to atone for the irresponsible behavior of their most notorious associate. "However they acquired it, and whatever public relations benefits they may gain from the donation, what matters most is that the quilt now belongs to the Waterford Historical Society," Agnes had declared as she prepared the quilt for preservation. "We'll care for it properly and ensure that it will be here to educate and inspire for many years to come."

The Waterford Historical Society had kept their promise, and Sarah had helped. Her first book, published by the Pennsylvania State University Press, was a study of the Authors' Album and included detailed biographies of each person who had signed the quilt, some of whom had long since slipped into obscurity. It was required reading for all eighth graders in the Elm Creek Valley School District, and teachers often brought their classes on field trips to Union Hall to see the quilt. Now students, teachers, parents, and citizens alike would be able to view the historic treasure at any time of year without needing to make arrangements for the quilt to be retrieved from protective storage.

Since then, Album quilts had held a particular fascination for Sarah. "I'm planning an Album quilt for your sister," she confided to James as they strolled on. "I've already pieced dozens of Memory Album blocks, and at the reception, I'll collect signatures from the guests."

"That's a great idea," said James, stopping short in front of another quilt. "But don't you think Caroline would prefer something like this instead?"

Sarah looked to see which quilt he meant and had to laugh. The quilt James indicated was another of her favorites, but it was very different from the Authors' Album. The intricate designs of the sixteen large blocks always reminded Sarah of the traditional Baltimore Album quilts popular in the first half of the nineteenth century, with appliquéd pieces creating still-life portraits in fabric—a basket of garden vegetables, a red banked barn, a farmhouse, a school, a ring of maple leaves and seeds, a wooden bucket half encircled by flowers, branches of elm leaves framing four lines of embroidered words, a book, and other tableaus. The most unusual block depicted what looked to be a large black kettle hanging above an open fire from a pole suspended between two bare-limbed trees. But whereas most Baltimore Albums offered flat, stylized images of elegant subjects—floral bouquets, nesting birds, wreaths, beribboned baskets, urns of greenery—this quilt depicted more ordinary, homey things, and the buildings, especially, used perspective to create more realistic portraits of daily life in the Elm Creek Valley.

"It's a beautiful quilt," Sarah said, tucking her hand into the crook of her son's arm as they walked on, "but it's not Caroline's style, and you know it. It's far too fancy and flowery for her taste."

"And you'd never be able to finish something like this in time."

"That too," Sarah confessed with a smile. "But the Memory Album quilt will be a perfect wedding quilt, don't you think? Their friends and family will write personal messages to the bride and groom, and when the blocks are sewn together and the quilt is complete, it'll be a wonderful memento of their wedding day."

"I couldn't agree more," James hastened to assure her. "I was just teasing about the Creek's Crossing Album. It's a masterpiece, but it doesn't suit Caroline and Leo."

"In a way it does," Sarah mused. "It was a wedding gift. In the days when this quilt was made, in the mid-nineteenth century, girls would learn to sew by piecing quilts as a part of their domestic training. In this region, a properly brought up young woman was expected to complete twelve quilt tops by the time she reached marriageable age. The thirteenth quilt was meant to be her masterpiece, a beautiful, tangible sign that she had learned all the womanly arts of needlework she would need as a wife and mother. When the young woman became engaged, all the bride-to-be's female friends and family would gather for a quilting bee, where the thirteen pieced and appliquéd tops would be quilted and everyone would celebrate the engagement."

"I remember," said James. "I read about the custom in Gerda Bergstrom's memoir. But this quilt top was made by one woman and given to another, so it didn't follow tradition perfectly."

"That's true." Thinking of that lucky bride from long ago made her yearn to see the bride-to-be she loved and missed dearly. "Do you think we can duck out of here discreetly? I want to be home to welcome Caroline and Leo when they arrive."

"It's not like they'll be showing up at an empty house. Dad and Grandma will be there, not to mention at least a few Elm Creek Quilters."

"I know, but I want to be there too."

James admitted that he didn't want to miss his twin sister's homecoming, either, but he suggested that rather than sneak away, they bid the president of the historical society a proper good-bye and explain that they were needed at home.

Soon they were on their way, James at the wheel of the Elm Creek Quilts shuttle, which hummed along almost noiselessly as they traveled south along the highway from downtown Waterford. After a time, James turned onto the narrow private road that wound through the leafy wood encircling the Bergstrom estate, and Sarah was struck by a sudden memory of the first time she had taken that route, riding along in Matt's red pickup truck as he tried to find the home of the reclusive woman who had hired him to restore the overgrown gardens. She remembered clutching her seat as the truck bounded jerkily up a gradual incline rife with potholes, hoping fervently that no one was approaching them from the opposite direction. She had doubted that both cars could stay on the narrow road without one of them scraping a side on a tree. Suddenly the leafy wood had given way to a clearing, and the road, which had become little more than two dirt trails an axle's width apart surrounded by overgrown grass, had climbed and curved around a two-story red barn built into the side of a hill. Just beyond the barn, the path crossed a low bridge over a burbling creek and then widened into a gravel road lined with towering elms. Then the manor came into view at last, and Sarah, who had been expecting a quaint cottage, could only stare in heartfelt admiration.

The road through the forest was paved now, and wide enough for two vehicles to pass each other safely at low, cautious speeds. Matt's sunlit apple orchard filled the once grassy clearing, but the manor still captivated Sarah whenever it came into view—three stories of gray stone and dark wood, its unexpected elegance enhanced by the rambling, natural beauty of its surroundings. Most important of all, it was home.

James parked in front of the solar charging station and plugged in the car. "Looks like Anna and Gina aren't back yet," he said, noting the absence of the other shuttle as they climbed the four stone stairs to the back door.

"Anna said they were going all the way to her favorite specialty market in Harrisburg." There, Sarah suspected, Anna and her daughter, Gina, had probably spent far more than they should have on delicacies for the wedding week. Soon after Caroline and Leo had announced their engagement, Anna and Gina had offered to cater the entire celebration as their family's gift to the bride and groom. At first Caroline had reluctantly demurred, since Gina was also the maid of honor and Caroline didn't want to burden her with too many responsibilities, but she couldn't withstand the combined persuasive power of the two Del Maso–Bernstein women. And thank goodness for that. Sarah couldn't imagine anyone else doing the job half as well—or with a quarter of the care and affection—as Gina and Anna would. Anna was Sarah's best friend, and their daughters, who were two years apart in age but had grown up together in the manor, were as close as sisters.

Together they went upstairs to the library, where Sarah put away her pad and James checked his personal messages and then those for Elm Creek Quilts. A breeze fragrant with ripe apples stirred the long cotton curtains hanging in the west windows, and Sarah jumped at the sound of wheels crunching fallen autumn leaves on the road they had just traveled. "At last," she cried, hurrying to the window and drawing back the curtain, but instead of Caroline and Leo's car, she spied the other Elm Creek Quilts shuttle. After it came to a halt in its usual place at the charging unit, Anna emerged from the driver's side and plugged it in, her long gray French braid slipping over her shoulder as she chatted merrily with her daughter. Then Gina appeared, climbing out the side door and reaching back inside to fill her arms with grocery bags, laughing at something her mother said. Gina's black, close-cropped curls were as dark as Anna's had once been, but she was petite and slender, whereas Anna was taller and had always carried a few more pounds than she preferred. Sarah was about to suggest that she and James hurry outside to help Anna and Gina when she heard the back door squeak open and bang shut. It was Jeremy, calling out a greeting to his wife and daughter as he descended the back stairs. The three made short work of distributing the bags among themselves, and within moments they had brought everything inside, the back door banging shut again behind them.

When Sarah sighed and let the curtains fall back into place, James joined her at the window, wrapped Sarah in a hug, and rested his chin on the top of her head. "Poor Mom, waiting by the window for her baby. You know Caroline wasn't planning to get here until suppertime."

"I know that's what she said, but I thought maybe they were able to set out earlier."

"I'd bet money that Caroline stayed at her desk studying until the last possible moment before they had to leave."

"She could study on the way, if Leo's driving." Sarah wondered if she should encourage Caroline to leave her pad at the manor instead of taking it on her honeymoon, but Caroline had been reading for twenty-two of her twenty-five years, and she wasn't likely to be parted from her beloved books now. That's all the twins were, twenty-five years old. Sarah recalled feeling quite mature and adult at that age, but from her new perspective, twenty-five seemed shockingly young to make a lifetime commitment. If only Caroline would have taken Sarah's advice and—

Sarah inhaled deeply and forced her misgivings out in the exhaled breath. Leo was a wonderful young man, and he and Caroline were very much in love. They were both reasonable, responsible young people, and Sarah had to trust that they knew what they were doing—and if not, that they would accept the consequences with maturity and grace.

Sarah didn't want Caroline to wait forever to marry, just until she finished medical school. Just until she had her degree and a job and a bit more security. But Caroline had pointed out that Leo had recently earned tenure at the elementary school where he taught second grade, and they could live very comfortably on his salary while Caroline finished school. "It's not like the days of yore when you were young, Mom, when teachers weren't respected and well paid," Caroline had said, a pleading tone in her voice. She wanted Sarah to be happy for her, to accept her choices wholeheartedly, and Sarah, remembering all too well how her mother had objected to her marriage to Matt, couldn't bear to voice objections that could be misinterpreted as dislike or disapproval. On the contrary, Sarah thought Leo was a wonderful young man, but he would be just as wonderful in a few years, after Caroline graduated from medical school, completed her residency, and had a job, an income of her own, and her independence. So what was the rush? And if Caroline was in such a hurry to marry, why hadn't she come home to Elm Creek Manor yet, so the week of preparations and festivities could begin?

"I know you miss her, Mom, but don't be sad," said James, giving her one last quick hug before letting her go, although she gladly would have held him longer. "Someday Leo might get an offer from a school in the Elm Creek Valley, and Caroline might set up her practice here in Waterford."

Sarah regarded him levelly. "You know, it's scary sometimes how easily you read my mind."

"It comes from working side by side so many years," James teased. "I know all of your quirks, all of your secrets."

Sarah's shudder was not entirely feigned. "I hope not all of them."

James merely laughed, and then he announced that he was going to help put away groceries and hurried off to the kitchen. Never before had a young man been so eager to help unpack grocery bags, Sarah thought wryly. James and Gina thought they had everyone fooled, but Sarah and Anna knew their friendship had recently developed into something more. How recently and how much more, they could only speculate, and as their hopes rose, they privately congratulated each other on their children's excellent judgment.

She reached for the curtain but, at the last second, resisted the temptation to peer out the window again and adjusted the tieback instead. Soon friends and relatives from near and far would descend upon the manor—cousins and classmates, in-laws-to-be and strangers-to-be no more, former Elm Creek Quilters, cherished friends—but it sometimes seemed to Sarah that if she closed her eyes and wished hard enough, she could climb the stairs to the nursery and find the twins sleeping in the crib, snuggled beneath the quilts Grandma Carol had sewn for them.

Twenty-five years had come and gone with a swiftness that might have been cruel except for the sweet, beloved memories of the days that had filled them.

They had been winter babies, longed for and cherished even before they were born. After Sarah got over the shock of discovering she was carrying twins, the pregnancy had proceeded uneventfully. She followed a healthful diet and exercise plan, the babies reached all of their prenatal benchmarks on schedule, and her friends were always nearby to reassure her when she worried or to help her relax when she became stressed. She planned her maternity leave with what only years later she realized was astonishingly naïve optimism. Though there were good days and bad, her pregnancy went along as well as she could have hoped—until that day in late November when Matt threw all her carefully wrought plans into disarray.

It was the Friday after Thanksgiving, a day Sarah and her friends always set aside as their very own annual quilter's holiday. While others throughout their rural central Pennsylvania valley were sleeping in or embarking upon the Christmas shopping season, the Elm Creek Quilters always gathered at the manor for a marathon of quilting to work on holiday gifts for loved ones or decorations for their homes. One might have expected Sarah to stitch quilts for her unborn twins, but she left that project to her mother while she sewed Twin Star Log Cabin blocks into a quilt for her father-in-law, Hank. Although he had often declared that he had no interest whatsoever in quilting, she hoped that if he had a quilt of his own, he might develop a greater appreciation for the creative and artistic work that Elm Creek Quilts fostered. If he did, he might stop pressuring Matt to quit his caretaking job and come to work for Hank's construction company. Later, Sylvia Bergstrom Compson Cooper—master quilter, Elm Creek Quilts founder, heart and soul of their circle of friends—remarked that it had been unfair to expect one quilt, however beautifully and lovingly made, to accomplish so much, but that was a lesson Sarah had yet to learn.

In the company of her friends, Sarah spent the snowy morning working on Hank's gift. At noon she and her friends set their quilts aside and gathered in the banquet hall for a potluck lunch of dishes made with leftovers from their family feasts the previous day. That year, in keeping with the season's spirit of gratitude, Sylvia had also revived a cherished Bergstrom family tradition. While remodeling the manor's kitchen earlier that autumn, she and Anna had discovered a long-forgotten cornucopia that had once served as the centerpiece of the Bergstrom family's Thanksgiving table. Into it, each member of the family, from the eldest patriarch to the youngest granddaughter, had placed an object that symbolized something he or she was especially thankful for that year. After the feast, each had drawn their item from the cornucopia and had explained what it signified. On that quilter's holiday, Sylvia had invited the Elm Creek Quilters to continue the tradition by sewing quilt blocks that represented their thankfulness and gratitude. Not to be left out despite their inexperience with needle and thread, the husbands in attendance found squares of fabric in the classroom scrap bag and contributed those to the cornucopia instead.

Even as they had climbed out of bed that morning, something in Matt's manner, something Sarah could not define, had warned her that something weighed heavily upon his thoughts. Even so, she completely missed his discomfort and embarrassment at lunchtime when she explained to one and all that the Twin Star block she had placed into the cornucopia represented her gratitude for her unborn children, and also for Matt, who had been by her side faithfully every day of her pregnancy, offering support and encouragement. The square of fabric he had placed into the cornucopia would have offered another sign, had she known to watch for signs. As the square cut from a landscape print of green trees on rolling hills was passed around the table, Matt explained that he was most thankful for his family. "I'm thankful for their support, their loyalty, their understanding, and most of all, their love," he said. "I owe my family everything, and it's a debt I doubt I'll ever be able to repay in full, but that doesn't mean I won't try."

His talk of debts and repayment puzzled her for a moment, but she quickly forgot it in the happiness of the quilter's holiday. Her joy was to be short-lived. As they cleared away the dishes, Matt took her aside and explained that his father had again pleaded with him to take over the construction company while he recovered from a flare-up of an old back injury. Hank couldn't afford to turn down jobs during such poor economic times, nor could he manage without someone he trusted on-site supervising the work. Sarah was surprised and hurt to discover that Matt had already agreed to go, without first discussing it with her, though it meant he would be a three-hour drive away for most of the winter, though it meant she would spend the rest of her pregnancy without him. But what could she do? Although he should have consulted with her before making any promises to his father, she knew he had weighed his decision carefully. If she asked him not to go, he would probably stay, but he would blame her if his father's business failed—and she didn't want to disappoint him.

So she consented, but not without exacting from Matt a solemn promise that regardless of any other consideration, he would not miss the birth of his children. She also warned him that if Hank decided he couldn't manage without Matt after the twins arrived, and if Matt agreed to stay on rather than allow his father's company to fail, she would not leave Elm Creek Manor to go with him.

They were at an impasse, and they knew it, and their inability to promise each other what they most wanted to hear left them bereft and unhappy.

Matt packed a bag and left on the Monday morning after Thanksgiving, promising to return late Friday afternoon. Restless, Sarah spent their first day apart in the library designing brochures for the next season of quilt camp and in the ballroom layering and basting Hank's quilt top. On Wednesday she attended her weekly childbirth class with Gretchen Hartley, who, before accepting a teaching position with Elm Creek Quilts and moving into the manor, had spent many years volunteering at a shelter for homeless pregnant girls in Pittsburgh and had assisted so many of them through labor that she probably could have moonlighted as a midwife. Matt phoned every evening, but Sarah was not really interested in his perfunctory reports about hanging drywall and scheduling inspections, nor did he seem particularly enthralled by her accounts of the babies' kicks and her weight gain. They were both tired and preoccupied, and Sarah's surging hormones occasionally sent her careering off on mood swings that Matt, understandably, found difficult to handle. She told herself that everything would be fine between them again when he came home for good.

On Friday evening, she was so relieved to hear his pickup truck pull into the back parking lot that she nearly ran down the stairs to greet him. He greeted her at the back door with a hug and a kiss, and then he dropped to his knees and pressed his cheek against her ample belly to tell the babies how much he had missed them. On Saturday she had hoped he would help her paint the babies' room, but he was so exhausted from the week on the construction site that after attending to his caretaker's duties around the estate, all he wanted to do was relax, and she felt guilty asking him to do anything more. On Sunday he packed his duffel bag again, and on Monday morning he left. The next week wasn't as bad as the first, as she grew accustomed to his absence, but she missed him with a hollow, aching loneliness that compelled her to count and recount the days until her due date when he would come home for good.

The Christmas season rekindled some of her joy. Matt agreed to take off work from Christmas Eve through New Year's Day, and she felt relieved and happy to have her husband close again, even though Hank spent the holidays with them also and all too frequently sat Matt down in the kitchen with cups of coffee and blueprints. Fortunately, Gretchen's husband, Joe, was a woodworker, and he kept Hank happily distracted in his wood shop from time to time, leaving Sarah and Matt to themselves. While Sylvia and Gretchen decked the halls and Anna prepared apple strudel and other delicious Christmas treats her friends loved, Sarah and Matt prepared the nursery. While they worked, they talked and laughed, dreamed and planned, and it was almost as if the conflict that had begun on the quilter's holiday had never happened.

Almost, but not quite. Hank's lukewarm response to the beautiful quilt to which she had devoted so much time, effort, and creativity disappointed her. "Well, isn't this a nice blanket," he said after unwrapping the gift. "It looks as nice as anything you could buy in a store." Less insulting but more annoying were his frequent reminders that he and Matt needed to depart before dawn on January 2. All week Sarah forced smiles to mask her irritation and offered cordial replies rather than spoil the holidays with complaints, but she reached her limit by New Year's Day, and she wished they had never invited Hank to join them for the holidays.

The next morning, Matt and his father threw their bags into the back of Matt's pickup and left soon after sunrise. After a week of Matt's company, Sarah felt the loneliness of his renewed absence as keenly as she had upon his first departure in November.

Winter was supposed to herald a seasonal slowdown in the construction business, but for McClure Construction, January seemed to be as busy as ever. Twice Matt had so much work that he couldn't afford to take the weekend off, and once a dangerous winter storm prevented him from making the trip home. Sarah comforted herself with the knowledge that the babies were healthy and that in a matter of weeks, they would be born and Matt would come home to stay, as he had promised. She didn't know what that might mean for McClure Construction, and she couldn't help worrying that in the end, despite Hank's assurances that he understood Matt couldn't work for him indefinitely, he might try to persuade his son to stay on.

"Matt wants to be with you and the children," Sylvia reminded her whenever her worries became too great a burden to bear alone. "He knows his most important duty is to care for you and those babies. Surely Hank will respect that and not ask him to spend so much time away from home. He can hire a foreman if he can't do the work himself. As fine a worker as Matt is, he isn't absolutely essential to his father's company, but he is essential to his wife and children."

But Sylvia frowned, and her gaze over the rims of her bifocals was steely, as if she were already composing the lecture she would deliver to both men if they failed to follow the obviously correct and proper course.

February arrived, cold and silver gray. As her due date approached, Sarah found herself ending every phone conversation with Matt with a pleading reminder that he needed to tie up any loose ends and prepare to return home at a moment's notice. Joe had finished baby-proofing the manor, the nursery was snug and cozy, and Sarah's overnight bag was packed and waiting in the closet by the back door. All she needed was her husband.

Her due date, February 3, came on a Monday. Early that morning she followed Matt out the back door of the manor, the brisk wind chilling her to the bone since she could no longer close her winter coat around herself. "Please don't go," she asked him, shivering and tucking her hands under her arms for warmth.

Matt tossed his duffel bag onto the front passenger seat, hesitated, and studied her. "Are you feeling any contractions?"

She was tempted to lie, but she couldn't do it. "Not yet."

"Then you know I can't stay, not when my dad's expecting me." He took her in his arms and kissed her on the cheek. "I promise, when the babies are really on the way, I'll be here."

She couldn't speak. Pressing her lips together, she waddled back to the manor without so much as a wave in farewell. The day passed with miserable slowness, although Gretchen, Sylvia, and Anna tried to distract her with books and quilting. That evening, Matt called to see if she had gone into labor yet, and in a surge of hormone-fueled distress, she burst into tears and yelled at him when he remarked that his father had been right after all; due dates were apparently mere estimates and it hadn't been necessary for Matt to stay home as Sarah had insisted. "If you're planning to wait until my water breaks and I'm eight centimeters dilated before you get in the truck, don't bother coming at all," she cried before slamming down the phone. She sobbed on Sylvia's shoulder for nearly an hour afterward, while her friends patted her back and alternately soothed her and reproved Matt in absentia. Their words were little consolation. Why wouldn't her husband come home when she wanted him so desperately?

"He wants to get as much work done there as possible before the babies arrive, because he isn't planning to go back," Anna surmised. "You should take that as a good sign. I'd be more concerned if he left unfinished business behind."

Sarah thought Anna made good sense, so she dried her eyes and accepted the cup of herbal decaf organic tea her friend had brewed for her. She knew she ought to try harder to see the situation from Matt's perspective. He didn't want to let his father down, and he knew Sarah was surrounded by devoted, caring friends. Maybe he didn't realize how much she needed him. Maybe he didn't understand that she was worried and anxious, and that the distance between them left her feeling bereft and alone even among her dearest friends.

Two nights later Sarah felt her first real contractions, and the long months of anticipation and excitement seemed suddenly to have flown by. She felt hopelessly ill prepared, despite the volumes of books she had studied, the classes she had taken, and the long conversations with Gretchen, who had proven to be an inexhaustible source of reassurance, patience, and wisdom. There was no turning back now. Ready or not, she was going to become a mother.

But she knew it could be hours or even days yet. Knowing Matt would already be asleep, she texted him with the news and asked him to set out for home as soon as he woke up. She would try to sleep, and she'd update him on the progress of her contractions in the morning.

After a restless night, she woke before dawn to strong contractions and the sensation that her bladder was about to burst. Huffing and puffing, she carefully climbed out of bed and tried to soothe away her worries with the thought that soon she wouldn't be pregnant anymore. She certainly wouldn't miss the waddle she had acquired or the frequent trips to the bathroom. She longed for a cup of real coffee, and she intended to celebrate her first day of motherhood with a piece of decadent dark chocolate and a glass of red wine.

Making her way back to bed, she groped on the nightstand for her cell phone. It was only five o'clock, and Matt had not returned her text. Sighing, she climbed back under the covers and tried to drift off to sleep, but found herself blinking up at the ceiling, watching the pattern of shadows shift with the approach of dawn and mentally rehearsing the ordeal to come. At six o'clock, she decided to time her contractions. First they were ten minutes apart, then nine, then—eleven? She must have counted wrong. She tried again, using the stopwatch feature on her phone. Eleven minutes. She set down the phone and flung an arm over her eyes, frustrated. Her contractions were slowing down? Her due date had come and gone, and now her labor was going in reverse? Well, she wouldn't tell Matt, whenever he finally got around to answering her text. He'd use that as an excuse to tile one more floor or install one more light fixture instead of coming home where he belonged.

Her cell phone buzzed. She snatched it up and read Matt's text: "Hope it doesn't hurt too much. How far apart now? Thought I'd leave after lunch if ok."

"Not ok," she immediately texted back. "Come home now."

She waited, but he didn't respond.

If Matt were awake to text her, he was awake enough to talk, so she called him. The phone rang and rang and eventually went to voice mail. He was probably already in the truck driving, with his phone inaccessible in the back pocket of his jeans. "Hi, it's me," she said after the voice mail tone. "I hope you're on your way home. Please call me as soon as you get this. I love you."

Fuming and worried, she lay down again and timed a few more contractions. Eleven minutes. Dr. Jamison had advised her not to go to the hospital until they were seven minutes apart, unless her water broke. She didn't want to report to the hospital only to be sent home again. She could imagine Hank's reaction if he thought Sarah had panicked and summoned Matt home for a false alarm.

Carefully, gritting her teeth whenever a contraction seized her, she showered and dressed, then made her way downstairs to the kitchen. Sylvia and Andrew were seated at one of the cozy booths sipping coffee and sharing a plate of buttered toast, while Joe sat at the old wooden table with the newspaper spread out before him, an empty bowl and spoon at his elbow, his weathered, calloused hands cupped around a steaming mug. Although she didn't see any bacon, she caught a faint whiff of it in the air, and the odor nauseated her as it hadn't since her first trimester. Holding her breath, she paused in the doorway and clung to the frame as she waited out a contraction.

Gretchen glanced up from the eight-burner gas stove and smiled just as Sarah's discomfort passed. "Good morning, sunshine. Are you hungry? I could make more oatmeal."

"That sounds wonderful, thanks." She ought to eat something, since she wouldn't be permitted anything but ice chips once labor really set in. She returned Sylvia and Andrew's greetings with a pained smile and eased herself into the adjacent booth.

"Whatever you do, don't go into labor today," Joe remarked cheerfully, turning the page and folding the local news section. "According to the paper, we're supposed to get ten inches of snow by evening."

"Oh, yes, I saw the weather radar online." Gretchen shook her head as she filled a measuring cup with oats and stirred them into a saucepan of boiling water. "A huge mass of white and blue is covering eastern Ohio and the entire western part of Pennsylvania, and it's heading our way."

"Are you kidding me?" Sarah exclaimed. They had to be. She had not hidden her contraction in the doorway as well as she had thought, and they were teasing her. "Please tell me you're kidding."

All eyes went to her face. "Oh, dear," said Sylvia. "Are you having contractions?"

"A few," said Sarah weakly. "It's probably nothing. Maybe they'll go away."

"You should call Matt," said Andrew.

"You should call your mother," said Sylvia, at almost the same time.

"I called Matt already, but I just got his voice mail." Sarah shifted in her seat to retrieve her phone from the pocket of her hooded sweatshirt. "It's only seven. Maybe I should wait to call my mom. I wouldn't want to wake her."

"Call her," Sylvia and Gretchen said in unison. Gretchen added, "She's probably awake already, and she'll want to set out right away to beat the storm."

"As Matt should," said Andrew, frowning. Though he usually kept his opinions to himself, especially when they were unfavorable, he hadn't been very successful at concealing his disapproval of Matt's recent choices. He appreciated filial loyalty as much as the next man, but he thought it irresponsible of Matt to leave Sarah during her pregnancy, since it wasn't absolutely necessary. "It's not like he's in the service or something," Sarah had overhead him tell Sylvia. He thought even less of Hank.

Another contraction seized Sarah as she dialed her mother's number, and she saw Sylvia and Gretchen exchange a knowing look. Her mother answered on the second ring. At

Sarah's news, she let out a gasp of delight and assured Sarah she would be there in an hour. "Is it snowing there yet?" Sarah asked, afraid to hear the answer.

"A few flurries for now, but I heard on the radio that a bad storm is on the way." Carol sounded breathless, and Sarah imagined her pinning the handset to her ear with her shoulder as she pulled on her heavy winter boots. If only Matt felt the need for such haste. "It'll be all right. The snow tires are on the car and I packed enough clothing for two weeks in case I get snowbound at the manor."

Despite her worries, Sarah felt somewhat relieved, and she told her mother she'd see her soon. While Matt was two hours farther west than her mother, the weather couldn't be too bad in Uniontown yet if only a few flakes were falling at her mother's house. If Matt left soon, he should arrive in plenty of time. All the books said first-time mothers had longer labors anyway. Everything would be fine. Everything would almost certainly be fine.

She dialed Matt's number, but again the call went to voice mail. Her annoyance rising, she left another, more urgent message warning him about the approaching storm and begging him to call her as soon as he could. "He's probably on his way," she told her friends as she hung up the phone, then she gasped as the strongest contraction yet seized her.

"Nine minutes," said Gretchen, setting a steaming bowl of oatmeal on the table before her.

Sarah had not noticed that Gretchen was timing her contractions. "I think if I just sit here and have a little breakfast, they might slow down."

Andrew's brow furrowed. "I don't think that's how it works."

Gretchen seated herself in the booth opposite Sarah and patted her hand. "Why don't you eat since you're hungry, and afterward we'll see where we are?"

Sarah nodded and picked up her spoon, but her mouth was dry. Matt was surely on his way, and that's why he couldn't answer the phone. All that really mattered was that he arrived before the twins did. That's what she told herself, but she couldn't help thinking that if he had come home on her due date as she had asked, he could have spared her this unnecessary worry.

She managed to finish some of her breakfast, and afterward, she gathered her iPod, already loaded with her favorite relaxing music, a small bag of handwork in case she felt up to quilting, and a novel she had received for Christmas and had saved for the occasion. She packed everything into a tote bag and rejoined her friends, who had evidently been discussing her circumstances as they tidied the kitchen.

Sylvia spoke first. "Gretchen thought that perhaps, since you're carrying twins, the nurses might bend their rules and admit you early."

"Especially with the storm coming," said Andrew. He glanced out the window, and Sarah instinctively looked too. Her heart sank when she spied a flurry of white flakes whirling in the wind. "It wouldn't hurt to be prudent."

"By the time we get there, they might not need to bend the rules to admit me," Sarah managed to say, dropping her tote bag on the old wooden table and holding on to the edge for support. This wasn't how she had imagined this day. She had envisioned holding Matt's hand as they drove to the hospital, resting on the sofa in the birthing suite as Matt unpacked their bags, lying in bed as he stroked her forehead and murmured loving words of encouragement. But she refused to spoil the most important day of her life with disappointment. "You're right. We should go. The worst they can do is send me home."

There was a mad scramble as her friends gathered up her belongings, checked and double-checked to make sure they hadn't forgotten anything, and helped her out to the Elm Creek Quilts minivan. Andrew loaded her suitcase in the back, where a matching pair of infant car seats waited, still swathed in plastic. Matt was supposed to have installed them already, but Sarah supposed it was just as well, since the infant seats would have left no room for the white-haired crowd piling into the minivan. "Everyone's coming?" she asked as she buckled herself into the front passenger seat.

"You'd ask us to stay home and miss all the excitement?" protested Andrew. Sarah must have looked alarmed, for he quickly added, "Don't worry. We'll stay in the waiting room unless you invite us in. We just don't want to be snowed in here and unable to come if you need us."

Nodding, Sarah gritted her teeth through a contraction before she remembered to breathe. As Joe steered the minivan out of the parking lot and over the bridge, she involuntarily imagined Matt stuck in a snowdrift on the shoulder of the interstate, unable to reach her. She shook her head to clear it. No, no, he was an excellent driver and the heavy four-wheel-drive pickup handled slippery roads well. With any luck, he was already a quarter of the way to Waterford.

At the hospital, the admissions nurse raised her eyebrows in mild surprise at Sarah's elderly entourage, but briskly took her vital signs, asked her a few questions, and agreed she should be admitted. Her contractions were becoming more painful by the moment, and although Sarah had been toying with the idea of attempting natural childbirth, on the teeth-rattling drive through the woods surrounding the Bergstrom estate, she had come down firmly on the side of narcotics. Sitting in the waiting room while the orderlies prepared an available suite, with Gretchen on one side rubbing her back and Sylvia on the other holding her hand, she waited in vain for her cell phone to ring and Matt's welcome and reassuring voice on the other end of the line.

At last they were shown upstairs, Sarah traveling via wheelchair, her friends trailing along carrying her bags and coat. "Grandparents?" the young orderly pushing her along guessed as they waited for the elevator. "Great-grandparents?"

Breathing through a contraction, Sarah managed something halfway between a shrug and a nod, glad that she wasn't obliged to speak. At the moment she couldn't remember the hospital's policies, and she was afraid that if she explained they weren't related, they wouldn't be allowed to stay.

The birthing suite was spacious for a hospital room, with a bed for her, a futon sofa for visitors that Matt could sleep on at night, a couple of armchairs, a bathroom, and a small closet into which Sylvia and Andrew promptly stowed her things. The orderly helped Sarah from the wheelchair onto the sofa as two nurses bustled about checking instruments. After wishing her good luck, Andrew and Joe escaped for the waiting room. On their way out, they passed a tall, attractive woman who couldn't have been much more than thirty. She wore a long white coat over her tweed skirt and blouse, and her raven hair was pulled back into a smooth chignon. "The doctor will want to check how you're progressing," explained one of the nurses, plump and matronly. "Let's get you up into bed, dear."

"Wait," said Sarah as the nurses helped her into the high hospital bed. "Where's Dr. Jamison?"

The doctor, for that was who she must have been, pulled a rueful face. "She was on her way back from vacation, but her flight was grounded at O'Hare this morning thanks to the storm. I'm the ob-gyn on call, Dr. Susan Granger."

Sarah heard Sylvia gasp in recognition as she numbly shook the doctor's hand, her dismay at her usual doctor's sudden absence warring with astonishment at hearing the familiar name completely out of its expected context. "You're Dr. Granger?" she echoed. "Are you related to Jonathan Granger?"

"If you mean the ophthalmologist at Hershey Medical Center," the doctor replied as she turned to the sink to wash her hands, "then the answer is yes. He's my brother."

"No, I mean the Jonathan Granger who was a doctor in the Elm Creek Valley back in the Civil War era."

Dr. Granger shot her a look of surprise as she dried her hands. "That Jonathan Granger was my great-grandfather. How in the world do you know about him?"

"Oh, my goodness, do we have some stories to share with you," exclaimed Sylvia, just as Sarah cried out in pain from the worst contraction yet. "But I suppose they'll have to wait for another occasion."

Before she knew it, Sarah was on her back with her feet in stirrups. Her momentary delight at the novelty of being treated by a descendant of the physician who had tended and befriended Sylvia's Bergstrom ancestors vanished with the crushing squeeze of another contraction. She mourned the absence of

Dr. Jamison, whose brisk efficiency had earned Sarah's respect and confidence throughout her pregnancy. While she was not particularly warm or maternal, she possessed an aura of reassuring competency that only years of experience could give. This young doctor did not.

"Dr. Granger," she gasped, her uncertainty augmented by the strangeness of addressing a young woman by that name, "forgive me for asking, but have you ever delivered a baby before? No offense, but you look—" The rest of her words were swallowed up in a wave of pain.

"No offense taken. I've delivered hundreds of healthy babies both as an attendee and a resident. Well, Sarah—may I call you Sarah?" Sarah quickly nodded, breathing in rhythm. "You're dilated to six centimeters, and the babies' heartbeats are strong and steady. Sometime today, you're going to become a mother."

Dr. Granger patted Sarah's knee, beckoned the nurse to assist her into a more comfortable position, and ordered an epidural. Mulling over the doctor's words, Sarah felt joy and fear and hope welling up within her from a deep, deep source she had not known existed. She was going to be a mother. She blinked away tears and thanked the doctor, who smiled reassuringly and left to see to her other patients.

Before long the epidural took hold and she felt far more comfortable. Then she remembered Matt and her mother, driving through the gathering storm. Sylvia had gone to the waiting room to update Andrew and Joe on her progress, so Sarah asked Gretchen to search her tote bag for her cell phone. She felt dizzy with relief to see a text from Matt—"How are you? How are the babies?"—although she wished he had mentioned when he expected to arrive. Before responding to him she called her mother to tell her that she was fine, that the babies were fine, and that she should come straight to the hospital rather than stopping by Elm Creek Manor. The roads were slippery and becoming more so, her mother reported, but the salt trucks and snowplows were out in force and Sarah shouldn't worry.

Sarah would worry less once she finally heard Matt's voice. She called his number and sighed with relief when he answered on the second ring. "Hey, honey," he said cheerfully. "How are you?"

"I'm feeling much better now that I'm hooked up to the epidural. Where are you? When do you think you'll get here?"

Matt laughed, but then he abruptly stopped. "Wait. Epidural? You're already at the hospital?"

"Of course I am. What did you think? Didn't you get my text this morning? Didn't you get my voice mail?"

"Well, yes, but all you said was—"

"I said you needed to come home!"

"You said you hoped I was on my way home, but you've been saying that for days."

"But this time I said it while I was having contractions!" Her panic soared. "Matt, where are you?"

Matt panted slightly, as if he were running. "I'm on a site."

"You're still in Uniontown?"

"Not for much longer. I'm leaving the building and running to the truck." Wind whipped past the microphone, drowning out most of his words. "I wanted to finish a few things, then what with the storm and everything I thought I'd call you after lunch and see if you really needed me to come home—"

"I really do." Her tears spilled over. She felt Gretchen take her hand; Sarah threw her a stricken look and forced herself to take a deep breath, to calm down for the sake of the twins. "If you had listened to me from the beginning—"

"I'm sorry." The truck's engine roared to life. "I'm really sorry. But you're not alone, right? Gretchen and Sylvia and your mom are there, right?"

"My mom's still on the way." No, she wasn't alone, but she wanted Matt. She needed Matt. "Just try to get here as soon as you can."

"I will. Sarah"—he hesitated—"I love you."

"Drive carefully," she said, and hung up. She set down the phone and burst into tears. She didn't need to explain; Sylvia and Gretchen had easily deduced what had happened.

"You're going to be fine," Gretchen soothed her. "I know you want Matt here, but if he can't make it in time, you're still going to be fine. Haven't we taken all the childbirth classes together? I'm not as handsome as Matt, but I think I can fill in for him as coach just fine if need be."

Sarah managed a shaky laugh. "You'll probably be a better coach, since you took the classes." She could not say the same for her husband. She fought to calm herself, to regain control of her breathing, to recapture the steady, even rhythm that had helped her ride the waves of discomfort not dulled by the epidural. She tried to put her husband and her disappointment and the storm out of her mind and concentrate on her babies, the beautiful babies she would soon hold in her arms. She was considering asking Sylvia to retrieve the book from her tote bag when a knock sounded on the door.

"Don't start without us," Gwen called, bursting into the room in a bright red wool coat that clashed merrily with her gray-streaked auburn hair. Following close behind was Diane, who beamed at Sarah before turning a wary eye upon the medical equipment surrounding her, and Agnes, petite and white-haired, her blue eyes joyful behind pink-tinted glasses.

Agnes hurried to her side and kissed her cheek, her rosewater scent lingering in the air. "Oh, my dear, you look beautiful."

Sarah had to laugh. "I couldn't possibly."

"I've been saying for years that Agnes needs new glasses," Diane agreed, and when Gwen glared at her, she added, "What? You want me to lie? Sarah's in labor with twins, not preparing for a photo shoot."

"Matt was going to take pictures," Sarah suddenly remembered. "I left the camera in the library."

"I brought mine," said Agnes, patting her purse. "I'll lend it to Sylvia."

"You aren't staying?" asked Sylvia.

"We figured you, Gretchen, and Carol would have everything under control," said Gwen. "Is she on her way?"

Sarah breathed through a contraction and managed a nod.

"We just wanted to say hello and wish you well, Sarah," Agnes said, patting her shoulder. "You couldn't possibly relax with all of us crowded in here."

"This isn't all of us." Diane looked around. "Where's the father-to-be?"

"He's on his way," said Gretchen, squeezing Sarah's hand.

"On his way from the manor, not from Uniontown, right?" queried Diane, glancing to the window, where thick clumps of heavy, wet flakes obscured the view. "If not, he'll never make it, and he'd be stupid to try."

Sarah winced.

"Don't pay any attention to her," Gwen said. "She's been a nervous wreck about driving in the snow ever since she slid off the road last year."

"Tim doesn't know it yet," said Diane, shuddering at the memory, "but someday we're retiring to Arizona."

"You can't leave," protested Gwen. "First Judy, then Summer, then Bonnie, and now you?"

"I didn't say we'd move anytime soon," said Diane, looking mildly affronted that Gwen would think her so near retirement age. "Anyway, Bonnie's coming back next month."

"I spoke to her a few days ago," remarked Sylvia. "She said she would be sorry to miss this happy day."

"She doesn't have to," said Gwen. "We can hook up a Webcam and stream the entire birth live on the Internet."

"No, thanks," declared Sarah, prompting laughter from her friends. She managed a smile and shifted in her bed. Quickly Gretchen was there to plump her pillow and adjust the blanket. The epidural was wearing off, and she was becoming more uncomfortable with each passing moment. Gretchen spoke to her gently and encouragingly, reminding her to breathe deeply and evenly, to rest and to relax. Sarah closed her eyes and nodded, remembering everything they had practiced in their weekly classes. How fortunate she was that Gretchen had offered to fill in for Matt, and that her other friends were close at hand. If she were lying in this hospital room utterly alone, she knew her strength and courage would falter.

"This takes me back," said Gwen, sitting down on the sofa and resting her elbows on her knees. "Remember how we all met? Well, not all of us, just those of us who were here before Sylvia's return to Waterford."

"It was at Bonnie's quilt shop," said Diane. "On a beautiful autumn Saturday."

"I was in charge of the Waterford Quilting Guild's annual charity raffle quilt," Agnes recalled. "Diane and I were shopping for fabric to make it."

"Bonnie was helping me and Summer at the cutting table," said Gwen. "Judy came in with a Baby Bunting quilt top, finished except for the border."

"She looked as if she were nine and a half months pregnant," Diane added for the benefit of Sarah, Sylvia, and Gretchen, who had not been present.

"That's perhaps not the best time to go fabric shopping," said Gretchen.

"She desperately wanted to finish the quilt before her baby arrived," said Agnes. "But it gradually became clear to the rest of us that she was in labor."

"It's hard to pinpoint what gave it away," said Diane, tapping her chin with a finger. "Was it when she kept groaning from the pain of the contractions, or was it when her water broke all over the quilt shop floor?"

"You're kidding me," said Sarah, shocked and delighted.

"The truly funny part is," said Gwen, "that when we insisted upon calling nine-one-one, she told us she couldn't be in labor yet because"—Diane and Agnes joined in gleefully—"her due date wasn't for three more days!"

"As if a baby could read a calendar," said Diane.

Sylvia laughed and Gretchen smiled, but Sarah said, "That's an easy mistake to make."

Gwen laughed so hard she had to wipe tears from her eyes. "Be that as it may, Baby Emily had no intention of keeping anyone's schedule but her own. The ambulance came and whisked Judy off to the hospital—"

"And you went along to keep her company," Agnes broke in.

Gwen nodded. "And while she was recovering, the rest of us got together and finished the Baby Bunting quilt so Judy would be able to bring Emily home from the hospital snuggled up in it, just as she had wanted. And that, as they say, was the beginning of a beautiful friendship."

"I can't believe I never heard this story before." Sarah had to wait for a contraction to rise, crest, and pass before she could speak again. "I thought you met through your quilt guild."

"A few of us knew one another in passing from the guild," Diane acknowledged, "but we weren't really close. I'd known Agnes since the time she babysat me as a girl, but Gwen—well, I thought Gwen was a loud, obnoxious hippie."

"You still think so," said Gwen cheerfully.

"Of course, but now I realize that's part of your charm," Diane teased. "I wouldn't want you any other way, now that I've figured out you're all bluster. If I ever suspected that you might actually *do* something to foist your liberal values on the rest of us, I might worry, but I know you're harmless."

"Oh, don't tell me that," warned Gwen, with a vigorous shake of the head that sent her beaded necklaces clicking. "You'll force me to do something to prove you wrong."

Everyone laughed, and for a moment Sarah forgot her anxieties, her weariness. But soon Gwen, Agnes, and Diane departed, explaining that they didn't want to wear her out and they thought they should try to beat the worst of the storm home. Before leaving, each hugged Sarah and assured her all would be well. As they headed out the door, Agnes reminded Sylvia to call them regularly with any news, even if the only news was that they were still waiting. If they didn't receive timely updates, Gwen might return and make good on her threat to set up a Webcam.

After they left, Sarah felt fatigue settle over her like the snow blanketing the winding mountain road into the Elm Creek Valley. She didn't want her book or her music or her quilting. She lay in bed with her eyes closed, relaxing while Gretchen or Sylvia rubbed her back or stroked her hair. She half listened and half dozed as her friends chatted quietly about the upcoming camp season, new classes, the long-arm quilting machine they had recently purchased and set up in the ballroom. From time to time the nurses came in to check her vital signs and the babies' heart rates, and occasionally Dr. Granger appeared to check her progress. Sarah dilated to seven centimeters, then eight. She had reached nine when her mother dashed into the room, unwinding her scarf and peeling off her gloves, her gray hair sparkling with melting snowflakes. "There's my girl," she exclaimed, hurrying to Sarah's side. Her quick, appraising glance took in Sarah, her chart, and her companions. "I assume Matt's out getting a sandwich or something?"

"Hmph." Sylvia glanced up from feeding Sarah ice chips and shook her head. "He's on his way, we hope."

"He's on his way," said Gretchen firmly, rubbing Sarah's back. "He'll be here soon, and even if he doesn't make it, we'll be fine."

Carol draped her coat over the back of an armchair and sat down. "He should have come home days ago."

"That's what I've been telling him all along," said Sarah

wearily. "If he misses everything, I won't get any pleasure out of saying, 'I told you so.'"

"He won't miss everything," said Sylvia, rubbing her shoulders and stroking her sweaty hair off the back of her neck.

Carol frowned. "He'd better not."

The epidural had completely worn off by then, but Sarah couldn't have another dose out of concern that it might slow down the labor. An hour after her mother arrived, Dr. Granger checked her again, but her brow furrowed slightly when she explained that Sarah had not progressed beyond nine centimeters. "We'll give you Pitocin to help move things along," she said, but her reassuring smile had lost its power to comfort.

"Why am I not fully dilated yet?" Sarah fretted wearily.

"I thought you were holding back on purpose to give Matt more time to get here," remarked Sylvia.

Sarah managed a smile, but it quickly faded as she continued inhaling and exhaling in rhythm. Matt had not called or texted since leaving Uniontown, not that she had expected him to. She wanted his hands on the wheel and his eyes on the road. He should have come home days ago. He never should have agreed to spend the winter away from Elm Creek Manor. "If Matt misses the birth of his children, after I begged him time and time again to come home," Sarah gasped between contractions, "I'll kill him."

"If Matt misses this, you won't need to," her mother replied, massaging her feet. "You're in no condition to kill anyone. I'll do it."

"Mother!"

"Don't look so shocked. It was your idea."

"I was speaking metaphorically."

"So was I."

"You sounded serious."

"So did you."

"Well, you sounded like you'd enjoy it a little too much."

Carol seemed about to reply, but her attention was suddenly drawn to one of the many monitors beeping and blinking around Sarah. "What is it?" asked Sarah. Her mother, a nurse, knew much more about what was going on than she did.

"I'll be right back," Carol said, and stepped out of the room.

Moments later, through a haze of fatigue and pain, Sarah was aware of her mother and a nurse holding a quick, hushed conference at the end of the bed. "We're going to give you some oxygen, dear," the plump nurse said, and quickly placed a mask over Sarah's mouth and nose. She could barely hear anything over the steady hiss of rushing air.

Moments later Dr. Granger appeared, examined her, and conferred with the nurse. "I'm afraid you still haven't progressed beyond nine centimeters," Dr. Granger told her, barely audible, wearing the same rueful look with which she had announced the delay of Dr. Jamison's flight. "And one of the twins is starting to experience heart decelerations. We're going to keep an eye on it, but I want you to consider the possibility of a C-section."

"What's a heart deceleration?" Sarah gasped, her voice muffled by the mask. Sweaty bangs clung to her forehead and fell into her eyes, but she felt a sudden chill.

"It's a transitory decrease in the baby's heart rate. It may suggest that the baby isn't receiving enough oxygen to withstand the rigors of labor."

Sarah propped herself up on her elbows and searched the doctor's face for clues. "Is . . . my baby going to be okay?"

"Just try to relax," her mother said, placing her hands on her shoulders and easing her back against the pillows. "Breathe deeply."

Sarah obeyed, suddenly terrified. She closed her eyes and took deep breaths, tears trickling down her cheeks. "I think a C-section right now would be a very good idea," she said shakily, and felt her mother squeeze her hand in reply.

The hiss of the oxygen mask filled her ears, drowning out the words of the doctor and nurses, but she knew from their carefully studied expressions that the matter was serious. Through her pregnancy, she had skimmed the chapters on Caesarian sections with a foolish superstition that if she prepared for such a measure, she would need it. She knew women carrying twins often required Caesarian deliveries even after a smooth labor, but she had dreaded surgery and had prayed she would avoid it. Now all she wanted was to deliver the babies as swiftly and as safely as possible, never mind what happened to her. The thought of the small, steady heartbeat faltering was too much to bear.

After what felt like an agonizingly long wait, though later she learned it lasted only a few minutes, Dr. Granger confirmed her recommendation for a Caesarian delivery. Sarah immediately assented and with a shaking hand signed the forms someone put in front of her on a clipboard. Once the decision was made, the team moved swiftly. The nurses prepared Sarah; Dr. Granger disappeared for a time and returned dressed in scrubs. Her heart pounded as an orderly pushed her bed out of the birthing suite and into the hallway.

"Sarah," said Matt, suddenly at her side, snow dusting his coat and hat. "I'm sorry. I'm so incredibly sorry I didn't get here until now."

None of her frustration and disappointment over his absence seemed to matter anymore. "I have to have a C-section."

"I know." He tore off a glove, held her hand, and walked beside the bed as the orderly wheeled her toward the operating room. "They told me."

Her words came out in a sob. "I don't know if the babies are okay."

"They're fine," he said firmly, squeezing her hand tighter. "I promise you everything's going to be fine."

She nodded, but how could he know? How could he promise her that?

"Are you the father?" someone unseen asked Matt. She heard him confirm that he was. "If you want to attend the birth, you'll have to put on these and scrub up."

Matt clasped her hand with both of his. "Sarah, I have to go for a minute but I'll be right back."

"Promise?"

"I swear I won't be gone long. I'll be right beside you the entire time."

She released his hand and heard him go. The operating room was unnaturally bright and cold. Dazed and exhausted, she sat up, supported by two nurses, and held her breath as they inserted the spinal block. By the time she was fully anesthetized and prepped for surgery, Matt had returned, barely recognizable in blue scrubs, cap, and mask, but she knew his eyes, full of love, concern, and reassurance. He stood by her side, just out of her range of vision, as Dr. Granger began the surgery, blocked from Sarah's view by a blue drape. She felt pressure but no pain, and then there was a wrenching, and then a sudden flurry of activity and a baby's cry and Dr. Granger declaring that she had a daughter, a beautiful baby girl.

"Can I see her?" Sarah called out feebly. "Can I see my daughter?"

Matt bent close to her ear. "They took her away, honey. They rushed her off to the neonatal unit."

"Is she okay?"

"I'm sure she's just fine." Matt rested his hand on her shoulder, and she could tell he was shaking.

He had barely finished speaking before Dr. Granger announced that she had a son—a strong, healthy son, by the sound of his wail, which was so outraged and indignant that the attendees laughed. "Can I see him?" Sarah called out, only to be assured that he was being examined and would be cleaned up, and she would be able to hold him soon. Matt could accompany the babies, if he wished.

He seemed torn between concern for the children and his determination to keep his promise not to leave her. "Go with them," she begged him. "Make sure they're okay."

Matt nodded and hurried away. Blinking away her tears, Sarah started at an unexpected touch on her shoulder. "They looked perfectly healthy—strong and beautiful," a woman hidden in blue surgical garb said. Sarah would have known the eyes even if she had not recognized the muffled voice—her mother's eyes, shining with unshed tears. Sarah had not realized Carol had been allowed into the operating room, and she was suddenly overwhelmed with gratitude that she was there. She placed her hand on her mother's and held on while the doctor closed her incisions. Her mother walked beside her as she was taken to the recovery room, and there, when she shivered from the cold, her mother made sure she was draped with heated blankets. When Sarah felt warmer and less disoriented, Carol stepped away for a moment and quickly returned to report that Sarah's son had an Apgar score of nine and her daughter's initial score of six had risen to eight five minutes after her birth. Matt had been allowed to hold both of the children, and Sarah would be able to soon. It was the same answer as before, and yet Sarah seemed no closer to holding them. After months of waiting and hours of labor, to be unable to cuddle or even see her children now that they had finally arrived frustrated and worried her.

"This is routine," Carol soothed when the nurse stepped away. "I know it's annoying, I know it's hard, but it won't be much longer."

The wait seemed interminably long, but at last she was taken back to the birthing suite where she had labored so long. Gretchen was waiting, and as a nurse attended to Sarah, two aides entered, pushing two contraptions that Sarah could best describe as tall, wheeled bassinets. Above the edge of one, Sarah glimpsed a tiny pink fist waving in the air, and she gasped out a happy sob. Her babies, at last. Her children.

Then Sarah was allowed to hold them, one at a time, while a nurse stood at her side watching attentively, since Sarah was still recovering from the anesthesia. "We're filling out the birth certificates," another nurse asked. "Do you have names for the children?"

"Yes, please do divulge the secret at long last," said Sylvia, seated on the sofa with the baby boy in her arms. Beside her,

Gretchen held out a fingertip for the child to grasp with a tiny fist. "You've been keeping us in suspense for ages."

"Not ages," said Sarah. "Only nine months."

"Please tell me you haven't selected any of those silly names you were teasing us with before," said Carol, leaning over to tuck a corner of the soft striped blanket out of the way so she could better see her granddaughter's sweet face. Sarah smiled, knowing her mother longed to wrap the babies in the pink-and-white and blue-and-white Sawtooth Star quilts she had painstakingly made for them, the first and second—and only—quilts she had made in her brief career as a quilter. Sarah was saving them for the babies' trip home to Elm Creek Manor.

"You mean Barnum and Bailey?" said Matt, who had just returned from the waiting room where he had shared the good news with Andrew and Joe. They had accompanied him into the birthing suite, looking as pleased and proud as if they truly were the baby's great-grandparents. "Peas and Carrots? Skipper and Gilligan?"

"That last one's not so bad," Andrew mused, mostly to see the look of alarm on Carol's face.

"Bagel and Schmear was always my favorite," Sarah remarked, but considering how attentive and helpful her mother had been throughout that long, difficult day, she couldn't bear to torture her a moment longer. "Yes, we've chosen names. Sylvia's holding James Matthew, and this little sweetheart is Caroline Sylvia."

A gasp of delight and recognition went up from the gathered friends, and Sarah thought she spotted tears of pride behind the loving smiles of the two women who had lent their names to the newborn girl. And their son, called James after

Sylvia's first husband and Matthew for his father—he, too, had a proud, honorable name that paid tribute to the McClure family as well as the Bergstroms. In the years since Sarah had moved to the Elm Creek Valley, the Bergstroms had come to seem like a second family to her, although she knew them only through Sylvia's stories and the quilts and words they had left behind.

The parents, grandmother, and honorary great-grandparents took turns cuddling the babies and phoning absent friends to share the happy news. Two healthy, beautiful babies and a healthy, relieved mother—in all their lives Sarah and Matt had never had better news to share.

A lactation consultant arrived to help Sarah nurse her children. That first feeding went less well than she had hoped—not at all like the blissfully easy, natural process described in the books stacked on her nightstand back home—but the consultant assured her that the babies were probably not very hungry so soon after their birth, and by the time her milk came in and her babies were ready, she would have it all figured out.

Sarah had never felt less certain that she had anything all figured out, but surrounded by some of the people she loved best in the world and knowing that the rest would celebrate the joyful occasion when they returned home to Elm Creek Manor, Sarah had faith that she, Matt, Caroline, and James would be all right. Everything would be all right.

Sarah saw a shadow through the summer curtain an instant before a horn honked. Heart soaring, she waved the curtain out of the way and saw, at last, Caroline's car rounding the bend by the old red barn, crossing the bridge over Elm Creek, circling the two towering elm trees that even then, in the warmth of late summer, sent yellow leaves dancing on the breeze, falling lightly to the pavement below.

As the car pulled to a stop, Sarah saw Matt striding across the bridge, coming in from the orchard to welcome his eldest child and her husband-to-be. She heard the back door squeak open and crash shut, and she heard James shout out a cheerful greeting. Friends and loved ones were there to bless Caroline's homecoming just as they—and others, never far from Sarah's thoughts—had been present on that winter day in early February twenty-five years before when Sarah and Matt had brought the twins home from the hospital. Hopeful, excited, apprehensive, overwhelmed—the new parents had brought their son and daughter home and devoted themselves to their care and nurturing. Sarah had wanted her children to be surrounded by love every day of their lives. For all too brief a time she was their world and she could grant them that great gift, but as soon as they began walking, they began moving away from her. Although James always circled back, smiling happily, arms open wide for her embrace, Caroline seemed ever set upon venturing beyond the gray stone walls of Elm Creek Manor, beyond the towering elms, over the creek and away, with just a glance over her shoulder to be sure Sarah was watching. And Sarah, who marveled at her confident, fearless daughter, had smiled and waved and fought the urge to beg her to stay—and tried, unsuccessfully, to hide her broken heart when she did not.

Sarah let the curtain fall and hurried to join her husband and son in welcoming their bright and happy girl to the childhood home she loved but found far too easy to leave.

For now, Caroline was home again, and Sarah could forget the pain of her absence, the many partings, the times when school, friends, college, work, or love had beckoned her away and she had gladly gone. For a few days more they could be a foursome again, the McClure family of Elm Creek Manor—father, mother, twins. Soon everything would change: Caroline would marry, and she would begin a new family with the man she loved.

Sarah knew her daughter's wedding day would be bittersweet, an occasion of joy and love that marked the end of Caroline's childhood even as it ushered in a future rich with hope and promise. But for now, Sarah would put away thoughts of the parting to come. She would enjoy the time they had together and not mourn its brevity even as it passed.

Her darling Caroline had come home.

· Chapter Two ·

"Caroline," Sarah called out as she hurried out the back door and down the stairs. She glimpsed her daughter's golden curls at the center of a laughing, welcoming crowd of family, friends, and a few of the teenagers who worked in the orchard after school. Sarah had to smile; the young people had never met the bride and groom, but they didn't want to miss the excitement and were glad for an excuse to take a break from the work of the harvest. Leo stood a bit apart as he unloaded suitcases from the trunk, watching the scene with proud amusement, no doubt accustomed to seeing his charming bride-to-be at the center of a circle of admirers. Sarah decided to welcome him first and wait her turn to greet her daughter. "Leo," she said, embracing him and rising up on tiptoe to kiss his cheek. "It's good to see you. How was the drive?"

"Not bad," he said, returning her hug cheerfully. His hair was thick and wavy, so dark brown it was nearly black, and a deep dimple appeared in his right cheek whenever he smiled.

"Our fuel cell died about an hour after we crossed the Pennsylvania border, so we had to wait while it was replaced."

That explained the delay. "Replaced, not recharged?"

"No, we set out with a full charge. It was only a month old too. The technician said the cell was faulty and we should demand a refund."

"Well, I hope you get one." Sarah glanced over at Caroline and saw her hugging her grandmother. As soon as Carol released her, Sarah hurried forward to hug Caroline before anyone else did. "My baby girl," she cried, embracing her.

Caroline laughed and hugged her in return. "Hi, Mom. You look great, so well rested."

"Don't be fooled," said Carol, brushing wisps of steel-gray hair from her face with a thin, wrinkled hand. She had retired from nursing fifteen years earlier and had moved into Elm Creek Manor at Sarah's urging five years after that, not because she couldn't live alone any longer, but because most of her friends had passed on or moved into retirement communities, and she had become lonely. "Your mother doesn't get nearly enough rest. She's always on the go."

"With the campers gone for the season, I've been catching up on my sleep," Sarah assured them both. "Caroline, sweetheart, you look wonderful. Have you let your hair grow out?"

"A little," said Caroline, playfully elbowing her brother when he reached over to tousle her long blond curls. "I still haven't decided whether I want to wear it up or down at the wedding."

"She spends hours in front of the mirror," said Leo, grinning as he joined the group and put his arm around Caroline's shoulders. "She tries on the veil with her hair up, then down, then up, then down—"

As Caroline's mouth fell open in a wordless protest, Carol said, "I'm sure she doesn't spend *hours* in front of the mirror."

"Thanks, Grandma. I'm not that vain." Feigning outrage, Caroline placed her hands on Leo's burly chest and gave him a little shove. Playfully, he staggered backward a few steps until he bumped into the vehicle and rocked onto his heels, leaning against the hood. Caroline laughed, reached for his hand, and pulled him to his feet.

"You'll be the most beautiful bride in the world, however you wear your hair," said Matt, clearing his throat, misty-eyed. Caroline flung her arms around him and kissed his cheek. They were almost the same height, their hair the same golden blond, although Matt's curls had thinned considerably since his own wedding day.

Together the friends and family helped the bride and groom finish unloading their vehicle and carry their things inside—suitcases packed full of clothes for the wedding week and their Hawaiian honeymoon to follow, cartons full of goodies to assemble into gift bags for the out-of-town guests, gifts for the bridal party, and other parcels and luggage, including a long garment bag that surely contained Caroline's wedding gown. Sarah had not yet seen it, and she was tempted to unzip the bag and take a peek. She and Gina had traveled to Connecticut to help Caroline search for the perfect gown and bridesmaids' dresses, so Sarah knew which style her daughter had chosen, but she had seen Caroline in the bridal shop's floor sample, four sizes too large and pinned in back to contour to her slender curves. Caroline had ordered hers in ivory, for she thought the floor sample seemed too bright, and she had found a vintage embellished silver belt in an antique shop, which she intended to substitute for the floor sample's tulle sash. From time to time, Sarah had tried to imagine the altered gown, but she had seen the floor sample too briefly and couldn't quite understand how Caroline's changes would improve it. Still, Caroline had always had a flair for fashion, something she had certainly not inherited from her mother, and so Sarah kept her doubts to herself. To paraphrase Matt, Caroline would be the most beautiful bride in the world, whatever she wore.

Carefully holding the garment bag draped across her arms so it wouldn't drag on the floor, Sarah followed Caroline through the back door, past the fragrant kitchen where Anna and Gina were busily preparing a welcome-home supper, and through the older west wing of the manor to the grand front foyer. Carrying her suitcase with one hand and her sling bag over her shoulder, Caroline led the way two flights up the curving oak staircase, glancing back at Sarah from time to time as she chatted about letters she'd recently received from extended family and longtime friends, some of whom were looking forward to seeing the McClures soon at the wedding, others who had sent their regrets and good wishes. Behind Sarah came Leo and James hauling the rest of the couple's luggage. Caroline would be staying in her childhood bedroom, of course, but Sarah had made up a suite down the hall for Leo. Back in Connecticut, Caroline had already moved into Leo's house, but out of respect for their parents and for tradition, they had accepted the wedding-week sleeping arrangements without complaint. Sarah imagined that privately the young couple joked good-naturedly about their parents' old-fashioned notions of appearances and proprieties, just as she and Matt might have in their place, more than three decades earlier, before they'd had children.

"Leo's mom and stepfather said they hope to get here tomorrow morning around ten," Caroline said when they reached her room, flinging her sling bag on her desk and dropping the suitcase in front of the closet door. "His dad and stepmom probably won't arrive until closer to lunchtime. His brother is coming Thursday morning with his wife and the kids, and his sister and her family hope to get in that evening. She wanted to come sooner, but their eldest son has a soccer game."

"I'll make sure everyone's rooms are ready." Sarah carefully laid the garment bag upon the bed. "Should I put Leo's parents on different floors? On different floors in separate wings?"

"We don't have to keep them apart," Caroline assured her, laughing. "The divorce is ancient history, and they get along really well now. You saw them when we all met to celebrate the engagement. Everyone was friendly, didn't you think so?"

"We met so briefly, it was hard to get a clear impression." Not to mention that they had met virtually, not in person. Although most people the twins' age and younger insisted that meeting friends in virtual reality was just as good as being there—or "only a pixel's difference" as the ubiquitous advertisement claimed—for Sarah there was no replacing a gathering of friends in the real world. Thousands of quilters from around the world apparently agreed, for every year from spring through autumn they filled the halls and classrooms of Elm Creek Manor for classes, lectures, and camaraderie. Quilt camp offered them some intangible benefit, a spiritual and creative nourishment they couldn't get from a view screen or virtual reality room.

"You'll like them when you get to know them better," said Caroline confidently.

"I'm sure I will," said Sarah. "As long as they're good to you."

"They are." Caroline smiled wistfully as she looked around her childhood room, her old favorite books, the Waterford High School state champion swim team photo on the desk, the beloved and threadbare panda on her pillow. She picked it up and stroked its head absently, and Sarah was suddenly, painfully reminded of Caroline cuddling the toy when she received it from Elm Creek Quilter Maggie Flynn for her third birthday. It didn't seem so very long ago.

"I'm going to miss this room," Caroline said, with unexpected yearning.

"You haven't spent much time in it since leaving for college."

"I know, but I always knew it was here, waiting for me. After Saturday"—Caroline shrugged, pulled a face, and flopped down on the bed, the panda on her lap—"it won't be the same."

"It won't be the same," Sarah agreed steadily, nudging her daughter off the garment bag and smoothing the wrinkles. "But it will always be yours."

"You should redecorate it for the quilt campers, not preserve it as some sort of shrine to me."

"We have enough rooms for quilt campers without giving them yours." Outside in the hall, James and Leo passed on their way back out to the car. She thought she heard one of them say something about a bachelor party, but she fervently hoped she was mistaken.

Unaware, Caroline smiled and rolled over on her back, careful to stay off of the garment bag. "Maybe we can redecorate for when Leo and I come to visit. Or we can redecorate for our children."

"Let's not get ahead of ourselves." Sarah knelt down to open Caroline's suitcase. If redecorating to suit the newlyweds would encourage Caroline to visit more often, she would spare no expense, but she wasn't quite ready to think of herself as a grandmother.

Caroline swung her legs over the side of the bed and sat up. "Oh, Mom, just leave it. I'll unpack after supper."

"You should hang up your things," Sarah protested, but she stood up and left the suitcase alone. "You don't want to get wrinkles in your nice clothes."

"I can always press them later."

"If you hang them up now, you won't need to press them later."

"They've been crammed in a suitcase all day. I'm sure they're already wrinkled."

Sarah muffled a sigh. It wasn't worth arguing about. "They're your clothes. Do what you want."

"When you say that, what you really mean is, 'Do it the wrong way, if you insist.'"

Not so many years ago, when Caroline was in her rebellious teenage phase, a comment like that would have sent Sarah's temper flaring. Now she had to laugh. "That's exactly what I mean." She took her daughter's hands and pulled her to her feet. "Anna's been in the kitchen most of the afternoon, making all of your favorite dishes."

Caroline's eyebrows rose. "Surely not all of them."

"No, not all, but close to it. You're right; unpacking can wait. Let's sit, enjoy a good meal, and talk for a while instead."

"As long as we don't have to talk about the wedding," Caroline declared, giving the panda a firm, defiant hug before returning it to her pillow.

Sarah regarded her with amusement. "Honey, I think you should expect the subject to come up."

"Then I'll change the subject. I'm so tired of talking about me, me, me, like I'm the only person in the universe. I want to hear about what's been going on around here—about quilt camp, and the apple harvest, and what's new with the Elm Creek Quilters—"

"You're interested in quilt camp?"

"I've always been interested in quilt camp," said Caroline. "Just because I've never wanted to work for Elm Creek Quilts doesn't mean I don't care about the Elm Creek Quilters." Suddenly she frowned. "I wish I'd paid more attention when they tried to teach me to quilt."

Sarah couldn't believe what she was hearing. "You do?"

"Just because I don't like to sew doesn't mean I don't admire beautiful quilts," said Caroline, looking away. "And wish that I had one."

Astonished, Sarah sat down on the bed beside her. "Sweetheart, you have dozens of beautiful quilts. You've saved every one ever made for you, from the pink-and-white Sawtooth Star Grandma Carol sewed before you were born to your graduation quilt." Sarah had lovingly sewn it herself, using the Commencement block and the green-and-white colors of Dartmouth.

"I know, and I love them all." Caroline sat up with a sigh,

crossed her legs, and rested her head on her mother's shoulder. "I mean I wish I had a wedding quilt, one I made myself. It seems ridiculous that Leo marries the daughter of the famous Sarah McClure, Elm Creek Quilter, and he won't even have a wedding quilt to commemorate the occasion."

Sarah was tempted to tell her about the Memory Album quilt, but she couldn't bear to spoil the surprise. "Leo doesn't need a quilt to commemorate the occasion. He's getting the world's most wonderful bride."

Caroline laughed in spite of herself. "And that's your completely unbiased opinion."

"Exactly." Sarah sighed, torn. The moment she had longingly awaited for twenty-five years had come at last: Her daughter wished she were a quilter. But as extraordinarily talented and capable as Caroline was, no crash course Sarah could offer would enable her to whip up a stunning wedding quilt in five days, not when they had so many other tasks to complete before the ceremony. "You could make a quilt to commemorate your first anniversary instead," she said. "That's what I did."

"Only because you learned to quilt after you got married. If you had been a quilter all along, you would have made a wedding quilt."

Sarah almost certainly would have. "I don't think this is something you need to worry about right now," she said, stroking Caroline's blond curls away from her face and kissing her forehead. "If you want a refresher course in quilting, I'd be very happy to teach you, but it'll have to wait until you return from your honeymoon. In the meantime, don't let it trouble you. Agreed?"

Caroline smiled. "Agreed."

. . .

They went down to the kitchen for supper, where it seemed that every one of the manor's year-round residents had gathered to welcome the bride and groom, summoned either by the sounds of their arrival or by the delicious aromas of cardamom and cumin wafting from Anna's kitchen. The eight booths and the long wooden table in the center, a Bergstrom family heirloom, offered more than enough seats to accommodate everyone for the welcome-home supper: the four McClures, Carol, and Leo; the three Del Maso–Bernsteins; Maggie Flynn and her husband, Russell McIntyre, both longtime faculty members; and Emily DiNardo, the youngest Elm Creek Quilter and eldest daughter of founding member Judy Nguyen DiNardo. Emily was the third second-generation teacher at Elm Creek Quilt Camp, a distinction in which both she and her mother, a professor of computer engineering at Penn, took great pride. The other two second-generation employees were James, of course, and Summer Sullivan, but Elm Creek Quilter Diane often argued that Gwen and Summer didn't count since they had both been a part of Elm Creek Quilts since its inception, whereas "second-generation" implied the bestowing of a legacy from one original member to a descendant. Gwen thought Diane's definition of "second-generation" was unnecessarily narrow, as suited her unnecessarily narrow mind—and, not surprisingly, the discussion had devolved from there. Second-generation or otherwise, Summer had been one of the quilt campers' favorite teachers in the early years, and although she had resigned from Elm Creek Quilts even before the twins were born in order to earn her Ph.D. in history at the University of Chicago, she remained one of Sarah's dearest friends. Sarah was thrilled that Summer and

Gwen would be making the trip from Palo Alto, where Summer was a professor at Stanford University and Gwen was enjoying her retirement, to attend Caroline's wedding.

Those who had not welcomed Caroline upon her arrival were awaiting her in the kitchen, and when she appeared there were again hugs, kisses, and good wishes all around. Everyone present had met Leo on earlier visits, and they offered him congratulations and teasing warnings that he had better treat their darling girl well, admonitions that he accepted amiably.

Before long Anna announced that dinner was served, and soon everyone was enjoying pleasantly spicy chicken doro wat, sweet potato peanut stew, lentils in savory broth, spinach sautéed in garlic, and the sour tang of injera flatbread—Caroline's favorite meal. She had fallen in love with Ethiopian cuisine in middle school when introduced to it by a new friend, Ayana, who had moved to the Elm Creek Valley in the seventh grade when her father accepted a short-term position as a visiting professor at Waterford College. Two years later, when the assignment concluded and Ayana's family moved away, the usually ebullient Caroline was inconsolable. It had been Gina's idea to remind her of happier times by re-creating the meals she had occasionally shared at her friend's house, so Anna learned a few East African recipes and encouraged Caroline to help her prepare them. At first Caroline balked, reluctant to be reminded of the friend who had, in her young eyes, abandoned her, but Anna's cheerful persistence eventually won her over. Caroline and Ayana had stayed in touch, and had even managed a few visits through the years when their academic and work schedules allowed. To Caroline's delight, Ayana, now living and working in Manhattan, had eagerly agreed to be a bridesmaid.

Thankful for the power of a wedding to bring together friends and family from near and far, Sarah enjoyed the meal and the conversation, hardly able to take her eyes from her radiant daughter, so full of hope and happiness and love. At the table beside her, Leo seemed content, affectionate, and happy, not at all overwhelmed by the number of people gathered for what was, for them, an ordinarily family dinner at home, nor did he seem fazed by their abundance of enthusiasm.

As Gina and James began to clear away the dishes and Jeremy jumped up to put on a pot of coffee, Russell raised his voice to be heard over the din. "How did you two meet?" he called to the bride and groom from the corner booth where he sat with Maggie.

"In college at an aughts party," Caroline replied from the center table, evoking knowing laughter from Leo, James, Gina, and Emily.

Sarah, Matt, Carol, Jeremy, and Anna had heard the story before, so they understood the reference, but most of the others regarded the young people with bewilderment. "A whats party?" asked Russell.

"An aughts party," Caroline repeated, smiling. "You know, aught-aught, aught-one, aught-two—"

"Or," Sarah broke in, "as we referred to it back in the day, the year two thousand, two thousand one, oh-two, oh-three . . ." She gestured, waving her hand to indicate the rest of the years of the decade rolling on and on.

"What does one do at an aughts party," asked Maggie, "aside from meeting one's future spouse?"

"Well, the girls straighten their hair," Caroline began, "and some of the more daring guys shave their heads."

"For a party?" asked Matt, incredulous.

James shrugged. "Some people take their partying very seriously."

"We scour thrift shops for aughts fashions, like skinny jeans and Crocs or Ugg boots," said Gina. "Some people dress Gothic, like vampires, or like Harry Potter."

"That's Goth, not Gothic," said Jeremy, "and Harry Potter was neither."

"James wore my old Dunder Mifflin T-shirt to an aughts party in high school once," Matt recalled.

"Yes, but no one understood it," said Caroline. "Everyone thought he forgot to wear a costume." To her brother she added, "You should have worn the Obama 2008 shirt instead."

"Next time I will," James assured his sister. "The guys wear their pants low on their hips so you can see their boxer shorts. Seriously, why did you people dress like that? You can't dance, you can barely walk, and you definitely can't ride a bike."

"No one rode bikes back then," Gina reminded him, nudging him with her shoulder. Even if Sarah had been completely unaware of their blossoming romance, she couldn't have dismissed the touch as a friendly or sisterly gesture. "They all drove around in their hundred-gallons-per-mile Hummies."

"That's Hummers," corrected Jeremy, "and not everyone drove them, and some of us did bike, like me, and some used public transportation, like your mother."

"And not everyone wore their pants so that they would fall off if you stumbled on a curb," said Anna, smiling as she brushed her long gray French braid off her shoulder. "If your father had dressed like that, I never would have dated him."

"Yes, you would have," countered Jeremy. "You couldn't resist me."

"If you had worn your pants falling off your rear end, I would have found a way."

Everyone burst out laughing, and as the young people went on to describe the parties and thus reveal what, to them, best represented the era, their elders were alternately amused and chagrined. Although Caroline, James, Gina, and Leo did not intend to be unduly harsh, people their age found it nearly impossible to discuss Sarah's generation—their follies, crimes, wars, mistakes, and outrages against the environment—without implicit criticism. Sarah could hardly blame them. Out of greed, self-indulgence, fear, and hatred, they had almost destroyed the world their children would inherit. A global youth movement in the teens had inspired governments worldwide to take action to pull the human race back from the edge of self-destruction. What kids Caroline and James's age sometimes forgot, however, was that their parents were the ones who had sacrificed to save the world they and generations before them had almost ruined utterly.

"So you're at this aughts party," said Russell, drawing the conversation back to his original question. "And Leo impressed you with his ability to keep his pants hovering above his knees with no visible means of support?"

"No," said Caroline, nearly drowned out by laughter. "I was hip-hop dancing with my friends and he was on the other side of the room catching the end of the *Lord of the Rings* movie marathon on this little old forty-eight-inch television."

"Little," Matt echoed, raising his eyebrows.

"Dad, for us, that's little."

"I saw her dancing and went over to introduce myself," said Leo.

"No, you came over and tried to impress me with your dance moves," said Caroline, smiling. "You didn't say a word to me."

"I let my moves do the talking."

"Then the movie ended and someone put on this old television show where professional dancers perform with movie stars and athletes—*Dance with a Celebrity* or something?" Caroline shook her head, puzzled by the show's title or perhaps the entire concept. "They were performing a waltz, and suddenly someone switched the sound system from the music files to the television."

"That someone was my roommate," said Leo with satisfaction.

"Roommate, some might say collaborator," teased Caroline. "So all at once, instead of hip-hop, the speakers are blasting an orchestral waltz, and the next thing I know, this guy takes me in his arms and starts whirling me around the dance floor."

"And then the guy stepped on her toes," said James, "so she slugged him, and she bumped into Leo as she stormed off the dance floor."

"Don't listen to him," said Caroline, shooting James a look of sisterly exasperation. "The amazing dancer was Leo."

"Hip-hop isn't my strength," Leo explained. "I'm better with ballroom, so I changed the music."

"Wait until you see what he's choreographed for our first dance," said Caroline. "We've been practicing the Viennese waltz and the quickstep."

"And a little salsa for later," said Leo modestly. "Just for fun."

James looked suitably impressed. "No kidding."

"Girls love guys who can dance," said Gina admiringly, and James's eyebrows rose in mild concern.

"Girls always have," said Sarah, offering Matt a sidelong look. His lack of rhythm was notorious in the McClure family. For their first dance as husband and wife, they had resorted to the traditional stand-and-sway to "Unchained Melody" by the Righteous Brothers—still one of Sarah's favorite songs. And Matt, for all of his inability to bust a move, remained her favorite dance partner.

"Maybe you could show me a few steps before the reception," said James to Leo in an undertone that wasn't quite low enough to pass undetected. Gina raised her coffee cup to her lips, but not quickly enough to conceal her smile.

Despite Caroline's earlier declaration that she wanted no wedding talk at supper, the story of how the couple met inevitably steered the conversation in that direction. To Sarah's surprise, Caroline needed no prompting to dash upstairs for her computer pad, which she had been using as a wedding planner. Over coffee and dessert, Caroline covered the schedule for the week, with Sarah and Leo filling in details here and there, and Anna and Gina speaking up whenever they had questions or comments about the many meals they had offered to prepare. Matt was taking care of all the flowers for the ceremony, which would be held in the gazebo in the north gardens, as well as for the reception in the ballroom immediately afterward. In case of rain, the ceremony would be moved to the grand front foyer, but Caroline was confident that wouldn't be necessary.

Sarah had numerous lists of her own—when extra chairs were to be delivered, when the men of the bridal party were to meet at the formal-wear shop on High Street for their final tuxedo fitting, when they would set up the ballroom, who would receive gift bags and when Sarah and Caroline might find time to assemble them—but the subject that concerned her most was the travel itineraries for their most important guests. From the very beginning, Caroline and Sarah had intended for Leo's immediate family and the bridal party to stay at Elm Creek Manor, but after the invitations were sent out, other friends and more distant relatives inquired about staying at the manor too. Sarah couldn't blame them, for who wouldn't prefer the beauty, comfort, and convenience of the historic manor to a hotel in downtown Waterford? She found it impossible to turn down any requests, and before long every guest suite was assigned. Unwittingly, Sarah had arranged it so that during the wedding weekend, Elm Creek Manor would be as fully booked as it was during the busiest week of quilt camp season. It was a daunting prospect, but Matt and Anna assured her that it would be no more difficult than any other summer week, and perhaps less so, since they had no classes or evening programs for quilt campers to organize. Sarah put her faith in her friends and in her many years of experience running Elm Creek Quilt Camp, praying Matt and Anna were right. She would rather have her dearest friends and family nearby than across town, not only for their enjoyment, but also for her own. The weekend would be so filled with activity, and the wedding guests in town so briefly, that Sarah could not hope to spend as much time as she wished with each and every one. Offering them rooms in Elm Creek Manor would give them that much more opportunity to see one another.

Sarah was grateful that, as busy as it would be, the wedding weekend would bring about many reunions with loved ones she had not seen in far too long. Letters, e-mails, phone calls, and virtual reality helped them to keep in touch over time and distance, but as she grew older, she appreciated time spent in the company of others more and more. She had cultivated this respect and esteem over the years with the help of a wise mentor and friend, Sylvia Bergstrom Compson Cooper. Sylvia had taught Sarah the value of family and community, and the peril of isolation, as their unlikely friendship took root and flourished as they worked side by side in Elm Creek Manor.

Sarah and Matt had been newlyweds not much older than Caroline and Leo when they moved to Waterford so Matt could take a job with a landscape architecture company. After a fruitless search for an accounting position in her new town, Sarah reluctantly agreed to work for one of the company's clients, an elderly recluse who had recently returned to town to prepare her family estate for sale after her sister's death. As part of Sarah's compensation, the curmudgeonly woman agreed to teach her to quilt, and as the summer months passed and her grand family estate was gradually restored to its historic splendor, Sylvia shared stories of the manor's golden age, stories from her childhood through her years as a young wife on the World War II home front. As Sylvia's apprentice, Sarah learned that after the master quilter's husband and younger brother had been killed in the South Pacific, her sister had broken her heart and betrayed her trust by marrying the man Sylvia blamed for their deaths. Estranged from her sister for fifty years, Sylvia had lost touch not only with Claudia, but also with all of their extended family.

Once there had been many Bergstroms, Sylvia reminisced, aunts and uncles and cousins scattered around Pennsylvania and as far away as California. Upon hearing of her sister's death, Sylvia had, at first, wanted no part of the family estate that held so many painful memories. She hired a private detective to find someone else to inherit the estate and relieve her of the weighty burden. Quickly—curiously quickly, or so Sylvia realized years later—the detective concluded that Sylvia had no living blood relations, that she was the last descendant of Hans and Anneke Bergstrom, the first members of the family to come to America. Even at the time Sylvia had wondered how the detective had reached his conclusion so soon, and how out of all the cousins and second cousins she had played with in childhood, not one had left a son or daughter behind. But she accepted his report, and on one frigid, lonely New Year's Eve, she resolved that despite her past mistakes, she would not fail to complete the last, crucial task that had fallen to her. She would find a buyer who would restore the manor to its former glory, who would fill the halls with love and laughter once more.

Then along came Sarah, with her idealism and her fanciful scheme to transform Elm Creek Manor into a quilters' retreat, and Sylvia realized that she had found the perfect steward for the Bergstrom legacy. With the help of their friends, the manor became again as wonderful as it had been in Sylvia's childhood—and in many ways, even more so, because its welcome extended beyond the Bergstrom family to a greater community of women and men who longed for such a place, if only for one week each summer. At Elm Creek Manor they could explore their untapped artistry and take creative risks within a nurturing, supportive community of others who understood their longing. Over the years, Sylvia forged cherished friendships, created a thriving business, rediscovered the artist within herself, fell in love, married—but for all her success and happiness, she yearned for family ties of her own, for a niece or nephew who shared the same roots and branches of the family tree, for a cousin with whom to reminisce about the same shared memories of holidays in the years gone by. Sharing stories of her ancestors with her new friends and reviving her favorite traditions were worthwhile and gratifying in their way, and yet left her feeling incomplete. She longed to celebrate with people who knew those traditions as their own, people with whom she shared a common heritage, but she knew this was not to be.

Even as Sylvia mourned the end of her proud family line, she vowed not to take for granted the new family she had created for herself through cherished friendships and marriage to Andrew. And yet she still wondered what had become of all those dear aunts and uncles and cousins, how it could be that they had left behind not a single descendant. Most of all she wondered about her favorite cousin, Elizabeth Bergstrom Nelson, who lived on so vividly in Sylvia's memory that it seemed impossible she had departed the world without leaving her mark upon it.

Sylvia admired her beautiful, vivacious cousin, loved her fiercely, and considered it the unhappiest day in all her five years when Elizabeth married Henry Nelson and moved away with him to Southern California, where he had purchased a thriving cattle ranch, sight unseen, with every dime of his life savings. Sylvia found some comfort in Elizabeth's letters, filled with enchanting tales of splashing in the Pacific Ocean, strolling down the streets of Hollywood, and plucking apricots and oranges from her own groves on the rolling, sun-drenched hills of Triumph Ranch in the Arboles Valley. But over the years, perhaps as Elizabeth's responsibilities as ranch wife and mother grew, her letters became fewer and farther between, until they stopped coming.

Sylvia never saw Elizabeth again, and forever after she puzzled over what had become of her and why she had broken off ties with the family who loved and missed her so dearly. Inspired by the success of other searches into Bergstrom family history, Sylvia decided to launch an investigation. She enlisted the help of Elm Creek Quilter Summer Sullivan, whose historical research skills had unearthed a wealth of information about Sylvia's ancestors before, and she also consulted longtime friend Grace Daniels, a quilter, former museum curator, and antique quilts expert. Elizabeth had left Elm Creek Manor with two precious wedding quilts made by the Bergstrom women, a Chimneys and Cornerstones scrap quilt and a more elegant Double Wedding Ring variation embellished with exquisite floral appliqués. Elizabeth never would have parted with such cherished gifts, and if they had not worn out or suffered another sad fate, she surely would have passed them down to her children. If the quilts could be found, their provenance could trace a path back to Triumph Ranch and Elizabeth.

While Grace addressed that daunting task, Summer searched online databases and archives for any mention of Henry and Elizabeth Nelson or Triumph Ranch. On the quilter's holiday before the twins were born, Summer called with news of an astonishing discovery. While poring over indexes to

California vital records and voter registration lists, Summer had found the names and birth dates of Elizabeth and Henry Nelson's three children. Not only that, but by exploring these new leads further, she had uncovered evidence of at least two grandchildren, one of whom, Scott Nelson, was born in 1961 and currently resided in Newbury Park, California.

And Summer had his address and phone number.

Sylvia could scarcely believe that after so much longing and searching, she had possibly found not only an answer to the question of Elizabeth's fate but also one of her descendants, a blood relative—a second cousin once removed, to be precise. Sylvia decided it would be best to contact him by letter, since a phone call out of the blue might be too disruptive, especially since Nelson was not an uncommon name, nor was Scott. He might be no relation whatsoever.

With hope and a prayer, Sylvia wrote to Scott Nelson to introduce herself and asked him to be in touch if he were indeed her cousin Elizabeth's grandson. On December 6, the Feast of St. Nicholas, he called. Not only was he the grandchild of Elizabeth and Henry Nelson, but he and his sister, Melissa, were also planning a Nelson family reunion over Labor Day weekend at a cousin's farmhouse on what remained of the old Triumph Ranch land. If Sylvia cared to attend, she would be able to meet Scott, Melissa, their cousins, and many other relations, including Elizabeth's great-grandchildren. Far from being the last living descendant of Hans and Anneke Bergstrom, Sylvia was one of many.

Overwhelmed with joy, Sylvia declared that she wouldn't miss the reunion for the world. "My sister can't wait to meet you," Scott replied. "I didn't know there was any such thing as a quilting celebrity, but apparently there is, and you must be one of them. Melissa's heard of your work, and something she calls . . . a quilt camp? Is that right?"

Laughing, Sylvia assured him it was so. "Is Melissa a quilter?"

Scott confirmed that she was, having learned from Grandma Elizabeth as a child. Melissa had inherited several of their grandmother's heirloom quilts—and among them, Sylvia soon learned, was the Chimneys and Cornerstones quilt Elizabeth had received as a wedding gift.

Tears of joy filling her eyes, Sylvia told Scott the history of the quilt, how Sylvia's great-aunt Lucinda had sewn it for Elizabeth in the months leading up to her wedding. Sylvia clearly recalled standing at Lucinda's knee as she had stitched the blocks and explained the symbolism of the pattern. The dark fabrics represented the sorrows in a life, the light colors the joys, and each of the red squares was a fire burning in the fireplace to warm Elizabeth after a long journey home. Sylvia hoped the Chimneys and Cornerstones quilt and memories of home had comforted Elizabeth during the long years she had been inexplicably estranged from her family.

"Maybe Melissa knows why Grandma Elizabeth lost touch," Scott said, after admitting that he had no idea why Elizabeth had severed ties. "They spent hours sewing together and talking. Grandma Elizabeth might have confided something to her that she never told me."

He promised to have his sister call her soon, and the very next afternoon, the phone rang again. It was evening, and Sarah was in the kitchen sipping a cup of warm milk with vanilla, when Sylvia entered holding the cordless handset to her ear.

From her bemused expression, Sarah guessed that Melissa apparently did consider Sylvia a kind of celebrity and was treating her as such. "Why, thank you," Sylvia said again and again, taking a seat in the booth opposite Sarah. "Oh, you're much too kind." Another pause, during which she shot Sarah a look of amazement and mild exasperation. "Melissa, dear, you're embarrassing me with so much praise. I hope you can learn to think of me simply as Cousin Sylvia or I don't know how we'll ever become true friends."

Sarah smothered a laugh, amused that Sylvia seemed to be utterly unaware of her eminence in the quilting community. Years before, one of her quilts, "Sewickley Sunrise," had been selected for the permanent collection of the Museum of the American Quilter's Society in Paducah, and earlier in her career she had traveled the country to lecture and teach at quilt guilds, but the founding of Elm Creek Quilts had garnered her more fame than any of her other professional or artistic achievements. Sarah had seen admirers become tongue-tied when Sylvia dropped by a camp workshop to offer advice and constructive criticism, and campers often arrived with permanent-ink pens and fabric swatches stabilized with freezer paper to collect her autograph. But despite all the admiration and praise she received, Sylvia could not think of herself as a celebrity. She had friends and acquaintances, not fans, for heaven's sake, and she certainly didn't have sufficient fame to overawe anyone, especially not a relative.

Fortunately Melissa managed to gather her wits, for the conversation turned from Sylvia to Elizabeth, a topic far more to the master quilter's liking. They enjoyed a lengthy chat about Melissa's first sewing lessons with Grandma Elizabeth, the quilts she had inherited from her grandmother, and how Triumph Ranch had come to be. But Melissa was at a loss to explain why her grandmother had fallen out of touch with the kinfolk she had spoken of so fondly and so often. Grandma Elizabeth had never said an unkind word about any of her distant family, except for a few rare remarks about her father, who was "a drinking man," and she had spoken with particular affection of Sylvia and her aunt Eleanor, Sylvia's mother. Melissa was also confused about how Elizabeth could have written home about Triumph Ranch in 1925, upon her arrival in California, when all the family stories and preserved documents agreed that Grandpa Henry and Grandma Elizabeth had not purchased the farm until 1933. "Is it possible you've remembered the dates wrong?" she asked Sylvia, but Sylvia was adamant that Henry had set out from Elm Creek Manor with the deed to Triumph Ranch in his possession. He had shown the papers to Sylvia's parents on Christmas a few months before the wedding.

By the end of their chat, which endured long after Sarah had finished her warm vanilla milk and left the kitchen, Sylvia and Melissa were no closer to solving the mystery. "Maybe by the time you come out for the reunion, we'll discover the truth," said Melissa, or so Sylvia told Sarah later. "Grandma didn't save many personal papers, but she did leave a journal and a few letters. I'll go through them and see what I can learn."

"In the meantime, I'll see if my quilting friends can track down Elizabeth's Double Wedding Ring," Sylvia said.

"You'll have to come to the reunion a few days early so we can spend some time together comparing notes," said Melissa. "Everyone will be so eager to meet you, we might not have an opportunity at the reunion."

"I don't think we should wait until the reunion to meet," declared Sylvia. "I know you're busy with your work and family, but if you can get away for a week or two this spring, I'd be delighted if you'd come to Elm Creek Quilt Camp as my guest."

Melissa was thrilled by the invitation, and over the next few days and several phone calls back and forth, she and Sylvia settled upon the third week of May for her visit. Sarah had never seen her dear friend so happy, with the exception of the Christmas Eve the year before when Sylvia married Andrew in the ballroom of Elm Creek Manor, surrounded by their closest friends.

Throughout the winter, Sylvia and Melissa became fast friends with weekly phone calls and occasional letters. Melissa read aloud to Sylvia from Elizabeth's journal, which she had kept sporadically in the late nineteen thirties and early forties, and Sylvia reminisced about the cousin she had so admired as a girl, telling Melissa the stories Sarah already knew well—the Christmas when Elizabeth had hidden the star for the top of the tree under Sylvia's pillow so that only she would win the prize for finding it, the New Year's Eve when Elizabeth had taught her the Charleston so they could show off at the St. Sylvester's Ball, the day of the newlyweds' departure when Sylvia had hidden Elizabeth's shoes in a vain hope that she would be obliged to stay at Elm Creek Manor. Melissa found it enormously funny that Sylvia had not bothered to hide Henry's shoes, for he couldn't leave soon enough to suit her. "Grandpa Henry was reserved and a little stern sometimes, but he was a good man," she protested, laughing. "I don't know why you disliked him so much."

"He stole Elizabeth from me," replied Sylvia. "What was

there to like about someone who would do such a dreadful thing?"

When Sarah repeated the story to Matt—over the phone, for Matt was off at one of his father's construction sites in Uniontown—he fell silent for a moment, and then said, "How do you feel about Melissa stealing Sylvia from you?"

Sarah laughed. "Oh, sure, I live in dire fear that someday Melissa's going to show up with a sack, stuff Sylvia in it, and carry her off to Triumph Ranch."

"I guess it's good that you can joke about it," said Matt, but he sounded dubious. "I'm glad it doesn't bother you."

"You're glad what doesn't bother me?" The only things that really bothered her in those days were her weight gain, her inability to tie her own shoes, Matt's ongoing absence, and the way far too many of their phone conversations, which they scheduled for every evening right before bed, left her feeling dissatisfied and short-tempered.

"That Sylvia hasn't had much time for you ever since Melissa came along."

"What are you talking about? I spend hours with Sylvia every day. We work together, eat together, hang out and quilt together—"

"Okay, fair point. You're right. I'm glad you aren't worried that Melissa is taking your place."

"That never occurred to me." At least not until Matt had planted the thought in the most insecure, anxious part of her brain. "Do you really believe Sylvia's friendship is so transient? Do you really think I was just filling in until a real relative came along?"

"I don't mean you've been filling in as her friend. I know

Sylvia cares about you and that her friendship is genuine." Matt hesitated. "You have to admit, though, in some ways you *have* been a surrogate relative to Sylvia. You took the place of a descendant when Sylvia believed she had no living family."

Sarah needed a moment to decipher his meaning. "When you say I took the place of a relative, are you referring to Sylvia's will?"

"Yes, I'm referring to the will. Do you really think Sylvia would have named you her heir if she had known that her cousin Elizabeth had grandchildren living in California?"

His question left Sarah speechless. Two years after founding Elm Creek Quilts, a health scare had prompted Sylvia to put her affairs in order and revise her will. Dividing the business entity Elm Creek Quilts into shares, she had kept a twenty percent stake for herself, had given twenty percent to Sarah, and had offered each of the remaining Elm Creek Quilters ten percent each. She had also given away two parcels of land: a lot near Waterford College, which she donated to the city for the creation of a skateboard park, and the apple orchard, which she gave to Matt. He was not waiting to inherit the property; although the orchard was surrounded by land belonging to Sylvia, Matt already owned the orchard, free and clear, just as the city owned the skateboard park. What Sylvia had promised Sarah in her will was that upon Sylvia's death, Sarah would inherit Sylvia's twenty percent share of the business, the manor, the grounds, and all her personal property.

This was what troubled Matt; this was what he thought Sarah would lose. But she could not lose something that did not yet belong to her, and if Sylvia had a change of heart and decided to keep the Bergstrom estate in the family, Sarah could not prevent that. Nor could she honestly argue that this would be a misguided choice. As a quilter herself and one of Sylvia's admirers, Melissa was unlikely to use a stake in Elm Creek Quilts to ruin it. Perhaps Melissa would be willing to continue Sylvia's current arrangement and lease the manor to Elm Creek Quilts for a dollar a year. But to ponder such potential upheaval in the distant future when Sylvia had not offered the slightest hint that she might revisit her decision—and all because she had finally found other descendants of Hans and Anneke Bergstrom, something that brought her great happiness—seemed ridiculously premature to Sarah, and made her feel slightly ashamed, grasping, and greedy.

"I won't be sorry that Sylvia's found Elizabeth's descendants," she told Matt firmly. "I'm happy for them, not concerned for myself. Sylvia entrusted the future of Elm Creek Quilts and the Bergstrom estate to me because she knows I'll cherish and protect them, not because she has to give it to *someone,* and in the absence of a blood relative, she might as well settle for me."

"And if, after Sylvia gets to know Melissa better, she decides to leave everything to Melissa instead?"

Sarah took a deep breath and rested her hand on her abdomen, where her unborn twins squirmed restlessly as if sharing her emotions. "If Sylvia believes Melissa deserves her trust more than I do, then I'll have to accept that."

"And that wouldn't disappoint you?"

"Of course it would. I'll be horribly disappointed. But not because I won't"—Sarah waved her arm to indicate the manor and everything in it, but over the phone, the gesture was lost on Matt—"not because I won't get her stuff. Because it would mean I've let her down. It would mean she no longer believed I was the best person for the job." But not only for the job—for the Bergstrom legacy, their history, stories, and traditions. Though she was not a descendant of Hans and Anneke Bergstrom, Sarah felt that she was their true heir. She could not respect and honor them more if she shared their blood. Sylvia understood that, or so Sarah had always thought. But she couldn't deny that Sylvia had originally intended to leave the estate to a Bergstrom, and she might be overjoyed that, contrary to all her expectations, she would be able to fulfill that wish after all.

Matt said nothing while Sarah's thoughts churned. She sat down hard on the edge of the bed, wishing he had never brought up the subject, wishing he had more faith in Sylvia. When the silence dragged out too long, she asked, "Are you still there?"

"Yes."

"Please don't worry about this."

"How can I not worry about it? This is our future. Our livelihoods are at stake."

"Okay." Sarah took a deep breath, thinking. "Say Sylvia does leave everything to Melissa. You'll still own the orchard, I'll still own my twenty percent stake in Elm Creek Quilts, and I'll still have my salary as head of the company. We don't pay rent and we don't have a mortgage, so we're saving and investing a lot more of our income than most couples our age. We'll be okay, Matt. Really."

"What if Melissa comes into her twenty percent and decides to fire you?" Matt countered, not mollified. "Or fire both of us? Do you really think we could earn a living off the orchard alone, assuming Melissa lets us cross her property to get to it?"

Muffling a sigh, Sarah lay down on the bed and closed her eyes. "Melissa couldn't fire me. She would have to convince two-thirds of the board that I had committed an act of gross negligence or irresponsibility, and none of my friends would vote against me unless I really, really deserved it. Which I wouldn't." She was suddenly, overwhelmingly exhausted by the pointlessness of the conversation. Every worst-case scenario Matt brought up, while theoretically possible, was so unlikely to occur that her time would be better spent dreaming up a plan to protect Elm Creek Manor from meteor strikes than anything Matt seemed to fear. Then, all at once, she understood. Matt loved Elm Creek Manor and was terribly afraid of losing it. He loved his orchards, the gardens, working with agricultural students from Penn State in the summer, offering tours of the estate to campers, residing in the historic manor season after beautiful season—all of it, as much as Sarah did.

Sarah wished she knew how to make Matt see the situation as she did. "I'll do everything I can to make our jobs at Elm Creek Manor as secure as possible," she promised. "There really isn't anything to worry about, so please, don't worry."

"I'll try," Matt said quietly. "I hope you're right."

After they hung up, she lay awake in bed, stroking her abdomen and wishing Matt were there. If he were home, he would see that nothing between her and Sylvia had changed despite her new friendship with Melissa. If he were home, distance would lessen his father's influence. None of these strange new disturbances in their marriage would have erupted if Matt were home where he belonged, with her, preparing for the arrival of their children.

Then came the snowy February day when the time for preparation had passed. The babies arrived, mere minutes after Matt's return to Waterford. After four days in the hospital—her stay extended due to the emergency C-section—Sarah, Matt, James, and Caroline went home to Elm Creek Manor. In later years Sarah would remember those first few weeks with the twins as a blur of happiness, worry, wonder, exhaustion, pain, and awe. As if to make up for his long absence, Matt was as attentive a father as she could have hoped, dragging himself out of bed at all hours to bring a crying infant to her to be nursed, changing diapers, burping, bathing—all with utter devotion and concern. He took care of Sarah as she recovered from pregnancy and surgery, too, so that all she had to worry about was regaining her strength, feeding the children, and delighting in their exquisite perfection. Sylvia, Gretchen, Anna, and Carol were also nearby to make sure she wanted for nothing. Years later, Sarah would look back and realize that it was unlikely any new mother of twins had ever had an easier time of it than she had, surrounded by an attentive husband and caring friends who saw to her every need.

The weeks passed, her son and daughter grew, and suddenly it was March and time for a new season of quilt camp. Before the twins were born, Sarah had confidently assumed that she would be ready to return to work part-time by then; she figured she could slip off to the library to catch up on paperwork when the twins napped and squeeze in a few extra hours of work after supper, when Matt would be around to care for them. Instead she discovered that the twins rarely napped at the same time, and whenever she did manage to steal a few moments for herself, all she wanted to do was crawl off to bed to try to make up for the broken, intermittent sleep of the night before. Sylvia told her not to worry; she had retired from teaching camp classes years before, and since she and Andrew didn't have any travel plans except for the Nelson family reunion that summer, she would be able and willing to take care of Sarah's usual duties until she felt ready to return. "Take all the time you need," Sylvia urged her. "Any number of people can run Elm Creek Quilts in the interim, but only you can be mom to those precious twins."

Sarah gratefully accepted Sylvia's help, but the implication that Sarah was not absolutely indispensable to Elm Creek Quilts reawakened the doubts that Matt had sown in her imagination weeks before. Not that she wanted quilt camp to fracture into chaos without her, but it would reassure her to think Sylvia and her friends needed her a little more. Even so, it was a tremendous relief to stop worrying about all the work she wasn't doing and focus entirely upon the twins. James was a good sleeper, cheerful and good-natured, while Caroline fussed whenever anyone but Sarah or Matt held her. She also had difficulty latching on, so that nursing was a chore both mother and daughter struggled to endure. After many tearful, bewildering days, Sarah and Caroline eventually forged a truce, but from the very beginning Caroline was as restless as her brother was content, and Sarah felt that she had to work twice as hard to please her. She never had to worry about James the way she did Caroline, that she was overtired or undernourished or simply not thriving. If Sarah had been obliged to worry about campers' accommodations and teachers' scheduling conflicts and evening programs, too, she would have found it impossible to get through the days.

May brought the fullness of spring to the Elm Creek Valley, and before long the twins were sleeping through the night, or nearly so, and Sarah gradually began taking back some of her usual duties from Sylvia. Between the demands of motherhood and work, she was so busy and preoccupied that she forgot to worry about Melissa or dread her upcoming visit or count the days until she returned to California. It was Matt who reminded her on the eve of Melissa's arrival by urging her to think of the following day of quilt camp as no different than any other.

"I was, until you said that," she replied gloomily, but Matt's attempt to reassure her only emphasized the significance of one of their arriving guests. When Melissa arrived, should Sarah make a fuss over her, as befitted the return of a long-lost Bergstrom descendant to Elm Creek Manor? Should she maintain her distance and treat Melissa warily, rather than let a potential rival learn her weaknesses? Should she treat Melissa as if she were any other camper, in order to send a clear message that Sarah was secure in Sylvia's trust and did not see Melissa as a threat? A few months earlier, Sarah would have pondered the options and agonized for hours over exactly what to say and do, but the twins left her no time for such ruminations. Without giving it more than five minutes' consideration as she sank into sleep, she decided that she would welcome Melissa as warmly as Sylvia had always welcomed Sarah's family, and she would do her best to make sure Melissa had a wonderful week at camp, which was exactly what she tried to do for all of their campers.

As it happened, aside from witnessing Sylvia and Melissa's joyful meeting at camper registration in the foyer and dining at the same table on several occasions, Sarah saw very little of Melissa throughout the week. Even so, Melissa made such a warm and friendly impression that Sarah found it impossible to think of her as a lurking, opportunistic enemy. Melissa had arrived at Elm Creek Manor, suitcase in hand and joyful tears in her eyes, with a happy embrace for Sylvia and a smile for everyone. At the Welcome Banquet that evening, seated at the head table as Sylvia's special guest, she overflowed with praise for the manor, the Elm Creek Quilters, and Sarah in particular, exclaiming that Sylvia had spoken of her so often and so glowingly that Melissa felt like they were already friends. She was quite an accomplished quilter, and as the week went on, both Gretchen and Gwen remarked that her cheerful willingness to help less experienced students made her a joy to have in class. She devoted her spare hours to Sylvia, and occasionally Sarah came upon them in the north gardens or in the library, engrossed in conversation about Elizabeth, Elm Creek Manor, and the elusive Triumph Ranch. Sarah was heartened to see a new energy in Sylvia's step, an ease in her smile, and only then did she truly understand how it had grieved her dear friend to believe she was the last Bergstrom. How could Sarah begrudge Sylvia a friendship that had obviously done her so much good?

At the show-and-tell over breakfast on the cornerstone patio on Saturday, Melissa was so effusive and genuine in her praise for the Elm Creek Quilters that Sarah believed with absolute certainty that she had no designs on Sarah's job and would be horrified by the very thought of ruining the idyllic retreat Sarah and her friends had created. When the Elm Creek

Quilts minivan was ready to take Melissa and a few other campers to the airport, she sought out Sarah and hugged her, thanking her profusely for a week that had been a dream come true. Sarah returned her embrace and was able to tell her, sincerely, that she was very glad Melissa had come.

After the last camper left, the Elm Creek Quilters cleaned up after them and prepared for the next group's arrival the following afternoon. A contemplative quiet settled upon the manor as it always did during the brief respite between sessions. Curious to hear whether Sylvia had learned anything new about her long-lost cousin Elizabeth during her many conversations with Melissa, Sarah searched the manor for her old friend and found her at last, and unexpectedly, in the spacious room on the third floor that had once been the Bergstrom children's nursery. Sylvia was sitting on the window seat and gazing wistfully out the window at the vast green front lawn, sewing basket on the floor by her feet, scraps of fabric spread out on her lap and on the faded blue cushion she sat upon.

"Sylvia?" Sarah asked her.

When Sylvia looked up, her face seemed drawn and tired. "Yes, dear?"

Sylvia seemed so melancholy that Sarah was reluctant to bring up Melissa, whom Sylvia obviously missed very much. "What are you doing up here?" she asked instead.

"Reliving some childhood memories of my cousin Elizabeth." Sylvia gave a light, self-deprecating laugh as she began to gather up her sewing. "The manor always seems so quiet after the campers leave, doesn't it?"

"If it's noise you want, I'm sure Matt and Gretchen would love to have you join them and the babies in the parlor."

"That's a fine idea. Nothing makes one forget one's own sorrows and disappointments than the smiles and laughter of a happy baby, and you've thoughtfully provided us with two."

It pained Sarah to think that Sylvia had any thoughts of sorrow and disappointment after enjoying such a lovely visit with Melissa. "Is everything okay? You seem unhappy."

"I'll be fine, dear. I'm just feeling a little lonely today, with cares weighing heavily on my mind. It will pass. A cuddle with sweet Caroline and that darling James is exactly what I need to set things right." She stood, smoothed her skirt, and then looked around on the floor as if she had dropped something.

Sarah spotted a few bright patches of pink and green and hurried over to pick them up. "Pretty colors," she said, handing the fabric pieces to Sylvia. They were not scraps, as she had assumed from their irregular edges, but carefully traced and cut shapes that resembled a complex pattern she herself had never attempted. "Are you making a Double Wedding Ring quilt?"

"Melissa and I are making one together—or rather, two." Sylvia tucked the fallen pieces into her sewing basket with many other similar shapes, some of which had been sewn into colorful arcs and semicircles of greens and roses in a gradation of hues. "Since it seems unlikely that Elizabeth's wedding quilt will ever be found, we decided to make two copies of it, one for her and one for me. I'm going to piece the rings for both quilts, and Melissa will do all the appliqué."

"That's quite a project," said Sarah, trying to imagine how they would collaborate on two such elaborate quilts when separated by more than twenty-five hundred miles.

"If you think that's ambitious, guess when we intend to have them completed."

"Christmas?"

"Oh, if only that were so. No, our deadline is the Nelson family reunion over the Labor Day weekend."

"Are you serious? With all those curved pieces and appliqué?" When Sylvia nodded, Sarah asked, "You mean that you'd like to have the *tops* completed by then, right?"

"I suggested that, but Melissa thought that unveiling finished quilts would impress everyone more than tops alone. Naturally, both will be quilted by hand as Elizabeth's original was. Melissa declared that we should set high goals for ourselves and adjust our expectations later if we must." Sylvia smiled as she tucked her arm through Sarah's and walked her to the door. "Remind you of anyone?"

"Summer Sullivan?"

Sylvia laughed. "I meant you, dear. Elm Creek Quilts exists because you weren't afraid to dream big. Even with your own professional future uncertain all those years ago, you saw before you a lonely old woman and her neglected old house and recognized extraordinary potential. It takes a very special person to see with the heart rather than the eye, with imagination rather than cynical assumptions."

Sarah's ability to accept praise graciously was inversely proportional to how deeply it touched her. "Well, I don't know about that. I might have dreamed up Elm Creek Quilts, but I needed all of our friends' help to make it happen."

"What great achievement is ever accomplished by one person alone?" Sylvia patted her arm as they walked down the hall, and then gestured toward the foyer two stories below, where in less than a day they would welcome more campers, full of anticipation and excitement for the week ahead. "And yet without you, none of this would exist."

"Without your generosity, it wouldn't exist either. Without Elm Creek Manor, there is no Elm Creek Quilt Camp."

"Yes," said Sylvia, her voice suddenly distant. "I'm mindful of that, my dear."

Her grip on Sarah's arm tightened as they reached the stairs, and her mouth pursed in an expression Sarah had learned from long familiarity indicated troubled thoughts Sylvia was not yet ready to discuss. Sarah did not pressure her to unburden herself, knowing she would speak when she was good and ready and not one moment before.

The weeks went by. The twins flourished, surrounded by love; Elm Creek Quilts thrived, introducing aspiring quilters to their time-honored art and encouraging experienced quilters to explore new artistic challenges. Piece by piece, Sylvia and Melissa re-created Elizabeth's wedding quilt, discussing their progress and working out problems over the phone several times a week, and sending partially completed sections back and forth through the mail significantly less frequently. Sarah expected Matt's concerns about their friendship to heighten once he discovered they were collaborating on such an extensive, emotionally rich project, but he said nothing of it. Nor, as Sarah had feared, did he propose that—what with the construction business entering its busiest time of the year and Sarah managing so well with the twins—he could spend a few weekends now and then helping out his father.

Sarah had expected and dreaded the request ever since the end of April when Hank came to Elm Creek Manor to meet his grandchildren, but from the moment he first saw the babies, Hank was so smitten that McClure Construction never entered the conversation. He predicted that Caroline would grow up to be "a knockout" and James the starting quarterback of the Nittany Lions. It was he who first called the children "Carrie" and "Jim," nicknames that Sarah fervently hoped would swiftly disappear from memory as soon as his visit ended, but unfortunately, "Jim" stuck, so that as the years went by, only his parents and Sylvia called him by his given name.

After Hank left, Sarah breathed a sigh of relief, but she still worried that her father-in-law might pressure Matt during his weekly phone calls, which were ostensibly about the twins but eventually drifted—or were steered—to McClure Construction. Remembering every unhappy moment of their winter apart, Sarah couldn't believe that Hank would go down in defeat so easily. Weeks passed, and whenever Matt hung up the phone after a chat with his father, Sarah expected him to announce that Hank had made a reasonable request for his only son to help him out on a particularly important project. By midsummer, unable to stand the suspense any longer, she asked Matt outright whether Hank still hoped he would resume working for the construction company.

"I'm sure he still hopes I will," replied Matt, "but I told him I couldn't. You need me, the twins need me, and it's our busy season here too."

"So he did ask you?"

"He did."

"And you told him no?"

"Of course."

"And he's okay with that? He's not trying to wear you down?"

"He drops a few hints now and then, but he knows where I stand. Our agreement last winter was that I'd help him out until the twins arrived. You didn't think he'd forget the plan, did you?"

Not forget but disregard, Sarah thought, though she didn't say so aloud. So the request had come after all and Matt had refused—but it seemed too easy, too good to be true, after the ongoing conflict of the previous winter. Still, rather than have Matt repeat verbatim every word of every recent conversation with his father until she was satisfied that Hank truly understood that Matt wasn't going to leave his family and Elm Creek Quilts for Hank and McClure Construction, she decided not to pursue it. For once Matt had done exactly what she needed him to do, and she was going to express her thanks by letting the matter drop.

The rest of the camp season went along as it did every summer, with happy reunions of far-flung friends, extraordinary lectures by master quilters and gifted instructors that inspired her anew, occasional mishaps she and her colleagues sorted out behind the scenes, heartfelt confessions at the Candlelight welcome ceremonies on the cornerstone patio, and new quilts, so many new, breathtaking, beautiful—or amusing, intriguing, whimsical, perplexing, exquisite, or simple—wonderful quilts. With a twin on each hip, Sarah bade the campers good-bye at the close of each week, enormously gratified that she had been able to participate in their creative journeys. Each summer reminded her that everyone had an artist within; some possessed greater natural ability, others more powerful desire to develop their gifts, but all people were blessed with creative abilities they could use to make the world a better, more beautiful place.

Nurturing those gifts, no matter how long they had been dormant or unrecognized, was the true mission of Elm Creek Quilts.

All too soon, Labor Day weekend arrived. Caroline and James were seven months old, babbling, pulling themselves up, and delighting one and all with their sweet innocence and joy. Bonnie departed for Maui, where she would spend the winter working for Aloha Quilt Camp at the Hale Kapa Kuiki Inn in Lahaina. Maggie and her boyfriend, Russell, left to travel around the South and Southwest teaching at quilt guilds. Gwen had already begun the fall semester at Waterford College, where she had been turned down, yet again, for department chair, an annual slight she shrugged off as a blessing in disguise, for more administrative duties would have obliged her to spend less time on her research. Sylvia and Andrew headed out to Southern California for the Nelson family reunion in the Arboles Valley, after which they planned to spend a week in Santa Susana with Andrew's son, daughter-in-law, and their two daughters. Matt was busy with the orchards, and although Sarah's days were full of diapers and sippy cups and board books and first words and first steps and never enough rest, she was as content as she was exhausted, and possibly happier than she had ever been.

In mid-September, Sylvia returned home from California, road weary but joyful, full of stories about her long-lost cousin Elizabeth, her husband, Henry, their children, their grandchildren, and their great-grandchildren. She had also brought a precious gift from Melissa, one of Elizabeth's heirloom quilts—not the lost Double Wedding Ring or the Chimneys and Cornerstones Sarah had heard of before, but a scrap Postage Stamp quilt with a leafy vine border pieced from fabrics Elizabeth had saved from feed sacks or collected as souvenirs on her rare travels away from Triumph Ranch. Admiring the precious heirloom anew as she showed it to Sarah, Sylvia remarked, "Melissa didn't mind giving it to me because she knows she won't be parted from it long. It will be hers again someday."

"Not for a very long time," said Sarah firmly. She didn't like it when Sylvia alluded, however vaguely, to her mortality.

Sylvia eyed her over the rims of her glasses. "Whether it's sooner or later, and I do hope it will be later, I would like Melissa to have this quilt back when I pass on, and I trust that you'll see to it, dear."

Sarah promised to take care of it when the time came, and, eager to move on to a more pleasant subject, she urged Sylvia to resume her tale of the Nelson family reunion. Regrettably, Sylvia and Melissa had not finished the Double Wedding Ring replicas in time to unveil them at the gathering; Melissa had not completed the appliqué centers, so Sylvia's piecing had stalled. They had set a new goal for Christmas, when they could display the quilts for a smaller but no less enthusiastic gathering of Nelson descendants.

"You mean you won't be spending the holidays at Elm Creek Manor?" asked Sarah, dismayed.

"I'm afraid not." Sylvia frowned slightly as she spoke, which told Sarah she had misgivings about her decision. "It will be strange to celebrate far from home, but if we go to California, Andrew will get to see his children over the holidays too. When we told his daughter about our plans, she said that her family would travel from Connecticut to join us at his son's house."

"But this will be the twins' first Christmas."

"Well, yes, and I do hate to miss that, but I'm sure you understand."

Sarah felt her breath catch in her throat, but she managed to keep her voice steady when she replied, "Of course I understand. I hope you have a wonderful time. Let me know if you'd like my help finishing up the Double Wedding Rings."

"Hmph." Sylvia waved a hand dismissively. "I don't believe we'll make that deadline either. But never mind. Quilting has always been as much about the process as the final product for me. Working on these quilts with Melissa has been a true pleasure. It's made me feel closer to Elizabeth and to all my long-lost loved ones than anything has since—well, since returning to Elm Creek Manor. It's hard to describe, but I feel a connection now, the ties of kin. It's a great comfort to me, so I'd be perfectly content if the work on these quilts continues for the rest of my life."

Her heart full of sympathy and understanding, Sarah embraced Sylvia and was shocked to feel how thin and frail her friend felt in her arms. Sylvia was growing older, but because the force of her personality was so strong, Sarah had been able to ignore the signs. But time took its toll even on the most vibrant of souls, and none of them could escape the slow but inexorable ravages of the passing years.

Tears of pain and loss sprang into Sarah's eyes, but she blinked them away before Sylvia noticed. She gave her friend one last, warm embrace and forced a smile as she released her. "You know what would be a wonderful Christmas gift for Melissa?"

"I see you don't believe we'll finish the quilts either," said

Sylvia dryly. "That was our intention, you know, to exchange them as our Christmas gifts."

"I know better than to bet against you in any quilting challenge," said Sarah. "This could be an extra gift—or a backup, just in case you don't finish the quilts. I think you and I should go through all the old Bergstrom photo albums, scan in pictures of Elizabeth and her parents and grandparents and the manor and everything, and make copies for Melissa and her brother. We could even carefully—very carefully—remove those portraits in the library and parlor from their frames and scan them too. We could arrange the copies in beautiful leather photo albums with 'Bergstrom' and the family emblem of the rearing stallion embossed on the cover or the spine."

"What a perfectly wonderful idea," Sylvia exclaimed. "I'm sure the Nelsons don't have any of those photos, because I know Elizabeth didn't take any copies with her. One didn't have copies of photos in those days; you made one picture and you took very good care of it. Or didn't, in which case the image was lost forever."

"Another good reason to scan in the photos you've saved," said Sarah. "A digital archive will give us a backup in case the originals are damaged."

"God forbid," declared Sylvia. "Sarah, my dear, I don't think I tell you enough how much I admire your ingenuity."

"You tell me more than often enough, but I'm hardly the first person to think of this sort of project. There are entire businesses designed to do exactly this."

"Well, you're the first person around here to think of it, so as far as I'm concerned that counts for a great deal indeed." Sylvia smiled, dispelling the illusion—if it had been an illusion—of fragility Sarah had glimpsed only moments before. "When can we get started?"

"As soon as you like," said Sarah, "after the twins have gone to bed."

Eager to begin, Sylvia started on her own without Sarah, paging through old albums and scrapbooks and choosing those she thought Elizabeth's descendants would most appreciate. She included the only known photograph of Anneke Bergstrom—petite, dark-haired, and beautiful in her early thirties—and the precious few of Hans Bergstrom, one a formal studio portrait of a young man recently arrived in America, several others of Hans in his forties posed with one or more of his prized horses, and another when he looked to be in his sixties, taken with several unidentified men in suits and hats in front of a white-columned building—presumably somewhere in Waterford. Others showed family gatherings, Sylvia as a pouting child on Elizabeth's lap, a wedding portrait of Elizabeth and Henry looking very much in love—and as Sarah scanned in each one, made copies, and helped Sylvia arrange them in albums, she realized what a treasure she beheld, and she understood a little better the pain Sylvia had endured believing for so long that she was the last of that proud family.

The Double Wedding Ring quilts were, as predicted, not finished in time for Christmas, but the albums were completed, lovingly wrapped, and delivered. When Sylvia phoned from California to wish Sarah and the others a Merry Christmas, she happily reported that the albums had caused quite a sensation, evoking tears and laughter and teasing threats of theft while the recipients slept. "I may have promised to make a few more," Sylvia said.

Enjoying Sylvia's delight, Sarah was able to forget, for a moment, how much she wished Sylvia had spent Christmas at Elm Creek Manor. "How many more?"

"Perhaps"—Sylvia hesitated—"perhaps as many as a dozen. Oh, I probably shouldn't have offered so much."

Sarah laughed and promised to help her, and shortly after Sylvia's return to the manor, they began. As they worked on the albums and planned for the next session of quilt camp, Sylvia spoke often—sometimes happily, sometimes wistfully—of Elizabeth, her family long departed, and her new family so many miles away. Sarah listened and offered comfort as she could, and determinedly quashed any sparks of jealousy that surfaced.

She knew that Sylvia loved her, and she knew that Sylvia had love in abundance. Her affection for Melissa did not mean she had any less to spare for Sarah. Sarah hoped that she could learn to love as faithfully and unselfishly as Sylvia did.

She smiled to think that in many ways, she remained Sylvia's apprentice.

· Chapter Three ·

Everyone lingered in the kitchen long after only crumbs remained of Anna's delicious apple tart, but eventually Sarah bade everyone good night, reminding them that they had a busy day ahead of them and warning the young people not to stay up too late. She gave Caroline one last hug, murmured, "Welcome home," into her golden curls, and went upstairs. Matt followed close behind, and soon, as a cool early-autumn breeze stirred the curtains in the darkness, they lay side by side beneath the twelve-block sampler in a Garden Maze setting she had given him as an anniversary gift, her first quilt, the one she had learned to make with Sylvia's wise guidance.

Just as she was about to drift off to sleep, Matt broke the silence. "Do you remember the days leading up to our wedding?"

Sarah shifted on to her side. "How could I forget?" A time that should have been sweet with happiness and anticipation had been soured by stress, worry, and the constant strain of dealing with her mother's tears and warnings. Although Sarah was grateful that Carol had eventually come to love and appreciate Matt, she wished her mother had foregone the lamentations on their wedding day and had instead offered reassuring, practical advice about how to weather the storms every marriage eventually encountered.

Quietly, Matt asked, "If we could do it all over again—"

"I would in a heartbeat," Sarah said, not even needing him to finish the question. Her heart knew the answer.

"I'm glad. I would too." He pulled her closer and kissed her on the forehead. Resting her head on his shoulder, she soon fell asleep.

In the morning when she woke, Matt was gone, up with the sunrise and out in the orchard. She imagined him strolling through the rows of trees, a cup of coffee in one hand and a faded baseball cap on his head, looking up into the heavy boughs and estimating the harvest. His own cultivars were prospering, especially the one he had named after her, Sarah's Gold, which was especially popular at the farmers' market held on the Waterford town square every Saturday from April through October. Sylvia had once declared that Gerda Bergstrom's apple strudel had never tasted better than when prepared with Matt's apples. That was on the Christmas before Sylvia's death, at age ninety-three, when the twins were ten years old.

How Sylvia would have enjoyed Caroline's wedding day! She had doted on the twins, cherishing them as the grandchildren she had never had. She had delighted in watching them grow from infants into bright, happy children. She had celebrated every early milestone as proudly as Sarah and Matt had, and had enjoyed the small, simple moments of ordinary days that Sarah, in her new-mother fatigue, might have overlooked if Sylvia had not pointed out how marvelous they were. Sylvia would have been particularly delighted to observe how James had grown into his role with Elm Creek Quilts, for she had been neither surprised nor disappointed that James, rather than his sister, had inherited his mother's love of quilting.

From the time the twins were born, visiting quilt campers often remarked to Sarah how fortunate she was to have a daughter. Someday, they told her, Sarah could teach Caroline how to quilt, and they would spend many wonderful hours together sewing, shopping for fabric, and visiting quilt shows. And Sarah had agreed that she was very fortunate indeed. Warm, pastel-hued visions of Caroline blossoming into a talented quilter under her mother's wise and gentle tutelage filled her head, and she dreamed of a distant future, when, after graduating with highest honors from an Ivy League university, Caroline would return home to run Elm Creek Quilt Camp by her mother's side. James would thrive in some other field, Sarah was sure, but her visions of his future were far less specific.

Caroline, expected from birth to become a quilter, had been taught and prompted and praised by the Elm Creek Quilters and a nearly continuous stream of visiting quilt campers since she was old enough to hold a needle, but after obediently learning the running stitch and completing a few small pillows and pot holders, one day she boldly and unexpectedly announced that she would much rather help her daddy in the garden. When Caroline was in middle school, Sarah had to cajole her into joining their quilting bees each quilter's holiday and National Quilting Day, a misguided practice she abandoned when

Gretchen delicately pointed out that Sarah couldn't force Caroline to enjoy quilting, and perhaps Caroline's time would be better spent exploring her own interests.

Caroline's interests changed from week to week; she would throw herself headlong into a new subject, absorb it with a keen focus Sarah would have thought impossible for a child so young, and then move on to something else that piqued her insatiable curiosity. To Sarah's dismay, Caroline's sewing basket and half-sewn blocks gathered dust in her bedroom until James dug them out from under her bed, where he had crawled one rainy autumn afternoon during a game of hide-and-seek. Methodically he finished his sister's abandoned projects, but Sarah didn't realize what an achievement that was until Anna remarked about it. No one had ever taught James to sew, at least not directly; he had absorbed the knowledge over the years spent in the company of quilters in almost the same way he had learned language. Russell, who had married Maggie by then and had become a permanent member of the faculty, became James's favorite teacher, and when James was in the sixth grade, Russell privately told Sarah that the boy had true artistic talent. Sarah, who had assumed that James's interest was a passing phase, took her first real look at her son's finished quilts and realized that Russell spoke the truth.

After that, partly out of shame for being so caught up in her disappointment that Caroline didn't care for quilting that she had neglected James's keen interest and genuine gifts, she allowed him to attend any Elm Creek Quilt Camp classes he desired, as long as the teacher didn't object and he didn't disrupt the class. James, who tended to play the class clown at school and put in the bare minimum of effort required to pass his academic subjects, transformed into a serious student when the subject was art. Sarah marveled at the change in him and was eternally grateful to the art teacher who had helped James find his way. In eighth grade, when James griped to his art teacher that he didn't see the point of any of his other classes, especially math, she promptly responded that artists had to know math so they could determine how much to charge their customers. They had to know math so they could manage their finances, budget for supplies, and manage their galleries, not to mention the complex geometric calculations that quilters in particular had to understand. They had to read and write well, so they could describe their work to others and apply for grants. They had to know history, to better comprehend art and artists in context. For every academic subject James insisted he would never use outside of school, his teacher countered with a practical application. Thus persuaded, if a bit jolted by the rude awakening, James redoubled his efforts in all his classes, and although he never breezed through a semester accumulating A's and the adoration of his teachers as Caroline did, he became a reliable B+ student. When he graduated high school with honors, Sarah gave that clever, inspiring art teacher a stunning Mariner's Compass quilt along with a sincere, heartfelt letter she could only hope expressed the depth of her gratitude.

In the years since, James had taken his hard-earned, well-deserved place within Elm Creek Quilts, second only to Sarah. From the time he was in high school he had wanted to lead Elm Creek Quilts someday, although he had not told Sarah that until his junior year at Penn State, when, after she and Matt spent most of the spring semester encouraging him to find a summer internship, he finally confessed that he didn't want to work anywhere but Elm Creek Quilt Camp. Since then, he had become Sarah's most trusted adviser and one of the most popular teachers on the faculty. Sarah marveled at his ability to manage the business, teach, and pursue his own art with equal, effortless ease. Best of all, he was happy in his work, a blessing she knew from her own experience never to take for granted.

With a sigh, she threw off the sheet and climbed out of bed. She had too much to do and no time to spare reminiscing. Leo's parents and stepparents would be arriving that morning, and by afternoon, most of the bridesmaids were expected as well. Sarah already had a list of chores for Caroline's friends—checking over the place cards, assembling programs, filling gift bags, tying bows around wedding favors—and she hoped the young women would be willing workers. Ayana had always been a helpful girl, so Sarah was counting on her, and Gina was as industrious as her mother—but like her mother, she would be busy in the kitchen and couldn't be spared for other tasks. As Sarah showered and dressed, she considered asking her own friends to pitch in when they arrived in a few days' time, and decided that whatever the bridesmaids couldn't finish, she would entrust to her friends. They had already agreed to help her with the Memory Album quilt, and she was sure they wouldn't mind additional duties.

Downstairs in the kitchen, Anna had set out a continental breakfast, which several of the manor's residents and guests were enjoying when Sarah arrived. Caroline sat close to Leo in the corner booth with Emily, while Jeremy and Russell sat at the long table discussing a football game. At the other end of the table, Carol sipped a cup of black coffee and worked a crossword puzzle, frowning at the computer pad as if sheer disapproval would transform it into the newsprint she preferred. On the other side of the kitchen, Maggie poured herself a cup of coffee and looked around for the sugar bowl, which someone had moved to the other side of the sink. Gina stood in the pantry with her pad and stylus, examining the shelves and making notes for what in all likelihood was yet another grocery list. James was absent, which Sarah had expected, as he went for a long run every morning before breakfast unless the weather was truly horrific. He was always training for one marathon or another and had a broad interpretation of what qualified as perfect running weather.

Sarah returned everyone's greetings and helped herself to coffee and a bagel, which she toasted, spread thickly with cream cheese, and sprinkled with cinnamon. She sat down across the table beside Jeremy, who warned her in a whisper that Caroline had made them all promise there would be no wedding talk at breakfast.

"She did, did she?" Sarah sipped her coffee contemplatively and glanced sideways at her daughter, who had everyone at her table laughing at an animated story about the mishaps of her fellow medical students as they crammed for a notoriously difficult exam. "Well, I made no such promises, and I have a long agenda to get through before breakfast." Raising her voice, she said, "If I could have everyone's attention, there's a lot to accomplish today, and I'd appreciate your help."

While everyone else nodded, Caroline raised her hands as if preparing to cover her ears. "Unless you're talking about quilt camp or the apple harvest, please, stop right there."

"Honey, this is your wedding," said Carol, astonished and mildly scandalized. "These are your plans for your family and your friends."

"I'm just trying to help make sure it all gets done," added Sarah, "on time and properly, and I can't do that if you forbid us to talk about it."

"Can't you wait until after breakfast?" Caroline pleaded.

"And have everyone go their separate ways before I can assign them some work? Not on your life." Sarah touched the screen of her pad and scrolled to her list. "Let's start with the rooms. There are fresh linens on all the beds of the second-floor west-wing suites—except those belonging to permanent residents, of course. You're on your own as usual." Jeremy laughed. "I need volunteers to help make beds—" She broke off as Caroline suddenly groaned and buried her head in her arms on the tabletop. "Sweetheart, are you sick?"

"Yes, sick of wedding talk." Caroline sat up and draped an arm over Leo's shoulders. "We should have eloped."

Leo made a noncommittal sound, neither nodding nor shaking his head, managing to avoid the appearance of choosing a side. A wise young man, Sarah thought.

"Everyone considers eloping at some point," remarked Anna, smiling as she leaned against the counter and sipped from a steaming cup of coffee.

"Usually not so close to the wedding date, though," said Maggie, a bit warily.

"This isn't funny," said Carol, looking in dismay from her granddaughter to her daughter and back. "What will people say if you elope? They'll think your family doesn't want you to marry poor Leo, and we all know he's such a nice young man."

Sarah suddenly imagined Caroline slipping out the back door of the manor before dawn on the morning of her wedding day, Leo trailing after her obligingly with suitcases in hand.

"Caroline," she said evenly, mindful of her mother's distress, "you may be sick of wedding talk, but many people have gone to a lot of time, trouble, and expense to arrange a lovely weekend for you. Before you consider running off for a quickie ceremony somewhere, I want you to think about how you would feel later, knowing you had disappointed all those people."

"We're not eloping," said Leo, smiling reassuringly, his dimple deepening. "We've spent hours practicing the Viennese waltz, and I intend to show off."

"You can show off in Vegas," Caroline pointed out.

She could not seriously be considering a Vegas wedding. Sarah took a deep breath and counted to ten silently. By the time she reached seven, she realized that Caroline had no intention of eloping and missing the one day she was guaranteed and entitled to be the center of attention—not that she was ever far from the center on an ordinary day. She just wanted to punish Sarah, a little, for defying the promise she had exacted from everyone else.

"Sylvia's mother eloped," Sarah mused aloud. "Her parents had wanted her to marry another young man, the son of a wealthy Manhattan department store magnate. Actually, originally Eleanor's elder sister was supposed to marry him, but a few days before the wedding, she ran off with her best friend's widowed father, who also happened to be her father's biggest business rival. So, with a wedding all arranged and guests arriving and the merger of family fortunes at stake, they expected Eleanor to step into her sister's place as easily as putting on the wedding gown she had left behind."

Distraction by narrative, a technique Sarah had perfected during the tantrums of Caroline's truly terrible Terrible Twos, worked its magic yet again. "Her sister eloped with her best friend's dad," Caroline paraphrased in disbelief, "so her parents expected her to marry the jilted groom?"

"Yes, and she would have, except the man she truly loved, Sylvia's father, arrived in the nick of time to whisk her away to Elm Creek Manor." Sarah remembered how she and Sylvia had pieced together the story from the scant evidence they had discovered in the attic while searching for Bergstrom family photos to scan in for Melissa's album. She realized with a bit of a shock that that had been almost twenty-five years before. "Eleanor and Frederick celebrated their wedding here a few weeks later, with the Bergstroms, their family, and friends. Not one person from Eleanor's side of the family attended."

"What happened to the sister?" Gina asked, drawn from the pantry by Sarah's story.

"Oh. Well, she and her husband went down with the *Titanic,* so their elopement story didn't end quite as happily." Sarah picked up her pad. "Not that anything so unfortunate would happen to Caroline and Leo if they eloped, of course. It's probably just a coincidence."

"It wouldn't hurt to play it safe," said Carol. "I'm not superstitious, but I've never known a wedding celebrated at Elm Creek Manor to end unhappily. Isn't that right, Sarah?"

As her mother threw her an urgent look, Sarah hesitated, remembering Sylvia's sister, and how her Elm Creek Manor wedding had led to the sisters' estrangement. She also thought of Sylvia's first marriage, which had been happy indeed but ended far too soon with her husband's death in World War II. But Sarah offered a half shrug and a noncommittal nod rather than contradict her mother and undermine the power of her words, which seemed to be having the desired effect. She didn't want to say anything to encourage Caroline to elope, and Carol's claim was, for the most part, true: Except for those two notable exceptions, all the weddings Sarah knew of that had been celebrated at the manor had led to happy marriages, despite their sometimes inauspicious beginnings.

Sylvia and Andrew's relationship was a case in point. Andrew's children had strongly objected when he announced his engagement to Sylvia, voicing concerns about Sylvia's health—which was fine, despite the stroke she had suffered a few years earlier—and their advanced ages, which from Sarah's new perspective didn't seem so advanced anymore. They insisted that if Andrew chose to marry, they would not attend and give tacit approval to what they knew would be a tragic mistake. Though disappointed, Sylvia and Andrew were not dissuaded—in fact, they moved up their wedding date by several months. Only Sarah, Matt, and the judge who performed the ceremony had been in on the secret that Christmas Eve, when the holiday celebration turned into a ceremony honoring Sylvia and Andrew's love and commitment. The only shadow upon the evening was the absence of Andrew's children and their families, but the newlyweds were resolved to win them over in time. In later years, after the breach was mended and all was forgiven, both Amy and Bob admitted that their greatest regret in life was that they had refused to attend their father's wedding. Privately Amy had told Sarah that one of her greatest joys was that her father had found a second love in his golden years, and that he and Sylvia had made each other very happy for the rest of their lives.

Anna and Jeremy's wedding could have been equally

fraught with tension, but if anyone adamantly believed they shouldn't marry, they kept their objections to themselves. Anna was Catholic and Jeremy was Jewish, and both of their families preferred for them to marry within their own faiths. But concerns about religious differences fell into a surprisingly distant second place behind their families' misgivings about the apparent haste with which the couple had decided to marry. Sarah, too, had been astonished when they announced their engagement a mere handful of months after they had begun dating, but of course, they had been friends for years before their relationship developed into something deeper and richer.

Anna had liked her neighbor across the hall from the start, from the first brief greetings they exchanged when they happened to leave their apartments at the same time to the numerous occasions he had held the outside door for her when she returned with her arms full of grocery bags. She learned his name when a few misdirected letters ended up in her mailbox, and a quick trip across the hallway to deliver them to him turned into a twenty-minute conversation. Over time, she discovered more about Jeremy in quick, casual exchanges whenever they crossed paths in the hallway or the lobby: He had written his master's thesis on the battle of Gettysburg, he taught two undergraduate classes at Waterford College each semester, and he had recently passed the candidacy exam to be accepted as a Ph.D. student in the Department of History. She considered asking him over for coffee some evening, but she lost her courage and settled for accidental meetings in and around their apartment building.

One night in mid-November, Jeremy knocked on her door bearing a large cardboard box and a hopeful expression. The

Waterford College Key Club was collecting nonperishable food items to make Thanksgiving baskets for needy families in the Elm Creek Valley, but the carton they had left in their building's lobby held only a few boxes of pasta, a canister of raisins, and a package of granola bars. Anna was impressed that Jeremy had taken it upon himself to solicit donations door-to-door, so not only did she contribute a few items from her pantry to the carton, she also accompanied him on the rest of his rounds. The evening ended with them back in her apartment baking whole-wheat chocolate cappuccino brownies from ingredients Jeremy had spotted on her pantry shelves. They enjoyed the decadent dessert warm right from the pan as they watched the *Peanuts* Thanksgiving special on television, sitting cross-legged on her sofa, licking chocolate from their fingertips, as comfortable as if they had been friends for years.

From then on, their accidental meetings in the hall usually turned into lengthy conversations unless one of them was running late, and at least once every two weeks Jeremy came over for dinner or dessert, testing new recipes Anna invented for the restaurant she hoped to open someday. They met less frequently after Anna began dating Gordon—Jeremy thought Gordon was a pompous blowhard, and Gordon didn't like Anna to pay attention to anyone but him—but they still talked almost every day.

Anna had been involved with Gordon for more than a year when Jeremy mentioned meeting a beautiful girl at the library, so the sharp sting of jealousy she felt at the news caught her completely by surprise. A few months later, when the stunning auburn-haired beauty moved in with him and turned out to be as friendly, kind, and interesting as she was gorgeous, Anna silently berated herself for not being more delighted for Jeremy, who was, after all, supposed to be her friend. Summer had always been thoughtful and friendly to her, helping her land the chef's job with Elm Creek Quilts and encouraging Jeremy to drive her back and forth to the manor on days the bus ride would be too inconvenient. Two months later, when Summer suddenly moved out of Jeremy's apartment and into Elm Creek Manor, Anna naturally assumed they had broken up, but apparently they remained a couple even after Summer's departure for graduate school in the fall. By that time Anna had broken up with the pompous Gordon, and she was secretly delighted when Summer's absence gave Jeremy more free time—which he seemed very glad to spend with her. Their old companionship resumed, stronger than ever, and Anna began to think of Jeremy as her best friend, although she realized Summer probably occupied that place of honor in his life.

Anna was content being just friends for a long time, but eventually she realized she felt much more than friendship for Jeremy, and she suspected he felt the same about her. She tried to conceal her feelings, because if her crush became public knowledge, things could become awkward for her around the manor. Summer and Jeremy remained a couple, at least officially. To Anna, however, it seemed Summer had been pulling away from Jeremy for months, beginning with the day she had moved out of his apartment and into the manor. Moving to Chicago and discouraging him from visiting too often seemed, to Anna at least, another way to distance herself. But Jeremy was determined to make it work, and Anna was determined not to interfere, no matter how much it hurt.

On one stormy Friday after Thanksgiving, Anna brooded

over her unhappy circumstances as Jeremy drove west through an early winter storm to spend the weekend with Summer. Although they never acknowledged any deepening of their friendship, Anna and Jeremy had become very close, closer than mere friends. The day didn't truly begin until they'd greeted each other with a text across the hallway that separated their two apartments, and the day didn't feel properly concluded until that last late-night good-night phone call. Jeremy had to be aware that he spent more of his time and attention upon the friend who happened to be a girl than he did upon his girlfriend, but Anna didn't know whether he had ever asked himself what that meant. Was he really unaware of what Anna felt for him? Had he not figured out that she repeatedly turned down Sylvia's invitations to move into a comfortable suite in the manor, with no rent to pay and easy access to the kitchen of her dreams, because she would miss him if he weren't living right across the hall? Did he not suspect, as she did, that he had begun describing them as "good friends" so often and so emphatically because he was afraid that he had begun to feel more for her than that?

She realized she had fallen in love with him, and she knew she couldn't go back to pretending she was content to be no more than a friend. When he called her en route to Chicago, she blurted out that she could no longer be his fallback girl—the lonely girl he called and texted and spent time with because he couldn't be with his girlfriend, the loyal best friend he ditched when the woman he preferred finally paid attention to him. Completely blindsided, Jeremy protested that he had never intended to treat her that way, and as the conversation escalated into an argument, Anna confessed that she was in love with him. Mortified, she hung up the phone, assuming their friendship was over.

But Jeremy had other plans. He turned the car around and drove back through the snowstorm to Elm Creek Manor. Anna was stunned to see him. Everyone else at the manor, including Sarah and Gwen, Summer's mother, assumed he had turned back because of the storm, and of course he could not explain the real reason. Even Anna could only guess—guess, and hope. She prepared herself to bear it if he had come home only because he valued their friendship and wanted to salvage it if they could. That would be better than nothing, if not all that she wanted.

In those first early days when everyone was snowbound at the manor, they left everything unsaid and treated each other carefully, tentatively. Only after the roads were plowed and they departed for their downtown apartment building in his dilapidated old car were they able to talk. "There's something I need you to know," Jeremy began, keeping his gaze fixed on the road straight ahead. "What happened between me and Summer, the way things ended—you are not the cause. I don't want you to think you split us up. We've been headed in that direction for a long time. I don't want you to feel any guilt about that."

Anna told him she wouldn't, and he took her hand.

Back at his apartment, they sat on the sofa with their arms around each other, laughing, a little tearful, overwhelmed by the relief and joy that came from finally admitting what they truly felt for each other. "I think I've been in love with you for three years," Jeremy said before he kissed her.

Only later did Jeremy tell Anna that after she had hung up

on him, he had called Summer and told her he was halfway to Chicago and was having second thoughts about his surprise visit.

Summer, who had sounded shocked and not at all pleased to hear that he was on his way, asked, "Second thoughts about the surprise or the visit?"

"The visit. The surprise is already spoiled, obviously, and was probably a bad idea from the beginning." Jeremy braced himself. "How would you feel if I called it off and went home?"

"I think that would be a good idea," said Summer, sounding relieved that it had been his idea and not hers.

"Okay," he said. "Good-bye, Summer."

"Good-bye, Jeremy. Wait—"

He had been about to hang up. "I'm here. What is it?"

"When you say, 'Call it off,' you don't mean just the trip, do you?"

Jeremy hesitated. "No. No, I don't. I'm sorry."

"Don't be," she said quickly. "Really. Don't. I think that would be a very good idea too."

He had expected as much. What surprised him most was what a relief it was to finally have it over. They bade each other good-bye without any promises that they would talk soon or remain friends. They both simply hung up the phone and went back to the lives they had already begun living separately.

And Jeremy raced home to Elm Creek Manor and Anna as fast as the storm allowed.

For a while, they told none of the Elm Creek Quilters about the transformation of their relationship, and later, Sarah reflected that she had not noticed any change. Jeremy had always driven Anna to work, they had always texted and called throughout the day, and he had always come by to drive her home afterward. They had always laughed and had long, earnest conversations and teased and joked. Gretchen remarked, once, that Jeremy and Anna certainly did seem very happy in each other's company. On another occasion, Gwen asked Jeremy if he would let her know when he planned to make another trip to Chicago, because she had some books to give to Summer if he wouldn't mind taking them. Jeremy had stammered out that he wasn't planning to go to Chicago anytime in the foreseeable future. Only in hindsight did Sarah understand, and she was disconcerted that she had missed the romance blossoming right in front of her. She reassured herself that she would have noticed the signs if she had not been so distracted by Matt's absence and the long-awaited birth of the twins.

But at last the twins came, and when Sarah was still recovering from surgery, Summer called her at the hospital to congratulate her. "A boy and a girl," she exclaimed, utterly delighted. "I'm sure they're perfectly beautiful."

Sarah assured her Matt would e-mail photos as soon as he had a chance. Summer promised to try to be patient, and she lamented and apologized that she couldn't be there, and hadn't been around all winter to help.

"Don't feel bad about that; neither was their father," Sarah reminded her. She had poured out her heart to Summer often throughout those lonely months.

"All the more reason I wish I had been," said Summer. "I wish I could get away, but I don't have any time off until the end of the quarter. As soon as I finish my last exam, I'm coming home for spring break."

"It'll be so good to see you." Sarah had missed her friend,

the only one of the founding Elm Creek Quilters near her own age. "I'll get your old room ready."

"No! You need your rest. Have someone else do it. Tell Matt to do it. Better yet"—her voice took on an edge—"let me tell him."

Perhaps Sarah had shared too much about her recent disappointment in Matt. "One way or another, your room will be ready. Unless"—she remembered the visit spoiled by the unexpected winter storm the previous November—"unless you're planning to stay at Jeremy's place?"

"No, definitely not," replied Summer. "I assumed he'd told you. We broke up."

"What? When?"

"After Thanksgiving, when he was going to visit me. He called from the road to tell me he was on his way, and we sort of agreed that he should turn around and go home."

"I can't believe you never mentioned it."

"I thought *he* would, since he's there. It's not like we had a huge fight or anything. Things just . . . ran their course. Mentioning that we had broken up would have been almost anticlimactic."

Sarah felt like the worst friend in the world. "I can't believe I was so wrapped up in my own concerns that I didn't realize you'd broken up."

"Sarah, give yourself a break. Your concerns included a stressful pregnancy and giving birth to twins. It's really no big deal. If ending things with Jeremy had broken my heart, you would have been the first person I would've turned to for a shoulder to cry on." She laughed dryly. "Trust me, I didn't do any crying over Jeremy. I was trying to extricate myself from that relationship for months, long before I left for Chicago. I mean, I like him, and I care about him, but I can't imagine spending the rest of my life with him, you know?"

"But he's so nice, and you're so nice—"

"That doesn't mean we're meant for each other."

"I guess, but—you're still friends, right?"

"I don't know if one could call us friends, considering that we haven't spoken since November, but there's no animosity, at least not on my side."

"So . . . you'll be okay seeing him when you come home for spring break?"

Summer seemed puzzled by the question. "I'm not planning to see him at all."

"You'll probably run into him, don't you think? He's at the manor all the time."

"Why? Doing what?"

"Dropping off Anna, picking her up after work. Talking to Agnes and Sylvia about local history. He's writing a paper on some nineteenth-century writer with ties to the area or something. He hangs out in the kitchen, mostly. He says he'd rather study there than at the library."

"Who could blame him? The library doesn't have a steady supply of coffee and pastries." Summer sounded amused. "Don't worry. We'll be civil. If Anna doesn't mind him hanging around, I won't either."

A few days before Summer's return to Elm Creek Manor, Sarah learned just how little Anna minded Jeremy's presence in the kitchen. Sarah was sitting in the rocking chair in the twins' room, nursing James while Caroline slept, when Anna knocked softly on the open door. "Sarah," she asked pensively, "do you have a minute?"

"Of course," said Sarah. "Is something wrong?"

"Well, I guess—I don't know." Anna sat cross-legged on the braided rag rug in the middle of the floor. "I need to tell you something, and I hope it won't upset you. I know you and Summer are close."

"Okay," said Sarah, steeling herself. "What is it?"

"Jeremy and I are seeing each other."

"Oh," said Sarah. "That explains a lot."

"Summer and Jeremy had already broken up before we started anything." Then Anna grimaced, reconsidering. "Maybe that's not completely accurate. We knew each other before Jeremy met Summer, and I admit I had feelings for him long before they broke up, and he did for me, too, but neither of us acted on those feelings until he and Summer were officially through. I swear."

Anna seemed so distressed that Sarah hastened to reassure her. "Anna, it's really okay."

"I just don't want you to think I'm the sort of person who goes around stealing her friends' boyfriends."

Sarah had to laugh, distracting James, who released her nipple and let out a noise of complaint. Soothing him with gentle pats and helping him latch on again, she said to Anna, "I would never think that about you."

"What about the other Elm Creek Quilters?"

"No one is going to think you stole Jeremy from Summer," Sarah assured her, leaving unsaid the obvious fact that no one would consider it even remotely possible to steal a boyfriend from the beautiful, brilliant, talented Summer.

"Not even Gwen? She's Summer's mother, and we have to work together, and I don't want things to be awkward—"

"You definitely don't need to worry about that," said Sarah. "Gwen likes Jeremy a lot, but she never considered him the love of Summer's life."

Anna looked somewhat reassured, but she picked at a loose thread on the rug, brow furrowed. "We're going to have to tell Summer when she comes home for spring break," she said. "I wanted everyone here to know first, rather than shock everyone at once. I'm really, really dreading this."

"Do you want me to tell her?"

"Would you?" Anna looked up at her, desperate and eagerly hopeful. "I hadn't thought of that, but, oh, that would be so much better than the three of us sitting down in the kitchen for some ugly, painful, dropping-the-bombshell scene. But I don't want to take the easy way out if that's not the right thing to do. Would it be better coming directly from Jeremy?"

Based upon what Summer had said about their relationship, Sarah didn't think it mattered. "I'll work the news into the conversation the next time I speak to her," she promised. "In the meantime, please, don't worry."

"I'll try." Anna got to her feet, visibly relieved. "I'll still be nervous the first time I see her, and her reaction is the least of my worries. Jeremy—"

When Anna didn't complete the thought, Sarah prompted, "Jeremy what?"

Anna smiled, a little sadly. "Jeremy might take one look at her, come to his senses, and dump me on the spot."

"What are you talking about?" protested Sarah, lifting James to her shoulder and patting him lightly on the back until he let out a tiny baby burp, smelling of milk.

"Nothing."

"Oh, come on. It's obviously something."

Anna hesitated. "Well, Summer is—perfect. She's skinny and gorgeous and smart and perfect. I bet she's never even had a pimple or any grade below an A-minus. I am—let's just say I'm the opposite. I'm the exact opposite of Summer."

"You're winter."

"Yes. Exactly. I'm winter." Anna shook her head as if she realized how ridiculous she sounded. "I know Jeremy loves me. I don't doubt that for a moment. But I can't help wondering whether he settled for me because he couldn't have Summer."

"You've got to be kidding." Sarah knew Anna was self-conscious about her weight, but she was pretty and smart and fun—how could she not realize that? "No one, I repeat, no one, would be settling if they end up with you. And I'm including eligible foreign princes and famous movie stars in that assessment."

"Then I know I can't take you seriously."

"If Jeremy wanted Summer he would have driven to Chicago that day," Sarah pointed out. "He would have made one last attempt to save the relationship. He didn't. He turned the car around and came back to you."

Anna considered that. "I guess that's true."

"You guess? Anna, I think that's all the proof you should need." Just then Caroline stirred in her crib and let out a forlorn wail. "Okay, time for the next shift. Will you help me switch babies?"

Anna handed her Caroline and took James, and played with him while Sarah nursed Caroline. Anna seemed happier, but whether Sarah's words had reassured her or James's sweet smiles had lifted her spirits, Sarah couldn't say.

The day before Summer's arrival, she called to remind Sarah about her travel plans. "Before you hang up," said Sarah as the call was winding down, "I wanted to mention that Jeremy is seeing someone."

"Really," said Summer, instantly curious. "Already?"

"Already?" echoed Sarah. "You broke up four months ago. Did you expect a year of mourning?"

"Of course not." Summer laughed. "It just seemed soon, for Jeremy. Well, good for him, I guess. We should both move on. Do you know who this new woman is? Someone from the History Department?"

"It's Anna."

Summer was silent for a long moment. "You mean Chef Anna?"

"Yes, Chef Anna." What other Anna could she have meant?

"I see," said Summer stiffly. "When did it start? When Jeremy and I were still together?"

"No. Definitely not. It didn't start until after Thanksgiving."

"How do you know?"

"Anna told me."

"Would she have admitted it if they had gotten involved earlier?"

"Anna told me and I believe her," said Sarah emphatically. "What's wrong? You said you'd been trying to extricate yourself from the relationship for months before you and Jeremy finally decided to part ways. Have you changed your mind? Were you hoping to get back together?"

"Of course not. I just hate the idea that they were sneaking around behind my back, making a fool of me."

"That didn't happen. You know I would have told you if I thought your boyfriend was cheating on you."

"You're right. You're right." Summer took a deep breath. "Okay. I know I'm overreacting. I'm just surprised." She took another deep breath and blew it out slowly, reminding Sarah of practicing her breathing with Gretchen during her childbirth classes. "It's good that you told me ahead of time. I can get all of this misplaced rage out of the way now, so I can be perfectly pleasant when I see them. I'll just take it all out on you instead of them."

"That's what I'm here for," Sarah replied, relieved that Summer sounded more like her usual self.

When Summer returned to Elm Creek Manor Friday evening, Anna and Jeremy had already gone home, so Summer's civility wasn't put to the test right away. She spent the weekend catching up with Sarah and Sylvia and the Elm Creek Quilters in residence, visiting her mother, and admiring the twins. On Saturday night she babysat so Sarah and Matt could enjoy a rare night out by themselves. Over a long dinner at their favorite restaurant, they talked about the babies and yawned incessantly, thanks to their mutual sleep deprivation.

Since camp wasn't in session yet, Anna didn't come in to work until Monday morning. Summer and Sarah were in the kitchen eating bagels, drinking coffee, and chatting when the couple arrived. Sarah could sense the tension in the air, but Summer rose with a smile as soon as they entered, hugged them and kissed them both on the cheek, and asked them how their winter had been, and how the manor had changed with two young babies around. The twins were a favorite topic of conversation around the manor, as well as a safe one, so everyone talked easily and comfortably as Anna put on a fresh pot of coffee and started her workday. Jeremy left soon afterward, but he returned at noon for lunch, and he spent the afternoon in the kitchen as he often did, reading dusty academic history books and typing notes on his laptop. Sarah expected Summer to keep her distance, but perhaps to prove that there were no hard feelings, she stopped by the kitchen and engaged Jeremy in friendly conversation, asking for all the History Department news and gossip she had missed since the previous autumn. Anna, working in the kitchen, listened in warily for a while, but eventually relaxed enough to join in the conversation from time to time.

The next day was much the same. Summer spent the morning playing with Sarah and the twins, met her mother for lunch, and joined Jeremy and Anna in the kitchen afterward for a lively conversation about mutual friends before leaving them to their work. On Wednesday, she showed up at the kitchen lugging her own backpack stuffed full of books and papers and her laptop, and asked if they minded if she joined the study hall. She said it so comically that Anna smiled and Jeremy promptly agreed, but Anna's smile faded as Summer slipped into the booth across from Jeremy and he moved his books to make room on the table for hers. From time to time, Summer would look up from her work to ask Jeremy's opinion on the apparent causal connection between two historical events, or to consult him about the reliability of a particular research source. Sarah glimpsed several such exchanges as she passed in and out of the kitchen, noting Anna's deepening worry every time. By Thursday Summer was teasing Jeremy, touching his hand when she wanted to make a point, interrupting their work with amusing reminiscences from back in the day—and Anna's expression had taken on a cast of bewildered resignation. Sarah seized any excuse to make more frequent trips to the kitchen, not quite willing to believe what she thought she was seeing, wanting to give her friend the benefit of the doubt, but when she overheard Summer invite Jeremy on a quick research trip to the Waterford Historical Society's archives at the college library, she couldn't let it continue.

"Summer, could you help me with the twins?" she asked from the doorway, as plaintively as she could.

Anna began to untie her apron. "I'll help," she said grimly, no doubt eager to escape her once beloved kitchen.

"No, you're busy," Sarah quickly replied. To Summer she added, "Please? Upstairs?"

Leaving her books and papers intermingled on the table with Jeremy's, Summer promptly rose and followed her out of the kitchen. "What's up?" she asked cheerfully as Sarah led her down the west wing toward the grand front foyer. "Are simultaneous diaper changes in order?"

Sarah grabbed her arm and pulled her into an alcove where she was sure they wouldn't be overheard. "What are you doing?"

"Helping you, I thought. Why are we hiding?" Summer lowered her voice to match Sarah's. "And why are you whispering?"

"No, I meant what are you doing in the kitchen with Jeremy?"

"What do you mean? We're studying, talking—"

"And you're touching his hand, and reliving the good old days, and inviting him on research dates at the library—"

Summer planted a hand on one hip and regarded Sarah in disbelief. "I did not ask him out."

"Oh, come on, Summer. I heard you."

"It wasn't a date. I didn't mean it that way."

"Do you want Jeremy back?"

"No! I explained that to you weeks ago."

"Then stop flirting with him."

"Who's flirting?"

"You are," Sarah countered. "Right in front of Anna, and it's breaking her heart. How can you not see that?"

Summer hesitated, on the verge of protesting, and then suddenly her defenses crumbled. "Did it really seem like flirting?"

"Yes. Jeremy hasn't responded, more credit to him, but I don't know how long any man can withstand this kind of temptation." She waved a hand to indicate Summer from head to toe, inside and out, head, heart, everything. "Are you trying to prove that you could have him, if you really wanted him?"

Summer's face fell. "I—I don't know. I didn't even know I was doing it. I guess—I guess I was more hurt than I realized that we broke up and the next day he was in love with someone else—"

"It wasn't quite like that."

For a moment, Summer studied the pattern on the marble floor. "I know. You're right. That wasn't fair."

"When you and Jeremy were together, Anna made a point of not interfering in your relationship even when it was in free fall," said Sarah. "Now that she and Jeremy are together, the least you can do is show her that same respect. Especially since you know in your heart you don't belong together." Sarah reached out and touched her on the shoulder. "Come and play with me and the twins. You can gather up your books and things later, after Anna and Jeremy go home."

Nodding, Summer followed her upstairs, where Matt dozed in the rocking chair, a wide-awake James in his arms, and Caroline kicked and wriggled and complained hungrily in the crib. Summer swept Caroline up in her arms and soon had her smiling and cooing, but there were tears in her eyes when she passed the baby along to Sarah to nurse.

For the rest of her visit Summer avoided the kitchen when Jeremy was around, and though she exchanged friendly greetings when they passed in the halls, she never lingered to draw him into conversation.

She returned to Chicago on Saturday, after hugging everyone good-bye and wishing aloud that her spring break had fallen one week later, so she wouldn't miss Bonnie's homecoming from Maui. Judy, too, would be coming for the weekend to celebrate National Quilting Day, and the Elm Creek Quilters were bursting with a surprise for their recently divorced friend: Judy intended to sell her share of Elm Creek Quilts to Bonnie for the same modest price Bonnie had sold her own share to Anna in order to protect it from her now ex-husband, Craig.

Sarah and Summer never again spoke of Summer's bewildering, uncharacteristic behavior, and over time, Sarah resolved to pretend it had never happened. No true harm was done, and some small good did come of it. One day in early June, Anna and Sarah were taking the twins for a walk in their double stroller when the subject of a new course Gwen wanted to teach came up. Talk of Gwen led to talk of her daughter, and Anna wondered aloud when Summer might visit again, adding that Summer's overly friendly behavior toward Jeremy during her last visit had bothered her quite a lot at the time, but in hindsight she was glad for it.

"Glad?" Sarah echoed. If someone flirted with Matt right in front of her, she would be furious. Fortunately, Matt was rather oblivious to flirtation, a quality that had slowed their courtship but probably granted him a sort of immunity to trouble now.

"I know it sounds strange, but I am." Anna stooped over to pick up the shoe Caroline had tugged off her foot and flung from the stroller. "Summer practically threw herself at Jeremy, and he wasn't even tempted. When it came down to it, he chose me."

Sarah wouldn't have characterized Summer's mild, inadvertent flirting as throwing herself at Jeremy, but since it seemed to comfort Anna to believe that, she let it go. Besides, it was obvious Jeremy and Anna adored each other, and Jeremy had chosen Anna, just as she had said.

When Summer visited for a week between the summer and autumn quarters, time had worked upon the tension lingering among the three, and so their second reunion truly did seem to be that of good friends. Anna's insecurities had dissipated as her relationship with Jeremy had grown, or so it seemed to Sarah, and when Summer and Jeremy discussed their grad school research, the conversation was animated and enthusiastic, as it would have been between any two graduate students intrigued by a historical puzzle. Sarah was proud of her friends, who had handled a delicate situation with sensitivity, generosity, and grace where others might have allowed once treasured friendships to collapse into acrimony.

Summer returned to school, and Elm Creek Manor settled into autumn. As winter loomed, some friends departed for warmer climes until spring, while Matt turned his attention to the apple harvest with the help of his student workers. Sarah cared for her babies and tried not to worry about Melissa, Sylvia's newfound second cousin twice removed. All seemed well that golden autumn, the trees scarlet and gold and brown, a chill in the air, and logs burning on the hearth in the evening.

November arrived, and with it anticipation for Thanksgiving and the special quilter's holiday the Elm Creek Quilters would celebrate the day afterward. That year, as she had done the year before, Sylvia had invited her friends to piece quilt blocks representing whatever they were most thankful for and place them into the cornucopia centerpiece. Sarah would have made a Twin Star block except she didn't want to reuse a pattern she had chosen the year before, so instead she pieced a Home Sweet Home block from red, blue, and tan cottons. She had not realized what blessings peace and contentment within the family were until she had lost and regained them.

As much as she looked forward to their quilter's holiday with its delicious potluck lunch, daylong marathon of quilting, and expressions of gratitude shared around the table, she was even more excited about—and preoccupied by—an event that would begin two days later. On the Sunday after Thanksgiving, Elm Creek Quilts would host the first of what they hoped would become an annual gathering called Quiltsgiving, and although Sarah found the name a bit corny, she loved the concept. A year before, Gretchen had proposed a winter camp during which they and their guests would make quilts for Project Linus, a national organization dedicated to providing love, a sense of security, warmth, and comfort to children in need through the gifts of new, handmade blankets, quilts, and afghans. All volunteers who attended Quiltsgiving would enjoy a week at Elm Creek Manor absolutely free of charge, but rather than working on quilts for themselves, they would make soft, comforting children's quilts for Project Linus. As the inaugural coordinator of the fledgling Waterford chapter, Gretchen had already delivered numerous quilts to the Elm Creek Valley Hospital, where they offered comfort to seriously ill children, and to the fire department, where they warmed youngsters rescued from fires and accidents. Gretchen hoped the first Quiltsgiving would result in many soft, bright, and warm quilts to donate to the local women's shelter, where mothers fleeing dangerous domestic situations were often forced to bring their children with nothing more than the clothes on their backs.

Sarah was determined to help Gretchen make their first Quiltsgiving a resounding success. One day in mid-November, she was working busily in the library while James napped and Caroline played with toys on a quilt spread out on the floor near the desk. Jeremy entered and asked if he could borrow Sylvia's "quilt block book," as everyone referred to her well-used encyclopedia of traditional quilt blocks.

"Is this for a research paper?" asked Sarah, finding the volume on one of the room's many bookcases and giving it to him.

"It's research," he said, "but not for a paper."

Sarah teased him for his evasiveness, but Jeremy merely grinned and escaped with the book without revealing another detail. She suspected she would find out what he was up to eventually.

On the Friday after Thanksgiving, the skies were clear and sunny, with only a trace of frost on the lawn that melted before midmorning—quite a contrast from the previous year's dangerous blizzard. As Sarah prepared her dish for the potluck luncheon feast, she reflected upon their last quilter's holiday and considered how much more than the weather had changed since that momentous day. She had become a mother; Matt had gone away but had returned with promises never to leave her again; Anna and Jeremy seemed more in love every day; Sylvia had been reunited with Elizabeth's descendants; Sarah's precious babies were talking and toddling. She could only imagine what changes the next season would bring.

All morning long, Sarah and her friends quilted in the ballroom. Sarah's mother had come for the holiday weekend, and she was making cozy flannel quilts for the twins, plaid squares alternating with machine-appliquéd, folk art Santa Clauses. Diane, who seemed incapable of planning ahead, was leafing through back issues of *Quilters Newsletter* looking for inspiration for a Christmas ornament exchange she had signed up for through her church.

"How many ornaments are you supposed to make?" Gwen inquired.

Diane didn't look up from her magazine. "Why do you want to know?"

"Just curious. It's a natural question. You say you're participating in an ornament exchange, and I ask how many ornaments you need to make."

"Twenty-five."

"Twenty-five?" exclaimed Agnes. "But you told me they're due a week from tomorrow!"

Agnes's revelation evoked exclamations of surprise, sympathy, and amusement from the circle of quilters, and laughter from Gwen. "How do you expect to finish them in time?" asked Carol.

Sylvia looked up from hand-piecing another arc for the reproductions of Elizabeth's Double Wedding Ring quilt to study Diane over the rims of her glasses. "I hope you aren't thinking of exchanging something you've slapped together at the last minute for the lovely ornaments your friends have likely spent weeks laboring upon."

"No," said Gwen. "She'll choose something complicated to show off, finish half of them on her own, then throw herself upon Agnes's mercy and beg her to finish the other half."

"And this," Diane said to Agnes, "is why I told you about the deadline in the car rather than announce it in front of everyone else."

When Agnes bit her lower lip guiltily, Gwen laughed and said, "Diane, don't you dare blame your failure to meet your responsibilities upon Agnes. It's her job as your friend to keep you honest."

"I'm not blaming her," Diane protested, "and I haven't failed to meet my responsibilities yet. Eight days is plenty of time to make twenty-five simple ornaments." She took another magazine from the stack and added in an undertone, "As long as I find a pattern soon."

Sarah, who respected the value of planning ahead as much as Diane disdained it, was busy cutting squares from light fabrics and brightly colored novelty prints to sew into nine-patch quilts during Quiltsgiving the following week. Later that afternoon, Anna was going to give her another lesson on the long-arm sewing machine they had purchased a few months before. Anna and Gretchen, who had used the enormous quilting machines while working in quilt shops before they joined Elm Creek Quilts, were the most experienced long-arm operators on the faculty. In the few weeks that they had been available, their one-on-one workshops had quickly become the most sought-after classes on the camp schedule.

Sarah had cut enough pieces for two twin-size quilts by lunchtime, when the Elm Creek Quilters, the resident husbands, and their guests gathered in the banquet hall for what Agnes called their "Patchwork Potluck" feast. As a rule, every dish had to be made from leftovers from their family Thanksgiving feasts the day before. Agnes always said no meal was better suited for quilters, who could be trusted to find creative, delicious uses for leftover turkey, stuffing, and vegetables just as they created beautiful and useful works of art from scraps of fabric.

When the table was set but before they took their seats, the Elm Creek Quilters and Carol placed their folded quilt blocks into the cornucopia centerpieces, taking elaborate precautions to prevent their friends from seeing what they had made. As they had done the previous year, the men contributed pieces of fabric scavenged from the women's scrap bag—except for Jeremy. When Andrew kidded him about lacking sufficient courage to face the challenge, Jeremy said casually, "Oh, I put mine in first, before the rest of you got here."

In later years, Sarah would remember the Home Sweet Home block she had contributed and the California block Sylvia had made in honor of her newfound relatives there, but all the other choices had faded in her memory in contrast to Jeremy's. After the gathered friends had enjoyed their feast, Sylvia reached into the cornucopia, withdrew a block or a piece of fabric, and invited the contributor to share what it represented. Since Jeremy had been the first to place something into the cornucopia, his was the last to be taken out, which Sarah soon realized had been his intention all along.

"Now, what could this be?" said Sylvia as she withdrew a ribbon-tied scroll from the cornucopia. When she promptly handed it to Anna, Sarah knew Sylvia was in on the secret, and whatever it was, they would all know soon.

With a curious glance from Sylvia to Jeremy, Anna untied the bow and unrolled the paper. When she held it up for all to see, Sarah recognized the drawing as a True Lover's Knot block, finely rendered in the style of a nineteenth-century woodcut.

"That's lovely," said Carol, who did not know the block name. "But what does it mean?"

"Yes, go on," Sylvia prompted Jeremy, smiling. "Tell us."

"This is the True Lover's Knot pattern," said Jeremy. "This year, I'm most thankful for Anna—her goodness, her generosity, her compassion for others, her unique sense of humor—" Several chuckles went up from around the table. "Anna, falling in love with you was like coming home to a place I didn't realize I'd been missing all my life. You're the only person I've ever known who accepts me for who I am, right in this moment, faults and all, and isn't waiting for me to become someone else. You're beautiful and wonderful and kind. I love you, Anna, and if you'll let me, I'd like to spend the rest of my life doing my best to make you as happy as you've made me."

Her eyes brimming over with tears, Anna looked as if she might speak, but Jeremy wasn't finished. He reached into the cornucopia, and as a soft murmur of joy and expectation went up from the gathered friends, he knelt beside Anna's chair and held up a small, elegant black box. When he opened it, Sarah couldn't see what was inside, but it was easy enough to guess.

"Anna," he asked as she began to cry, "will you marry me?"

Unable to speak, she nodded. Her hand shook as Jeremy slipped the ring on the third finger of her left hand. They embraced, and the room rang with the sounds of cheers and congratulations.

They married at Elm Creek Manor in March the following spring. At first their families were surprised and concerned that they would have such a brief engagement, but the couple deflected their worries with reminders of how many years they had known each other as good friends before they had fallen in love, and they asked, rhetorically, since they were certain they wanted to spend the rest of their lives together, why not get started? They retained a sense of humor when elderly aunts and gossipy neighbors assumed Anna surely must be pregnant, since time would dispel that rumor soon enough. The most compelling reason for choosing a March wedding date, Anna confided to Sarah and Sylvia when she asked if they could hold the celebration at Elm Creek Manor, was that she didn't want the nuptials to interfere with quilt camp, and neither she nor Jeremy wanted to wait until after Labor Day to begin their new life together.

It was a lovely, simple wedding, with elements from Jeremy's Jewish and Anna's Catholic faiths. In the four months leading up to the ceremony, they participated in weekly pre-Cana group counseling sessions through the Waterford College Campus Ministry and attended a weekend Engaged Encounter retreat. Although older relatives had warned them they would never find a priest and rabbi willing to share the officiating duties, and no Catholic priest would ever validate a marriage that was not held within the four walls of a church, Anna's pastor and Jeremy's rabbi knew each other well, having offered many ecumenical services at the college through the years, and they proved all the naysayers wrong.

After a winter of preparations, the wedding day arrived, breezy and warm, with the fragrance of lilac blossoms filling the air. Both sets of parents escorted the bride and groom to the cornerstone patio where an intimate group of their family and dearest friends waited near the quilted *chuppah* Jeremy's and Anna's sisters had made from a blue-and-gold quilt top Anna had begun as a Chanukah gift for Jeremy. Suspended by four poles held by Anna's brothers and Jeremy's best friend, the canopy represented the new home they would create together, its four open sides reminding them of their essential place within their families, circle of close friends, and community. Before the blessing of the wine, there were readings from the Torah and the New Testament; they exchanged rings and read aloud an interfaith *ketubah*. Their aunts and uncles offered the traditional Seven Blessings, and afterward, Jeremy wrapped a glass in a soft cloth and crushed it underfoot, signifying the irrevocability of their vows. If anyone present believed that the wedding was neither Catholic enough nor Jewish enough and therefore imperfect, they kept their grumblings to themselves. In any case, Sarah found the ceremony very moving, and she believed that if Anna and Jeremy lived together as harmoniously as they had created their wedding celebration, bringing together significant elements from their individual traditions, they would live together very happily indeed.

After a honeymoon in Myrtle Beach, Anna moved across the hall into Jeremy's apartment until his lease ran out, and then they moved into a third-floor suite of Elm Creek Manor.

They seemed blissfully happy, Sarah often thought. The simple pleasure of working in the kitchen together seemed to bring them joy; Jeremy would read and take notes and write his dissertation in his favorite corner booth while Anna cooked and baked and worked magic with simple ingredients to create the most delicious meals Sarah had ever tasted.

In April of the following year, not long after the twins celebrated their second birthdays, Anna gave birth to a daughter—more than a year after the wedding, which must have been enough to satisfy the elderly aunts and gossipy neighbors who had been counting. Two months later, Jeremy successfully defended his dissertation and earned his doctorate with the highest honors in his department. It was a day Sarah had long looked forward to for the newlyweds' sake and dreaded for her own, because Jeremy's graduation meant that his time at Waterford College had ended, and he, Anna, and their adorable dark-haired baby, Gina, would move on.

In the months leading up to Jeremy's graduation, he had applied for every relevant position published in *The Chronicle of Higher Education* and had participated in several interviews at universities scattered across the country. Anna confided to Sarah that she fervently hoped an assistant professor position would become available at Penn State's University Park campus, not because their History Department boasted any extraordinary resources for his specialization, but because the commute to Elm Creek Manor would be long though not impossible, and she could remain their head chef. They all knew the odds were against it, and no one was surprised when Penn State posted no suitable openings that year. Jeremy considered remaining at Waterford College and doing a postdoc until a position reasonably close to Elm Creek Manor miraculously appeared, but he and Anna both knew that this perfect job might not ever come along, and his career would stall if he didn't take advantage of more certain, more promising opportunities.

In midsummer Jeremy received an offer from the University of Arlington, and after taking a few days to discuss his options with Anna and his graduate adviser, he accepted. Jeremy moved to Virginia at the end of July, but Anna remained behind with baby Gina so she could finish out the camp season.

On the Sunday before Labor Day, the Elm Creek Quilters threw a farewell party for their departing friend. Jeremy returned for the cookout, which began as a picnic along the grassy shore of Elm Creek behind the manor until rain forced them to retreat to the front verandah. But the occasion wasn't spoiled; Joe and Andrew managed to finish cooking all the burgers, steaks, and spareribs before the rain began to fall, and on the broad verandah there were comfortable Adirondack chairs for the adults to relax in and plenty of space for the children to play. The storm lifted as the sun set, and in the cool and misty evening the twins chased fireflies on the front lawn while Gina watched drowsily from her mother's lap.

At the end of the party, Sylvia presented Anna with a small but precious gift—a nine-block Winding Ways quilt, similar to those she had made for the founding Elm Creek Quilters years before, when Judy and Summer became the first to leave their circle of friends. Sylvia had chosen fabrics that represented each of her friends' unique qualities. The mosaic of overlapping circles and intertwining curves, the careful balance of dark and light hues, and the unexpected harmony of the disparate fabrics and colors evoked the sense of many winding paths meeting, intersecting, parting, creating the illusion that the separate sections formed a single quilt. Sarah remembered the words Sylvia had spoken as she had presented the panels to the original Elm Creek Quilters a few years before. "The Winding Ways quilt will remind us of friends who have left our circle to journey far away," Sylvia had explained. "When one of our circle must leave us, she'll take her section of the quilt with her as a reminder of the loving friends awaiting her return. The empty places on the wall will remind those of us left behind that the beauty of our friendship endures, even if great distances separate us. When the absent friend returns to Elm Creek Manor, she will hang her quilt in its proper space, and the loveliness of the whole will be restored."

As there were eight founding Elm Creek Quilters and nine panels, Sylvia had dedicated the one in the center to all the Elm Creek Quilters yet to come. That section would always remain on the library wall, despite the comings and goings of the people it represented. "That way," Sylvia explained, "as long as Elm Creek Quilts endures, no matter what becomes of the founding members, this section at the heart of the quilt will remain." In this way, Anna, too, had been included in the original quilt even though she had joined their group later, but Sarah thought it was only right that someone who had contributed so much to the success of Elm Creek Quilts should at last have a section all her own.

The next day, Anna, Jeremy, and Gina left early in the morning so that Jeremy would be back on campus when classes resumed after the long holiday weekend. The confluence of the end of camp season and Anna's departure plunged Sarah into melancholy. She found herself wandering into the library and gazing at the Winding Ways quilt with its missing panels, a painful rather than fond reminder of her absent friends. Bonnie would return from Hawai'i in the spring, and the other friends would visit now and then, but it would not be the same, and she felt their absence keenly.

Reluctant to contemplate Anna's impending departure, Sarah had postponed the search for a new head chef throughout the summer, making the excuse that she was too busy with the demands of the current camp season to contemplate staffing needs for the next. But with Anna gone, she could delay no longer. Earlier that summer, Anna had compiled a list of former culinary school classmates and student interns from her days as a chef with Waterford College Food Services, but when Sarah, Sylvia, and Gretchen contacted them, those who were interested in the job lacked the proper experience or didn't seem like a good fit, and those who might have worked out quite well declined their offer for one reason or another. The job didn't pay enough, or the location was too remote, or the prospect of limited advancement was too discouraging. Throughout the winter, they advertised the position, collected résumés, and interviewed dozens of candidates, but they found no one worthy of Anna's kitchen. As March approached and the search became more urgent, Sarah finally realized why they had failed thus far. "We're never going to find someone as perfect for Elm Creek Quilt Camp, as perfect for us, as Anna was," she told Sylvia and Gretchen. "Anna is one of a kind, and we're not going to find another Anna. At this point, we need to stop dismissing candidates simply because they aren't Anna and find someone who can do the job well and be pleasant enough to work with."

Once they set their sights lower, they found someone.

Maeve, who had worked at the Hotel State College for a year after her restaurant in Altoona closed, seemed like a good, if imperfect, fit. She prepared three delicious meals for fifty campers five days a week, and her welcome banquets and farewell breakfasts possessed an air of elegance without being too fussy. Sarah wasn't thrilled that Maeve created only seven menus, one for each day of the week, and repeated them every week throughout the summer, but she could tolerate that because the lack of variation affected only the permanent residents of Elm Creek Manor. Most campers attended only for a single week's session, so they had no idea that the chicken cordon bleu they enjoyed on Monday tasted exactly like the chicken cordon bleu Sarah had eaten the previous Monday and the Monday before that. What Sarah couldn't tolerate, and had to speak privately to Maeve about far too frequently, was her brusque manner with campers who wandered into the kitchen between meals in search of a cup of tea, a glass of lemonade, or a quick snack. The kitchen was for the chef and her assistants, Maeve insisted. Guests should remain outside. Sarah pointed out that the very reason they had installed eight booths when they remodeled the kitchen was so that campers would be comfortable if they wanted refreshments outside of regular meal hours. She reminded Maeve that part of her job was to welcome their guests, and if she couldn't interrupt her work to fetch them a snack, she should delegate that task to an assistant or leave a bowl of fruit on the wooden table so campers could help themselves. After one of these conferences, Maeve's behavior would improve for a while, but her aloof, unwelcome demeanor inevitably returned.

It was a relief when, on Labor Day, Maeve thanked Sarah

for the rewarding experience but announced that she wouldn't be returning the following summer. Henry took over after her, but his habitual lateness obliged Sarah to start breakfast without him several days a week until he finally wandered off for a smoke after lunch one July afternoon and never returned. His replacement, a recent culinary school graduate named Marjorie, was friendly, hardworking, and energetic, but she couldn't break an egg without dropping the shells in the bowl or bake cakes without singeing them or use the gas burners for any purpose whatsoever without scorching the pan and filling the kitchen with billowing clouds of smoke. When guests began complaining about the frequent false alarms from the smoke detectors, Matt ruefully suggested that they remove the batteries, invest in a few more fire extinguishers, and take out a second insurance policy. Sarah and Sylvia adamantly refused, so Marjorie had to go. A retired elementary school lunchroom cook filled in for the rest of the summer, and although she was something of a curmudgeon, she tolerated campers in the kitchen, and her meals were nutritious, if bland and institutional.

Every winter after Anna left, Sarah confronted the same nerve-racking challenge of finding a suitable chef in time for a new season of quilt camp. Her heart sank when the good chefs were ready to move on after a single summer, and she spent countless hours searching for last-minute replacements when one employee after another didn't work out. If Anna had not eventually returned to Elm Creek Quilts, out of sheer frustration Sarah might have gone into early retirement—but to her eternal gratitude, Anna had returned. If she had not, Sarah suddenly realized, not only would Elm Creek Quilts have suffered, but Sarah would have missed out on many years with the woman who had become her best friend, and James probably would not have fallen in love with Gina.

Sarah was sure it was love, although she had only observed a few stolen kisses, overheard a few murmured endearments. When James gave his heart, he gave it completely, and he had known and cared for Gina almost his entire life. Gina was a compassionate young woman and wouldn't trifle with any man's feelings, least of all James's. Surely they were in love, although why they went to such trouble to conceal a relationship that would inspire rejoicing in the hearts of everyone who knew them, Sarah and Anna could only speculate. Whatever their reason for secrecy, Sarah knew James loved Gina.

She hoped Gina loved him in return.

· Chapter Four ·

As the day unfolded, Sarah delegated wedding preparation tasks to her friends and family, prepared for the arrival of Caroline's future in-laws, and contemplated the paths her children had chosen. Caroline's had taken her far from Elm Creek Manor, while James's had kept him close to home—and she dared hope, albeit selfishly, that his love for Gina would ensure that he would remain at Elm Creek Manor always.

Then Sarah caught herself, and had to laugh. She knew her children as well as anyone could, and she had faith in their potential to find their own places in the world, to embark upon meaningful work that would become as satisfying and rewarding to them as Elm Creek Quilts was to her. When they did, she would celebrate those successes, even if they took Caroline and James far from home. She knew they would always return, if not to stay.

Sarah, Maggie, and Emily had suites ready for Leo's family by the time his mother and stepfather arrived at half past ten along with his two half sisters, one a senior in high school, the other a sophomore, both dark-haired, pretty, and given to sighing and exclaiming that it was all so romantic. Anna waited to serve lunch until after Leo's father and stepmother arrived about two hours later. Sarah watched for animosity between the two couples, but just as Caroline had assured her, they greeted one another cordially and chatted pleasantly throughout the meal.

Soon afterward, other guests arrived, in pairs and in groups—a few aunts, uncles, and cousins of Leo's; Ayana and her husband; Matt's childhood best friend and his wife; and several others who came so quickly one after the other that they must have been on the same flight. Sarah, Caroline, and Emily helped everyone find and settle into their rooms, and after everyone was settled, Sarah corralled the bridesmaids in the parlor and put them to work filling gift bags and tying bows on small boxes of chocolates that would serve as the wedding favors.

Once Sarah stopped by the kitchen to admire the final sketches Gina had made of the wedding cake, which was sure to delight the eyes as well as the taste buds. The bottom tier of the rich, luscious almond cake would be shaped as a square, the second a hexagon, the third a circle, and fourth a small square. Caroline had requested a chocolate-almond filling, and after much testing and sampling, Gina had invented one for her. Gina abhorred the taste of rolled fondant and had recommended a Swiss meringue buttercream flavored with Kahlúa instead. After frosting the entire cake smooth and glossy, Gina planned to adorn each layer with a different piped design: a crosshatch with marzipan dragées placed at the junctions for the bottom layer, elegant swirls for the hexagonal second tier, tessellated diamonds for the third, and vertical stripes for the top. A band of smooth marzipan would encircle the bottom of each tier like a satin ribbon, and a bouquet of gum paste lilies and roses in autumn hues would cascade from the top. The cake would be lovely and unique, just like the bride for whom Gina would create it.

As Gina put her sketches away, Sarah glanced out the window and spotted Matt in the parking lot helping Leo's elderly great-uncle carry luggage indoors. Hurrying outside to assist, Sarah slung a garment bag over her shoulder and led the way to the first-floor suite Leo's great-uncle and great-aunt would share. In the early days of Elm Creek Quilt Camp, all guest rooms had been on the second and third floors, but the building had no elevator, so everyone had to brave the grand oak staircase. Sarah had thought nothing of it until one of their annual campers, a longtime friend of Sylvia's named Grace Daniels, remarked that her MS made it difficult to climb all those stairs, but quilt camp was worth the effort. After that, Sarah began to wonder about the many quilters for whom stairs were not merely difficult but impossible. It troubled her to think that they had been excluded from the enriching experience of quilt camp all because Sarah had not considered their needs. By the next season, Joe had installed a ramp to complement the stairs to the back door, and Matt had remodeled three unused rooms on the first floor into accessible suites. They were available upon request, and during the camp season, they were never empty.

By late afternoon, Caroline and her bridesmaids had finished all the tasks Sarah had assigned them and were relaxing on the verandah, reminiscing and catching up on all that had come to pass since their lives had taken them in different directions. Caroline was in medical school; Ayana worked on Wall Street; Cameron was a barista and part-time musician in Chicago; Rachel was taking time off work to care for her seven-month-old in Boulder, Colorado; Mariah was attending Yale Divinity School; and Gina—Gina, of course, was the assistant chef at Elm Creek Manor, and if she had any other plans for her immediate future, personal or professional, she didn't mention them within Sarah's hearing. When the other young women mentioned their husbands or boyfriends, Gina engaged in the conversation without saying a word about her own affairs of the heart, and Sarah couldn't help wondering why.

By evening, her curiosity got the better of her. After supper, Sarah managed to get her son alone for a few moments as they helped clear the table. "Sweetheart," she began, "can we talk for a moment?"

"Don't worry, Mom," he said, smiling knowingly as he stacked plates dangerously high. "I've talked to Leo. He and Caroline have definitely ruled out eloping."

"Well, of course they have. I never really thought they would. That's not what I want to talk about." She hesitated. "I know about you and Gina."

Startled, he set down the plates on the table with an alarming rattle of china. "Know what about me and Gina?"

"That you two are involved, or seeing each other, or whatever people your age call it these days. In my day, we would have said you're dating."

"Oh." He gathered up knives and forks. "You're okay with that?"

"Okay? I'm delighted. I adore Gina, and I can see that you two make each other very happy." She gripped the back of a chair and steeled herself. "I don't want to pry, but I was hoping you would tell me why you're keeping your relationship a secret."

He shrugged as if he had assumed their reasons were obvious. "This time should really be about Caroline and Leo. We didn't want to steal their spotlight."

"You wouldn't have," Sarah protested. "We would have given you your own spotlight."

James laughed. "A spotlight, our own or anyone else's, is the last thing we want." He piled the knives and forks on the stack of plates and hefted the whole thing with a cheerful tinkling of china.

"Careful," Sarah couldn't resist warning as he left the banquet hall for the kitchen.

"When am I not?" he called as the door swung shut behind him.

Her gaze lingered on the door, but her thoughts were far away. Why would James believe that the revelation that he and Gina were dating, which they all had suspected anyway, would be enough to divert the attention from Caroline and Leo's wedding?

The friends Sarah most longed to see, her beloved Elm Creek Quilters, arrived within hours of one another the following morning. After putting the bridesmaids and the couple's other willing friends to work clearing the ballroom of quilt camp supplies and equipment, Sarah found herself pacing from window to window, checking the time, unable to focus on any task. At last, while making up more suites for their guests, she spotted a taxi shuttle crossing the bridge over Elm Creek. Immediately she dropped what she was doing, hurried downstairs, and flung open the back door just as the vehicle came to a stop in the parking lot. "Summer," she cried as her friend emerged from the backseat.

"Sarah," Summer shouted in reply. She dropped her bag on the ground and ran across the parking lot to embrace her. Her long auburn hair spilled down her back, bearing only a few faint traces of gray, and she was almost as slender as she would always remain in Sarah's memory of those first wonderful years of Elm Creek Quilts, when everything was new, and all their adventures awaited them. Suddenly Summer gasped and remembered her mother, still seated in the back of the cab, and the driver, awaiting the fare. Summer paid him and helped Gwen from the car as the driver removed their luggage from the trunk.

"Kiddo," Gwen cried, wrapping her arms around Sarah. "Let me look at you. You don't look a day older since I last saw you—well, not many days, anyway. Still running every morning?"

"Walking, mostly." Sarah closed her eyes, welcoming the feel of Gwen's sturdy arms around her. At seventy-eight, Gwen was stocky and stooped; she walked with a cane and wore her steely gray hair blunt-cut at the chin. But her voice still rang with confidence, as it always had, a faint trace of her Kentucky accent lingered despite decades spent in the north, and she carried with her the scent of curry and cinnamon.

"Tell me something." Gwen grasped Sarah's shoulders, held her at arms' length, and peered up at her, shaking her head in bemusement. "How can it be possible that your baby girl is old enough to get married?"

"I'm not convinced that she is old enough," Sarah confessed, just as Matt arrived. He greeted mother and daughter with warm hugs, endured Gwen's teasing about his disappearing hair good-naturedly, and carried their bags inside while Sarah offered her arm to Gwen. Anna met them at the back door and embraced them both, all the old rivalry with Summer long forgotten.

"Enrique sends his love, and his regrets," Summer said as she, Gwen, Sarah, and Anna sat down at the long wooden table where they had shared countless meals and conversations through the years. "He wanted to be here, but with the new semester just begun and the kids in school, it made more sense for him to stay home."

"Of course it does," said Sarah, pouring each of them a glass of iced tea. "We'll miss him, but maybe you can all come to visit another time."

"When should we get started on the quilt?" Wincing, Gwen quickly glanced over her shoulder and breathed a sigh of relief when she saw no one there. "Sorry. What a fine guest I would be if I spoiled the surprise within five minutes of my arrival."

"I thought we should wait for the rest of our friends," said Sarah. "But I don't suppose they'll feel left out if we start without them."

"We can wait," Summer said to Sarah, and then turned to Gwen. "You've been traveling all day. Just relax for a while."

Gwen's eyebrows rose as she stirred two heaping teaspoonfuls of sugar into her glass. "You say that like I hiked all the way from California. I'm seventy-eight, not one hundred and eight, and thanks to reform laws I myself championed in Congress, I've benefited from the excellent care of skilled physicians without ever fearing that illness, injury, or unemployment would leave me the devastating choice of treatment or bankruptcy. Thank you, and you're welcome."

"You're absolutely right." Summer raised her palms in a gesture of appeasement. "My mistake. Feel free to run laps around the manor if you like."

"Don't think I couldn't," countered Gwen, grinning as she brandished her cane, evoking laughter from her friends. "Now tell us, Sarah, how many blocks do you need each of us to make?"

"I've already sewn the blocks," Sarah explained. "I'll need your help collecting the signatures."

Her friends cheerfully replied that they would be happy to help however Sarah needed them. She knew they felt as she did, that it was a rare and wonderful treat to be working together on a quilt again, as they had done so often in years long past. They were especially happy to collaborate on a wedding gift for their beloved Caroline, especially one they knew she would cherish as a precious memento of her wedding day. Sarah had pieced dozens of Memory Album blocks in Caroline's wedding colors of blue, sage green, ivory, and dusty pink, choosing elegant florals and rich tone-on-tones to give the quilt visual depth and texture. In the corners of each block were four right triangles, two large and two small, their vertices framing and drawing the eye toward a large, symmetrical cross at the center. Pieced from a creamy ivory solid, the central crosses were the natural focal point of each block, and it was there that Sarah would ask the wedding guests to sign their names and write a few words of love and warm wishes for the bride and groom. She had ironed freezer paper to the back of each block to stabilize the fabric, making them much easier to write upon, and she had purchased several new permanent-ink pens made especially for cloth. She planned to divide the blocks among the Elm Creek Quilters and have them surreptitiously collect signatures from the other guests at the reception. With any luck, Caroline and Leo would be too distracted by their friends, their family, and the joy of the occasion to notice the Elm Creek Quilters strolling from table to table, pens in hand, their handbags stuffed with fabric that suspiciously resembled quilt blocks. Then again, what could be any less suspicious than an Elm Creek Quilter toting fabric around the manor, even at a wedding?

On Sunday morning after the bride and groom embarked on their Hawaiian honeymoon, Sarah and her friends would bring together all of the Memory Album blocks, admire the signatures, read the heartfelt messages, and unite them in a single, beautiful quilt, a chorus of loving voices wishing the newlyweds a future blessed with happiness, joy, and love. A quilt such as this, a future treasured family heirloom, required nothing less than their most exquisite hand quilting, so after the top was complete, Sarah would layer it with soft bamboo batting and backing, and together she and her friends would quilt it, working their needles in feathered plumes and crosshatches through the three layers, adding dimension and texture with every stitch. They might not be able to finish the entire quilt before her friends' visit ended, but that was fine, because Sarah intended to present the quilt as a gift to the newlyweds at Christmas, and she would have plenty of time to add the last stitches and bind the edges before then. Even so, it wouldn't hurt to begin earlier than she had intended.

Sipping her iced tea, Sarah said, "I suppose we don't have to wait until the reception to start collecting signatures. A good third of the guests are staying right here at the manor, and many of them have already arrived. We could begin going from room to room whenever we like. Of course, we'll have to make sure Caroline is busy elsewhere and won't suddenly turn the corner and see us."

"I'll be in charge of keeping her occupied," offered Gwen. "The prospect of distracting Caroline while the rest of you scurry up and down the halls with your quilt blocks and pens is rich with comedic possibilities."

"Try to be subtle about it, though," said Sarah. "She'll know something's up if you aren't acting naturally."

Gwen regarded her with amusement. "You can't have it both ways. Which do you want from me, subtle or natural?"

"If Caroline heads upstairs while we're collecting signatures, try to delay her in a way that's authentically you and yet not an obvious stall tactic," said Summer, smiling. "Tell her some of your stories from Congress, like the one about the time you filibustered that offshore drilling proposal—"

"Summer Sullivan, I taught you better than that. That wasn't a filibuster. You can't filibuster in the House, only in the Senate. I just had a lot to say on the subject." A gleam appeared in Gwen's eye. "I think I know just the story to share with our young bride if she tries to venture upstairs when she shouldn't."

"Don't go too far," said Anna, alarmed. "Don't say anything that will give her cold feet."

"That might not be such a bad thing," said Sarah, and when everyone looked at her, she added, "That was a joke."

"Uh-huh," said Summer skeptically. "Anyway, collecting signatures ahead of time is better all around. If we start earlier, and get as many signatures as we can before the wedding, we'll run less risk of running out of time at the reception and missing someone."

"And Caroline's less likely to suspect we're up to something if we're going from room to room delivering fresh towels than if she sees us going from table to table at the reception."

"Agreed." Summer turned to her mother, feigning regret. "I'm sorry, Mom, but your comedic stall tactics probably won't be necessary."

"I'll keep a few in reserve just in case." Gwen finished the last refreshing sips of her iced tea. "Should we get started?"

"Caroline's upstairs in her room with her bridesmaids debating what to do with her hair on Saturday," Sarah said. "I think we should wait until they're busy somewhere else in the manor. We can wait until the rest of the Elm Creek Quilters arrive and are ready to get to work."

"Who's not here?" asked Gwen. "I thought we would be the last to arrive. Let me guess who's running late. Diane?"

"We're expecting her any minute," said Anna. "Emily and Maggie are out running wedding errands, but they'll be back soon, and I know they can't wait to see you."

"Russell's helping Matt in the north gardens," added Sarah. "He wants every flower in place for the ceremony. Emily says that her parents will be coming in from Philadelphia later this afternoon."

"It'll be so nice to see Judy again," said Gwen. Judy and

Gwen had been best friends before Judy left Waterford College for a faculty position at Penn the autumn before the twins were born. "I miss her so much I ache. What about Bonnie?"

"Didn't she tell you? She's not coming," said Sarah, and when their faces fell, she added, "I'm as disappointed as you are, but it's a long way to travel. Caroline and Leo are staying at the Hale Kapa Kuiki throughout their honeymoon, so Bonnie and Hinano will have a belated celebration with the kids then."

"But what about seeing us?" protested Gwen. "No offense, Sarah, but this weekend isn't just about the kids. Sure, it's a long trip, but Bonnie and Hinano could take the suborbital transport and cut their flight time in half. That jet packs a lot of power."

"You know Bonnie never liked flying," said Summer. "She prefers for us to come to her."

"And as long as she lives in Hawai'i, we'll always be willing to go," said Sarah. After Bonnie became part owner of a charming inn in Lahaina on Maui, she had extended an open invitation to the Elm Creek Quilters to visit anytime. All of the founding members had gladly accepted, sometimes to work as visiting instructors, but often simply to enjoy a relaxing vacation in paradise. Sarah and Matt first visited the Hale Kapa Kuiki when the twins were three years old. Sarah went once a year after that, and when the twins entered high school, she began extending her visits. For the past few years, she had spent nearly every January enjoying the beauty and aloha spirit of Maui. Sometimes Matt joined her for a week or two, but he had always tolerated the cold, the snow, and the limited sunlight of a Pennsylvania winter better than she did, and didn't need to escape it.

Bonnie's first visit to Maui had been a different sort of escape, and even more necessary. Her marriage was in its death throes, and Craig, boiling over with malice and greed, was determined to prolong the misery of the divorce proceedings as long as he could. In a cruel stroke of misfortune, Bonnie had also recently lost her beloved quilt shop, Grandma's Attic, and was reeling from the dual losses of her marriage and her livelihood. Then an entirely unexpected invitation came from her college friend Claire, the owner of a quilt shop on Maui, who proposed that Bonnie come work for her for the winter and help her establish a quilters' retreat in a historic inn on the ocean. Gratefully Bonnie accepted, and as she passed the winter surrounded by warmth and beauty and occupied herself with interesting, challenging work, she found her stress and anxiety ebbing away. Even though she still had to deal with the acrimony of the divorce, putting thousands of miles between herself and her belligerent future ex-husband gave her respite, sparing her the misery of facing him across the table in a lawyer's office. Naturally, Craig being Craig, he managed to inflict a great deal of pain and unhappiness as she wrested herself free from their failed marriage, and ultimately she was forced to sell her share of Elm Creek Quilts so he couldn't claim part of it in the division of their marital property.

Sarah remembered those tumultuous months with regret and Craig's behavior with disgust. All along, the Elm Creek Quilters had known that once the divorce was final, Judy intended to sell her share of the business to Bonnie—but they couldn't tell Bonnie that and risk having her new share declared a joint marital asset. Sarah could only imagine how devastated Bonnie must have been, thinking herself abandoned by her friends when she most needed their support. What courage Bonnie had shown, and what selflessness, in deciding to sell her share rather than risk harm to all that they had created together! The Elm Creek Quilters had known that Bonnie could regain her position as a part owner of the business as soon as her divorce was final, but Bonnie had not.

And so, unaware of her friends' plans, Bonnie made plans of her own. She had grown accustomed to owning her own business and was not content to be a member of the Elm Creek Quilts faculty and nothing more, so when Claire offered her the chance to buy in to the Hale Kapa Kuiki, she accepted. Sarah would never forget the day Bonnie returned from Maui, met Sarah's infant twins, discovered Judy waiting in the newly remodeled kitchen—and at last learned the secret her friends had been keeping from her so many months. Bonnie's surprise was everything her friends had anticipated, but their surprise was even greater when Bonnie revealed that she would now be part owner of *two* quilters' retreats—and that she had discovered a new love in Hawai'i.

In Sarah's opinion, no one deserved a second chance at happiness more than Bonnie, but she wasn't as wholeheartedly delighted for her friend as the other Elm Creek Quilters seemed to be. Bonnie had been involved with Craig since college, and her marriage had only just ended. Rebound relationships rarely endured, and after all Bonnie had been through with Craig, Sarah worried that she would be badly hurt by another breakup. Was it wise, Sarah wondered, to embark upon a new relationship so soon? "What, if anything, about falling in love is wise?" Anna said with a laugh when Sarah came to her with her concerns. Anna was newly in love with

Jeremy then, and perhaps not as objective as she otherwise would have been.

Sylvia provided the reassurance Sarah sought by reminding her that Bonnie was by nature sensible; that the demise of her marriage had made her more cautious, not less; and that the thousands of miles that would separate Bonnie from her new sweetheart would oblige her to proceed slowly. Much relieved, Sarah realized that time and distance would prove whether Hinano was worthy of Bonnie. If he kept in touch throughout the spring and summer, if their affection grew rather than dwindled, then Sarah would believe that their feelings for each other were real and strong and not the ephemeral infatuation of a holiday fling. She hoped Hinano was every bit as wonderful as Bonnie said he was, and she prayed Bonnie wouldn't get hurt.

As spring blossomed into summer and another season of Elm Creek Quilt Camp continued with the usual delights and mishaps, Bonnie seemed happier and more full of life than she had been in years. Sarah often overheard laughter coming from Bonnie's classroom as she taught her favorite courses with renewed enthusiasm. Bonnie spoke often of Hinano, a widower, ukulele player, and music shop owner. His only child, a son, had recently graduated from the University of Hawai'i on Oahu with a degree in oceanography. His aunt Midori, the cook and housekeeper for the Hale Kapa Kuiki, was a talented traditional Hawaiian quilter and the first friend Bonnie had made in Lahaina. An expert on Hawaiian history and culture, Hinano had introduced Bonnie to some of the islands' most magnificent natural wonders and fascinating historical treasures: sunrise at Haleakala, the Queen's Quilt in the Iolani Palace in

Honolulu, the view of Kahului from the Waihee Ridge, the beauty and stunning history of the ʻIao Valley. Already he was planning other excursions for when Bonnie returned to Maui after Labor Day—which, Sarah gathered, couldn't come soon enough to suit either of them. They kept in touch with frequent phone calls and daily e-mails, and although hearing from Hinano always lifted Bonnie's spirits, an undercurrent of longing flowed through all of her stories about him, and about her Hawaiian home.

Bonnie also spoke often with Claire and Midori, who kept her informed about Aloha Quilt Camp's exciting launch, successful first sessions, and occasional calamities, which she helped resolve over the phone. The teachers Bonnie had recruited and hired were working out beautifully, and the evening programs she had designed based upon Hinano's recommendations delighted their campers, introducing them to the history and culture of Hawai'i beyond the popular tourist destinations. Whenever Claire e-mailed her photos from the Hale Kapa Kuiki—the outdoor classroom on the lanai, the welcome luaus on the beach with the sun setting over the Pacific, the campers enjoying excursions into the rain forest—Bonnie shared the pictures with the Elm Creek Quilters, seeming both happy and wistful as she gazed upon the scenes. After a busy day at Elm Creek Quilt Camp, Bonnie often could be found in the kitchen exchanging e-mails with Claire on her laptop, reading over her notes from the previous winter, or perusing tourist guidebooks for Maui—all in preparation for returning to Lahaina after the summer. Bonnie missed not only Hinano, Sarah realized, but also Claire, Midori, the Laulima Quilters, the Hale Kapa Kuiki with its pineapple garden and ocean views, and the excitement of launching a new business and watching it flourish. At times Bonnie seemed relaxed and happy, enjoying her students, her daily morning walks around the estate, the anticipation and peace of a Sunday-morning breakfast at the manor before the next week's campers arrived—but other times she seemed eager for the days to pass swiftly so she could return to Hawai'i, to Aloha Quilt Camp, and to Hinano.

Soon after Bonnie had returned to Pennsylvania, Sylvia repeated her offer to allow Bonnie to open a smaller version of her defunct quilt shop in Elm Creek Manor, both to cater to their campers, who sometimes forgot to pack some of the fabric, thread, and notions required for their classes, and also to draw local residents to the manor in hopes of fostering better relations between Elm Creek Quilts and the local quilting community. Sarah knew that Sylvia also wanted to help Bonnie reclaim something of what she had lost when the doors to Grandma's Attic quilt shop closed for the last time. The other Elm Creek Quilters thought "Grandma's Parlor" was a wonderful idea and had found Bonnie's lack of enthusiasm puzzling. Sylvia mentioned the idea once or twice more that summer, but as the end of August approached, Sylvia confided to Sarah that she doubted Bonnie would ever take her up on the offer. "She's found something else to fill those empty places in her heart," she said, smiling fondly.

Summer ended. Bonnie returned to Hawai'i, Sylvia worked on the replicas of Elizabeth's wedding quilt, Sarah helped her archive her family photos as she made albums for Melissa and her brother, and Jeremy proposed to Anna. In February, not long after the twins celebrated their first birthday, Sylvia became the first Elm Creek Quilter to accept Bonnie's invitation to visit the Hale Kapa Kuiki. After spending a week enjoying the sunshine, balmy breezes, and stunning beauty of the tropical paradise, Sylvia and Andrew returned with enchanting stories of their vacation and high praise for Aloha Quilt Camp and Hinano. He was a perfectly lovely gentleman, Sylvia declared, very kind, very talented, and very good to Bonnie. Aloha Quilt Camp was off to a wonderful start, and with its excellent location and accomplished faculty, Sylvia was confident that Bonnie, Claire, and their colleagues would enjoy tremendous success. Although Sylvia's reports reassured Sarah, she knew that only visiting Aloha Quilt Camp and meeting Hinano herself would put her lingering worries to rest.

But Sarah's visit to Maui would have to wait. Matt was eager to go, but Sarah found the prospect of traveling with toddler twins for more than fourteen hours one-way, plus layovers and plane changes, too daunting, and she couldn't bear to leave the twins at home. When the twins were three years old, Matt and her mother conspired to make the long-anticipated trip possible. For Christmas, Matt surprised Sarah with a floral batik sarong, two airline tickets to Maui, and Carol's promise to care for the twins at Elm Creek Manor during their absence, with the able assistance of the other Elm Creek Quilters in residence.

They departed in mid-January, mere hours before the annual Storm of the Century was predicted to bury the Elm Creek Valley in snow, and arrived in a glorious paradise of perpetual summer, bathed in sunlight and warmed by the aloha spirit. They rented a car at the airport and drove southwest across the island, past fields of sugarcane, rugged green mountains, and a volcano whose top was concealed by thick white clouds. The air was fragrant with flowers, the mountains sublimely beautiful. Matt drove while Sarah read the map, and as they reached the western side of the island and turned north, they passed through a tunnel. On the other side, the ocean appeared before them, endless and blue. Sarah forgot the map and gazed out at the water as they drove along the cliffside, the ocean to their left, vast and deep, the foothills of deeply forested mountains rising to their right.

Before long the rural landscape gave way to roadside fruit stands, public beaches, small restaurants, and turnoffs leading into newer hillside neighborhoods. Following the directions Bonnie had sent, they soon arrived in Lahaina, where Matt turned off the highway onto a street lined with shops, restaurants, and art galleries. To her delight, Sarah recognized several landmarks that had appeared in Bonnie's photographs and stories—the enormous banyan tree in Courthouse Square, the church where the Laulima Quilters met weekly, the Baldwin House, and the Old Lahaina Luau. Their journey ended at a quaint Victorian inn surrounded by palm trees, through which Sarah glimpsed waves crashing on tide pools encircled by black lava rock. A wreath of hibiscus flowers hung on the front door of the inn, and the banisters of the wraparound porch gleamed white as if freshly painted. Identical banisters framed the balconies on the second and third floors, which Sarah knew from Bonnie's description were partitioned into separate units called lanais, one for each guest room. Some, like Bonnie's, faced the ocean, offering her spectacular views of glorious sunsets as she relaxed in the peace and solitude of her room at the end of a busy day. Others looked out over the lush courtyard garden or offered charming views of Lahaina's Front Street. Sarah and

Matt hoped for an ocean view, but since Aloha Quilt Camp was fully booked for that week and they were staying gratis, they would be happy with whatever Bonnie and Claire offered them.

As Sarah and Matt left the car, Bonnie came out onto the front porch to welcome them, followed by a white-haired, barrel-chested Hawaiian man Sarah immediately recognized from her friend's photos as Hinano. "Aloha," Bonnie cried, hurrying down the steps to embrace her friends and drape beautiful leis of fragrant white blossoms over their shoulders. She was radiant, Sarah marveled, more full of joy and happiness than Sarah had ever seen her. She was struck by the thought that for the first time since Grandma's Attic closed, Bonnie looked perfectly at home.

Hinano, too, greeted them with warm alohas and helped them carry their luggage into the Hale Kapa Kuiki. In the foyer, tables adorned with fragrant tropical floral arrangements flanked the entrance, directly across from a grand staircase that climbed to a second-floor landing, where it split into two staircases and continued up to the third floor. To the left of the staircase was a cozy sitting room decorated with bamboo furniture and historic photographs. A built-in bookcase loaded with many well-read volumes stood between a pair of windows overlooking a lush garden. Sarah glimpsed a few middle-aged women sipping coffee at a small table outside and heard the low murmur of other unseen guests chatting. To the right of the staircase was a dining room, the dark wooden table set with woven Polynesian linens and fine white china. On a sideboard stood two large glass pitchers—one of lemonade and another of iced tea—and a silver fruit bowl filled with pineapples and mangoes, with plates and glasses nearby so guests could help themselves. Gentle breezes wafted in through the open windows, stirring the sheer curtains. It was an enticing fusion of Polynesian and Victorian décor, comfortable, elegant, and lovely.

As soon as they crossed the threshold, a petite woman who looked to be near Bonnie's age or perhaps a bit younger bounded into the foyer. "You must be Sarah," she exclaimed, startling her with an unexpected hug, her long blond ponytail bouncing perkily. *"Aloha. E komo mai."*

"And you must be Claire," said Sarah, grinning as Claire turned to Matt, who lost the battle to substitute a handshake for a hug. "Aloha, and—what was the other?"

"*E komo mai* means welcome," said Hinano as he set their suitcases in a small alcove off the sitting room, his deep voice a pleasant rumble. "More literally, 'Come in.' "

"And please do," said Claire, linking her arm through Sarah's and leading her into the inn, down the hall past the staircase. "Bonnie's told me so much about you, I feel like we've been friends for years."

"I feel like I know you too," Sarah replied, including Hinano with a smile. She smelled pineapple and nutmeg as Claire led them into the kitchen, where a small Japanese woman in her midsixties was placing four loaf pans into the higher of two large wall ovens. A few other loaves of banana bread cooled on a wire rack on the island in the center of the room.

"Aloha," the woman greeted them, smiling over her shoulder as she closed the oven door and set the timer. Her smile was both cheerful and knowing, and Sarah had a feeling that her single appraising glance took in much more than it seemed. She wore a long red dress with a pattern of white hibiscus flowers, and she wore her long black hair in an elegant chignon.

Bonnie introduced the woman as Midori Tanaka, the inn's manager, cook, and housekeeper, although, after hearing Bonnie's stories over the past three years, Sarah couldn't have mistaken her for anyone else. Midori offered Sarah and Matt glasses of iced tea spiked with pineapple juice and slices of warm banana bread, quickly proving that her baking merited every word of praise Bonnie had lavished upon it.

When they finished their refreshments, Bonnie took Sarah and Matt upstairs to leave their luggage in their room, a spacious suite with a queen-size bed and a private lanai facing the ocean, just as they had hoped. While Matt stepped outside to take in the view of the waves crashing upon the beach, Sarah admired the exquisite jade-green-and-white quilt spread upon the bed. The jade-green appliqué appeared to have been cut from whole cloth, trimmed like a paper snowflake in stylized shapes resembling large, broad, deeply lobed leaves, boldly symmetrical. Concentric lines of exquisitely fine quilting covered the white background, echoing the appliquéd shapes.

"Midori made this quilt," Bonnie remarked, following her gaze. "She calls it *Haku La'ape,* after the Hawaiian word for the monstera plant. Isn't it a masterpiece? She and the members of her quilt guild made all the quilts for the inn, and no two are the same. When we pass through the garden, I'll show you a monstera, and you'll see what a good likeness the quilt is."

Sarah knew from a Hawaiian quilt design workshop she had observed Bonnie teach at Elm Creek Quilt Camp the previous summer that most traditional Hawaiian quilt patterns were inspired by nature. As much as Sarah admired the unique, intricate appliqué style, it seemed so complex and difficult to master that she had never attempted one, despite Bonnie's encouragement. Perhaps one day, she thought, unable to resist running her hand lovingly over the soft, exquisitely formed surface before following Bonnie and Matt from the room.

Bonnie led them on a tour of the inn that ended in the central lanai, a courtyard enclosed by the wings of the building on three sides and a lush garden on the fourth. A footpath through the palm trees led to a secluded white-sand beach where guests of the inn could relax in the shade of broad umbrellas or stroll along the shore. The more adventurous campers rode the waves on boogie boards or went snorkeling, marveling at the multicolored fish and the slow, graceful sea turtles Hinano called *honu*.

One section of the courtyard lanai was partially enclosed, with a roof and half walls running the entire length of one wing of the inn. This, Bonnie explained, was where Aloha Quilt Camp classes met. It was efficiently arranged, with several custom-made sewing tables offering ample space for two dozen quilters, three ironing stations near the back, and an angled mirror suspended above the front table so that the students could easily view the teacher's demonstrations. The Hale Kapa Kuiki lacked sufficient space to offer multiple classes simultaneously, which the Elm Creek Quilters managed by dividing the manor's large ballroom into smaller spaces with movable partitions. It was a fair trade, Sarah thought, to be able to work in such beautiful surroundings.

Fatigued from their long day of travel, Sarah and Matt were perfectly content to relax on the beach while Bonnie and Claire returned to the work of quilt camp. Later that evening, their hosts invited the entire camp to a luau in their honor, where they feasted on *kalua* pork that had cooked all day in an underground oven called an *imu*, steamed chicken *laulaus*, vegetable long rice, *lomi lomi* salmon, macaroni salad, and taro rolls, with coconut pudding *haupia* for dessert. After the meal, Hinano and three of his friends provided enchanting traditional Hawaiian music on ukulele, guitar, and drums, and a group of lovely young women performed the hula and other Polynesian dances. It was a wonderful evening, almost overwhelmingly so, and Sarah and Matt slept well that night, lulled into peaceful dreams by the sound of the ocean.

Each morning, Sarah and Matt enjoyed breakfast on the courtyard lanai with Bonnie, the campers, and the rest of the Aloha Quilt Camp faculty. Sarah was delighted to meet the characters who had populated Bonnie's letters and stories: Kawena Wilson, a master of the Hawaiian quilt from the Big Island; Arlene Gustafson, a traditional quilter from Nebraska and author of three best-selling pattern books; and Asuka Fujiko, an innovative quilt artist from Tokyo who specialized in machine quilting techniques and had won numerous awards for her breathtakingly intricate quilts. Watching Bonnie among them, Sarah realized that Bonnie had created another group of friends as creative, supportive, and fond of one another as the Elm Creek Quilters.

Each day after breakfast, Sarah and Matt spent hours exploring Maui together. They had not had a night alone without the twins since their birth, nor had they gone on a real vacation—which Sarah defined as a getaway that did not include spending the holidays at the home of a relative—since before Sarah's pregnancy. At first the abundance of time together felt unexpectedly awkward, and without the children or Elm Creek Quilts to discuss, their conversations sometimes lagged. This troubled Sarah, because it seemed like a very bad sign that spouses should run out of things to say to each other. When she made a little joke of it to Matt, his brow furrowed as he replied that he hadn't noticed anything and she shouldn't worry, so she tried not to.

Fortunately, the tension or awkwardness or whatever it was eased by the third day of their vacation, and Sarah began to feel as if they were on a second honeymoon. They held hands as they window-shopped in Lahaina and asked other hikers to photograph them together as they climbed the Waihee Ridge to Lanilili Peak and descended the Sliding Sands Trail into Haleakala. The rest of the week flew by. As much as Sarah missed the twins, on the last day she packed her suitcase with a heavy heart. She had discovered peace and contentment during her all too brief visit to Maui. She understood now why Bonnie loved it so much, and she wondered how her friend could bear to leave it every spring, even for Elm Creek Manor and the dear friends awaiting her there.

Since their flight wasn't scheduled until late afternoon, on the day of their departure Sarah and Matt joined Bonnie and Hinano for lunch at Aloha Mixed Plate, where they could enjoy a tasty meal and a view of the ocean one last time. They lingered at the table as long as they could, but at last, regretfully, Matt glanced at his watch and said they had to leave for the airport.

As Sarah began to rise, Bonnie said, "Before you go, there's something else I need to tell you."

"Take all the time you need," said Sarah, settling back into her plastic chair. "With any luck, we'll miss our flight and we'll have to stay. Honestly, Bonnie, I don't know how you can leave this beautiful place year after year."

"Elm Creek Manor is beautiful, too, and I miss my friends," said Bonnie, smiling. "It also helps to know that Maui will be here waiting for me to return. But . . . actually, that's what I wanted to talk to you about." Bonnie and Hinano exchanged a quick glance. "I have some news, and I didn't want to tell the other Elm Creek Quilters over the phone. Since I can't tell them in person, I'd like to tell you, and have you spread the word, if you wouldn't mind."

Sarah's heart plummeted. Such a foreboding preamble could only mean that Bonnie was about to resign from Elm Creek Quilts. "Okay," she said, reaching for her water glass and taking a sip, though only a few drops and several cubes of ice remained. "What's the news?"

Bonnie beamed and took Hinano's hand. "We're getting married."

"What?" exclaimed Sarah, her fears forgotten. "That's wonderful!"

"Congratulations," boomed Matt, reaching across the table to shake Hinano's hand.

"Mahalo," said Hinano, putting his arm around Bonnie's shoulders and grinning with pure delight.

Sarah pushed back her chair and went around the other side of the table to hug her friend. "I can't believe you didn't tell me sooner. I can't believe you kept this a secret from me all week!"

"Me, neither, unless you just got engaged this morning?" asked Matt.

Bonnie and Hinano laughed. "About a month ago," said Hinano. "So now you know, and now you'll have a good excuse to come back to Maui, for the wedding."

"As if we needed an excuse," said Sarah, laughing. "But wherever you hold your wedding, we wouldn't miss it for the world."

"I'm hoping you can convince all of the Elm Creek Quilters to come," said Bonnie. "It wouldn't be the same without them. Anna, Judy, and Summer, too, even though they've left the manor."

"Of course," said Sarah. "You know what Sylvia says, 'Once an Elm Creek Quilter, always an Elm Creek Quilter.' Agnes might need a little convincing—you know she doesn't travel much—but I can't imagine anyone would want to miss your wedding."

"We'll have it during the winter so it won't interfere with quilt camp," Bonnie promised, but then her smile faltered, and she stepped back from Sarah's embrace. "There's one other thing. Once we're married, I won't want to be away from Hinano, and he can't afford to shut down his music shop for an entire summer to come with me." She glanced at Hinano, who smiled ruefully and nodded, encouraging her to continue. She took a deep breath and turned back to Sarah. "I'm afraid this coming summer will be my last with Elm Creek Quilt Camp. After the wedding, Hinano and I will remain here in Maui throughout the year."

Tears sprang into Sarah's eyes. Unable to speak, she nodded and hugged Bonnie again. She was glad for her friend, who had endured so much heartbreak on her way to her happy ending, but already she mourned her departure and couldn't imagine Elm Creek Quilt Camp without her.

"You'll tell the others?" asked Bonnie, a little worriedly. "It was hard enough to tell you, and I knew you'd understand and be happy for me. I can't bear to break the news to everyone."

Sarah agreed, assuring Bonnie that everyone would understand, and everyone would celebrate her happiness. They would miss her, but they loved her unselfishly. They wouldn't regret her departure if they knew her new path would lead her to greater joy and fulfillment, even if it meant leaving them behind.

Just as Sarah predicted, their friends back home welcomed the news of Bonnie's engagement with delight, and her decision to leave Elm Creek Quilts with regret and understanding. "It was only a matter of time," said Diane as they gathered in the manor's kitchen before a staff meeting to prepare for the upcoming camp season. "A new job, a new love, a home on the ocean—what do we have to compete with that?"

"Friendship," Gwen retorted.

"Her children and grandchildren," added Agnes. "Well, we don't have them here at the manor, of course, but they're in Pennsylvania."

"I'm sure Bonnie will come back to visit often," said Sylvia, "and we will certainly visit her."

But it wouldn't be the same, and they all knew it.

Before they settled down to camp business, they discussed the equally important matter of Bonnie's wedding quilt. Gretchen, a devoted traditionalist, suggested that they make a Double Wedding Ring, but Sylvia declared that she had made enough Double Wedding Rings for one lifetime and would be very happy never to make another. As the others proposed and debated other possibilities, Sarah mulled over Sylvia's declaration. She hadn't seen Sylvia work on the reproductions of Elizabeth's wedding quilt in many months. The last she had heard, Sylvia had finished enough rings for one quilt, had sent them off to Melissa, and was awaiting the appliqué sections Melissa had promised to contribute. Perhaps the pattern had proven too difficult for Melissa, or perhaps they had abandoned the project for other reasons. But Melissa and her friendship with Sylvia remained a sensitive topic for Sarah, so although she was curious, she didn't inquire.

While Sarah was lost in thought, her friends settled upon the Wedding March pattern for Bonnie and Hinano's wedding quilt. When Agnes mentioned that she had plenty of country homespun prints to contribute, Sarah roused herself from her reverie to point out that she didn't think those were Bonnie's favorite fabrics anymore. "I've seen Bonnie's room at the Hale Kapa Kuiki, and there isn't a scrap of barn red or navy blue plaid anywhere," she said. She remembered something Claire had told her while showing her around Plumeria Quilts, her shop across the street from the inn: In Hawai'i, quilters preferred brighter colors. Transplanted mainlanders brought their color preferences with them, but over time, they gradually adopted brighter palettes, as Bonnie apparently had.

They decided instead to use a combination of florals and solids in tropical hues, and with that settled, Sarah introduced the first item on her agenda: gathering suggestions for new classes and workshops. What her friends didn't know was that originally that item had been second on the list, right after hiring Bonnie's replacement, a subject so unpleasant to contemplate that Sarah had deleted it from the document before printing it out. Bonnie would be with Elm Creek Quilts for another summer, and there would be plenty of time to think about recruiting a new teacher after Labor Day. Sarah only hoped that the task would prove easier than the annual nightmare of finding a replacement for Anna.

Bonnie and Hinano chose the first Saturday in January for their wedding, and all of the Elm Creek Quilters, past and present, traveled from wherever the winter found them—Waterford, Chicago, Philadelphia, or Virginia—to celebrate their special day. Aloha Quilt Camp closed for the week so that the Hale Kapa Kuiki could accommodate the couple's out-of-town guests, the majority of whom were the bride's friends and family, since most of Hinano's lived in Hawai'i. In the days leading up to the wedding, the Elm Creek Quilters enjoyed a happy reunion at the inn with the friends who had left their circle—Summer, who brought a handsome, dark-haired fellow graduate student named Enrique as her date; Judy, accompanied by her husband, Steve, and daughter, Emily, who had become a rather accomplished quilter for her age; and Anna, Jeremy, and little Gina. This time Sarah and Matt had brought the twins along instead of leaving them home with their grandmother, and the three children played together happily, running races in halls of the Hale Kapa Kuiki, searching for tiny fish swimming in the tide pools, marveling at the pineapple growing in the garden of the courtyard lanai, and begging macadamia shortbread cookies from Midori. Anna and Sarah chatted as they kept an eye on the children—Sarah, bemoaning the impossibility of finding anyone half as perfect for Elm Creek Quilt Camp as Anna had been; Anna, confessing that she missed the cheerful bustle of the manor during camp season and worried about Jeremy's grueling pursuit of tenure, which left them little time to enjoy family life. But mostly they and the other Elm Creek Quilters spent their time admiring the beauty of the Hale Kapa Kuiki, enjoying their reunion, helping Bonnie with last-minute preparations for the wedding, and rejoicing in Bonnie's happiness.

On Saturday evening just before sunset, the guests gathered for the ceremony on the white-sand beach just beyond the inn's lush gardens. As they seated themselves in the rows of chairs arranged before a shade canopy of woven palm fronds adorned with plumeria and hibiscus blossoms, one of Hinano's best friends played the ukulele and sang gentle, romantic melodies in English and Hawaiian. The ceremony began with the seating of Bonnie's daughter and younger son, their spouses, and their children, followed by Hinano's father, son, and aunt Midori. Then Hinano entered, smiling broadly, clad in a short-sleeved dress shirt and slacks, with a wreath of dark green leaves upon his brow. Accompanying him was the *kahu,* or minister, who sang a Hawaiian chant as they approached. The *kahu* was dressed similarly to Hinano, but he wore a printed cloth draped over his left shoulder and midsection, a lei of honey-colored *kukui* nuts, and no wreath. In his hands he carried two leis, one of fragrant *maile* and another of *pikake,* or white jasmine. By his side hung a large white conch shell in a knotted carrier, and when he finished chanting his *mele,* he raised the shell to his lips and blew a long, low, sonorous call. Sarah's heart thumped and tears of joy filled her eyes as everyone rose and watched Bonnie process down the aisle on the arm of her eldest son, clad in a simple but elegant ivory dress and carrying a bouquet of lavender anthuriums, white orchids, and *pikake*. When they reached the front, C.J. kissed his mother on the cheek, shook Hinano's hand, and seated himself in the first row beside his wife.

The *kahu* spoke simply but eloquently of the meaning of marriage, the importance of aloha between a husband and wife, and the special blessing of discovering new love after loss. Then he handed the *maile* lei to Bonnie, who presented it to Hinano as she spoke her vows. In turn, Hinano recited his vows and presented the *pikake* lei to Bonnie. They exchanged rings, kissed, and as the *kahu* pronounced them husband and wife, their friends and family took to their feet, cheering and applauding.

The gathering moved to the Hale Kapa Kuiki lanai for the reception, which was a grand luau rich with delicious food, beautiful music, joy, and much aloha. Sarah was distracted by the twins, who—at Caroline's instigation, of course—scampered down the path to the beach to look for *honu* whenever Sarah's back was turned, but she enjoyed herself nonetheless. Bonnie and Hinano looked so happy together, so much in love. Sarah wished them many, many years together and hoped they would always cherish each other as much as they did that day.

Later that night, after Matt took the drowsy twins upstairs to bed, Sarah sipped a glass of chardonnay and listened as Hinano and his son, Kai, joined the band for a set. She wondered if she and Caroline would ever collaborate on a quilt as full of beauty and harmony as the music Hinano and Kai created together. She had longed for a daughter with whom to share her love of quilting, but Caroline ran away when Sarah called her, climbed down from her lap when Sarah tried to hold her close, and would rather puzzle out the words in a picture book than admire the bright colors and soft touch of fabric Sarah showed her. She was still too young, Sarah decided. One day she would fall in love with quilting as Sarah had and their mutual interest would draw them closer. In the meantime, Sarah would try to be patient.

Bonnie, radiant in her wedding gown, found Sarah as she sat listening to the ukulele and guitar, lost in thought. Sarah offered her friend more hugs and congratulations, and told her truthfully that she had never been to a more beautiful wedding, or one more blessed with aloha. "I have you to thank for it," Bonnie replied.

"Me to thank for what?" asked Sarah. "What did I do? I just flew in to enjoy the celebration like everyone else. I didn't even set up any of the chairs on the beach. Matt and Claire's husband did that."

"What did you do?" Bonnie put her head to one side and regarded her with fond amusement. "You made me the happiest woman in the world, that's all."

"I think maybe you've had too much champagne," Sarah replied, draining the last of her wine. "I didn't marry you; Hinano did."

Bonnie laughed. "But I never would have met him if not for you."

"How do you figure that?"

"Elm Creek Quilts saved me, and you created Elm Creek Quilts," said Bonnie. "After I lost my quilt shop and my marriage fell apart, I can't imagine what I would have done without Elm Creek Quilts. It gave me a home, a paycheck, and a reason to get out of bed every morning when I felt like I had lost everything. You probably don't know this, but Claire was inspired to create Aloha Quilt Camp because Elm Creek Quilts was such an enormous success. And because I was an Elm Creek Quilter, Claire offered me the consultant's job when she could have hired any number of experienced local quilters." She reached for Sarah's hand. "I never would have met Hinano if not for that job, which depended upon my experience with Elm Creek Quilts, which depended upon you."

"Claire might have invited you to Maui for a vacation," Sarah offered lamely. "You might have met Hinano then."

"It wouldn't have worked out the same way, even if I had happened to wander into his music shop." Bonnie shook her head. "Sarah, honestly, it never ceases to amaze me how you can't believe a word of praise spoken about you. Most people demand credit and recognition for every minuscule thing they do, but you act like it's dishonest, somehow, to accept praise you've rightly earned. You seem to think you don't deserve it."

Usually Sarah didn't, as in this case. "I'm truly glad if I played any role in bringing you and Hinano together," she said sincerely.

"You definitely did, and I'll be grateful to you for the rest of my life." Bonnie squeezed her hand and rose, her soft ivory silk dress stirring in the gentle ocean breeze. "I wish you knew how much good you've contributed to the world by creating Elm Creek Quilts. I think I'll make it my mission to keep telling you until you understand."

"I'm not Elm Creek Quilts," said Sarah. "It's so much more than one person."

"But it all began with you." Someone called to Bonnie then, but she threw Sarah one last smile over her shoulder as she turned to go. "And even if you don't believe it, Hinano and I owe our happiness to you. Thank you."

"You're welcome," Sarah said, since it seemed rude to argue with the bride on her wedding day.

Weeks later, back home in Pennsylvania, where the rolling Appalachians were shrouded in white and the stark, bare-limbed trees cast thin shadows beneath the midwinter sky, Sarah confronted the task of finding Bonnie's replacement. Alone in the library, she studied the Winding Ways quilt on the wall beside the fireplace, its missing panels a constant reminder of her absent friends. Should she search for an instructor whose interests mirrored Bonnie's and simply have that person take over her usual classes, or would it be better to find the most talented quilter available and let her teach her own specialty, whatever that turned out to be? She spent hours laboring over a new help-wanted ad to post on their Web site and run in a few quilting magazines, until finally, frustrated with her inadequate description of everything the job entailed, she wandered downstairs and found Gretchen, Sylvia, and Maggie in the kitchen.

"Will you tell me what you think of this?" Sarah implored, and read aloud her most recent draft. Sylvia suggested a few additional details for the job requirements, and Gretchen recommended rearranging a few sentences near the end. Maggie sat quietly, sipping her tea, her hazel eyes looking anywhere but directly at Sarah, the furrow of her brow telling Sarah she wanted very badly to offer her opinion. "How about you, Maggie?" she finally prompted. "You've been awfully quiet. You don't think my writing is all that bad, do you?"

"No, in fact, I think it's great. If I didn't work here already, I'd apply for the job." Maggie hesitated, her long, slender fingers toying with her teaspoon. "It's just that before you go to the expense and trouble of recruiting a new teacher, I'd like to recommend someone, although I admit I'm anything but an objective, disinterested party."

Immediately Sarah guessed whom Maggie wanted to put forward: Russell MacIntyre, a talented art quilter who happened to be her long-distance boyfriend. Years before, when Summer and Judy had announced their plans to leave Elm Creek Quilts, Sarah and her colleagues had launched a nationwide search for two new instructors. Of the five finalists, Maggie had been their favorite and first choice, for she was a quilter of unique qualifications. Russell had ranked second.

Two days after her twenty-fifth birthday, Maggie had been walking home from the bus stop when she passed a garage sale and discovered a sampler quilt being used as a tablecloth for a display of glassware. Although she had made only two quilts in her lifetime—one a Girl Scout badge requirement, the other a gift for her sister's newborn—one look told her that this quilt, despite its dusty, disheveled appearance, was something special. The woman running the garage sale was astonished by Maggie's interest in the bedraggled quilt, which she had kept in the garage since moving to the neighborhood twenty-six years before. Her mother-in-law had bought it at an estate auction, and when she tired of it, she had given it to her son to keep dog hair off the car seats when he took his German shepherds to the park. Bemused, the woman apologized for its condition and asked five dollars for it, which Maggie gladly paid.

At home, she moved the coffee table aside and spread the quilt on the living room carpet. Despite the years of ill treatment, the quilt was free of holes, tears, and stains, and the geometric patterns were striking beneath the layers of dust and dirt. All one hundred of the two-color blocks were unique, and each had been pieced or appliquéd from a different print fabric and a plain background fabric that might have been white once, but had discolored with age and neglect. Along one edge, embroidered in thread that had faded to pale brown barely distinguishable from the background cloth, were the words "Harriet Findley Birch. Lowell, Mass. to Salem, Ore. 1854." The discovery astounded her. How had a 133-year-old quilt ended up as a tablecloth at a garage sale?

With the help of the Courtyard Quilters, a quilting bee comprised of residents of the Sacramento retirement home where she worked, Maggie relearned her long-forgotten sewing skills and made a replica of the fragile antique. Fellow customers of the Goose Tracks Quilt Shop admired her quilt so much that the owner invited her to teach a class so that they could make their own versions. The success of that class led to another, and another, which brought her to the attention of local quilt guilds, who invited her to lecture and teach. As her fame in the quilting world spread, Maggie wrote a pattern book, *My Journey with Harriet*, which quickly sold out of its first edition and went into its third printing within a month. All along, Maggie had kept her job at the retirement home, enjoying her work and her friendship with the Courtyard Quilters, but one day, years of budget cuts and rumors of corporate mergers culminated in the unsettling announcement that another health care organization had bought them out and intended to shut them down.

With unemployment looming, Maggie applied for a faculty position with Elm Creek Quilts and was invited to an interview, where, although she did not know it at the time, her knowledge, skills, and insight into the spirit of Elm Creek Quilts impressed her interviewers—even Diane, who had been particularly hard on all of the candidates in the vain hope that none of them would take the job and Judy and Summer would be compelled to stay.

On the flight home, while Maggie was hand-piecing a quilt block and mulling over her visit to Elm Creek Manor, a man moved to the empty seat across the aisle and struck up a conversation about quilting. They were both a little embarrassed to discover that although they didn't recognize each other, they had previously met; the man turned out to be Russell MacIntyre, a renowned contemporary art quilter from Seattle, and a few years earlier, they had both been seated at the head table at the awards banquet of the American Quilter's Society's show in Paducah. It soon came out they were both returning home from interviews with Elm Creek Quilts, and after the initial awkwardness of learning that they were competitors passed, they chatted all the way to Seattle. As the plane touched down, they exchanged business cards and agreed to have lunch the next time they were scheduled at the same quilt show. They disembarked and parted ways, and Russell had almost reached the security checkpoint when he realized he didn't want to wait for another unlikely synchronicity of their travel schedules. He checked the monitors for Maggie's connecting flight, sprinted to the gate, and just as she was about to disappear down the jet bridge to her plane, he called out to her, and they arranged to meet the following week when he traveled through California on a teaching tour.

After that, they spoke every night on the phone, and they enjoyed a wonderful weekend together when Russell's travels brought him near Sacramento. Two weeks after that momentous plane ride, Sarah called Maggie with an offer of employment. Maggie, confident that Russell would surely be chosen for the second vacant spot on the faculty, gratefully accepted. And indeed, after hanging up with Maggie, Sarah had called Russell—but Russell, unaware that Maggie had already been hired and trusting her dire assessment of her performance during the job interview, turned down the offer so that he could remain on the West Coast, closer to her. By the time Russell spoke with Maggie, realized his mistake, and called Sarah back to rescind his refusal, Sarah had already offered the position to the Elm Creek Quilters' third choice, Gretchen. Disappointed but undaunted, Russell quickly agreed to work as a visiting instructor whenever they needed a substitute.

In all the years since, Maggie and Gretchen had proven to be wonderful additions to the faculty, and whenever Russell filled in for an Elm Creek Quilter who needed a week off for vacation or family obligations, he received glowing reviews from his students. As his romance with Maggie blossomed, he began visiting the manor more often even when quilt camp wasn't in session. But for the most part, he continued to reside at his home in Seattle when he wasn't traveling from quilt guild to art gallery, lecturing and teaching, although both he and Maggie wished it could be otherwise. They were in love and wanted to be together, but their careers kept them mostly apart.

Of course now that Bonnie was leaving, Maggie would want them to hire Russell to replace her. As Maggie waited pensively for the verdict, Sarah and Sylvia exchanged a long look that communicated volumes. When Russell had interviewed for the two vacant faculty positions nearly four years earlier, the Elm Creek Quilters had intended to hire him. During his time as a visiting instructor, he had been amiable, productive, and diligent, never bemoaning the misunderstanding that had cost him the permanent faculty job. He had won the approval of the Elm Creek Quilters and the admiration of his students, and also—and this was by no means the least of Sarah's considerations—having him join the faculty would make Maggie very happy.

Sarah raised her eyebrows at Sylvia, a silent inquiry, and Sylvia returned the barest of nods. "I think that's an excellent idea, Maggie," Sarah said. "Do you think he'd be interested in the job?"

"I know he would," Maggie exclaimed, bounding to her feet. "I'll go call him." She bolted for the doorway, where she hesitated. "As long as it's official?"

Sarah laughed, and Sylvia said, "It's official, my dear. Please let him know our intentions, and if he's interested, Sarah will call him later to work out the details."

Thus Russell joined the Elm Creek Quilters, and Maggie's happiness made the loss of Bonnie a little easier to bear. A few months later, Maggie and Russell married in the ballroom of Elm Creek Manor, a commitment they had long spoken of and wished for, but had deferred until they could be together. When Sylvia learned this, she declared that if she had known why they were deferring their marital bliss, she would have created a new position on the faculty especially for him. "You could have fired someone to make room," Gwen remarked. "I nominate Diane."

"Too late," retorted Diane, but like everyone else, she knew Gwen was only teasing. Although the departures of founding members never failed to introduce them to wonderful new teachers like Gretchen, Maggie, and Russell, the absence of dear friends sometimes made them wistful for the early days of Elm Creek Quilts, when their imaginations were full of plans and their days with hard work, when success was but a fond dream and the likelihood of failure daunting.

So many years had passed, and now only Sarah remained of the original Elm Creek Quilters. The others had passed on, or had followed winding ways in pursuit of other dreams. But as Sylvia had predicted so many years before, despite the departure of beloved friends, Elm Creek Quilts endured.

And that reminded Sarah of an important task they needed to fulfill. "Before we start collecting signatures on the Memory Album blocks," she said, rising and smiling fondly at her friends, "we have an errand in the library."

Gwen and Summer knew what she wanted, and as the friends left the kitchen, the mother and daughter paused in the back foyer long enough to take from their luggage their panels of the Winding Ways quilt. A contemplative hush fell over them as they climbed the grand oak staircase—slowly, to accommodate Gwen's stiff knees—made their way down the second-floor hallway, and passed through the French doors to the library. Summer hung the two long-absent panels in place, her mother's in the upper left corner, her own just below it. An empty place would remain in the lower right corner where Bonnie's panel belonged, but soon Diane's panel would fill the space beside it, and Judy's the space next to that. Although the center panel had originally been intended to represent all future Elm Creek Quilters, over the years they had come to think of it as Gretchen's own. She had been with Elm Creek Quilts so long and had contributed so much that they often forgot she was not a founder.

And then the quilt would be almost complete, despite the absence of other beloved friends, because although Sylvia and Agnes and Gretchen could not be among them except in spirit, their sections of the Winding Ways quilt hung proudly, displayed in their memory.

· Chapter Five ·

After admiring the Winding Ways quilt a little longer and reminiscing about days long past, Sarah took the Memory Album blocks from their hiding place in the bottom drawer of the large oak desk and divided them evenly among her friends. They also divided up the wings and floors of the manor, and, pens in hand, went forth to collect signatures and messages of love, hope, and congratulations for the bride and groom.

Sarah worked one side of the third-floor west wing while Anna took the other side, but Anna moved from door-to-door more quickly, not only because several of the rooms on her side of the hallway were not yet occupied but also because everyone wanted to chat with the mother of the bride, and they were not about to pass up a rare opportunity when Sarah was not surrounded by well-wishers, as she was likely to be on the day of the wedding. Sarah meant to stop by each room only long enough to explain the project and collect signatures, but she ended up spending ten minutes chatting about Elm Creek

Quilts with Leo's sister-in-law, an aspiring quilter; fifteen more talking over old times with her favorite cousin, a children's book illustrator from Duluth; and nearly an hour sitting cross-legged on the bed with her former college roommate, reminiscing about their favorite Penn State experiences—Nittany Lions football games, midnight snacks of grilled sticky buns at The Diner on College Avenue, and Thon, the annual dance marathon dedicated to raising funds to find a cure for pediatric cancer. Enjoying her friend's company and their shared memories of long ago, Sarah quickly lost track of time.

When she finally bade her former roommate good-bye and promised to continue their conversation later, it was time to meet Anna, Gwen, Summer, and the other Elm Creek Quilters in the library. Comparing notes, they discovered that several strokes of bad luck had prevented them from collecting more than a handful of signed blocks apiece. Most knocks on their guests' doors had gone unanswered, since almost everyone was either out visiting with friends elsewhere in the manor or were enjoying the beautiful autumn day by exploring the estate. Maggie had narrowly escaped disaster when she had turned a corner and bumped into Caroline, barely managing to stuff the blocks into her bag before the bride-to-be got a good look at them. When Sarah admitted that a conversation with an old friend had kept her from collecting more signatures, her friends exchanged guilty looks, burst out laughing, and confessed that they, too, had spent more time standing in the hallways chatting with one another than knocking on doors.

"We'll try again this evening, when people are more likely to be in their rooms," Sarah decided, collecting the blocks, signed and unsigned, and concealing them beneath a few empty folders in the bottom desk drawer. Before their next outing, she would sort the blocks and check off the names of guests they had already reached, so they would know where to focus their attention.

The Elm Creek Quilters went downstairs to join the manor's other residents and guests in the banquet hall for a delicious meal that was sure to build anticipation for the grand wedding feast yet to come. Gina and Anna earned well-deserved praise as their guests savored the spinach lasagna, sautéed green beans, and rosemary rolls, with Gina's heavenly mocha ganache cupcakes for dessert. After the other guests left the banquet hall, the Elm Creek Quilters cleared away the dishes, tidied the kitchen, and lingered over coffee at the long wooden table where they had held countless business meetings and had shared nearly as many delicious meals through the years. Sarah couldn't bear to break up the fun by asking everyone to get back to work collecting signatures, so the blocks remained in the library for the rest of the night.

They sat in the drawer undisturbed all the next morning, too, for from the moment Sarah woke she was preoccupied with other wedding preparations, fielding phone calls from the minister and the musicians. After lunch, running late for an errand downtown, she delegated the Memory Album project to Summer, who assured her she would collect as many signatures as she could as discreetly as possible. "I'll tell my mom to be prepared to distract Caroline," she promised with a grin. "She's been looking forward to it."

"I wouldn't want her rehearsals to go to waste," Sarah replied, sorry that she would miss whatever theatricals Gwen had contrived. She hoped Gwen didn't resort to slapstick. The priceless Bergstrom family antiques were even more priceless and antique than they had been when Elm Creek Quilts began, and they wouldn't serve well as props.

Calling for James—and finding him in the kitchen with Gina, wearing a suspiciously happy grin—she enlisted his help rounding up the groomsmen while she went to the north gardens, where she found Matt pulling weeds from the rose terraces while Russell swept fallen leaves from the cobblestones. The freshly painted gazebo gleamed white in the autumn sunshine, and a cool breeze stirred the chrysanthemums, sedum, purple coneflowers, and black-eyed Susans blooming amid the decorative grasses. It would be a picture-perfect setting for a wedding, as long as the weather cooperated.

When Matt spotted her, he rocked back on his heels and brushed the dirt from his hands. "Is it time already?"

"Just about. You have a few minutes to clean up while James is getting the boys together, but if you're too busy here, I could pick up your tux for you." She secretly hoped he would insist upon coming, because he knew much more about fitting a tuxedo than she did. For all the time she had spent in front of a sewing machine, her knowledge of fabric and stitchery was limited to quilts. "If it doesn't fit perfectly, Emily could alter it for you. She's been sewing her own clothes since the fifth grade."

"Stay home and miss all the fun?" Matt stood and wiped his brow with the back of his forearm. "I'm not going to miss this, especially since the search for a wedding gown was girls only. But if you have too much to do here—"

"I wouldn't miss this for anything either," she said, smiling. James and his friends rarely dressed up, and she would enjoy seeing them in tuxedos. Also, someone had to keep a sharp, critical eye out for mistakes. If the shop gave them the wrong suits or mismatched their shoes or hemmed their pants legs too long, she wanted to be on hand to insist that they make things right. Leo and James, especially, ought to be capable of noticing such problems on their own, but she could imagine glaring errors going undetected until Caroline spotted them in the wedding photos.

By the time Matt had washed his face and hands and changed his shirt, James, Leo, and the other groomsmen had gathered in the kitchen, where they munched Gina's freshly baked cookies and joked about forgoing tuxedos and donning Halloween costumes for the ceremony instead. Sarah thought she heard the dreaded phrase "bachelor party" come from the corner booth, but when she fired a curious glance in the three groomsmen's direction, they returned smiles of perfect innocence. Yes, something was definitely afoot.

When Leo's parents returned from a walk through the fragrant orchard, they all climbed aboard the Elm Creek Quilts shuttle and set out for the formal-wear shop, crossing the bridge over Elm Creek, rounding the barn and passing the orchard, traveling through the red and gold and russet woods of the Bergstrom estate, until they came to the road that led to downtown Waterford. Students toting backpacks and cups of coffee filled the sidewalks on their way to and from apartments and classes at Waterford College, but Matt turned off on Church Street before they reached campus. A block from the town square, they passed an old churchyard enclosed by a low iron fence. Few citizens had been buried there since a larger cemetery was established east of town in the 1950s, but the Bergstroms had owned a family plot, and many generations had been laid to rest in the shadow of the old church steeple. Involuntarily, Sarah gazed at the churchyard and sighed as they drove past. Matt took her hand and gave it a gentle, comforting squeeze.

They reached the formal-wear shop, one of several businesses occupying the renovated original city hall, one of the oldest buildings in the Elm Creek Valley. The phrase "Creek's Crossing, Penn," engraved in stone above the main entrance, paid homage to the town's first name, almost forgotten except by local history buffs. Sarah had discovered the name—and the reason local officials had changed it—within the pages of a memoir written by one of Sylvia's ancestors, Gerda Bergstrom. Although dozens of customers every day passed beneath the engraved words without noticing them, whenever Sarah saw them, she felt the strong, sudden pull of history, so vividly had Gerda described her arrival in America, the founding of Elm Creek Farm, her family's dangerous and important role as stationmasters on the Underground Railroad, and the conflict that had divided Creek's Crossing in the years leading up to the Civil War. Thanks to the Waterford Historical Society, the story of the town's fascinating past was better known now than it had been when Sarah and Matt had moved there, but for all the society's hard work and research, Sarah was sure many more secrets awaited discovery.

As Matt and Leo led the other young men and Leo's parents into the building, Sarah paused on the front portico and turned to admire the grand Greek Revival edifice across the street, where only a few days before she had spoken at the dedication of the new quilt gallery named in honor of her old friend and fellow Elm Creek Quilter, Agnes. Nearly as old as the former city hall, Union Hall had been restored to its stately 1863 appearance and was tended by a dedicated staff of docents and local historians. Over the past two decades, it had become Waterford's most recognized landmark and the jewel of the historic district. As Sarah watched a groundskeeper trim hedgerows in the front garden and a group of schoolchildren on a field trip follow their teacher up the white marble front stairs and through the tall double doors, she marveled that the historic building had ever fallen into such disrepair that it had once been slated for destruction. The story of its rescue still served as both a warning and an inspiration to preservation societies across the country—and Agnes was the story's heroine.

The twins had been in third grade, Sarah recalled, when the *Waterford Register* ran a front-page article about a proposal to replace the long-vacant and neglected building with a complex of modern, efficient condominiums. A local realty company had appeared before the town zoning commission and had offered to take the eyesore off their hands, but their proposal had encountered a few snarls: The city of Waterford didn't actually own the property and therefore couldn't authorize the sale, and several members of the board were reluctant to permit a modern, multiresidential high-rise in the middle of the town's historic district. According to the article, University Realty president Gregory Krolich expected to "iron out the wrinkles" in a closed-door meeting to be held the following week.

"Wait. Did you say Gregory Krolich?" Sarah interrupted Andrew, picking up her coffee mug and sliding into the booth beside him. He and Sylvia often read bits of the newspaper aloud to each other over breakfast, and the familiar name had caught Sarah's attention as she served the twins their oatmeal.

Andrew jerked his thumb at the page. "That's the name, all right. Why? You know the fellow?"

"Hmph," sniffed Sylvia. "I should say she does. She thwarted his attempt to buy Elm Creek Manor from me back in the day. He told me he intended to transform it into student housing, which I thought was a fine idea—it certainly would have livened up the place—but Sarah did a bit of sleuthing and discovered that he planned to tear down this wonderful manor and put up condos in its place."

"He's the guy who worked with Craig to buy Bonnie's condo after Craig locked her out," added Matt, scowling. "The man has no scruples."

"My old nemesis," Sarah muttered, picking up the folded paper and skimming the article. "He never saw a lovely historic building he didn't dream of running over with a bulldozer. And seriously, what is his obsession with condos? Does everything have to be replaced with a condo?"

"Condos are lucrative," said Matt. "It's all about the bottom line."

"I don't disagree that old Union Hall is an eyesore," said Sylvia, "but a contemporary high-rise would stick out like a sore thumb on that street. Well, this is why we have a zoning commission. They won't let the project go through."

"Don't count on it," said Sarah darkly. "I bet 'closed-door meeting' is code for a smoke-filled back-room deal where Krolich will pay his way into an exemption."

"Surely not," protested Sylvia. "The zoning commission wouldn't even let Diane's husband build a skateboard ramp in their own backyard. These condos would be an even more egregious violation of city ordinances."

"Diane and Tim didn't have the resources to bribe the entire commission," said Sarah, "and they wouldn't have bribed anyone, even if they could have. If Krolich isn't planning to bribe the commissioners, and if they aren't eager to take the money, why postpone the decision until this top-secret meeting? Why hold it behind closed doors?"

Andrew's lined face furrowed in worry. "Would they really do that? Make and take a bribe so boldly?"

"They won't call it a bribe," said Sarah. "Krolich will do something like offer in trade a fantastic deal on some other piece of property University Realty owns. The commissioners will convince themselves it's in the best interest of the community to take the deal as they pocket their finder's fees. Or if not that scenario, something like it. You wait and see."

"We can't let them get away with such shenanigans," declared Sylvia. "You thwarted him once, Sarah. You can do it again."

"Me? What could I do about this—what's it called—Union Hall? I don't know anything about that place." She studied the photo and vaguely recalled passing a large, sad, forlorn, apparently vacant building on her way to the gym or the hair salon. "In the case of Elm Creek Manor, all I did was tell you the truth about Krolich's intentions, and you decided not to sell to him. That was easy. This—" She shook her head and set down the paper. "I wouldn't know where to begin. He's told the commission he plans to tear it down, and they're okay with that."

"It sounds like their only objection is what he plans to put in its place," said Matt. "If Krolich changes the design to fit in with the surrounding buildings, they might not object."

"And if they do, Krolich's money will help them forget." Sarah hated to see Krolich succeed at anything after all the trouble he had caused Sylvia and Bonnie, but she wasn't sure how to fight him this time. As far as she knew, this Union Hall, whatever it had once been, had been vacant for years, a magnet for vandals and litter. If it were beyond saving, perhaps it ought to be razed and replaced with something more useful and less hazardous—but not these condos, and not only because they didn't suit the historic district. Sarah would rather have almost anything on that lot as long as Krolich wouldn't benefit from it.

"Perhaps Agnes knows more," said Sylvia, turning the page with a disapproving shake of her head. "She's a member of the Waterford Historical Society, and they surely won't stand by and let Mr. Krolich run roughshod over the zoning commission."

They all nodded in agreement, but later, no one remembered to ask Agnes about the conflict. It wasn't that they didn't care, but other, more relevant concerns occupied their time, and it was easy to forget the troubles facing an old, abandoned building downtown. Sarah supposed none of them gave the matter another thought until a few days later, when a smaller follow-up article appeared in the *Register,* buried on page twelve amid a mosaic of advertisements. The executive board of the Waterford Historical Society had demanded to be included in the closed-door meeting, not only because they wanted to preserve the building due to its historical and architectural value to the community, but also because they owned it.

"If they own it, why have they allowed it to fall into such a state?" asked Gretchen, as once again the manor's permanent residents discussed the news of the day over breakfast.

Joe scanned the rest of the article. "Apparently their budget won't cover any maintenance except for the bare minimum to keep the pipes from bursting and the roof caving in. 'Although the Waterford Historical Society currently uses the building only for storage,'" he read aloud, "'their long-range plans include a complete renovation and restoration and the eventual reopening of Union Hall as the organization's headquarters and a museum of local history.'"

"An admirable goal," remarked Sylvia. "Well, if they're the proper owners and they don't wish to sell, that should be the end of the matter."

"I suppose," said Sarah dubiously. In theory, that indeed ought to be the end of it, but she knew Gregory Krolich didn't give up that easily.

Sure enough, the following Wednesday, Sarah had just settled the twins down to their after-school snack and homework—in separate booths in the kitchen, so they wouldn't distract each other—when Agnes called, distressed. The Waterford Historical Society had been denied admission to the meeting, where it was rumored that Krolich had made a persuasive case for the city to invoke their power of eminent domain, declare the property neglected and abandoned, and sell it to University Realty. Agnes was so angry and upset that it was difficult to understand whether these things had already happened, were about to happen, or merely might happen if the Waterford Historical Society did not take immediate action. Agnes, who had welcomed Bonnie into her home when Craig and Krolich had conspired to sell her condo out from underneath her, disliked Krolich as much as Sarah did. "Union Hall is a treasure," she said, her voice trembling with outrage. "We can't allow that dreadful man to tear it down."

"What can we do?" Sarah asked. "Chain ourselves to the front doors as the wrecking ball approaches?"

"Let's pray it never comes to that." Instead, Agnes explained, the Waterford Historical Society was planning a volunteer workday to clean up the property, inside and out. Presenting a more attractive appearance would not solve the larger, long-term problems facing the building, but it would make it more difficult for the zoning commission to condemn the property. Unfortunately, the society's membership had dwindled in recent years, and they had few volunteers to call upon. Agnes wondered if she could search the Elm Creek Quilts database for the names and e-mail addresses of local former students who might be willing to help. "Quilters are always willing to pitch in during a time of need," said Agnes. "That's why I thought of our campers. If camp was in session right now, I could ask for helpers when everyone gathered for lunch, but since it's October—well, if this weren't so important, I wouldn't ask you to divulge their contact information, but we absolutely must save Union Hall."

Sarah had never heard Agnes so adamant. "I'm fine with it, but I'll have to ask Sylvia." She promised to call back soon.

Sarah found Sylvia sewing in the parlor. Sylvia mulled over Agnes's request and agreed that Agnes could have the contact information for her own former students, and that she herself would contact the Waterford Quilting Guild and ask them to spread the word. "If we lose any students because their former teacher wrote to them, I believe those are students we can do without," said Sylvia, justifying her decision. Sarah agreed and hurried off to assemble a list of e-mail addresses for Agnes.

The workday took place on the third Saturday in September. Sarah couldn't attend because she and Matt spent most of the day standing on the sidelines of soccer fields, cheering on the twins in back-to-back matches on opposite ends of the valley. Sarah meant to stop by for a few hours between soccer and supper, but just as she was hurrying out the door, Anna called, and as usual, they had so much catching up to do that the conversation ran well over an hour.

Unfortunately, Anna had little good news to share. She and Jeremy liked Virginia and they loved their little family, but ever since the move, they had both encountered one professional disappointment and bewildering complication after another. Gina had grown into a sweet, delightful six-year-old, she had many friends in her neighborhood, and she adored her first-grade teacher. For those blessings, Anna was grateful beyond measure, but she missed her work and friends at Elm Creek Manor with a longing that had not eased over the years. After Gina became old enough to attend half-day preschool, Anna had launched a personal chef business, catering parties and delivering a week's worth of fresh, delicious gourmet meals to clients' homes. Although she enjoyed the creativity of the work and the flexibility of her schedule, her client list had grown little since she started the service, despite numerous referrals by satisfied customers. Unless things turned around soon, Anna wasn't sure how much longer she would be able to stay in business.

She was even more concerned about Jeremy's career. Although he had begun his work as an assistant professor buoyed by enthusiasm and optimistic ambition, he soon discovered that the History Department was splintered into three warring factions, each seeking to profit at the others' expense. During his first few months on the job, Jeremy attempted to stay out of the fray, treating everyone with professional cordiality and demurring when asked to offer an opinion on old grievances that had occurred before he had joined the faculty. He was not aware that his every action, from meeting one colleague for coffee to collaborating with another on a conference paper, was scrutinized and analyzed for signs of his true allegiance. By second semester, most of his colleagues assumed he was allied with a faction other than theirs, and burgeoning friendships suddenly cooled. Worst of all, in his second year on the job, he offended a particularly influential professor who not only happened to lead the most powerful faction, but also was married to the dean of the college.

Jeremy wasn't even sure what he had done to earn such withering enmity. True, he had missed a department meeting to attend Gina's dance recital, and he had not attended a lecture the professor offered in recognition of her recent publication in the *Journal of American History* because he had been up all the previous night grading exams. Since the lecture was open to the entire campus he had assumed he would not be missed, but apparently his absence was noticed and gave offense. When another colleague, a gray-haired associate professor who had managed to navigate the lonely territory between factions for more than a decade, warned him about his inadvertent slight, Jeremy attempted a friendly apology, but he was coolly rebuffed. He figured his prospects in the department dimmed after she was named department chair the following semester, and they became utterly bleak when she appointed herself to his tenure committee.

"Isn't there anything Jeremy can do?" Sarah had asked at the time. "If she's completely biased against him, can't he ask for her to recuse herself?"

Anna explained that the tenure system didn't work like a courtroom, and appealing to the department chair to appoint someone else would be no use because the professor in question *was* the department chair. Her thoughts leaping to the most logical conclusion, Sarah hesitantly asked what would happen if Jeremy were denied tenure. Would he remain an assistant professor as long as he worked for the university, or would he ever have another chance to be promoted to associate professor, perhaps after the current department chair stepped down?

"I wish," said Anna. "If he's denied tenure, they'll keep him on the faculty until the end of the school year, and then they'll let him go. That's to give him time to find a place at another university. But with so many new Ph.D.'s graduating every year, who wants to hire someone who was denied tenure at another school?" She choked up. "It's just not fair. He's worked so hard. He's published a book from his dissertation and a whole slew of papers in good journals, he's served on committees, and his teaching evaluations are some of the strongest in the College of Arts and Letters. How can his whole career get derailed by one mean person?"

Sarah had no idea. The whole situation seemed bizarre and wrong, and all she could do to reassure Anna was to remind her that the other members of the committee, who weren't biased against Jeremy, might overrule the department chair. Even if he didn't earn tenure, his record of publications and successful teaching would surely win him a position somewhere else. Surely his more reasonable colleagues would vouch for him when he explained that he had been denied tenure for purely political reasons.

The dismaying course of events had unfolded over several years and would soon reach its conclusion, for better or for worse. The tenure committee would decide Jeremy's fate within the next few weeks, and he had feverishly redoubled his efforts to prove himself. Anna hardly saw him anymore, she lamented, her pain and loneliness clear to Sarah even over the phone line. He worked seven days a week, from morning until long past Gina's bedtime, and he couldn't afford to attend her school events anymore. Jeremy promised that his workload would lessen tremendously after he earned tenure, and the three of them would take a long-awaited and well-deserved vacation. "I hope he can make it until then," said Anna. "I'm worried about him. The stress of the past few years is taking its toll. I'm afraid he'll have a heart attack or something."

"Really? It's that bad?"

"Yes, it's that bad. I thought graduate school was grueling, but this is insanity. Not the research or the teaching or even the boring committee meetings—that's all fine. No one can fault him for his actual work, but the office politics are killing him. He might get tenure, but at what cost? I'm telling you, Sarah, this is not the kind of family life either of us wanted."

Sarah wished with all her heart that she could do something to help. All she could do was try to reassure Anna that the situation was temporary and that it would soon be over, one way or another. And one way or another, Jeremy would land on his feet.

By the time they hung up, Anna seemed somewhat comforted, but Sarah was more worried about the couple than ever. They had talked so long that the afternoon had waned, and it was too late for Sarah to head downtown to volunteer at Union Hall. In the end, out of all the Elm Creek Quilters, only Gretchen responded to Agnes's call for help. Somewhat guiltily, Sarah and Sylvia greeted Gretchen at the back door when she returned home later that evening, weary from a long day of sorting through dusty artifacts haphazardly packed into cartons and trunks in an upper gallery of Union Hall. Too exhausted to chat, Gretchen went upstairs to freshen up and change clothes while her husband microwaved some leftovers for her supper. Sylvia put the kettle on, and when Gretchen returned to the kitchen, Sylvia and Sarah joined her and Joe at the long wooden table, sipping tea while Gretchen ate and told them about her day.

About thirty people had turned out for the workday, Gretchen reported, and they had divided themselves into three teams. The first group worked outside, trimming hedges, raking leaves, and yanking weeds from overgrown flower beds. The second, made up of people with carpentry skills or construction experience, fanned out through the building, inspected every room, made a very long list of necessary repairs, and began working on them. Gretchen was assigned to the third team, which took inventory of the storage rooms, sorting, identifying, and cataloging everything from collections of personal documents and shoe boxes stuffed with yellowed newspapers to books and daguerreotypes. It was hard, discouraging work. For each fascinating historical treasure the workers discovered, they found a half dozen so damaged by water, time, or mold that they had to be immediately discarded. "Some papers were so fragile they disintegrated the moment we picked them up," Gretchen lamented. "Others were so blackened by mold that scarcely any of the words remained legible. But someone, years ago, must have thought they were valuable enough to save, or they wouldn't have been stored in the gallery in the first place. I hate to think what knowledge has been lost, all because the building wasn't properly maintained."

"It's a shame," said Sylvia, with a quick upward glance that told Sarah she was thinking of the historical treasures she had found in the manor's attic, clues that had illuminated the mysteries of her heritage. Since her return to Elm Creek Manor after her fifty-year absence, Sylvia, Sarah, and Summer had investigated many of the trunks and cartons, but much had remained undisturbed.

Thinking of all that they had discovered, Sarah could only imagine what could have been learned from documents and artifacts stored in a public building nearly as old as the town itself, if only they had been properly preserved. "Why didn't the historical society take better care of the things entrusted to them?" Sarah asked.

"They don't have the staff," said Gretchen. "In their defense, they thought they had stored everything in a safe, dry place. The gallery is on the second story, not tucked away in a corner of a damp basement. The water damage came from a leaking pipe within the walls, the leak so small it went unnoticed until yesterday, when the volunteer carpenters found it." Gretchen finished her supper and touched her napkin to her lips with a mournful sigh. "Their resources are so limited that for more than fifty years, they've kept most of their research archives in a special local history room of the Waterford College Library rather than maintain the collection themselves. The college took on the responsibility—and the expense—so that the archives would be available for their students and faculty."

"Good thing they did," said Joe. "At least that part of the collection didn't get damaged."

"Lots of other things survived storage unscathed too," said Gretchen. "We finished going through only about two-thirds of the boxes, and the ones that remain are closer to the center of the room, away from that damp wall. Agnes is optimistic that their contents will be in better shape."

Sarah hoped Agnes was right, and she resolved to attend the next workday her friend arranged, even if she had to skip the twins' soccer games.

But her first visit to Union Hall came much sooner than that. The next morning, Agnes phoned with the news that the volunteers had made an astonishing discovery late Saturday night after Gretchen had left, and the society's president was eager for the Elm Creek Quilters to meet her at Union Hall to examine the find. Maggie, especially, was most urgently invited to attend.

"Why me?" asked Maggie, bewildered, but in her excitement Agnes had hung up without explaining.

"I don't know," said Sylvia, equally perplexed. "I assume they've turned up an antique quilt or two, but why they should need any of us, I can't imagine. Agnes is certainly qualified to appraise whatever it is they've found."

Sylvia's observation was spot-on, because not only was Agnes a very experienced quilter, she also had a certain expertise in antiques, for she had learned quite a lot over the decades assisting her second husband in his work. What could the historical society volunteers have discovered that required more than Agnes's expert eye, and why did they need Maggie in particular?

Gretchen begged off, craving a quiet afternoon at home with Joe after the hard work of the previous day, so Sarah, Sylvia, and Maggie had a quick lunch before driving downtown to Union Hall. The front lawn was sparse but newly mown, the wrought-iron fence painted obsidian black, broken windows replaced, and hedges neatly trimmed. "No one would mistake this for an abandoned building now," remarked Sylvia, smiling in satisfaction as Sarah parallel-parked the Elm Creek Quilts minivan in the first available spot she found, half a block away on the opposite side of the street.

Agnes was waiting for them on the portico, clasping her hands in anticipation, her blue eyes shining behind pink-tinted glasses. "Do hurry," she called to her three friends as they made their way up the cobblestone walk.

"It's waited this long," Sylvia called back, taking Sarah's arm as they reached the limestone staircase. "It can wait a few minutes longer."

"It can, but I'm not so sure about Agnes," said Maggie. "Agnes, honey, take a deep breath. You look like you're about to burst."

Agnes obeyed, but she remained just as fidgety and flustered as before. "I can't help it. This is simply too wonderful. I think we've found the key to saving Union Hall." Beckoning them to hurry, she pushed open one of the large double doors and disappeared into the building.

Quickening their pace—but not without a faint sigh of amusement from Sylvia—her friends climbed the limestone steps, each sloped slightly in the middle, worn from the footsteps of more than a hundred years' worth of visitors. They passed between the two freshly whitewashed central pillars and followed Agnes into the foyer, which could have been as lovely as Elm Creek Manor's, if it were not in such shabby condition. Many footsteps, perhaps those of the previous day's workers, had left tracks in the layer of dust on the gray-blue marble floor, and dozens of engraved copper plaques affixed to the walls flanking the front doors were tarnished and dull. Boxes of cleaning supplies were pushed up against the wall next to an enormous mahogany antique curio cabinet that looked heavy and out of place in the understated elegance of the Greek Revival architecture. Directly across the foyer from the front entrance was a wide doorway leading into a large, dark room—the theater, Sarah guessed, barely making out a stage at the far end—but the doors themselves were missing, leaving behind only four rusty hinges as evidence that they had ever been. Plaster peeled from the molded ceiling high above, where a chandelier hung, half of its tapered bulbs dark and all of them coated in dust. Somewhere unseen, hammers banged and power tools buzzed.

"If you think this is a mess," said Agnes, correctly interpreting their silence, "you should have seen it the day before yesterday."

Agnes had no sooner closed the outer door behind them when two women who looked to be in their fifties—one tall and sturdy with long sandy blond hair, the other short and stout with more silvery gray than black in her wiry curls—

hastened toward them from a side room. The dark-haired woman went straight to Sylvia. "You must be Sylvia Bergstrom," she said, clasping Sylvia's hand in both of hers. "I'm Patricia Escher, president of the Waterford Historical Society. It's a true pleasure to meet you. Your family has enriched our town's history in countless ways, but I suppose I don't need to tell you that."

"Thank you," said Sylvia graciously. "The Bergstroms do have a rather storied past. Some of them were downright notorious in their day."

"Oh, but that just makes them more interesting," exclaimed the other woman, pushing her glasses back upon the bridge of her nose. "Stationmasters on the Underground Railroad, war heroes, prosperous businessmen, suffragists—name an important event in the Elm Creek Valley during the last one hundred and fifty years and you can bet a Bergstrom was in the middle of it."

"Perhaps," said Sylvia dryly, "but on at least one occasion that propensity for activism landed my ancestors in the Creek's Crossing prison. It certainly made them their share of enemies."

"No one makes history without making a few enemies," the woman replied, offering Sylvia her hand. "I'm Leslie Reinhart, vice president of the historical society."

"Leslie's people have been in the Elm Creek Valley even longer than yours, Sylvia," said Agnes. "Her great-great-grandfather was the town's first postmaster."

"It's good to meet you," said Sylvia. "I'm intrigued by your request for our visit. What is this treasure you've discovered?"

"Not one treasure, but several, and two in particular that I think will fascinate you." Patricia beckoned the visitors to follow her and Leslie into the side room, a small office with barely enough room for a desk, two armchairs, a cluttered bookcase, and several tall filing cabinets. Five small cacti in terra-cotta pots sat on the windowsill, and an ancient computer blinked a luminous green cursor at them from the desktop between an overflowing wire basket labeled "In" and an identical, though empty, basket labeled "Out." As the women crowded into the room, Sarah's gaze went to a steamer trunk that sat open in the narrow space between the armchairs and the back wall. It looked to be half full, but the folded quilt on top concealed whatever else lay beneath.

Leslie's breathless anticipation was all the invitation Sylvia needed. She stooped over and withdrew the bundle from the trunk, and as she carefully unfolded it, Sarah and Maggie quickly came forward to help so that it would not touch the floor. Sarah drew in a breath as she took in the sight of the fabric unfurling; she had expected an antique quilt, of course, but not one so lovely or so well preserved. It was a sampler quilt, the fabrics a glorious bouquet of Turkey red, Prussian blue, dark green, navy, brown, and light tan, faded but not worn. A quick count of rows and columns told Sarah there were 121 blocks, each apparently unique, separated by striped sashing and quilted with tiny stitches in an intricate pattern of scrolls, feathered plumes, and flowers. Elegant floral swags fashioned in appliqué twined around the sampler center, with the phrase "Union Forever" embroidered along the top border and "Water's Ford, Pa." along the bottom.

"How astonishing," breathed Sylvia, peering at the quilt as light from the overhead fixture glinted on her glasses. "The fabrics look to be mid- to late nineteenth century. Maggie, do you recognize any of these blocks?"

At once, Sarah understood why Patricia and Leslie had wanted Maggie in particular to examine the quilt. In the years since Maggie had discovered and re-created the Harriet Finley Birch sampler, she had become an expert on nineteenth-century samplers, concentrating her research on those comprised of dozens of small blocks. This newly discovered quilt fit perfectly into that category.

Maggie studied the quilt, her expression a mixture of wonder, delight, and curiosity. "A few of them are traditional blocks," she said, gesturing to one near the upper left corner. "That's Crosses and Losses, although like many traditional blocks, it's known by several names. This is a Double Four-Patch, of course, and that appliqué block over there is called Tea Leaves."

"I know this one," said Sarah, surprised to discover amid all the unfamiliar patterns a block she herself had made years before, in honor of her children. "That's Twin Star."

Maggie nodded, her gaze fixed on the quilt. "Most of these patterns are completely new to me. Each has at least one slight variation that transforms it from a more familiar, traditional pattern into an original design."

"I wonder what the quilter's source for all of these variations was," said Sarah. "Did the local newspaper print patterns, like *The Kansas City Star* did? Or do you think she simply made them all up on her own?"

Sylvia bent closer over the quilt, examining one block carefully, and then another, and then a third, frowning as she compared them. "These blocks don't appear to me to be the work of a single quilter," she declared. "Even if you account for the improvement in skill one might acquire in the course of working upon such an ambitious project, the quality of piecing varies significantly from one block to another."

"I think so too," said Maggie, nodding.

"That question, at least, we can answer," said Patricia, reaching out to turn over a corner of the quilt. "The thread has lost so much of its dye that I couldn't tell you its original color, but on the other side, someone embroidered a few important details about the quilt's provenance."

Sylvia ran her hand over the back of the quilt, searching for the embroidery by touch. "Ah. Here it is." The thread blended in with the muslin so closely that Sarah, standing only a few feet away and knowing exactly where to look, couldn't see it. Sylvia held the corner of the quilt close to her eyes, then farther away, but then she shook her head, frowning. "I can't make out a single word. Sarah, bring your young eyes over here and give it a try."

"My eyes aren't that young anymore," Sarah pointed out, but it was true that she still had excellent near vision, a small compensation for the annoying myopia that obliged her to wear glasses whenever she drove a car or watched a movie. Scrutinizing the back of the quilt, she managed to discern the small, delicate letters, the script as elegantly formed as if the quiltmaker had written with pen and ink. "'The Loyal Union Sampler, made by the Ladies of the Elm Creek Valley in Wartime. Completed July 4th, 1862. Union Hall, Water's Ford, Penna.'" Below those lines, the thread became slightly darker, the embroidered letters noticeably larger and rounder. "I think the last two lines were added later, possibly by a different person. 'Presented to the Waterford Historical Society in loving memory of Faith Cunningham Morlan, 1813–1882.' "

"Union Hall, Water's Ford," Sylvia echoed. "That suggests the quilt was completed within this very building, which strikes me as a bit odd. I tend to finish my quilts at home."

"Maybe those 'Ladies of the Elm Creek Valley' were a guild, and maybe they held their quilting bees here," said Maggie, her gaze traveling over the surface of the quilt as if she were learning each star and mosaic by heart. "They thought it was important to mention that the quilt was made in wartime. It could be that Faith Cunningham Morlan lost a husband or a son in the fighting and her friends made her this in his honor. Maybe this is a memorial quilt."

"I confess I never made the connection between Union Hall and the Civil War," remarked Sylvia. "I assumed the name referred to a labor union that might have met here long ago. The building's age alone would have suggested otherwise, if I'd been paying attention."

Sarah had made the same assumption. "Do we know anything about this Faith Cunningham Morlan?" she asked Patricia and Leslie.

"We found a Faith Anne Morlan listed in the 1850, 1860, and 1870 federal censuses," said Patricia. "Her family owned a farm in the foothills of the Four Brothers Mountains in the north end of the Elm Creek Valley."

"We didn't have time to research more thoroughly than that," added Leslie, a note of apology in her voice. "We've been"—she gestured with weary resignation to the water stain on the ceiling, an apt symbol of Union Hall's disrepair and a reminder of all the work yet to be done if they were to fight off

Krolich's plan to have the building condemned—"a little preoccupied lately."

"Of course," said Sylvia. "We understand perfectly."

"If only Summer were here," said Agnes. "She knows your archives at the Waterford College Library better than any of us. She has a gift for uncovering important information in the most obscure sources."

"Jeremy too," said Sarah, her conversation with Anna the previous day still fresh in her thoughts. To Patricia and Leslie, she added, "He's a friend who earned his Ph.D. in history from the college. Unfortunately for us, he no longer lives in Waterford."

Patricia and Leslie exchanged a quick glance. "You don't mean Jeremy Bernstein, do you?" asked Patricia.

"That's exactly who I mean," said Sarah. "Do you know him?"

"I'm familiar with his work," said Patricia. "He's written quite a few excellent pieces on Pennsylvania history. I think he would be particularly interested in the other quilt we wanted to show you." She beckoned to Leslie, who helped her take a second folded bundle from the trunk. Handing the Loyal Union Sampler to Maggie, who folded it carefully on the bias and cradled it in her arms, Sarah took hold of one edge of the second quilt as Patricia and Leslie unfolded it.

This, too, was a sampler quilt, but in a markedly different style than the first. Instead of many small blocks, almost all of them pieced, the second quilt boasted sixteen large appliqué blocks that looked to be eighteen inches square, three times the size of those in the Loyal Union Sampler. The intricate designs reminded Sarah of quilts made in the Baltimore Album tradition, with appliquéd pieces creating still-life portraits in fabric.

The quality of the work was flawless, the calico flowers, leaves, and figures sewn meticulously by hand to the soft muslin backgrounds, bleached to a snowy white by the sun. The sixteen blocks were arranged in four rows of four and separated by light tan sashing with Turkey red cornerstones, and an appliqué border of elegant swags gathered by roses framed the whole.

"'Creek's Crossing, Elm Creek Valley, Pennsylvania, 1849,'" said Maggie, reading aloud the words embroidered upon one of the blocks.

"There's more on the back." Patricia gestured for them to turn over the quilt and indicated the lower right corner.

"'Creek's Crossing Album,'" Sarah read. "'Appliquéd by Miss Dorothea Granger, 1849. Quilted by Mrs. Abel Wright, 1850. Presented to Mrs. Wright by Miss Granger in celebration of her marriage, 1847, on the occasion of her arrival to her new home.'"

"Are you certain you read those dates correctly?" queried Sylvia. "A seven can often resemble a nine, especially in antique embroidery."

Sarah examined the stitches more carefully. "I'm sure this says 1849, and that definitely says 1847. It looks like Miss Granger was two years late with her wedding gift." She felt a faint tug of memory, which suddenly snapped into focus. "Wait a minute. Those names, from Gerda's memoir—Dorothea Granger is Dorothea Nelson's maiden name. Mrs. Abel Wright must be their friend Constance Wright."

As Leslie nodded eagerly, Patricia said, "Agnes has told us about your great-great-aunt's memoir, Sylvia. I can't tell you what I would give to read it. What a marvelous glimpse into the past it must offer."

"You're welcome to see for yourself," said Sylvia graciously. "I'd be happy to lend it to you for a little while. I'm sure you, of all people, would take very good care of it."

As Patricia thanked her, Leslie said, "Now you understand why we've heard of Jeremy Bernstein."

The Elm Creek Quilters exchanged puzzled glances before Sarah spoke for them all. "No, sorry, not really."

"He's the author of the definitive biography of Abel Wright," said Patricia. "I believe the book grew out of his dissertation. You didn't know?"

"I thought Jeremy's dissertation was about a local nineteenth-century author," said Maggie. "I never really discussed it with him, but I overheard him talking about it from time to time. He wrote a lot of it in the Elm Creek Manor kitchen."

"He was smitten with the chef," added Agnes with a smile for Patricia and Leslie. "They're married now."

"The Abel Wright from Gerda's memoir was a dairy farmer," said Sylvia, puzzled. "As well as a conductor on the Underground Railroad. Gerda never mentioned that he possessed any literary gifts. Are you sure we're talking about the same man?"

"Oh, yes, I'm sure," said Leslie. "The author Abel Wright was also a dairy farmer until he left the Elm Creek Valley for Colorado. His first book, an account of his experiences serving with the Sixth Regiment of the United States Colored Troops, was published in late 1865, after the war had ended."

"Why didn't Jeremy tell me so?" asked Sylvia, indignant. "I

let him read Gerda's memoir, I answered as many of his questions about the Wrights and the Bergstroms as I could, and he couldn't find a moment to tell me that Abel Wright was an accomplished writer?"

"Jeremy sent you an autographed copy of his book when it was published," Sarah pointed out. "Didn't you read it?"

Sylvia looked abashed. "I confess I never found the time, but I'll surely read it now."

"Let me borrow it when you're done."

"You'll enjoy it," said Patricia. "Abel Wright had quite an exciting life. He ran a station on the Underground Railroad, but he also served in the more dangerous role of conductor, venturing into the South to sell his cheese and transporting runaway slaves to freedom in the North when he returned home. He met Constance on one of those trips, but when she refused to risk running away, he saved up enough money to buy her freedom. They married while she was still a slave, which would account for the discrepancy between the dates on the back of the quilt. They married in 1847, but Abel couldn't purchase her freedom and bring her home to the Elm Creek Valley until two years later."

"How sad that slavery kept them apart so long," said Agnes. "How sad and how cruel."

"Abel, Constance, and their two sons were members of the infamous Creek's Crossing Eight," Patricia explained. "In 1859, the Underground Railroad stations the Bergstroms, Nelsons, and Wrights ran were betrayed, and the stationmasters—as well as the Wrights' two young sons—were jailed for breaking the Fugitive Slave Act."

"Children were thrown into jail?" asked Maggie, shocked.

"For a few days, yes," said Leslie. "But none of the Creek's Crossing Eight were ever brought to trial. There was such a public outcry that the authorities were compelled to release them without charging them with anything. The Fugitive Slave Act was extremely unpopular in the North, and when word of the arrests spread, the officials were shamed and ridiculed from New York to Minnesota. The notoriety proved so damaging to the local economy that, a few years later, the town council voted to change the name to Water's Ford, which over time evolved into Waterford."

Sarah knew that from Gerda's memoir. "And when the Civil War began, Abel joined an African-American regiment?"

"Not immediately, of course," said Patricia. "African-Americans weren't allowed to form regiments until well into the war. Abel Wright joined the Sixth United States Colored Troops at Camp William Penn in Philadelphia in July 1863, and he served honorably until he lost an arm fighting in the trenches at Petersburg about a year later."

"Oh, how terrible," exclaimed Sylvia.

Patricia nodded. "If not for his wound, however, he might not have become a writer. He gave a famous speech at Howard University in which he explained how he had reconciled himself to the loss of his arm, not only because it was in service to his country and helped prove the valor of men of color, but also because 'in being obliged to set down the rifle,' he 'took up the pen.' You really should read his books if you're at all interested in local history. They're out of print now, of course, but the Rare Books Room at the Waterford College Library has a copy of each."

Sarah had a sudden thought. "Does he mention the Bergstroms in his books?"

Sylvia let out a soft gasp, as if that had not occurred to her, while Patricia and Leslie exchanged a startled glance. "I honestly don't recall," said Leslie. "He mentions many friends and neighbors, and the occasional enemy, but I wasn't looking for references to the Bergstrom family when I read his books, so I wouldn't have taken note of it."

"It would be easy enough to find out if he did," said Agnes. "I'm good friends with the librarian in charge of the collection, and I've visited the Rare Books Room quite often. I know exactly where to look for Abel Wright's books."

"I'd love to hear the results of your research, but we have another task we'd like you to take on first," said Patricia, looking from one Elm Creek Quilter to another. "We hope you'll be willing to help us in what is turning out to be—well, I don't think it's overstating things to call this our most desperate hour."

"None of us wants to see Union Hall torn down," said Sylvia staunchly as she motioned for Agnes to help her fold the appliqué sampler, "and we're not very fond of the man who wants to do it. We'll help however we can."

As Sarah, Maggie, and Agnes chimed in their agreement, Patricia breathed a sigh of relief and Leslie smiled, blinking away tears.

"What do you need?" asked Sarah. "Helpers for your next workday?"

"A raffle quilt?" asked Agnes. "That's always a good fundraiser."

"We'll gladly take you up on both of those offers," said Leslie. "But more than anything, we need you to help us prove that Union Hall is worth saving, and we think these quilts are the key."

"Sprucing up the place won't be enough to protect us from the zoning commission," Patricia added. "Not if they go along with Mr. Krolich and recommend that the city council exercise their power of eminent domain. A building's age isn't enough to grant it special protection. We need to prove that Union Hall bears unique historical significance. If we can find evidence that it does, Union Hall could be added to the National Register of Historic Places, and that would bring us tremendous benefits—not only protection from the wrecking ball, but tax breaks, so we could afford to maintain the building properly."

"And we could apply for grants so that we could finally turn Union Hall into a museum," said Leslie with longing. "That's been a part of the mission of the Waterford Historical Society since its inception. It would be so wonderful to finally do it."

Sarah needed no time to reflect upon the value of the goal—of course it would be better to preserve Union Hall as a museum rather than destroy it and put up yet another score of condos in its place. But if the building's age alone wasn't evidence enough of its historic value, what could be? "You said you believe these quilts are the key," she said. "How would they prove that Union Hall is historically significant?"

Patricia hesitated. "We don't know. That's what we hope you'll discover."

Leslie gestured to the two beautiful antique quilts, one in Maggie's arms and the other in Sylvia's. "You agree that these are two unique and remarkable quilts, don't you?" The Elm Creek Quilters nodded. "Well, the first sampler was completed in this very building during the Civil War in the same year Union Hall was built, and it was donated to the historical society. The other quilt was appliquéd by a renowned local abolitionist and suffragist, and quilted by the wife of the Elm Creek Valley's most revered author of the day—and it, too, found its way into our collection. This can't be mere coincidence."

"Somewhere in the intertwined histories of the Bergstrom, Wright, and Nelson families is the telling detail that will prove the historical significance of Union Hall," said Patricia emphatically. "I don't know what that detail is, but I know it's out there. We just have to find it."

"We don't have much time," said Agnes, frowning worriedly. "Of course we'll help you. You can count on us. Whatever evidence we need, we'll find it before that dreadful man can knock a single chip out of a single stone of the foundation of this wonderful building."

Sylvia raised her eyebrows at her sister-in-law in what was, perhaps, a mild rebuke for promising more than anyone could guarantee, but she quickly concealed any concern she might have felt as Patricia and Leslie thanked them profusely for joining their cause.

The Elm Creek Quilters were eager to get to work, but first they carried the Loyal Union Sampler outside, placed a clean cloth over the portico railing, and gently draped the quilt over it so Maggie could take snapshots of the entire quilt and each individual block. She planned to research the unfamiliar blocks to see if their names or origins offered any clue about the quilt's history. Afterward, Agnes accompanied Leslie back inside to continue taking inventory, but the other Elm Creek Quilters returned to the manor, where Sylvia went straight upstairs to the library for Jeremy's book. After finding Matt in the orchard with the twins and telling him about the day's astonishing discoveries, Sarah went to her room to call Jeremy.

Anna answered the phone, and in a strained and hushed voice she explained that Jeremy was spending a rare Sunday afternoon working in the yard and watching movies with Gina instead of toiling away in his office. The tenure committee had met, they had presented their case to the senior faculty, and their votes were due the next day. There was nothing more Jeremy could do to prove himself. Even those faculty members who had not yet turned in their ballots had already made up their minds. Now all he could do was wait and try to rest.

Sarah didn't want to bother him, so she told Anna to tell him that everyone at Elm Creek Manor was pulling for him, and that when he had a chance, she'd like to ask him a few questions about Abel Wright. Anna immediately brightened. "That'll make his day," she said. "He loves it when friends show an interest in his research. I'll bring him to the phone."

"No, it can wait," said Sarah, although it couldn't wait long. "Let him enjoy a few days off. I'll talk to him about Abel Wright when he calls to share the good news about the vote."

"I hope it's good news," said Anna fervently. "But either way, he'll call you later this week."

For the next few days, Sarah waited for the phone to ring and for Sylvia to finish reading Abel Wright's biography so she could borrow it. While she waited, she reread Gerda's memoir to refresh her memory about the Bergstrom family's first years in Creek's Crossing. Meanwhile, Gretchen and a few other volunteers resumed taking inventory of the remaining boxes and cartons in the east gallery, but they found nothing as remarkable as the quilts, and nothing to prove that Union Hall had made a significant contribution to local history. Agnes joined Gretchen for a few hours each day, but she spent most of her time calling council members to plead the historical society's case, researching Krolich's previous dealings with the city online, and poring over the minutes from previous city council meetings to see if she could spot any trends, signs of unsavory dealings, or hints that particular members might be sympathetic or hostile to their cause. Maggie concentrated on the Loyal Union Sampler. She searched through the pattern reference books in the manor's library and in her friends' personal collections, but found less than a third of the Loyal Union Sampler blocks in published sources. That she tracked down so few suggested—astonishingly—that the unidentified blocks were original to that quilt. The names of those that she did discover—Emancipation, Fort Sumter, Gettysburg, the states of the Union—revealed a distinct pattern that mirrored the quilt's title.

On Wednesday, Jeremy e-mailed Sarah with the long-awaited news that the faculty vote had gone as he had hoped rather than as he had expected: His colleagues in the College of Arts and Letters had apparently given more credit to his record of scholarship and teaching than to his department chair's review, for they had voted to grant him tenure. "I don't know this officially, of course," he added. "The whole process is shrouded in secrecy. In these situations, though, the college grapevine is rarely wrong."

Sarah would have been jubilant in Jeremy's place, but he sounded only guardedly optimistic. The vote was merely advisory, he explained; although the dean very rarely countermanded the faculty vote, he could still decline to forward

Jeremy's case to the provost. In a situation where the tenure committee's opinion strongly disagreed with the faculty vote, the dean might prefer to err on the side of caution and save his recommendations for junior faculty who received unanimous praise—especially considering that at the end of the day, he would have to face the chair of the tenure committee across the dinner table. But at least Jeremy wasn't out of it yet.

"Anna said you're interested in Abel Wright," he wrote. "I heartily encourage you to pick up my book (or borrow Sylvia's copy), and I'd also be happy to answer any questions you might have. E-mail or call, whatever works best."

Sarah decided that e-mail would probably be more convenient for him, so she clicked "Reply" and explained the plight of Union Hall and the historical society's urgent effort to save it. She described the quilts and asked him if he could shed any light on them, or offer any other leads that might help them find the elusive evidence they sought. "The city council is expected to decide whether to exercise their right of eminent domain within the next few weeks," she concluded, "so please get back to me as soon as you can."

Rather than sit in front of the computer impatiently awaiting a response, she forced herself to go about the ordinary business of her day—which on that day meant maintaining the Elm Creek Quilts Web site, responding to campers' inquiries, paying bills, and her least favorite perennial task, editing the previous year's help-wanted ad to begin the process of recruiting a new chef. Later, the twins came home from school, the manor's permanent residents ate supper together, and as evening fell, Caroline settled down to write an extra-credit report for her earth sciences class while Matt took James to his Cub Scout meeting. Sarah was fixing herself a cup of tea and considering how to pass her solitary evening when, to her surprise, she glanced out the window over the sink and spotted the headlights of a car crossing the bridge over Elm Creek. Soon thereafter she heard someone enter through the back door, and then, astonishingly sprightly for eighty-three, Agnes hurried into the kitchen carrying a manila envelope, her hound's-tooth wool coat unbuttoned as if she had been in too much of a hurry to button it.

"You'll never guess what my friend the librarian found," she cried as Diane entered at a far more leisurely pace, set her purse on the table, and draped her long leather coat over the back of a chair with an air of patient resignation. Agnes relied upon Diane for rides around Waterford, and she would never impose after dark unless she thought it was very important.

"Tell me," said Sarah as the kettle began to whistle shrilly. "Tea?"

"Nothing for me, dear, thank you," said Agnes breathlessly, taking a few pieces of paper from the envelope and laying them out side by side on the table.

"Decaf green tea with lemon and honey for me," said Diane. "If you have it. Agnes, let's at least get you out of that coat."

"Hmm? Oh, yes. Of course." Agnes shrugged out of it and hung it over the back of a chair. "Sarah, is Sylvia awake? She can't miss this."

"She went to bed an hour ago. Should I wake her?"

"No, no." Agnes seated herself, a trifle disappointed, and motioned for Sarah to come over. "It can wait until morning."

"Then why couldn't it have waited until morning for us?" protested Diane.

"Oh, hush," chided Agnes. "You weren't doing anything anyway."

Diane shrugged as if that were true but beside the point. Curious, Sarah carried two steaming cups of tea to the table, with lemon and honey for Diane, milk for herself, and a spoon for each of them. "So what did your friend find?" she asked, taking the seat beside Agnes. "This is the friend who works at the Rare Books Room, right?"

"Of course," said Diane, stirring honey into her tea. "How many librarian friends do you think she has?"

"One can never have too many librarian friends." Agnes nudged the papers closer to Sarah. "A few days ago I told her about our investigation, and this afternoon, when I stopped by the Rare Books Room to read more of Abel Wright's first book—you can't check out books from the Rare Books Room, you know, you have to read them right there. Some books in their collection are so fragile you have to wear white cotton gloves when you handle them, and some you're not allowed to touch at all. A librarian will turn the pages for you when—"

"Agnes," Diane interrupted mildly. "My TiVo is paused and waiting for me back at home. The point?"

"Oh, yes, of course." Agnes tapped one of the black-and-white pages, which appeared to be a photocopy of a page from an old magazine. "I told my friend about our quest, and she said the name 'Loyal Union Sampler' sounded familiar. She searched the archives, and lo and behold, she discovered this article from the November 1863 issue of *Harper's Monthly*."

"'Pennsylvania Ladies Wield Their Needles for the Union,'" Sarah read aloud, but then she fell abruptly silent, transfixed by the illustration beneath the headline, a meticulous black-and-white engraving of the Loyal Union Sampler. "This is it. This is the quilt from Union Hall."

Agnes nodded, beaming. "Read on."

"Diane, would you go get Maggie?" Sarah asked. "She's researching patterns in the library. She should see this."

While Diane went to fetch Maggie, Sarah read the entire article, an account of how a group of ladies from the Elm Creek Valley had collected donated quilt blocks to make the elaborate sampler. Once it was complete, they had raffled off not only the quilt, but also the patterns and templates for its blocks, to raise money to build Union Hall, a grand edifice in Water's Ford, Pennsylvania. The Union Quilters, as they called themselves, had hosted many successful fund-raisers in the hall's theater, garden, and galleries, with the proceeds benefiting the 49th Pennsylvania, the 6th United States Colored Troops, and the Veterans' Relief Fund for the infirm soldiers of the Elm Creek Valley and their families. Not only that, the women had formed a body corporate, meaning they themselves owned and operated Union Hall, a remarkable accomplishment for the fairer sex, which they would not have been obliged to undertake if not for the absence of their brave husbands, sons, and fathers serving in the war. The story of the Union Quilters served as yet another example of how patriotic women of the North proudly used their feminine talents to serve their country.

"Feminine talents," said Agnes indignantly. "Remarkable accomplishment for the fairer sex, indeed. I'd say that was a remarkable accomplishment for anyone, woman or man."

"Unfortunately the article doesn't mention any of the women by name," said Sarah just as Diane and Maggie entered the kitchen. "But if these Union Quilters formed a corporation and owned the building—not only owned it but organized every stage of its construction—there must be official records somewhere."

She handed the photocopies to Maggie, who read them eagerly. "This is astonishing," Maggie said. "You have no idea how much I wish I had this much historical documentation of the Harriet Findley Birch quilt. This article places Union Hall at the heart of Waterford's Civil War history. A building constructed by local women to support the local regiments at war and the wounded veterans who had come home—what could be more historically significant than that?"

"I'm going to Union Hall first thing in the morning to share the good news with Patricia and Leslie," declared Agnes, returning the photocopies to the envelope. "We'll start the application process for the National Register of Historic Places right away. Krolich wouldn't dare try to destroy the building now."

"Let's not congratulate ourselves too soon," cautioned Diane, putting on her coat. "If Krolich hears that we have a plan in the works, he might pressure the city council to push the measure through so he can destroy Union Hall before it's designated an official historically important building."

Sarah agreed. "We'll have to keep this a secret. Don't tell anyone about the article or our plans to have Union Hall added to the register. Let Krolich think the way is clear, and he might lower his guard."

"That doesn't sound like him," said Agnes.

"I don't think secrecy works in our favor," said Maggie. "I think we should tell everyone what we learned and what the historical society wants to do. We should send certified letters to the city council members and the press, and include copies of the *Harper's Monthly* article in each one. That way, they won't be able to condemn Union Hall and later pretend they had no idea how important it was."

"Maggie's right," said Sarah. "I'll run upstairs to the office and make the copies right now."

"I'll write the letters to the city council," said Maggie, flexing her fingers as if she couldn't wait to put hands to keyboard. "And another for Krolich."

"And I'll take them all to the post office," said Agnes. "Oh, I wish I could be there to see that wicked man's face when he reads Maggie's letter and sees how we've thwarted his plans!"

Sarah wouldn't mind a glimpse of that herself. As her friends offered suggestions for what to include in the letters and worked out how Maggie would get them to Agnes, Sarah hurried upstairs and made a dozen photocopies of each page of the article, saving one copy for Sylvia. She was certain that the Bergstrom women and their friends had participated in the making of the Loyal Union Sampler—in fact, she wouldn't be surprised to discover that they themselves were the Union Quilters. If they were, the official records of their incorporation and the construction of Union Hall might be somewhere in the attic of Elm Creek Manor, stored with other relics of bygone days.

Sarah left the extra copy of the article on the table of Sylvia's favorite booth so she would see it when she came down to breakfast, which, during the off-season, was almost always at least an hour before Sarah dragged herself out of bed. The next morning, Sylvia was as delighted by the news as Agnes had been, if less ebullient in expressing it, and she agreed with Maggie's plan to spread the word about Union Hall's newly discovered history. As for whether her great-grandmother and great-great-aunt had counted themselves among the Union Quilters, Sylvia couldn't be certain. She couldn't recall her parents or grandparents mentioning Union Hall except in passing as a place where they had attended concerts, lectures, or wedding receptions many years ago, and although Gerda had written her memoir in 1895, it focused on the years between 1856 and 1859, with few details of her life before or after. About the tumultuous Civil War years, Gerda had said only, "So much I could write of that dark, unforgiving time, but I cannot divert from this history to recount it now, not when I am so near the end. Perhaps I will chronicle those events someday, if I can bring myself to do it, if I live long enough." If Gerda had ever completed a second volume of memoirs, Sylvia had not yet found it.

In the absence of documented proof, Sylvia and Sarah pondered what they knew about Gerda, Anneke, Dorothea, and Constance from Gerda's memoir and concluded that the women surely would have been involved in making the Loyal Union Sampler and building of Union Hall. Even Gerda, who had loathed sewing, would have been compelled by her staunch abolitionist beliefs to support the Union cause. "Now that Union Hall is safe," mused Sylvia, "perhaps Agnes and her librarian friend will have time to help me do the research and find the proof."

Remembering Diane's warnings, Sarah cautioned Sylvia that Union Hall was not yet safe—and soon Diane proved to be dismayingly prescient. Two days later, Agnes phoned, outraged and distressed over confirmation from a friend on the staff of the *Waterford Register* that the city council had called an emergency session late the previous night so that Krolich could address the new evidence submitted by Maggie Flynn on behalf of the Waterford Historical Society. In a circular argument that defied all logic, the city council decided that while the history of Union Hall as reported in the *Harper's Monthly* article offered an interesting bit of local trivia, it was not historically significant or it would have been common knowledge. It certainly did not sufficiently prove that the building merited special consideration. None of the Union Quilters had been mentioned by name, for example, so it was impossible to connect the building to any important historical figures. And while Union Hall apparently had served as the site of fund-raisers for local Union regiments, so had other locations, like the town square and a handful of churches and civic buildings, some of which had been razed decades before without public outcry. Union Hall was not, therefore, unique, and the city council could find no legal reason not to exercise their right of eminent domain.

Sarah's heart plummeted, but she took a deep breath and asked, "So it's over?"

"Of course it's not over," exclaimed Agnes. "It's not over until Union Hall is torn down, God forbid, and that won't happen, not if I have to handcuff myself to the front doors. Gwen promised to join me."

"Forgive me if I don't," said Sarah. "It's not that I don't relish the excitement, but someone needs to stay free to pay your bail."

Agnes laughed. "Of course. Now, dear, you mustn't lose hope. Leslie and Patricia are moving ahead with the process of having Union Hall added to the National Register of Historic

Places. They've already contacted the State Historic Preservation Office, and they're confident that Union Hall will meet the National Register Criteria for Evaluation and be declared eligible for consideration."

Sarah was glad to hear it, but she had read about the process on the National Park Service Web site and she knew it could take months for the review board to make a final decision. "We have to convince the city council to wait," she said. "Or, failing that, we have to stall them somehow, force them into a delay. Once they condemn Union Hall, it's over. Krolich will have bulldozers on the front lawn within minutes."

"We'll figure out something," said Agnes. "Now, I'm off to the Rare Books Room to finish reading Abel Wright's first book, and if all goes well I'll begin the second. If the *Harper's Monthly* article isn't sufficient evidence for that council of nincompoops, we'll just have to keep looking until we find something that is."

Sarah wished her luck.

She was just finishing up her lunch and contemplating whether to phone Jeremy when Agnes called back, as furious as Sarah had ever heard her. "Abel Wright's books are gone," she cried. "There's just an empty gap on the shelves where they used to be!"

Her suspicions soaring, Sarah nonetheless asked, "Is it possible someone else checked them out?"

"No, no! You're not allowed to check out books from the Rare Books Room. Remember? They're too valuable. You have to read them right here."

"Maybe they were misshelved."

"I returned them to their proper place when I was done with them yesterday, but even if another patron did take them down after that, my librarian friend and I and two student volunteers have spent the past two hours shelf-reading, and there's no sign of them. Hold on." Agnes covered the mouthpiece and Sarah overheard a brief, muffled exchange. "My friend just found the security tags in the trash, still attached to pages torn from the books."

"Someone stole them." Sarah's thought whirled. "But why? And why now?"

"The timing's no coincidence, that's for sure. They've sat on those shelves undisturbed for years except when Jeremy was researching his dissertation, and now, when we need them most, they vanish. The evidence we need is in one of those books, and Mr. Krolich knows it." Agnes's voice shook with anger. "I'm going down to his office right now to give him a piece of my mind."

"Agnes, wait. Don't provoke him—" But Agnes had hung up.

Quickly Sarah raced downstairs, threw on her coat, and snatched up her purse and keys. She paused by the orchard only long enough to shout an explanation to Matt, then drove downtown and parked across the street from campus a block east of the offices of University Realty, hoping to intercept Agnes on her way from the library. Moments later, she spotted her white-haired friend making her way down the sidewalk to the corner, her purse slung over her shoulder, her mouth pinched in fury as she waited for the light to change. Sarah scrambled from the car and ran to meet her on the other side of the crosswalk. "Agnes—"

Agnes didn't even slow down. "You can come along if you like, but don't try to stop me."

Sarah knew it was futile to try to dissuade Agnes from confronting a bully, so she nodded and fell in step beside her.

"That despicable man," Agnes muttered as they passed the shops and restaurants along Main Street. "It irks me to call on him in his new offices, but I won't let him spoil my happy memories of this place."

They paused beneath the steel-gray-and-blue sign that hung above the entrance to University Realty. Once, from that same post, the red-and-gold sign for Grandma's Attic had welcomed quilters to Bonnie's quilt shop, and beautiful quilts, books, and bundles of fabric had brightened the front window display where foam board advertisements of properties for sale and rent now stood. When Krolich had bought the building years before, he had not only conspired with Bonnie's ex-husband to force her to sell their condo, but he had also raised the rent on her first-floor shop and those of the other commercial tenants seventy-five percent. At the time Bonnie had wondered why Krolich would impose such an outrageous rate hike, which was all but guaranteed to drive away his tenants. It was Agnes who had uncovered the plot. While investigating Craig's hidden assets, she had phoned University Realty in the guise of a prospective tenant and had learned from an unsuspecting receptionist that Krolich intended to move their own offices from the converted Victorian house they had outgrown into Bonnie's building, which was more spacious and closer to campus.

Even now, years later, with Bonnie happily remarried and running Aloha Quilt Camp in paradise, the thought of Krolich wheeling and dealing from the office where Bonnie had once ordered fabrics and notions for quilters throughout the Elm Creek Valley filled Sarah with anger and disgust, but she forced her feelings aside, held open the door for Agnes, and followed her inside.

The large center island Bonnie had used as a cutting table was gone, as were the rainbow-hued aisles of bolts of fabric, replaced by cubicles where a half-dozen men and women in business attire talked on phones, shuffled paperwork, or typed on keyboards, their eyes glued to their computer screens. The wall shelves, once filled with books, notions, and sewing machines, had been removed; framed posters of dramatic nature and sports photos with inspirational captions in bold typefaces now hung in their place. Through the glass window at the back of the main room, Sarah glimpsed sleek, dark, modern office furniture, each piece likely worth twice as much as the secondhand stainless steel and Formica furniture with which Bonnie had furnished the office. Sarah felt a sharp, sudden pang of nostalgia for Grandma's Attic and hoped Bonnie would never see the changes Krolich had imposed upon the shop.

Agnes went straight to the receptionist's desk and gave the young brunette her sweetest granny smile. "Hello, dear. I'm here to pick up some books from Mr. Krolich. Is he in?"

"I'm sorry, but he's at lunch."

"Oh, my, and I walked all this way, so many blocks." Agnes looked stricken. "I don't suppose he left the books with you? They're old books, even older than I am."

"I'm afraid he didn't." The young woman bit her lower lip and checked her desk just to be sure. "Would you like to make an appointment and come back another time?"

"Oh, that won't do at all. I need those books right away." Suddenly Agnes brightened. "He probably left them for me in his office. Mind if I take a quick peek?"

The receptionist hesitated as if she sincerely wished she could help them, but she said, "I don't think I should."

Sarah put an arm around Agnes's shoulders as if Agnes were so frail she needed support simply to stay on her feet. "She walked all this way, so many blocks," Sarah reminded the young woman. "Did I mention she's eighty-three?"

"Yes," Agnes promptly interjected. "We don't know how much time I have left."

Sarah thought that was pushing things too far and shot Agnes a warning look, but after a moment, the receptionist shrugged and stood. "I guess it wouldn't hurt."

"Sit down, Brianna," a man said behind them. The receptionist promptly clamped her mouth shut and sat down hard, and Sarah and Agnes turned to find a man in a black wool coat entering the agency. Someone had removed the bell Bonnie had hung on the door, Sarah realized, or it would have tinkled merrily to warn them of his arrival. Gregory Krolich looked thinner than Sarah remembered, his hair grayer at the temples and sparser, combed back into stiff furrows and shiny with product. When he smiled, his teeth seemed too bright against his tanned skin, a curious anachronism given the autumn chill.

He regarded Sarah curiously. "I know you. We met, many years ago, at the Bergstrom estate."

"Yes," said Sarah evenly. "We also ran into each other once here, when it was still Bonnie Markham's quilt shop."

He nodded as if suddenly all was understood. "I don't suppose you're bringing me the good news that Mrs. Bergstrom has finally decided to sell? Or perhaps she's finally died, and you're interested in disposing of the property?"

Sarah bristled. "Sylvia's fine, thanks very much."

"You'll never get your hands on Elm Creek Manor," snapped Agnes, "and you won't tear down Union Hall either!"

"That place is an eyesore," Krolich said. "It's a hazard and a blight, and it lowers the property values of every other building on the block."

"That place is a historic treasure, and you know it, or you wouldn't have stolen Abel Wright's books!"

His brow furrowed and he shook his head. "I'm sorry, but I have no idea what you're talking about." His gaze met Sarah's. "Is your friend really . . . quite all right in the head?"

"Don't mock me, young man," said Agnes. "You have no idea who I am, but I know you. I know your type. You're a bully and a thief and you're used to trampling over everyone else to get your own way. Well, you may have taken Grandma's Attic from us, but you didn't get Elm Creek Manor, and you won't get Union Hall. I know you stole those books, or had someone steal them for you, but they aren't the only copies in existence. One way or another we're going to find the evidence we need to convince the city council not to make any back-room deals with you."

Krolich offered Agnes a faint smile, but the corners of his mouth quirked with annoyance. "You're feisty, and that's charming, but you apparently mistake me for one of the little old ladies in your quilting bee. This is business, and in business, profit trumps sentiment. If you have any proof that I've committed this theft, any witnesses who can place me at the scene of the crime, I suggest you call the chief of police. Oh, and when you do, remind him that I have two extra tickets for the next Penn State home game, if he and his wife would like to join me and my wife on another road trip to Happy Valley."

Agnes glowered at him, balled her hands into fists, took one step forward, and might have done something she would regret later if Sarah had not placed a hand on her shoulder to restrain her. "Once Union Hall is listed on the National Register of Historic Places, the city council won't let you touch it, no matter what bribes you offer," said Sarah.

"You may be right," said Krolich, with an oily smile. "In which case you'd better hurry if you hope to stop me."

Sarah knew that prolonging the exchange of threats would only waste valuable time. "Come on, Agnes," she said, glaring at Krolich. "I'll drive you home."

On the sidewalk outside the office, Agnes fumed, "I despise that man. He's behind the theft of Abel Wright's books, I know it."

"Of course he is," said Sarah as they walked to her car. "Which means he believes they have information that would help us. Do you think the Waterford Public Library has copies?"

"I know for a fact they don't, but Pattee Library at Penn State might."

"I know that library fairly well." Sarah had spent many hours studying there and perusing the stacks as an undergraduate.

Sarah helped Agnes into the front passenger seat, and as they drove away, Agnes said, "If they do have the books, they won't be in circulation. I doubt that I could get them through interlibrary loan, and I can't drive there to read them."

"I could," said Sarah. "I could read all day, spend the night in a hotel, and come back the next morning for more, as many days as it takes, until I find the evidence we need or I finish the books."

"Would you, Sarah? That would be wonderful."

"As long as Matt's okay with single-parenting for a few days." Though it was hardly single-parenting, considering that Sylvia, Maggie, and Gretchen, as well as their spouses, would be around to assist. "But maybe we don't need to make the trip. Jeremy must know Abel's books thoroughly. I'll ask him if he knows what Krolich doesn't want us to see." Jeremy had not yet responded to her last e-mail. Ordinarily she wouldn't bother him again so soon, but the theft of the books added urgency to her request.

Dropping off Agnes at home along the way, Sarah drove back to Elm Creek Manor, where Matt was in the kitchen fixing the twins an after-school snack. The children listened wide-eyed as Sarah told Matt about the theft of the books and Agnes's impromptu visit to University Realty. James was impressed that Agnes had stood up to a bully, while Caroline was horrified that someone had damaged and stolen rare books. "Why hasn't anyone called nine-one-one?" she demanded. "Why isn't that big jerk in jail?"

Sarah explained that the library had immediately reported the theft, but they had no proof that Krolich or someone working for him was to blame. "Don't they have security cameras?" Caroline persisted. "Are you telling me there are security cameras, like, everywhere else in Waterford, but not in the Rare Books Room?"

"I'm sure the library has security cameras. For all I know, the police are reviewing surveillance footage as we speak." Sarah doubted very much, though, that Krolich would have strolled into the library and committed the theft himself when he could pay an unscrupulous student fifty bucks to do it for him. He didn't even need the books; he only needed to keep them away from Agnes and the historical society long enough to push his measure through the city council.

After settling the twins down with their homework, Sarah went upstairs to the library to check her e-mail, and when she found no reply from Jeremy, she called his cell phone. He didn't answer, so she left a voice mail explaining the latest developments, then called the Del Maso–Bernstein home and left a message on the family answering machine too. If no one responded by the next day, she would check online to see if Pattee Library did indeed have copies of Abel Wright's books, and if so, she would plan a road trip to University Park.

When the following evening arrived and Sarah still had heard nothing from either Jeremy or Anna, she grew concerned. It was not like them, no matter how busy they were, to let urgent e-mails and messages go unanswered for so long. After supper, Sarah and Matt lingered at the table to discuss her trip and speculate about their friends' silence. Sarah feared Gina was ill or Jeremy had been denied tenure, but Matt thought it was more likely that the family was on vacation. "In the middle of the semester?" asked Sarah, skeptical, but Matt pointed out that the family both deserved and needed time off after all Jeremy had gone through lately, and Jeremy himself had promised Anna a vacation.

When there was still no word from Jeremy or Anna the next morning, Sarah kissed the twins good-bye, explained that she was going out of town for a few days, and sent them off to school. Then, back upstairs, she went online to reserve a room at a hotel within walking distance of the Penn State campus and packed enough clothes for a few days. When she came downstairs lugging her suitcase, her laptop in a smaller bag slung over her shoulder, she found Matt in the kitchen packing her a lunch and snacks for the road. "Call me when you get there?" he asked, helping her carry everything out to the car.

"Of course." They kissed good-bye, and Sarah set out.

The long drive gave her ample time to consider all that had happened since the discovery of the two antique quilts. She wondered what Krolich knew about Union Hall that they didn't—not only what he knew, but also how he had come to know it. He didn't strike Sarah as particularly well-read or intellectually curious. Whatever he had learned about Union Hall, he hadn't stumbled across it in the pages of Abel Wright's books. Something or someone else must have warned him of the evidence they contained.

The weather was sunny and clear but cool, the trees on the rolling Appalachians long past their peak of autumn color. Sarah reached University Park by late morning, parked in the hotel lot but didn't check in, and walked up the hill to the Pattee Library, her laptop bag slung over her shoulder. While the librarian retrieved Abel Wright's books from Special Collections, Sarah discreetly checked her messages before obeying the posted signs and shutting down her cell phone. Matt had sent a text wishing her a safe drive, but otherwise there was no news from home, nor any word from Jeremy.

The librarian returned with six volumes that smelled faintly of age and attics, their covers worn and faded, the pages yellowed. Sarah left her driver's license in lieu of a library card and carried the books to an isolated carrel. Since Agnes had already read most of Abel Wright's first book, Sarah opened the second and soon became engrossed in the spellbinding tale of his Underground Railroad years. It was midafternoon before hunger compelled her to break for lunch, and after returning the books to the Special Collections desk, she walked downtown to a favorite restaurant from her college days only to discover that the Stage Door Deli had become the Fraser Street Deli. Startled and a bit disappointed, she nonetheless ordered a sandwich, reflecting on how many years had passed since her graduation, and how all things must change. Waiting for her lunch, she turned on her phone to check for messages—and found a startling text Diane had sent hours before: "Urgent! Everyone meet at Union Hall at noon!"

"Oh, no," Sarah muttered, dialing Diane's number. The call went straight to voice mail. She next dialed Agnes's home, but the line was busy. She called Elm Creek Manor, but after three rings the answering machine picked up. That struck her as the strangest of all; usually at least one of the manor's residents was around any time of day to answer the phone. One by one she called each of the Elm Creek Quilters, but reached only busy signals or voice mail. She sent out a flurry of texts, and at last received a cryptic response from Diane: "On phone. Will explain later."

"Should I come home?" Sarah quickly texted back, but Diane didn't reply.

Torn, Sarah finished her lunch, returned to the library, and reclaimed Abel Wright's books from Special Collections. Though distracted by concerns about what could possibly be going on back in Waterford, she continued to read and take notes, surreptitiously checking her cell phone from time to time in case Matt or her friends had returned any of her messages.

Special Collections closed at six-thirty, but Sarah managed

to finish reading Abel Wright's second book before she had to leave. Sylvia would be delighted to hear that he had mentioned the Bergstrom family several times. Not only that, but in the chapter when he told of his wife's deliverance from slavery in Virginia to freedom in Pennsylvania, he mentioned a visit from the Granger family and a quilt that nineteen-year-old Dorothea had given to Constance to welcome her to her new home. Although the description was brief, certain details convinced Sarah that the quilt in question had to be the elaborate appliqué sampler discovered in Union Hall. The passages verified the embroidered details on the back of the quilt, but that evidence only confirmed the historical significance of the quilt, not the building in which it was found.

Sarah was intrigued by all she had learned that day, but her frustrations and worries remained. The Loyal Union Sampler was linked to Union Hall but not to Abel Wright. The appliqué album was definitely linked to Abel Wright but not to Union Hall. The crucial evidence linking quilts *and* author *and* Union Hall still eluded her, and she doubted she would find it in Abel Wright's third book, which was another memoir covering the postwar years and Reconstruction, or the three books that followed, collections of essays and treatises on a variety of social and political subjects. Sarah would have to read the books to be sure, but considering that Union Hall was built in 1863, it seemed unlikely that it would figure in Abel Wright's later work.

As soon as she exited the library, she called Matt's cell phone and was relieved when he picked up. "What's going on at Union Hall?" she asked. "I've had two alarming texts from Diane, but otherwise I haven't heard anything all day."

"I don't know much," said Matt, his voice barely audible over the exhaust fan above the stove. Likely he was fixing himself and the twins hamburgers for supper. "Agnes found out that the city council was holding an emergency closed-door session today when someone from the *Waterford Register* called her for a comment."

"Another closed-door session?"

"Apparently so. The reporter told Agnes that the council was expected to vote to condemn Union Hall under their right of eminent domain."

"Already?" Sarah hurried down the hill past Old Main, where tall, stately elms sent golden leaves dancing to the grass and sidewalks below. "This is unbelievable."

"Surely you didn't expect Krolich to waste any time."

"No, but I thought the council might." A fallen elm leaf caught in her hair, and she plucked it out and tossed it over her shoulder. "What happened?"

"Agnes called all hands on deck to try to figure out some way to stall them. I don't know if she succeeded. Gretchen and Maggie joined the meeting at Union Hall, but they haven't come home yet."

Just then, Sarah's call waiting beeped. "It's Diane," she said, checking the screen. "Can I call you back after supper?"

"Please do. I want to know everything," Matt said, and hung up.

Diane had much to tell. After the reporter alerted Agnes to the unexpected city council meeting, she summoned all the friends of the Waterford Historical Society to Union Hall so they could organize their response and attempt to delay the vote. Agnes's first thought was to organize a march on city hall, but Gwen, who had fond memories of antiwar protests at Berkeley, pointed out that they could march and protest and burn Krolich in effigy until they were hoarse and footsore, but the city council could still proceed blithely along behind locked doors, ignoring them. What they needed to do, Gwen proposed, was to prevent at least six council members from attending the meeting. "If they can't form a quorum," Gwen explained, "they can't hold a binding vote."

"How exactly do you suggest we keep them away from city hall?" Diane asked. "Ambush them on the sidewalk and carry them off in a sack?"

Gretchen suggested they send two or three people to each council member's home and to civilly and politely explain the historical society's position. "Even if we can't convince all twelve members to save Union Hall today," she added, "we might be able to convince six of them to stay home from this meeting tonight. We're not asking for the moon, just a little more time to search for proof that Union Hall is historically significant. If the council members are even moderately reasonable people, they'll see the merit in postponing the vote."

"What if they won't listen to us?" a member of the historical society called out over the chorus of voices chiming in their agreement. "What if they don't answer the doorbell? What if while we're on the front porch, they're sneaking out to the garage through the side door?"

"We're their constituents," Gretchen said. "They have to listen to us."

Gwen burst out laughing, but then caught herself. "Oh, you're serious. I'm sorry, Gretchen. I thought you were joking."

"If they won't listen to the voters," Agnes declared, her

blue eyes taking on a steely glint, "I bet there's someone each of them will listen to."

Agnes's plan required a bit of research, but several of the friends of Union Hall had brought their laptops and were able to log on to the Internet via the free Wi-Fi at a café down the block. Others used their smartphones. Within a half hour, thanks to Waterford's relatively small population and to the lengthy biographies posted on the council members' election Web sites, they were able to track down the names, addresses, and phone numbers of the council members' mothers. Then, while teams of two or three went to each council member's home to speak with them, Agnes had other friends call their mothers. She assigned callers to mothers with swift insight, never failing to find some small connection between them—they attended the same church, or they lived on the same street, or their husbands were co-workers, or they had both served on the same fund-raising committee when their children were in the high school marching band together many years before. Before anyone dialed a single number, Agnes instructed them to tell the mothers that an irreplaceable city treasure was in jeopardy, and all the historical society wanted was the opportunity to prove it. All they asked for was time to finish their research and have the National Park Service determine whether Union Hall possessed unique historical significance. Should the mothers agree that their voices deserved to be heard just as much as Mr. Krolich's did, the Waterford Historical Society would be deeply grateful if they would call their children and urge them to be patient, to listen, and to give them a chance to make their case.

The calls, the visits, the scrambling to reach mothers who

were not at home, the gentle persuasion, the protests as some council members pushed past their visitors in their haste to get to their cars—it went on all afternoon and into the evening. A few of the mothers declared that they did not get involved in their children's politics and hung up on the callers. One mother tearfully admitted that her son had not spoken to her in years. Several were appalled to learn how Krolich was trampling on the historical society's right to equal treatment, and they vowed to keep their children on the phone until they agreed to preserve Union Hall or it was too late for them to leave for the council meeting. At least one drove to her daughter's house, blocked the end of her driveway with her own car, and joined the friends of Union Hall on the front porch, ringing the doorbell and calling to her daughter through an open window until embarrassment compelled the younger woman to invite them in. When the appointed hour arrived, four council members had made their way to the chambers in city hall, two had feigned illness, and six had called the mayor to explain that upon further reflection, they saw no reason to rush to a vote in yet another closed-door emergency session, or to deny the Waterford Historical Society an opportunity to explain why preserving Union Hall would benefit the community. To that end, they urged the mayor to invite the society's president to address the council at their next regularly scheduled meeting.

Thanks to Agnes, a quorum had not met that day, the vote was not taken, Union Hall had been granted a reprieve, and the historical society would be allowed to make their case for saving Union Hall. Sarah was thrilled, but she cautioned, "Krolich won't give up. For every argument the historical society makes for preserving Union Hall, he'll have a counterargument."

"Don't I know it," said Diane darkly. "He'll have tax revenue projections on his side, and so far all we have are nostalgia and sentiment. Unless you found something today?"

"I learned a lot, but nothing that you'd call conclusive proof of Union Hall's historical significance."

"You'll keep looking, though, right?"

"Of course. How can I give up after one day at the library after all Agnes went through today?" Sarah fell silent, reflecting upon her friend's actions, not only that day but ever since Union Hall had become threatened. "Why do you suppose Agnes cares so much about Union Hall? Why is the history of Waterford so important to her? It's not like she has deep roots in the Elm Creek Valley—she moved to town when she married Sylvia's younger brother. I could understand her passion if generations of her family had lived here, but why care so much about the history of an adopted hometown?"

Diane paused. "You really don't get it?"

"No, I don't."

Diane had known Agnes longer than any of them except Sylvia. They had been neighbors throughout Diane's childhood, and Agnes had often babysat her. "Her parents disowned her when she married Richard," Diane said.

"That much I know."

"Did you know she hasn't had so much as a postcard from any of her relatives in almost sixty years? Waterford isn't just an adopted hometown to her. It's her home, her only home, and Union Hall was once the pride and joy of the town. She's not going to let it be eliminated and forgotten as if it never existed."

And Sarah understood.

She asked Diane to keep her posted, and then she ended

the call and checked in to the hotel. Exhausted, she ordered room service for supper and called home to speak to the twins and update Matt on the day's developments. Gretchen and Maggie had come home, exultant in victory, and added a few other details to Diane's story. The friends of Union Hall knew they had not won yet, but they believed the momentum was turning in their favor.

That night Sarah slept restlessly in the unfamiliar bed, and she woke to the sound of her cell phone buzzing on the nightstand. Groping for it, she blinked sleepily at the caller ID and was startled awake when she read Jeremy's name. "Hello?" she said, sitting up in bed and drawing the covers around her. "Jeremy?"

"Hi, Sarah." He sounded tired and drained, not as if he had woken too early but as if he had not slept well for days. "How are you?"

"I'm fine, but the question is, how are you? How are Anna and Gina? I haven't heard anything from you in so long, I was beginning to worry."

"Anna and Gina are fine. I'm sorry I've been out of touch. I'm even sorrier that I gave you cause to worry." Jeremy inhaled deeply and sighed. "The thing is, it's been kind of a bad week."

Sarah suspected she knew why, but hoped she was wrong. "What happened?"

"I didn't get tenure."

"What? Why not? How did that happen? Anna said the faculty voted in your favor."

"They did, and as required, the tenure committee forwarded everything to the dean of the college. And . . . that's where it all fell apart."

"The dean turned you down?"

"The dean turned me down."

"The dean, who's married to the chair of your tenure committee, a woman who inexplicably hates you."

"That's the one." Jeremy sighed heavily. "He weighed the evidence and decided I wasn't a strong enough candidate to warrant forwarding my dossier to the provost."

"That's not fair. How were you ever supposed to get an unbiased decision out of those two?"

"I don't have a good answer for that."

"Can you go over the dean's head?"

"I could but . . ." Jeremy's voice trailed off. He cleared his throat and continued. "It would get ugly. It would mean legal action, and I don't think I have the stomach for that. I also don't think I have much of a case, and I definitely can't afford the legal bills."

"I'm so sorry, Jeremy. This is just wrong, so wrong."

"Thanks." He sounded numb, drained of all emotion. "I couldn't agree more."

"What are you going to do?"

"Look for another job. I actually started sending out CVs months ago. It's standard procedure for anyone going through tenure review, but in my case it seemed especially prudent."

"How long do you have?"

"How long do I still have a job here, you mean? Until the end of spring semester. With any luck, I'll have something else lined up by then, and if I'm very lucky, it will be within a tolerable commute so we won't have to move. The way my luck's been lately, though . . ."

He didn't need to complete the thought.

Sarah thought it was deplorable that he would have to finish out months of teaching and committee work for that department with everyone knowing he had, essentially, been fired. "If there's anything I can do, you know all you have to do is ask."

"I appreciate that," he replied. "All the more since I haven't responded to your questions."

"For perfectly legitimate reasons."

"Maybe, but they were easy questions to answer and the need was urgent. I should have stopped wallowing in self-pity long enough to get back to you. I hope it's not too late."

Thanks to Agnes, it wasn't. "Your timing couldn't be better. Does this mean you know something that could help us save Union Hall?"

"I think so. Have you read Abel Wright's fifth book?"

"No, only the second. Agnes has read the first, and I was going to start the third today."

"You might want to skip ahead to the fifth. In one of the essays about halfway through the book, Wright discusses ownership of land and property, especially the ownership of community assets, and how that can raise families out of poverty. He describes how the women of Water's Ford incorporated in order to maintain control of a grand hall constructed for the purpose of hosting fund-raising events to benefit local soldiers and veterans. Then, almost as an aside—because for all of his accomplishments, Wright was a modest man—he suggests that he was the architect and the construction foreman."

"He says he built Union Hall?"

"Not single-handedly, of course." Jeremy hesitated. "And he doesn't come right out and say it. He uses a lot of passive voice in that section, as if he expected his reader to know who the architect and foreman was, so it would have been unnecessary and perhaps even boastful for him to name himself. Keep in mind that he was writing for a contemporary audience. He wasn't thinking of what a reader more than a hundred years in the future might need explained."

"Abel Wright built Union Hall," said Sarah decisively. "It makes perfect sense. In 1863, he wanted to serve his country, but men of color weren't permitted to enlist yet. Naturally he would use his skills to serve another way."

"That's a logical conclusion," said Jeremy, "especially if you take into consideration that he helped build the first library in Creek's Crossing several years before that, and the architectural styles are similar. Anyone familiar with Abel Wright's publications and the literary conventions of the time would take the statements in his essay to mean that he designed and built Union Hall. However, I don't know if anyone meeting that description sits on the city council."

"You can be our expert witness. You can tell them."

"I'd be happy to," he said. "Anna and Gina would love an excuse to visit Elm Creek Manor. Just tell me when you need me."

"It might be as soon as next week. Can you get a sub to take over your classes?"

"Probably, and if I can't, I'll just cancel them. What are they going to do, fire me?"

Sarah was glad to hear humor in his voice. "It's their loss, Jeremy."

"Anna says the same thing, but you know, it's my loss too. Aside from the departmental politics, I like it here. My students are bright and motivated. We like our house and we have great neighbors. Gina loves her school and she has nice friends there. Anna's personal chef business is doing okay—not fantastic, but okay. We aren't looking forward to starting over somewhere else."

"It'll be all right," she said, hoping it was the truth. She asked him to give her love to Anna and Gina, and they hung up.

Quickly she showered, dressed, and had a bite to eat at the free continental breakfast served in the lobby. After packing and checking out, she made one last trip to Special Collections to find and photocopy the passage from Abel Wright's fifth book that Jeremy had mentioned. Then, after stopping by the campus bookstore to buy Nittany Lions sweatshirts for Matt and the twins, she drove home.

Matt welcomed her with kisses, and after telling him what she had learned, she spent most of the afternoon on the phone with her friends, sharing her discoveries and hearing the story of Agnes's triumph over and over, with each narrator offering some new detail the others had not known. Sarah was very proud of her friend, and when Agnes announced another workday and brainstorming session at Union Hall, Sarah promised to be there.

The next day, as she helped Leslie repair the red velvet curtain that had once hung proudly above the main stage, she asked about the first library in Creek's Crossing, the one Abel Wright had helped build.

Leslie looked puzzled. "I wasn't aware that Abel Wright was involved in the library's construction—but of course, I didn't know he had built Union Hall either. Unfortunately, the original building was torn down in the 1950s after the new library was built on Second Street."

"Don't tell me; let me guess," said Sarah dryly, working her needle through the plush, heavy velvet. "They built condos on the site."

"You're almost right," said Leslie, smiling. "It was student apartments."

"I guess I can't blame Krolich this time."

"No, he would've been only a teenager then, perhaps younger. His predecessor arranged that sale."

Sarah froze with her needle stuck in the velvet. "You mean University Realty handled the transaction?"

"They called themselves College Realty in those days, but yes, it was the same company." Leslie sighed and brushed lint from the heavy folds draped over her lap. "Same company, very different sense of civic responsibility. Before the original library was razed, they took care to preserve important artifacts—the cornerstone, several brass plaques engraved with the names of generous donors, a framed declaration by the town council celebrating the library's tenth anniversary—things of that sort. They kept some for themselves, but others they donated to the historical society. Some of them are on display here, others"—she nodded to the ceiling to indicate the upstairs galleries, where dozens of unsorted storage boxes remained—"others are still packed away."

"They saved the cornerstone?" asked Sarah.

Leslie nodded. "They incorporated it into the foundation of the new library. It's on the north side of the front entrance, opposite the cornerstone for the new building."

"Does the old cornerstone include any information other than the date the first library was built?"

"I think it has only the year, but don't quote me on that," said Leslie. "I see it so often I don't really pay attention. If you're curious, why don't you stroll over there and take a look? It's no more than a five-minute walk."

"I think I will," said Sarah, pushing herself to her feet and promising to return soon.

The day was cold and overcast, with strong gusts of wind that warned of a storm approaching. Sarah pulled up the hood of her jacket and tucked her hands into her pockets as she made her way a few blocks west of Union Hall to the Waterford Public Library. She found the old, preserved cornerstone exactly where Leslie had told her it would be, but she was disappointed that it provided the year of its dedication, 1850, and nothing more.

She studied the cornerstone, thinking, then headed back to Union Hall. Halfway there, she took her cell phone from her pocket and called Jeremy. He answered on the second ring, and after asking him how his job search was faring—not well, he said, but he was trying to stay optimistic—she got to the point. "How did you know Abel Wright built the first library in Creek's Crossing?" she asked. "He didn't refer to it in his second book, the Underground Railroad memoir, and that was the one that covered the year 1850. Unless I missed it."

"You didn't miss it," said Jeremy. "Thanks to his characteristic modesty, he didn't mention it. I stumbled across that detail in a book published by the town chamber of commerce in the early twentieth century. The title was something like *Waterford: The First Hundred Years,* and it was meant to commemorate the town's centennial. It wasn't a best seller by any definition, not even in the Elm Creek Valley. Apparently there was some controversy over what year actually marked the centennial, which isn't surprising, considering the various names the town has gone by. Some people apparently refused to buy the book for that reason alone."

"The authors included a photo of the library in the book?"

"Yes, as well as a photo of a plaque that apparently had been mounted inside the front entrance. The names of the library board, the first librarian, and many of the people who had a hand in the construction were engraved upon it. I noticed Abel Wright's name right away because it was the last one, and it was the only name out of alphabetical order." He paused. "That leads me to believe his name was added later, but I don't have a good explanation for why."

Sarah thanked him, wished him luck, and hung up. She wondered what had become of that plaque, whether it had been given to the Waterford Historical Society and was in one of the upstairs galleries awaiting discovery—or whether it was locked away in a vault at the new offices of University Realty, where Krolich might have seen it, and perhaps other documents and artifacts alerting him to the historical and cultural significance of Union Hall.

The cloudburst struck when she was half a block from Union Hall. The wind drove icy drops into her face as she ran the rest of the way, holding her hood closed with one hand, darting up the front stairs and through the tall double doors. Inside, she stood on the mat and caught her breath, brushing rainwater from her jacket and hair as she scanned the foyer walls. Her gaze rested upon the engraved copper plaques on the walls flanking the doors; she had noticed them on her first visit, when they were still tarnished and dull, not polished and gleaming as they were now. Most of the plaques had been polished, anyway; a few were partially covered by the enormous mahogany antique curio cabinet. Heavy and dark and stuffed with mementos, it didn't suit the light elegance of its surroundings. Sarah suspected that someone had put it there because the foyer was the only first-floor room other than the theater large enough to accommodate it, and hauling it upstairs to one of the galleries would have been out of the question.

Sarah wiped her wet feet on the mat, studying the incongruous curio cabinet and mulling over her conversation with Jeremy. Then she drew closer. The floor had been mopped and polished, but she could still make out the faint scuff marks on the gray-blue marble leading from the wall beside the door to the theater, the only room on the lower level larger than the foyer—

The marks led not from the wall to the theater, she realized with a start, but from the theater to the wall.

The curio cabinet was pushed back as far against the wall as it could go, leaving only a dark, narrow space about a quarter of an inch wide behind it. Pressing her cheek to the wall, Sarah peered into the crevice, and in the shadow she could barely make out the shapes of more small copper plaques like the others she had already seen—and one significantly larger.

Sarah knew the curio cabinet would be too heavy for her to move, but she couldn't resist shoving it with her shoulder just in case. When it didn't budge, she called Leslie out from the theater and hurried upstairs to the east gallery to round up a few more volunteers. With the help of two pairs of furniture slides Patricia kept in her desk drawer, they managed to move the heavy cabinet away from the wall.

Then they discovered what the curio cabinet had concealed—a tarnished bronze plaque chronicling the provenance of Union Hall. The Union Quilters who had conceived and executed the project were listed, and Sarah felt a thrill of excitement as she read the names, which included Dorothea Nelson, Gerda Bergstrom, Anneke Bergstrom, Constance Wright, and several other women whom she recalled from Gerda's memoir. And then, at once, they all saw the name of the architect and foreman of construction—Abel Wright.

Armed with that information, at the council meeting two weeks later it was easy to persuade the city council not to exercise their right of eminent domain and to deny Gregory Krolich's bid to purchase the property. When questioned, he denied any knowledge of how the curio cabinet happened to be right in front of the plaque bearing the crucial information the historical society had sought. Neither Patricia nor Leslie nor any members of the society could recall exactly when or why it had been moved from the theater to the foyer, but they knew the cabinet had been in its current location for years. No one had questioned the move. Everyone had assumed another member of the society had done it for some good, albeit unknown, reason.

A few days later, Patricia produced photos taken at an event held in 1988 to commemorate the 125th anniversary of Union Hall—and one photo clearly showed the recently discovered plaque in the background, with the mahogany curio cabinet nowhere in sight. The Waterford Historical Society had invited business and civic leaders from the town and representatives from the college to an open house, hoping to launch a capital campaign to restore the building and transform it into a museum. Though the event generated a great deal of interest and promises of help, their attempts to raise funds languished in the recession of the early 1990s, when they were forced to put their plans on hold indefinitely. When Sarah learned that representatives from University Realty had attended, she surmised that Krolich surely had been one of them. While attending the event, he could have noticed the plaque, recognized Abel Wright's name from the Creek's Crossing Library artifacts owned by his company, and secretly returned later with his own personal brute squad to move the curio cabinet. He had concealed the truth and bided his time, confident that with each passing year, Union Hall would become less valuable in the eyes of the community, until the time was right for him to seize it.

Unfortunately Sarah never could prove her suspicions, but it was enough for her that justice was served in other ways. A few weeks after the city council decreed that they would not condemn Union Hall, an alert clerk at a local used bookstore called the police when a young man in a Waterford College sweatshirt tried to sell them six books, each more than a century old and bearing the stamp of the Rare Books Room on a flyleaf. Under questioning, the student confessed that "some guy in a suit" had paid him one hundred dollars to steal the books and hold on to them for a few months until he could dispose of them in his own hometown hundreds of miles away. It was fortunate indeed for the historical society that the student had needed beer money before semester break, that he had seen the books as a source of quick cash, and that he could pick Krolich out of a lineup. Charged with felony theft, Krolich agreed to a plea bargain to avoid a seven-year prison term and was instead sentenced to nine months in a medium-security prison, a thousand hours of community service, and restitution. His reputation ruined, his career in a shambles, Krolich left the Elm Creek Valley to appear on a reality television show in one last vain attempt to restore his credibility before he disappeared into obscurity.

Krolich was still in prison when the long-abandoned capital campaign to restore Union Hall began anew. Media coverage of the effort eventually reached Thomas Wright II, Abel's great-grandson and director of the Abel Wright Foundation, a nonprofit organization dedicated to preserving the author's legacy and promoting literary and history education in the public schools. After visiting Union Hall and viewing relics from his great-grandfather's past that he had not known existed, Thomas Wright II gave the historical society's project the full support of Abel Wright Foundation, contributing one million dollars to the restoration fund and promising, once the renovations were complete, to donate Abel Wright's personal papers and possessions to them as well. To spare the Waterford Historical Society the financial burden of maintaining the acclaimed collection, the foundation would also endow a chair in Waterford College's Department of History. In addition to the usual duties of tenured faculty, the Abel Wright Professor of American History would be responsible for maintaining the Abel Wright archive and promoting his legacy through teaching, scholarship, and service.

As the author of the definitive biography of Abel Wright and the expert whose knowledge had helped thwart the attempts to condemn Union Hall, Jeremy was at the top of the short list of candidates for the newly endowed position. A year after losing his bid for tenure in Virginia—and just in time to officiate the ceremonies honoring Union Hall's appointment to the National Register of Historical Places—Jeremy returned to Waterford College as a full professor, to the delight of his former graduate adviser and the rest of the faculty. For weeks after he, Anna, and Gina moved back to Pennsylvania, he went about his new duties with an expression of joyous disbelief, as if he had forgotten what it was to be happy and secure in his work and he did not expect it to last—and yet day after day, it did.

If anyone was happier than Jeremy, it was Anna, restored to her role as head chef of Elm Creek Quilts. And no one was happier—or more relieved—to see Anna back in her beloved kitchen at Elm Creek Manor than Sarah, who had missed her friend terribly and was thankful beyond measure to be spared the annual task of searching for her replacement. She had learned all too well that no one could fill Anna's place except Anna herself—although in recent years, both Sarah and Anna had agreed that Gina and James would be able successors and might even surpass their mothers.

"Mom?"

Sarah tore her gaze away from Union Hall—beautiful, honored, and in danger no more—to find James standing in the entranceway, "Creek's Crossing, Penn" engraved in stone above his head.

"Mom?" he said again. "Are you okay?"

She smiled. "Yes, sweetheart. I was just lost in thought. I'm sorry I kept you waiting."

"Are you coming in?" He smiled back, but he looked puzzled, and perhaps even concerned. "We're dressed and awaiting inspection."

"I'm coming," she said, and followed him inside.

· Chapter Six ·

Inside the shop, the young men looked handsome and sophisticated in their formal suits, but their jokes and playful teasing reminded Sarah of the young boys they had once been. Because their wedding would take place in the afternoon, Caroline and Leo had chosen traditional morning dress for the men's attire, gray cutaway coats that slanted from waist to thigh and fell to the knee in back; striped trousers, also gray; white dress shirts with folded collars; gray waistcoats; and four-in-hand neckties. Matt and Leo's father were similarly attired, and as the tailor and his assistants took measurements and pinned seams, Sarah and Leo's mother alternately admired the men, teased them for admiring themselves in the full-length mirrors, and threatened to make them dress up more often, since they all looked so handsome in their fine clothes.

Most of the garments were in perfect order, but a few needed alterations. Rather than wait at the shop, Leo's brother, the best man, arranged to pick up the remaining jackets and trousers early the next morning. The men changed back into their comfortable jeans and sweatshirts, and soon the entire party was on the way back to Elm Creek Manor.

As soon as the Elm Creek Quilts shuttle cleared the leafy wood and rounded the barn, Sarah glimpsed a very expensive, chauffeur-driven vehicle in the parking lot behind the manor.

"Who could that be?" Leo's mother wondered aloud.

"Fifty bucks says it's my mom's friend Diane," said James. "Her son is Michael Sonnenberg."

"*The* Michael Sonnenberg?" asked a skeptical groomsman.

"The Michael Sonnenberg," confirmed Matt, with a grin for Sarah, for they both remembered the days when the good citizens of Waterford had referred to Diane's eldest son disapprovingly as "*That* Michael Sonnenberg."

"Is Michael Sonnenberg coming to the wedding?" asked Leo's brother, awestruck.

"Sorry, no," said Sarah. "He couldn't make it. You can meet his parents, though."

Leo's brother nodded politely, but he couldn't hide his disappointment.

Sure enough, as the shuttle crossed the bridge over Elm Creek, Sarah watched the chauffeur open the passenger door and Diane and her husband, Tim, emerge. At the same moment, the back door of the manor swung open and out came the Elm Creek Quilters to welcome them. Sarah watched as the newcomers stood at the foot of the stairs basking in the warm greetings, and as soon as Matt parked the shuttle, she hurried to join the throng. Diane seemed impossibly youthful, slim and impeccably dressed in a tailored mauve skirt and jacket, her blond curls perfectly styled. "Welcome home," Sarah said, hugging her. "You look wonderful. I swear you seem younger every time I see you. Has Michael built a time machine too?"

Diane laughed, pleased. "No, not yet." She lowered her voice. "I might as well tell you, since I'm sure you've already guessed: I had some more work done."

"Again?" exclaimed Gwen. "What's left of you that hasn't already been lifted, plumped, filled, or lasered?"

"Looking this good at my age requires vigilant maintenance," said Diane. "Which you would know if you weren't still working the aged-hippie look."

Gwen shrugged, planting both hands on her cane. "It suits me."

"It doesn't suit me," declared Diane. "Thank goodness Michael is so generous. It's either that or he's nursing a guilty conscience. I'm sure he's well aware that his childhood escapades caused most of my wrinkles and gray hair. It's only fair that he foot the bill for the repairs."

Everyone laughed, more from the sheer delight of being together again than from Diane's quip, which they knew was only partially truthful. Diane had not had as much work done as she implied, but Michael certainly had been generous with his wealth. As an unhappy, alienated youth in Waterford, he had given his parents much cause for worry, but they had never given up on him. Somehow—Diane credited prayer and an assertive determination to remain involved in his life—he had left juvenile delinquency behind, graduated from high school, and achieved unexpected success as a computer science major at Waterford College. From there he went on to graduate school at MIT, where he confounded his professors by concentrating on gaming platforms, a focus they considered a waste of his talent. After earning his Ph.D., he turned down several lucrative job offers to work on an invention that he swore would revolutionize the gaming world. Though his parents wished he had chosen gainful employment and had saved his pet projects for the weekends, they took out a second mortgage on their beloved home on the Waterford College Arboretum to help him launch his business, which at the time was little more than a single patched-together prototype and a wildly fantastic plan. It turned out to be the best investment they had ever made.

Eventually even a nongamer like Sarah knew all about Michael's invention, the Vertex, a gaming device about the size and shape of a smartphone that was unlike any handheld game that had preceded it. The graphics, according to James, were "epic," and for the cost of an annual subscription, the user could connect to a huge library of games and applications via the Internet, and one player's device could connect to others wirelessly through a mesh network infrastructure. For a more immersive playing experience within the home, the Vertex could be plugged into a base console that allowed the games to be played on a large, high-definition screen, limited only by the quality of the player's media equipment. Using the base station, friends could play together using one Vertex, or they could bring their own devices and plug them into the same console for even greater flexibility and interaction.

As Michael's company had taken off, his marketing department had encouraged Vertex gatherings by offering gamers bonuses and prizes in both the virtual and actual worlds, which had sparked positive reviews and word-of-mouth and propelled sales beyond the company's manufacturing capabilities—and the short-term shortage only increased demand. The devices also linked each player to an online social network where they could show off their accomplishments, challenge one another to duels or multiplayer tournaments, and socialize. Over time, Vertex bricks-and-mortar stores—a cross between shops, showcases, and cafés—opened in larger markets, offering gamers places to meet, play, and see the latest games and hardware. In more recent years, the company had moved beyond games to other social and business applications, and had begun hosting an annual convention, VertexCon, where they launched new products to great fanfare. Celebrities eager for publicity found excuses to plug their new projects at the convention, and Sarah was no longer surprised to see reports in the news media of Michael's romantic involvement with one gorgeous starlet or another.

Rumors abounded about a new, extremely classified product Michael was collaborating on with one of the nation's leading theoretical physicists, a friend from his MIT days. After swearing Sarah to secrecy, Diane had tried to explain the project to her, but Diane's own understanding of physics and computer engineering was so limited that all Sarah learned from her was that the project was called Event Horizon, it drew upon the physicist's research into black holes, it had something to do with holograms, it would revolutionize virtual reality, and it could quite possibly transform the telecommunications industry. Sarah, who sometimes had trouble thinking of Michael as a successful, multimillionaire inventor and businessman rather than the scowling teenager who had been arrested for illegal skateboarding in downtown Waterford, was amazed anew with each successively more impressive accomplishment. Even Diane, who had believed in her son's potential when everyone, from his teachers to the police, had dismissed him as incorrigible, seemed unable to believe what he had achieved. "When I think of how many times throughout his childhood I told him to put down those video games and go do something productive, I want to kick myself," Diane once famously said in an interview, never imagining it would become one of the most oft-quoted statements about her son.

Michael ran his empire from a campus in Boulder, Colorado, a reasonable distance from his parents' home in Denver, where they had moved upon Tim's retirement from the Waterford College Chemistry Department, after one blisteringly hot summer in Paradise Valley had convinced Diane that Arizona was not for her. Their younger son, Todd, was an assistant district attorney for the City of Philadelphia, but thanks to Michael's fortune, they were able to travel to see him, his wife, and their three daughters often. And naturally, whenever the Sonnenbergs returned to Elm Creek Manor, they traveled in style.

No sooner had Diane and Tim settled into their suite than another, less expensive, and more familiar vehicle pulled into the parking lot. Emily flew outside to welcome her parents and escorted them into the kitchen, where their friends gave them a warm welcome. "I always feel like I've come home when I walk through that door," said Judy, hugging each of her friends in turn.

"We always have room for one more teacher if you want to come back," teased Sarah.

"Don't tempt her," said Judy's husband, Steve, as he put one arm around Judy's shoulders and the other around his daughter's. "Whenever she's mired in grading a particularly dismal batch of exams, she threatens to resign and beg you for her old job back."

"You wouldn't have to beg," Sarah told Judy, hoping her friend's dream job had not become unduly stressful. If it had, Judy certainly hid it well, for she seemed as vibrant and youthful as she had been as an Elm Creek Quilter. Slim and petite, with only the barest trace of fine lines on her golden skin, she wore her glossy black hair simply, tucked behind one ear and cut straight across beneath her shoulder blades. In the early years of Elm Creek Quilt Camp, Judy had taught hand-piecing and hand-quilting classes, and through the years her preference for the relaxing, more contemplative pace of handwork had endured. As she had explained to Sarah soon after they first met, "I work with computers and lab equipment all day. The last thing I need is another machine in my life."

Emily was eight years old when Judy was offered a coveted position as a professor with the Computer Engineering Department at the University of Pennsylvania, and Steve, a journalist, found a job on the staff of *The Philadelphia Inquirer*. The family moved to Philadelphia, and for many years, the Elm Creek Quilters watched Emily grow up through photographs and yearly visits.

When Emily was in fourth grade, Judy taught her to piece, appliqué, and quilt by hand, and proudly e-mailed photos of her creations to her friends at Elm Creek Manor. After Emily mastered those skills, she begged Judy to teach her to use the sewing machine, and when she was in middle school, an indulgent neighbor gave her serger lessons on wintry Saturday afternoons. Emily, whose tastes ran to the eclectic, soon began creating abstract, impressionist quilts and sewing her own clothes. In high school she was the queen of the drama club, not only because of her brilliant comedic timing and pure soprano voice, but also because of her gift for costuming. But art remained her first love, and after spending her first two years after high school in an independent study program in France and Italy, she enrolled in the California College of the Arts in San Francisco. There she earned her bachelor of fine arts degree with highest honors, and after spending a year in Oakland working for a nonprofit organization that promoted art education in inner city public schools, she enrolled in the prestigious School of the Art Institute of Chicago, where she earned her master of fine arts in fiber and material studies. Her work, an intriguing amalgam of quilting, weaving, and sculpture, received critical praise in student shows, and thanks to Russell's connections in the art world, some of her pieces were displayed in prestigious galleries in Seattle, Atlanta, and Louisville. She won a few awards, enjoyed a few brief but glowing magazine reviews, and even sold a few pieces. But all too soon she learned what her parents had privately worried about ever since she first expressed her dream of becoming an artist: It was a desperately difficult way to make a living.

Perhaps to atone for those many tearful conversations years earlier in which Judy had urged her smart and diligent daughter to major in science or engineering and enjoy art as a relaxing hobby, Judy resolved to help Emily pursue the artist's life without fear of starving to death in a cobwebby garret. Emily's first medium had been quilting, she had teaching experience, and everyone at Elm Creek Manor adored her, so Judy did not feel as if she were imposing upon their friendship when she asked Sarah to consider Emily for the faculty of Elm Creek Quilt

Camp the next time they had an available position. For Sarah this was welcome news. In recent years they had relied upon visiting instructors to fill vacancies, which allowed them to vary their course offerings from year to year and introduce their regular campers to different celebrities from the quilting world each summer. Although this system offered some advantages, the smooth operation of quilt camp over the long term depended upon a consistent core faculty, and their numbers had been dwindling. Sarah gladly offered Emily a permanent position on the faculty, as well as room and board at Elm Creek Manor.

Emily gratefully accepted, honored and delighted to be invited to join the renowned group of quilters she had admired since childhood, the women who had inspired her to become an artist. She spent her summers teaching Elm Creek Quilt campers contemporary art quilting, color theory, embellishment, clothing design, and a host of other classes as quirky and intriguing as she was. When autumn came, she retreated to the private studio Sarah had invited her to create in the expansive room on the third floor that had once been the Bergstrom children's nursery. As the winter winds blew and snow dashed upon the windowpanes, Emily lost herself in the eternal springtime of creation. She had friends about her when she craved companionship, solitude when she needed to be alone. The quilt campers' positive energy nurtured her creativity, she often said, and she couldn't imagine anything about her profoundly blessed life she would change.

Judy, who visited as often as she could and worried that Emily spent far too much time alone, had confided to her friends that she would change only one small matter—she wished Emily had a husband, or at least a boyfriend. Gwen found this enormously funny and pointed out that she had been single most of her life and was much happier for it. "Perhaps," Judy had replied in an e-mail exchange that included all of the original Elm Creek Quilters, "but you had Summer."

"So it's grandchildren you want," teased Anna.

"Maybe she'll meet someone later in life," offered Maggie, who had met Russell in her late thirties and married him at forty-four.

"Emily doesn't seem lonely," Sarah reassured Judy. "She's bright and happy and cheerful. She's made friends in town—artists, musicians, writers, and the occasional mathematician. I promise you, she isn't a hermit."

At the time, Judy seemed relieved to hear it, but as the years went by and Emily remained contentedly single, her worries returned. Although she feigned nonchalance, she was delighted when Emily mentioned that she planned to bring a date to Caroline's wedding. Emily had met Miles, a biology professor at Waterford College, after he purchased one of her tapestries from a small gallery downtown that specialized in the work of regional artists. Miles had volunteered to select a gift from the Biology Department for a visiting professor whose appointment was ending, and he had requested Emily's contact information so he could consult her about how to properly pack the tapestry for the professor's flight home to Switzerland. After exchanging a few e-mails, Miles invited Emily to dinner, ostensibly to thank her for her help. Later he confessed that he had seen her photo at the gallery—*after* he bought the tapestry, he emphasized—and he couldn't forget her beautiful dark eyes and the faint amusement in her smile.

Emily and Miles had gone out several times since then, and he had joined the Elm Creek Quilters and their campers for supper at Elm Creek Manor occasionally throughout the summer, but Judy and Steve had not yet met him. Sarah suppressed a smile as she watched Judy and Emily together, suspecting that Judy would like nothing more than to take her daughter aside and interrogate her about her new friend.

After lingering in the kitchen for nearly an hour to catch up on everyone's news, Judy and Steve followed Emily upstairs to their usual suite. Afterward, Judy and Emily met the other Elm Creek Quilters in the library so that Judy and Diane could restore their Winding Ways panels to their proper places on the wall beside the fireplace.

"It's nearly complete," remarked Emily, admiring the segmented quilt.

"Yes, nearly," said Judy, putting an arm around her daughter's shoulders as all eyes went to the empty space in the lower right corner where Bonnie's panel belonged. Sarah tried to remember how many years had passed since it had last hung in its proper place—ten years? Twelve? It seemed impossible that Bonnie had been away from the manor so long. It was easier to remember the last time all nine panels had hung on the wall together and the quilt had been whole. On the day of Agnes's funeral eleven years before, all of the Elm Creek Quilters, past and present, had returned to the manor to honor their beloved friend, the most sincere and indefatigably optimistic member of their circle. Before that, the last time the quilt had been displayed in its entirety was on the day of Sylvia's memorial service. Gazing at the incomplete Winding Ways quilt, Sarah found it impossible not to wonder what occasion would next reunite the remaining Elm Creek Quilters—and whether that occasion would be full of grief. At least Caroline's wedding had brought most of them together for a celebration of life and love.

Someone sighed, and Sarah knew that she was not the only one whose thoughts had taken a melancholy turn. It was her responsibility as hostess to make sure their reunion didn't become maudlin. Looking around the circle of friends, she said, "We have an hour before dinner, so I'll offer you your choice of activities: You can put your feet up and relax, you can help me collect signatures for Leo and Caroline's wedding quilt, or you can help Anna and Gina in the kitchen. What do you say?"

"Forgive me, but I've had enough going door-to-door to last me a lifetime," said Gwen. "I'd rather chop vegetables or stir soup or whatever the master chefs will trust me to do."

"I thought you loved campaigning," said Diane. "Pressing the flesh, talking about yourself, being the center of attention—that's kind of your thing, isn't it?"

"I enjoyed getting out to meet the people and discuss the issues," Gwen clarified. "I didn't like the perpetual marketing of myself or the endless fund-raising."

"Mom loved the work of legislating," said Summer, putting an arm around her mother's shoulder and smiling at her with proud fondness. "She relished taking on the corporate villains and improving the lives of ordinary citizens. She enjoyed making a difference."

Diane folded her arms and shook her head mournfully. "If only you had put all that determination to work for the right political party."

"You voted for me," Gwen pointed out as everyone laughed.

"Twice for city council and five times for Congress, or so you said."

"Those were first, last, and only times I've ever voted for a liberal," Diane declared. "And I wouldn't have done that for anyone but you."

"And I appreciate it," said Gwen, grinning. Everyone there knew Diane had done much more than simply vote for her longtime friend. She had dared wear a "Sullivan for Congress" button to her Republican women's club meeting and had candidly explained to her friends and acquaintances why she was breaking party loyalty to support a self-professed bleeding-heart liberal. Diane had even planted "Sullivan for Congress" signs in her beautifully manicured front yard, despite the unappealing way the blue cardboard clashed with her roses. And although she had not intended to, Diane had inspired Gwen to run in the first place.

Sarah remembered when the seed was first planted. She was in labor with the twins, and several of the Elm Creek Quilters had come to her bedside to encourage her. Conversation turned to how the friends had first met, and after describing her first impression of Gwen—that she was "a loud, obnoxious hippie"—Diane had added, "I've figured out you're all bluster. If I ever suspected that you might actually *do* something to foist your liberal values on the rest of us, I might worry, but I know you're harmless."

"Oh, don't tell me that," warned Gwen, shaking her head vigorously. "You'll force me to do something to prove you wrong."

Although none of her friends realized it at the time, Gwen had taken Diane's words to heart. Was she really all talk and no action? Had she become too settled, too complacent? She hated to think of herself as harmless, an old curmudgeon who complained and censured, who pointed out problems but never took action to solve them. For days she brooded over Diane's inadvertent criticism, and for a few months afterward, she resolved to become more engaged in her community. She wrote letters to the editor of the *Waterford Register* when she disagreed with an editorial, attended city council meetings when important issues arose, and participated in town hall meetings when important political figures visited campus. But over time, eroded by the pressures of her academic career and commitments to Elm Creek Quilts, her resolve weakened, and she fell back into her old habits of shaking her head in disgust and dismay as she read the morning news and airing her complaints to like-minded friends—that, and little more.

Then Union Hall came under attack, and although Gwen was too busy with graduate student advising and a heavy undergraduate course load to do much more than commiserate, she looked on in admiration as Agnes led the successful grassroots campaign to preserve the historic building. While it had been Gwen's suggestion to prevent a quorum from meeting, without Agnes to figure out how to do that and how to motivate everyone to make it happen, Union Hall would have been reduced to rubble. What use were brilliant ideas, Gwen mused, if she lacked the resolve to implement them? She didn't like to think of herself as a spectator calling out plays from the sidelines. She wanted to be in the game.

She tested the waters by running for city council on a progressive platform of environmentalism, preservation of historic sites, improved relations between the town and the college, and eliminating waste and fraud in city services. Ten candidates, including five incumbents, vied for the six seats up for election on the second Tuesday of April that year. Gwen won one of them handily, thanks to her strong performance in the race's sole debate and an unexpectedly high turnout of eligible student voters. Her experience on the city council gave her an opportunity to explore the role of a legislator without obliging her to quit her day job. She soon discovered that she had a gift for negotiation and implementing policies, and she was proud of the measures she had enacted that made Waterford a greener, more efficient, more tolerant, and more sustainable city.

As her first term approached its end, she ran for and won reelection. A few weeks into her second term, she considered all she had accomplished for the city of Waterford and all the greater good she might do if she held a higher office. After careful thought, she formed a nominating committee of influential local party members she had met through her work on the city council and began raising funds. Friends warned her that she would face a tough battle, one made even more difficult by her late entry into the race, and she would probably lose. The incumbent from her district had served a member of Congress for more than twenty years and had a satisfactory if not remarkable record to show for it. He also possessed enough name recognition and personal wealth to ensure that every two years he would run unchallenged in the Republican primary and trounce his opponent in the general election by double digits.

Gwen knew she couldn't win unless she used his firmly entrenched position to her advantage, and she started with securing her party's nomination. None of the more prominent Democrats in the district wanted to challenge him, preferring to wait until he retired rather than attempt to unseat him. Someone had to run against him, though, so when Gwen's name came up, the local party authorities were relieved to put her on the ballot, although they warned her that they couldn't afford to sink much money into what would likely be a losing race.

Gwen thanked them graciously, amused that they were impressed by her willingness to be the sacrificial lamb—but Gwen had no intention of losing. She took a leave of absence from Waterford College and devoted herself to meeting as many constituents of the twenty-second congressional district as she could. She spoke at every community gathering that would have her, listening to the people's concerns, asking questions, and making plans. She learned that the citizens weren't particularly enraptured with the incumbent, but although he hadn't accomplished anything remarkable, he hadn't done anything to disgrace the office, either, and that was about the best you could expect from a politician anymore.

Their willingness to settle for the bare minimum from their elected representative appalled Gwen. She began breaking away from her stump speech to make long, impassioned entreaties for her listeners to demand more from their government, to make elected officials earn their taxpayer-funded salaries. She began to draw sharp distinctions between what she would do—work hard to improve the lives of the people of central Pennsylvania—and the coasting downhill toward retirement that her opponent apparently planned to do. She insisted upon speaking with straightforward honesty rather than cloaking her responses with vague generalities designed to offend as few people as possible, a trait her own advisers as well as her opponent's people considered a weakness until, astonishingly, she began gaining in the polls. By October she had closed the gap to single digits, but while her party leadership was pleased that her inexplicable rise had forced the Republican party to invest money into a campaign that a few months earlier was considered a sure thing, they still expected her to lose.

Late at night on the second Tuesday in November, Gwen won the election by two percent of the vote. Pollsters declared that the incumbent had been undone by complacency: He had not campaigned vigorously because he had not faced a serious challenge since his first campaign and had never perceived Gwen Sullivan as a serious threat. The national party leadership had not pumped additional money into his campaign in the final days because a loss in the twenty-second district was inconceivable and they couldn't afford to divert funds from closer, more urgent races. Most significant of all, his loyal supporters had believed his confident predictions of certain victory and had stayed home in droves. If Gwen had challenged her opponent in a presidential election year when voter turnout was higher, she might not have stood a chance, but her message resonated with enough new and disgruntled voters to put her over the top.

For a while, bemused pundits asked themselves how a single-mother, liberal college professor who advocated gun control and green energy could have unseated a longtime incumbent backed by the GOP, NRA, and FOX in rural central Pennsylvania. For a while, they floated theories about idealistic young voters and tossed around new buzzwords like "pizza dads" and "minivan moms." But eventually they found something else to talk about, and Gwen went to Washington and got to work.

She kept her promises, too, and two years later she won re-election by a five-point margin, and by twice that two years later, until she began to joke that she had become the longtime incumbent she had once unseated. Her friends assured her she resembled him only in longevity. She never took her position for granted, never pretended to believe anything she didn't in order to win a vote or a donation. When she finally retired from Congress after five successful terms, having achieved most of the goals she had set to accomplish so many years before, Waterford College begged her to return to the faculty. She missed academic life, so she accepted their offer and taught for one last, celebratory year before retiring for good. After spending the summer at Elm Creek Manor—for the first time, enjoying camp as a quilter and artist in residence rather than as a teacher—she moved out to Palo Alto to be closer to Summer, her son-in-law, and her grandchildren. There, though ostensibly retired, she wrote her memoirs and several children's books about American political history. She had left public office, she often declared, but she wasn't going to settle for being a spectator on the sidelines ever again.

But her days of door-to-door campaigning were over, not because she didn't care about causes, but because her knees weren't up to the task. Sarah watched as Gwen rose stiffly from her chair, leaning heavily on her cane. "I'll help Anna and Gina in the kitchen," she said, "but I'll take a few unsigned quilt blocks and pens with me. If anyone comes by for a snack, I'll hit them up for a signature."

"Thanks, Gwen," said Sarah.

"I'll join you, Mom," said Summer, bounding up from her seat on the armrest.

As the mother and daughter left the library, Sarah distributed unsigned Memory Album blocks and pens to the rest of her friends and reminded them which guests they still needed to call upon. This time luck was with them, and by the time Anna and Gina called everyone for dinner, for the first time Sarah hid more signed blocks than unsigned in the desk drawer.

Supper was another culinary triumph spent in the warm company of cheerful, loving friends and family. Sarah's heart swelled with happiness as she watched Caroline and Leo together, so joyful, so perfectly at ease, so very much in love. Leo would be good to her daughter, she realized, and Caroline would never take him for granted. For a moment, she forgot the stress of wedding preparations and simply watched her daughter and loved her, and felt her misgivings ebbing away. They were not too young. They knew their hearts and minds, and surely Caroline, at least, had no illusions that the love they felt that day would endure through the years without attentive care.

A sense of reassurance and peace fell upon her, easing her troubled heart. Later that night, for the first time in weeks she drifted off to sleep without running through her mental to-do list and working herself into such a state of worry that she couldn't justify going to sleep until she crossed off one more item.

The moon had set and Matt was snoring softly beside her when she woke, disoriented, to the sound of footfalls and muffled laughter in the hall. Climbing out of bed and making her way carefully in the darkness, she opened the bedroom door to find James, Leo, and the other men of the bridal party in the hallway stealing toward the staircase, their shoes in their hands. She blinked at them dumbly for a moment, and then someone muttered, "Run!"

Choking on laughter, they made haste for the stairs, James bringing up the rear.

"James," she called in a stage whisper, stepping into the hallway and shutting the door behind her. "James, don't you dare pretend you don't hear me."

Reluctantly, James slowed to a walk as the other young men disappeared down the staircase.

"What is going on?" Sarah asked, striding toward him. "Why aren't you boys in bed?"

James looked pained, as if he were mulling over the wisdom of telling her the truth. "We're going out."

"Going out? At this hour? Where?"

He held up his hands in a placating gesture. "We aren't doing anything stupid. We're just going downtown for a night out with the guys."

Her suspicions soared. "This is it, isn't it? The bachelor party."

"Yes, Mom, it's a bachelor party." He glanced over his shoulder, but the other young men had long since departed. "And if you keep me here to debate it, they're going to leave without me, and not only am I the most responsible of the crew, I'm also the designated driver." He folded his arms across his chest and regarded her, and after a moment, she realized he was unconsciously imitating her own posture. "Well?"

She shoved her hands into the pockets of her nightgown. "Go ahead," she whispered. "Keep them out of trouble! Especially Leo." When he nodded and turned to go, she caught him by the arm. "And no strip clubs."

"He's marrying my sister," James exclaimed, a little too

loudly. "Do you really think I'd let him do anything that would upset her?"

Sarah shook her head. No, of course he wouldn't. She released his arm, and he gave her a quick kiss on the cheek before hurrying off after the other young men. She returned to her room, unsettled and wide awake, and climbed carefully into bed to avoid waking Matt. James was the most trustworthy person she knew. If he said they weren't going to do anything stupid, he meant it. Besides, he was twenty-five, and Leo and most of the groomsmen were a few years older. If they were intent upon a night of wild abandon, there was very little she could do to prevent it.

She resisted the urge to sit in the kitchen nursing a cup of herbal tea and watching through the window until she saw headlights crossing the bridge over Elm Creek, as she had during the twins' high school years whenever they were out late. Somehow she managed to fall asleep, but in the morning, worry overcame fatigue and shook her awake early. Matt slumbered on, oblivious to the night's adventures, so she climbed gingerly from bed to shower and dress. He stirred as she left the room, and mumbled something about the orchards, but when he rolled onto his side and sank back into sleep, she closed the door without a sound.

Downstairs, she peered out the back door, relieved to see all the vehicles present and accounted for. She put on a pot of coffee and glanced at Anna's meal planner notebook lying open on the counter, wondering if she should start breakfast and deciding that she could at least wash apples and peel oranges for the fruit salad. Anna and Gina soon arrived, and as the mother and daughter cheerfully accepted her offer to help, Sarah resisted the urge to ask Gina if she knew where the young men had gone the night before, and what time they had returned.

She expected, and feared, that they would lie abed all morning and creep downstairs at noon, bleary-eyed and clutching their pounding skulls, desperate for a hangover remedy. To her surprise, the young men showed up for breakfast not much later than usual, joking and grinning and hungry for waffles and scrambled eggs. Later, after the dishes had been cleared away, Sarah caught James lacing up his running shoes on the back stairs and dragged the story out of him. The young men had spent a few hours at the Wolves' Den, a campus bar whose name referred to the Waterford College mascot rather than the sort of wild bacchanalia one might seek for a bachelor party. They shot some pool, drank a few beers, talked, and utterly destroyed a group of frat boys in a Vertex soccer match on the big screen. "Knowing the boss of the guy who wrote the app gave us something of an edge," James said, grinning. "Michael adds cheat codes not even his programmers know about until the players talk them up online."

"So no one got trashed."

He stifled a laugh. "No one's gotten 'trashed' in fifteen years, Mom."

"You know what I mean." Sarah tried to remember the word the kids used. "No one got blonked."

He put his hands on her shoulders and looked her in the eye. "No one got blonked," he assured her, "and if they had, I would have gotten them home safely. You know you can trust me."

"I trust you," she said. "And I hope you trust me."

"Of course I do," he said, surprised.

"Then tell me, what's really going on with you and Gina?"

He released her shoulders and inched a step backward, suddenly wary. "Why? What have you heard?"

"Nothing, which is why I'm asking you."

He glanced at his watch. "Sorry, Mom. No time to talk. I have to go now or I won't be back in time for . . . stuff. Wedding stuff." With a wave, he darted off at a pace more suitable for a sprint than a cross-country run.

"You can't evade the question forever," she called after him as he raced over the bridge. Sighing, she went back inside, narrowly avoiding a collision with Caroline in the back foyer.

"Anna said I'd find you outside," said Caroline, relieved. "Can you help me, Mom?"

"Sure, honey. What is it?"

Caroline took her by the arm and led her down the west wing toward the front foyer. "I'm having trouble finding something to wear tomorrow."

"Okay," said Sarah, eyeing her daughter curiously as Caroline led the way up the grand oak staircase. "This is just a suggestion, but why not wear that beautiful wedding gown you picked out a few months ago?"

Caroline managed a laugh. "I'm definitely wearing the gown, but I need a few things to wear with it or carry. Something old, something new, something borrowed, and something blue."

" 'And a silver sixpence in her shoe,' " Sarah completed the Victorian rhyme. "Sweetheart, you don't have to follow that tradition. It's meant to bring good luck, but you're not superstitious and I know you can't really be worried about warding off evil spirits."

"Of course not, but I'd like to follow the tradition anyway. Didn't you?"

Sarah had, in fact. Brides wore or carried something old to represent their families and continuity with the past, and so Sarah had carried a beautiful lace handkerchief her grandmother had given her. Her wedding gown had counted as something new, a symbol of hope for a bright future, success, optimism, and the new union she and Matt would create together. A bride borrowed something to remind her that she would be able to rely on friends and family throughout her married life, and accordingly, Sarah had borrowed a rhinestone tiara from her best friend, had attached a fingertip veil and white silk roses, and had worn it as her headpiece. The baby blue lace trim on her garter had sufficed for something blue, which represented purity, faithfulness, and loyalty.

"Your gown is something new," Sarah mused as they paused outside Caroline's room, "and the antique silver belt is something old. Finding something blue is usually the biggest challenge."

"I have that covered," said Caroline. "Dad's going to weave a beautiful dark blue ribbon into my bouquet."

It didn't sound like Caroline needed Sarah's help after all, since all that remained was something borrowed. "You could borrow some earrings from one of your friends."

"No, I want to wear the pearl earrings Leo gave me last Christmas." Caroline fixed her with a tentative, hopeful smile. "According to tradition, it's important for a bride to borrow something from a happily married person, so that she can carry some of that person's marital bliss into her own marriage. I'd like to borrow something from you."

Sarah hesitated. "Why me?"

Caroline laughed, surprised by the question. "Why not? You're my mom, and you're happily married. Right?" she asked, suddenly concerned.

"Of course I am," replied Sarah quickly. "Well, let me think." And then, suddenly, she knew the perfect piece to lend to her daughter.

She took Caroline's hand and led her farther down the hall to the room Sarah and Matt shared. An old jewelry box the size and shape of a small cabinet sat upon the bureau, and as Caroline seated herself upon the bed and absently traced the outline of the Hands All Around block in the sampler quilt, Sarah withdrew a shallow, rectangular case from a lower drawer. Sitting down beside her daughter, she lifted the lid, smiling as Caroline gasped at the sight of the beautiful pearl necklace.

"These belonged to Sylvia," said Sarah, gently removing the pearls from the case and unfastening the clasp. Her eyes widening, Caroline drew her blond curls out of the way as Sarah fastened the pearls around her neck. "She wore them on the day she married her first husband, James, the man your brother is named after. Sylvia's mother wore them on her wedding day too. They belonged to her own grandmother, who might have worn them as a bride herself, for all I know." Sarah smiled. "Perhaps then, so long ago, they were her 'something new.' "

Caroline rose and went to the mirror above the bureau, her mouth slightly open in astonishment as she admired them in the reflection. "They're so beautiful. Why don't you ever wear them?"

Sarah laughed. "Caroline, honey, those pearls are very precious. That's not a necklace I can throw on for a day at quilt camp."

"Then you should definitely add some special occasions to your social calendar so you'll have an excuse to wear them." Caroline turned, beaming, and flung her arms around Sarah. "Thank you so much, Mom. They're perfect. They'll even complement my earrings."

"And they qualify as something borrowed. Someday they'll be yours, of course—"

"Oh, Mom, don't talk like that."

"Don't talk like what?"

"Don't bring up your—you know, your mortality, not the day before my wedding."

"I'm not bringing it up. I'm only letting you know that someday—" The sight of Caroline's unhappy frown cut her short. "Very well. Please borrow my pearl necklace and consider the tradition satisfied. I want them back in perfect condition for all the balls I'll attend throughout the upcoming social season."

"Absolutely," said Caroline, her good humor immediately restored. Reluctantly, she lifted her hair again so that Sarah could remove the necklace, and after returning it to the velvet-lined case, she thanked Sarah again and carried it off to her room, hugging it to her heart.

Sarah watched her go, smiling fondly, thinking of how happy Sylvia would have been to see Caroline wearing the pearls, a beloved and rare heirloom from her mother's side of the family. Sylvia had left nearly all of her family heirlooms to Sarah along with the estate, and like Caroline, Sarah had hated to hear Sylvia talk about her eventual passing and had changed the subject whenever it arose. She knew Sylvia intended her to be her heir, but Sarah avoided any discussion of the details.

One day shortly after her ninetieth birthday, Sylvia had enough of Sarah's nonsense, as she called it, and summoned her onetime apprentice for a frank and difficult discussion of her affairs. Sarah had no choice but to listen to Sylvia's instructions, nodding and blinking away tears as Sylvia told her the location of her private papers, the contact information for her lawyer, and the documents pertaining to her burial, which, ever efficient, she had arranged in advance.

"There," Sylvia declared when she had finished. "That wasn't so bad, now, was it?"

"Yes, it was," retorted Sarah, sniffing and dabbing at her eyes with the cuff of her blouse. "You know I hate to think of this kind of stuff."

Sylvia gazed heavenward. "Refusing to discuss 'this kind of stuff' won't prevent it from happening. But now the unpleasant task is done, and you're free to think of something else."

Sarah nodded and gulped air.

"Sarah, dear." Sylvia clasped her hand. "Please don't be unhappy. This day comes to us all. Remember what I told you when I wrote my will so many years ago, after I suffered the stroke?"

Sarah nodded, for she had never forgotten her beloved friend and mentor's words. "I need to know that the estate will be cared for when I'm no longer here to see to it myself," Sylvia had told Sarah, with all their friends standing witness. "I need someone who understands that the true value of Elm Creek Manor doesn't reside in its price per acre. You are that person."

The memory of Sylvia's plainspoken praise warmed Sarah's heart, and in a sudden upswell of love for her friend, she realized that her sorrow was nothing next to the deep and profound gratitude she felt for Sylvia, who had shared her life, her home, and her history generously for as long as Sarah had known her, asking nothing in return.

Well, that was not entirely true.

"Why are you smiling?" asked Sylvia. "Not that I wish to discourage you."

"I was thinking of the day we met."

"Oh, not that," said Sylvia, exasperated. "Why would you want to remember that day? I was thoroughly unpleasant to you."

"Yes, you were." Sarah still remembered the heat and humidity of the day, oppressive in downtown Waterford, where she had concluded another dismal job interview, less so in the cool shade of the elms surrounding the manor. "You had hired the landscape architecture company Matt was working for, and they had sent him out to take photos of the grounds. You were cranky—"

"Because Matt was late."

"As a matter of fact, we were five minutes early, which was pretty good considering how difficult it is to find Elm Creek Manor when you've never been here. You called me 'Uh, Sarah'—"

"That was how you introduced yourself. 'I'm—uh, Sarah. I'm Matt's wife.' Honestly, I don't know why you would want to make this particular trip down memory lane."

"You offered me a glass of lemonade, and when I accepted, you told me to get it myself because you weren't going to wait on me." She had to laugh as Sylvia waved her hands as if to ward off embarrassment. "Then you whisked Matt away to take the photos and left me behind in the kitchen."

"And you decided to go exploring."

Sarah nodded, remembering how she had wandered into a sunny, pleasant sitting room, larger and wider than the kitchen, with overstuffed furniture arranged by the windows and before the fireplace, and cheerful watercolor landscapes on the walls. A small sewing machine had sat on a nearby table, a chair pulled aside as if someone had left it only moments before. On the largest sofa Sarah had discovered a beautiful quilt, which she had unfolded for a better look. Small diamonds of all shades of blue, purple, and green had been joined into eight-pointed stars on a soft ivory background. Tiny stitches had formed smaller diamonds within each colorful piece, and the lighter fabric was covered with a flowing, feathery pattern, all made from unbelievably small, even stitches. A narrow, leafy vine of deep emerald green meandered around the edges, framing the delicate stars in foliage. She would have admired the quilt longer, had Sylvia not suddenly reappeared and scolded her.

"I thought you might spill lemonade on my quilt," Sylvia made an excuse.

"I wouldn't have."

"Well, I didn't know you then. For all I knew, you might have been a very reckless and irresponsible young woman."

"Yes, I'm sure that's exactly the impression I made in my best business suit and sensible heels."

Sylvia laughed and removed her glasses to wipe a tear from the corner of her eye. "Oh, I'm utterly ashamed of myself. I can't think of a single word to say in my own defense. I was a dreadful hostess, I freely confess. And yet you came to work for me anyway."

"Matt wanted me to, and I needed a job." But they both knew those were not the only, nor the most compelling, reasons Sarah had accepted Sylvia's offer to work as her assistant, helping her prepare for a sale that, thankfully, never happened. "I fell in love with that beautiful quilt, and I knew you could teach me to make one of my own."

"And so I did." Sylvia's gaze was far away. "I wonder whatever became of that quilt."

"It's on the bed in one of the third-floor suites," Sarah said. "Do you want it?"

"No, dear. That's exactly where it should be, offering warmth and comfort to our guests." Sylvia gave Sarah's hand a brisk pat and smiled, and with that affectionate gesture all the lingering unhappiness between them broke and fell away.

In the time that followed, their friendship endured and thrived. Sarah cared for Sylvia in her sunset years, and she was among the few at Sylvia's bedside when she passed away at the age of ninety-three, peacefully, her hand in Andrew's. Hundreds of friends, colleagues, and former students came to Elm Creek Manor for her memorial service, but only those closest to her attended her burial in the small family plot in the old cemetery on Church Street. Melissa, her brother, and their spouses flew out from California to pay their respects, and Sarah was touched to see how genuinely saddened they were by her passing. Sylvia had been their sole link to their Bergstrom ancestors, and although they had known her only briefly, they would be forever grateful that she had mended the broken chain.

Andrew took the loss of his beloved wife harder than anyone, and although Sarah and her friends did what they could to comfort him, he was bereft and lonely. Without Sylvia, Elm Creek Manor no longer felt like home to him. If he had not sold his RV, he might have driven away, traveling coast to coast as he had after his first wife's death, until the solitude of the road eased his grief. Instead he accepted his son and daughter-in-law's long-standing invitation to join them in California. They found him a condo in a retirement community near their residence in Santa Susana, and a month after Sylvia's death, he packed his belongings and moved away. It was a tearful parting, and Sarah promised Andrew that they would keep a room for him if he ever decided to return, but she suspected he would not. She hoped that in time, the sunny skies of Southern California and the cheerful company of his granddaughters would temper the sharpness of his grief.

Andrew departed a few days before Sylvia's will was released. Sarah had expected a dramatic scene in the lawyer's office in which all the relevant parties gathered to hear a formal reading of the will, but apparently that happened only in the movies. Thus she learned by certified mail that, except for a few quilts and other possessions Sylvia wanted set aside for the Elm Creek Quilters and other cherished friends, Sylvia had bequeathed almost her entire estate—the grounds, the manor, and almost all of her possessions—to Sarah. Sylvia returned the Postage Stamp quilt Elizabeth had made to Melissa, and had also left her a few Bergstrom family heirlooms and her twenty percent share in Elm Creek Quilts.

Only Sarah owned so large a share; the other Elm Creek Quilters with a stake in the company each owned ten percent. What Melissa would do in her role as part owner from so far away, Sarah could only guess, but it was likely that she would do little more than vote on crucial development matters, accept her portion of the profits, and perhaps enjoy a free week of quilt camp every so often. She might even wish to sell her share to other members of the permanent faculty, as Judy and Bonnie had done. Whatever Melissa decided, Sarah would help her.

Thus Matt's fears were proven groundless and Sarah's faith in Sylvia justified.

The lawyer's letter also stipulated an important task Sylvia had wanted Sarah to complete. In the bottom drawer on the right-hand side of her father's oak desk, Sylvia had left a list of cherished friends and special gifts she wished each of them to have in remembrance of her. Upstairs in the library, Sarah found a thick, padded envelope hidden beneath a box of empty file folders. As often as she had worked at that desk, she had never noticed it before, and it occurred to her that the drawer was an excellent hiding place she could use herself if she ever had anything important to keep out of sight.

The list, and Sylvia's expressions of affection and gratitude to the friends who had blessed her life with their companionship, support, laughter, honesty, and love, brought fresh tears to Sarah's eyes. To several of her favorite students and quilt campers, Sylvia had left sewing tools, pattern books, and quilts in progress, with the request that they finish the quilts, if they were so inclined, and think of her whenever they used them. To the other Elm Creek Quilters she had left quilts that each had especially admired, along with instructions to divide her fabric stash in an equitable fashion. "Perhaps you should let Gwen, with her proven skills for negotiation, determine the method," she had written, "and Diane, no complaints out of you, dear."

There were other gifts, simple and surprising and humorous and touching, and one in particular that Sarah knew would be gratefully received: Sylvia had left Matt the red banked barn Hans Bergstrom had built and several acres of land surrounding it adjacent to the orchards. Matt used the barn more than anyone, Sylvia had noted, and he had earned it.

The last two items on the list were the most surprising and the most unexpected. "Within a window seat up in the nursery," Sylvia had written, "you will find two wrapped boxes. The larger one is for Caroline, the smaller, for James. I was not blessed with grandchildren, Sarah, dear, but your twins are as precious to me as if they were my own, and I am grateful you allowed me to be such an important part of their childhood. My only regret is that I will not be here to witness all of the important milestones in their lives. I hope that these small gifts will help them to remember me on a particularly significant day. Please give these gifts to the twins on their wedding days with my love." A word was crossed out, and then Sylvia continued. "However, it is highly unlikely that they will marry on the same day, and I don't want it to seem as if I'm favoring one twin over the other. Therefore, you may give both gifts on the wedding day of the twin who marries first." Another crossed-out word followed. "It occurs to me that perhaps neither of them will choose to marry, and I don't wish to imply that they should or must. Gwen would certainly chastise me for that. If Caroline and James decide to remain single, please give them these gifts on their thirtieth birthday. There, that should do nicely."

Sarah smiled through her tears, the words so true to Sylvia's intonation that she could almost imagine she heard her friend's voice. She left the letter on the oak desk and headed upstairs to the nursery, a name James, Caroline, and Gina had dismissed as babyish, preferring the more dignified "playroom." More recently they had begun calling it the game room, and Sarah wistfully suspected that soon they would abandon play altogether. She wondered what they would do with the nursery then. It would be a shame if the spacious, well-lit room went to waste, but its remote spot on the third floor of the manor made it inconvenient for quilt camp activities.

On her way down the hall to the stairs, Sarah ran into Gretchen. Sarah told her about Sylvia's letter, and that Sylvia had wanted Gretchen to have her old Featherweight sewing machine in hopes that she would create an artistic masterpiece with it. Tears sprang into Gretchen's eyes. "She's so generous to think of me. She knew how much I admired her Featherweight."

"She remembered all of those dearest to her, even the twins." When Sarah explained that Sylvia had left gifts for Caroline and James in the playroom, Gretchen's curiosity was immediately piqued and she offered to help Sarah find them.

Upstairs, board games, books, and LEGOS were scattered on tables and floors, and someone had left the television on, still hooked up to the video-game system and merrily chirping electronic music. With an exasperated sigh, Sarah shut it off, wondering how long it had been playing to an empty room.

Each of the seats along the windows overlooking the front lawn lifted up to reveal a storage space beneath. Forgotten toddler toys and board books and dust bunnies filled most of them, but one had been scrupulously cleaned and cleared of everything except a plastic shopping bag from a downtown Waterford department store that had closed in the 1960s. Inside, Sarah and Gretchen discovered two boxes, one large and one small, each carefully wrapped and tied with ribbons. The tag on the larger box read "Caroline" in Sylvia's spindly handwriting, the other, "James."

"This feels like a book," mused Gretchen, turning James's gift over in her hands.

Sarah gave Caroline's gift a gentle shake, and the contents shifted an inch or two from one side of the box to the other. "I haven't a clue what this is." Carefully she pushed down on the top of the box. "It's soft. It could be a quilt."

Gretchen smiled. "It's almost certainly a quilt. Consider the source."

"I wonder . . ." Sarah inspected the paper and ribbons. "We could unwrap them very carefully, see what's inside, and wrap them up again—"

"Sarah," exclaimed Gretchen, scandalized. "The twins should receive their gifts exactly as they are, lovingly wrapped by Sylvia herself."

"But the twins are only ten," Sarah protested weakly, for she knew Gretchen was right. "They might not marry young or at all, and their thirtieth birthdays are twenty years away. Curiosity might kill me before then."

"It won't," said Gretchen firmly. "The years will pass more swiftly than you can imagine. You'll just have to be patient and tell yourself that one day you'll know what Sylvia left your children."

Gretchen fell silent, and her gaze dropped to James's gift, which she still held in her wrinkled, blue-veined hands. Sarah knew that Gretchen was thinking that she herself might never learn what Sylvia's lasts gift were. Sarah's throat tightened. She could not think of another loss, not so soon.

They returned the gifts to the bag and the bag to its hiding place in the window seat. Then they softly closed the door to the nursery—playroom, game room, who knew what incarnation it would take next. The years would unfold, and time would tell.

Sarah returned to the library and Sylvia's list. In the days that followed, she distributed Sylvia's gifts to those friends who resided in the manor, and called or wrote letters to those who did not. One by one the other gifts were claimed by grateful, tearful friends, students, and colleagues, and when each recipient came to the manor, they shared heartfelt, joyful memories of the master quilter they all loved and admired—and so Sarah, too, received another, wonderful gift from her departed friend, the gift of stories.

Sylvia's gifts for the twins had remained undisturbed for fifteen years, and in the interim the playroom had become Emily's studio. Gretchen was no longer with them and would not discover what the gifts were, a likelihood she and Sarah had both silently considered when they found the wrapped and ribbon-tied parcels in the window seat on that long-ago day.

Just as Gretchen had foretold, the years had passed swiftly, far too swiftly. The twins were grown, the time had come, and soon Sarah would know what her friend and mentor had left behind as a last, loving gift for her children.

· Chapter Seven ·

For Sarah, Friday morning passed in a blur of activity—decorating the ballroom for the reception, setting up chairs in the north gardens, folding programs, and delegating whatever tasks she could to any willing volunteer. To her relief, Carol took charge of welcoming guests, showing them to their rooms with cordial efficiency and making everyone feel at home. Lunch was a quick but tasty affair, a sandwich, soup, and salad buffet that Gina and Anna arranged on the front verandah. Then Sarah was glad to pause, catch her breath, and have a bite to eat. She sat on one of the old Adirondack chairs, munching a tuna salad and arugula wrap and sipping a mug of warm apple cider as she watched younger guests play soccer, croquet, and tag on the broad green lawn.

Balancing a mug of cider, a bowl of clam chowder, and a plate with a roast beef and provolone sub, a side of chips, and a pickle, Matt pushed a chair closer to hers with his foot and carefully sat down. "Save room for dessert," said Sarah. "Anna made pumpkin tartlets."

"I saw them," Matt replied, glancing back at the buffet table in anticipation. "That's why I took only a six-inch sub instead of a foot-long. Don't worry, I'll still fit into my tux tomorrow."

"I wasn't worried," Sarah assured him, amused. "I'm sure you've been working up an appetite putting the gardens in order. How do they look?"

"Exactly as Caroline wanted them, but they'll never be as beautiful as the bride." Matt gazed out at the front yard, where Caroline was playing freeze tag with Leo's younger cousin, coltishly lovely in a comfortable pair of jeans and a forest green Dartmouth sweatshirt. Her golden hair shone in the autumn sun, and her laughter rang out, clear and happy. Sarah and Matt exchanged a smile, proud and wistful.

"They grew up so much faster than I expected," said Matt. "Remember when they were babies and everyone always told us to enjoy every minute, even while we were up to our elbows in diapers and a good night's sleep was nothing but a fond memory?"

"They were right."

"They were right," affirmed Matt. "I can't believe it's been twenty-five years."

"The days were long, but the years were short." Sarah leaned back and smiled ruefully. "I miss those little babies. I miss my toddlers and my fifth graders and every stage in between and every one that followed."

"Remember how we always used to say, 'This is the perfect age. They're absolutely perfect just as they are.' And then a year later, we'd say, 'No, we were wrong; *this* is the perfect age. They're even more wonderful now.'"

"I remember," said Sarah. Then she laughed. "We'll probably say the same thing about our grandchildren."

"Probably."

They finished their lunches in the companionable silence of longtime spouses who could speak volumes with a single glance or the smallest gesture, watching the games on the lawn and wishing that time wouldn't pass so swiftly.

A month before the wedding, Sarah, the consummate organizer, had planned her schedule for the wedding week down to the last minute, allowing extra time for unforeseeable disasters both small and significant. Only then would she be certain to finish everything in time so that she could relax and enjoy the wedding day, with all the hard work behind her. An hour before the rehearsal, and only fifteen minutes behind her master schedule, Sarah crossed off the last item from her list of wedding preparation duties with great satisfaction and relief. There were other tasks, of course, that had to wait until the day of the ceremony, but Caroline and James had encouraged her to delegate those to her friends, the best man, and the bridesmaids. Caroline had also made her promise that she would not spend Saturday morning going from one helper to the next, making sure everything would be done properly and on time. "This isn't quilt camp," Caroline had reminded her after supper on the day of her arrival. "You don't have to manage everything. You're the mother of the bride, not the wedding planner."

"We don't have a wedding planner, and mother of the bride or not, I'm the hostess, not a guest," Sarah had pointed out. "I can't sit down, put my feet up, and swill a cocktail until I'm sure everything is perfect."

"It's not going to be perfect," Caroline had told her firmly. "It's going to be lovely and I'll be very happy, and I say that knowing that it's not going to be perfect. Things are going to go wrong—"

"Not with the rehearsal dinner or the wedding supper," Gina broke in cheerfully. "And definitely not with the cake."

"Okay, the food will probably be perfect," amended Caroline, amused. "But things are going to go wrong, and that's okay. I refuse to be upset if the napkins are the wrong color or if we run out of wedding favors, and you should too."

Sarah agreed to try, finding it an odd sort of role reversal that the bride was delivering that speech to her mother instead of the other way around.

At four o'clock in the afternoon, the wedding party and the bride's and the groom's immediate families gathered in the north gardens for the rehearsal. Despite the early hour, the crisp sunshine of the day was waning as gray clouds pillowed in the western sky. The wind had picked up, scattering fallen leaves over the carefully swept stones.

"We all knew we were taking a chance on an outdoor wedding in September, in Pennsylvania," said Carol, shivering in her thin sweater as Sarah led her to her seat in the front row. "Still, I suppose it's better than if they had eloped."

The minister began with a brief, cordial welcome, glancing frequently at the skies. "We'll finish before the rain falls," he promised. The minister walked them through the ceremony, explaining the different elements with gracious good humor, and even the six-year-old ring bearer and four-year-old flower girl, Leo's nephew and niece, listened carefully so that they wouldn't miss a word. Thunder rumbled low in the distance as the minister asked them to take their places for a quick run-through, and everyone quickly obeyed. A few ladies clutched their hats as a gust of wind swept through the garden, making the evergreens sway and sending autumn leaves swirling.

"I should have waited until tomorrow morning to set out the chairs," Matt said in an undertone as he passed Sarah on his way to line up for the procession with Caroline. Sarah silently agreed. Setting up the chairs early had been the twenty-second item on her to-do list—which, like Caroline's choice of an outdoor wedding, depended upon fair weather. She prayed that the storm would blow over—but if it didn't, the following morning she would muster up a team of teenagers, arm them with towels, and send them out to dry off the chairs so their guests wouldn't be forced to sit in puddles of rainwater.

She didn't want to think about all the other plans that would have to change if the storm lasted throughout the next day.

Thunder rumbled again, closer. The minister climbed the stairs to the gazebo, turned to face them, and began. As James escorted Sarah to her seat in the front row on the left, she glimpsed the mother of the flower girl and ring bearer peer anxiously at the sky, clutch her husband's arm, and whisper urgently to him. Then Leo and his brother passed Sarah's chair on their way to join the minister in the gazebo. Sarah thought she heard the best man warn Leo that maybe the storm was a bad omen, and she watched in satisfaction as Leo paid him back with an elbow to the side.

Then the groomsmen escorted the bridesmaids down the aisle in pairs. James winked at Sarah as he passed, Gina on his arm, and he smiled when they parted at the steps of the gazebo and took their places on opposite sides of the aisle. "Ordinarily you'll process in at a more stately, moderate pace"—the minister paused for another, more insistent thunderclap—"but given the circumstances, we should move things along." He gestured for the ring bearer and flower girl to speed up, and after a moment of uncertainty, during which Sarah guessed they were weighing the minister's words against their mother's earlier exhortation that under no circumstances should they run, they beamed and scampered down the aisle.

Just as the minister motioned for everyone to rise, Sarah felt a cold, heavy drop of water splash on the back of her hand. It was just a bit of dew blown down from the treetops, she told herself, that was all. Her confidence faltered as Matt escorted Caroline down the aisle at a pace rivaling the young children's. Another gust of wind blew the minister's notes from his grasp, and then came the unmistakable tap of a raindrop on stone, followed by another, and as an exclamation of dismay went up from the bridal party, the taps quickened and became a staccato patter that drowned out the minister's suggestion that they seek shelter. Snatching up purses and wraps and cameras, everyone raced for the gazebo, crowding toward the center to escape the windblown rain. As soon as she had Carol safely under cover, Sarah worked her way through the crowd to Caroline's side, but words of comfort and reassurance faded on her lips when she found her daughter shaking water from her curls and laughing, not at all distressed. "I know you have a backup plan, Mom," she said. "You always have a backup plan."

"My backup plan was to move the rehearsal to the front foyer," said Sarah, eyeing the driving sheets of rain in consternation. In minutes the golden sunshine of midday had sunk into the cold steel-gray of dusk. "We can't ask people to run a quarter of a mile in this cloudburst."

"We'll wait it out," said Leo, putting his arm around Caroline and pulling her close. She smiled and shivered in the sudden chill, rubbing her bare arms for warmth. Quickly Leo pulled off his sweater and held it up, gesturing for Caroline to raise her arms so he could slip it over her head. She smiled and thanked him, and they both laughed to see how the sleeves completely hid her hands, and the bottom ribbing fell almost to her knees. She looked like a little girl playing dress-up, even as she briskly and efficiently made cuffs of the sleeves so she could hold Leo's hand. They were among the few who didn't mind the close quarters, but Sarah wished she had more breathing room and fewer elbows and knees bumping into hers. She was damp, cold, and uncomfortable, and her toes hurt from being trod upon in the mad dash to squeeze beneath the gazebo roof.

Lightning flashed and thunder rolled. Sarah alternately wished that someone within the manor would remember the rehearsal and come to their rescue with the dozens of umbrellas stored in the back hall closet for the quilt campers' use, and hoped that her friends would use common sense and stay inside out of the storm. After twenty minutes, the thunder quieted, the lightning flashed no more, and the downpour lessened to become a steady drizzle. Someone suggested dubiously that they make a run for it, but no one seemed eager to leave the shelter of the gazebo.

"Here comes a rescue team," called one of the groomsmen, and everyone turned to look where he pointed. Sarah glimpsed two tall figures in blaze-orange rain ponchos making their way into the garden, a bundle of umbrellas under each arm. As they approached the gazebo, she recognized Jeremy and Russell, and she joined in the chorus of thanks as they distributed the umbrellas. In pairs and trios, they hurried off to the manor, parents carrying children, grandsons offering their arms to grandparents while granddaughters held the umbrellas high enough to shelter them all.

Anna and Maggie met them in the foyer with soft, thick towels, and after removing their wet shoes and drying off as best they could, everyone but the bride, the groom, and their parents dispersed to change into dry clothes for dinner. "I suppose that's it for rehearsal," the minister remarked. "You seem like a smart bunch, though. I'm sure the walk-through will suffice."

The others chimed in their agreement, so Sarah refrained from suggesting that they practice one last time in the foyer when the bridal party returned downstairs for dinner. It didn't have to be perfect, she reminded herself, just as Caroline had said. As long as Caroline and Leo ended up happily married at the end of the day, it didn't matter if they processed in at the wrong pace or if shyness overcame the flower girl and she ran to her parents instead of accompanying her brother to the gazebo.

Matt offered the minister a change of clothes, too, but he declined, reminding them that he had been beneath the shelter of the gazebo roof when the rain began to fall and only his shoes and the cuffs of his trousers had gotten wet in the walk from the garden to the manor. Sarah showed him to the parlor and asked him to make himself at home until dinner, and then she, too, hurried upstairs to change.

Soon afterward, the bridal party, their families, and the minister gathered in the banquet hall for a delicious Italian banquet. Even though the dinner took place in Elm Creek Manor, in keeping with tradition, Leo's parents were the official hosts. Leo's mother had been delighted to discover that Anna was also of Italian heritage, and for the past several weeks they had corresponded almost daily as they collaborated and planned the menu. The antipasti course included bruschetta, slices of bread topped with diced tomato, olive oil, garlic, and herbs; fried squares of polenta; and a savory assortment of cheeses and cured meats. For the *primo piatto,* or first course, the guests enjoyed a delicious Italian wedding soup and small portions of *ravioli con burro e salvia,* ravioli with butter and sage, one of Leo's favorite dishes. Sarah was already quite full by that time, but she couldn't resist sampling a few bites of the grilled herb chicken with sautéed eggplant and green beans Anna and Gina served for the *secondo piatto*. For dessert, Gina offered the guests their choice of tiramisu or raspberry gelati. A few of the young men requested both, and since she and her mother had made more than enough for all, Gina was happy to comply.

As the guests enjoyed their desserts with coffee or tea or cocoa for the children, Leo's father rose and toasted the bride and groom, reminiscing fondly of the day Leo had told them that he had met the love of his life. Next Matt stood and raised his glass, choking up as he spoke of his beloved daughter and the time he first realized she had fallen in love. Leo's toast to the bride followed, and Sarah's eyes filled with tears as he spoke movingly of all that he cherished about Caroline, and all he intended to do to nurture their marriage for the rest of his life. He sat down to a crash of applause, and Caroline needed a few moments to compose herself before she rose and offered her own toast to her husband-to-be and both sets of parents. Beneath the table, Matt's hand closed around Sarah's as Caroline spoke. Their daughter smiled through her tears and said that she knew she had not always been the easiest child to raise—a confession that evoked a soft chorus of disbelieving murmurs—and that she was grateful for her parents' unconditional love, unwavering faith, and strong example of loving commitment they had set for her throughout her life. "I've found the man I want to spend the rest of my life with, and for that I feel truly blessed," she said. "I hope that our marriage will be as resilient, as strong, and as full of enduring love as those our parents enjoyed."

Matt smiled proudly, his gaze fixed on his daughter as he released Sarah's hand to join in the applause. Sarah felt her smile faltering as she, too, applauded, and she hoped anyone who might have witnessed her sudden distress would attribute it to the overwhelming emotions of the day. She felt a sharp pang of worry as she watched Caroline take her seat and accept Leo's kiss with a loving smile. She knew that some children idealized their parents' marriages, but that was not in Caroline's nature. Sarah and Matt's marriage was far from perfect, and although they had shielded the twins from their disagreements and difficulties, especially when they were very young, Sarah had never lied or pretended all was well when it was not. Had they protected the children too much? Caroline could not possibly realize how hard her parents had worked, and how they had sometimes struggled, or she would not wish for a marriage like theirs.

Sarah knew Matt would agree that, thanks in part to the

crises they had overcome together, their marriage was healthy, their expectations realistic, and their commitment strong. But that didn't mean Sarah wanted her daughter to hold up her parents' marriage as any sort of ideal, especially on the eve of her wedding. Sarah wished Caroline had not ended her toast with hopes that her marriage would resemble her parents'. Caroline should insist upon something much better from the very first, and not require the surmounting of obstacles to set her and Leo on the right path.

The applause faded and the buzz of conversation resumed as the guests finished their desserts and coffee. As the rehearsal dinner came to an end, Sarah joined Matt, Caroline, Leo, and his parents at the door to bid their friends and families good night. After the last guest departed, Sarah urged Caroline to go to bed early and rest up for the busy, momentous day ahead, but Caroline insisted upon helping Sarah, Anna, and Gina clear away the dishes and tidy the kitchen. Not to be outdone, Leo, James, and Matt joined in, too, and together they finished the work quickly.

Afterward, Sarah followed Caroline upstairs, wishing that they had found more time during the busy week of wedding preparations to spend alone together. She felt as if she had not prepared Caroline sufficiently, and yet she didn't know what she would have done differently, what wisdom she could impart at this late hour that would illuminate the path her daughter had chosen. But as she kissed her daughter good night, she felt urgently compelled to correct her daughter's grave misunderstanding about her parents' marriage. She would not have Caroline embark upon her new life with Leo guileless, mistaken, and unprepared.

"Caroline," she said. "Your toast—it was lovely, for the most part, but something you said troubles me."

Caroline looked surprised. "What do you mean?"

"You said that you hoped your marriage would be like mine and your father's." Sarah groped for the right words to express her dismay without worrying Caroline or criticizing Matt. "Marriage is hard work, sweetheart. Your father and I love each other very much, and we're very happy now, but it hasn't always been easy."

Caroline smiled, relieved. "Oh, that. I know that, Mom."

"No, I don't think you do. No one lives happily ever after. You have to work at it."

"I know, Mom," said Caroline, hugging her. "But you're the one who's mistaken. I didn't say I wanted my marriage to be exactly like yours—that would be impossible, anyway—but you and Dad do have a marriage worth admiring. You heard what I said in my toast, but did you really listen?"

"Of course I did. I heard every word."

"Are you sure? Because if you had, you would have heard that I admire your commitment and I consider it a wonderful example for Leo and me. I don't know the specific details of whatever conflicts you had, and I don't need to know—that's between you and Dad. What I do know is that you didn't just give up and walk away when times got tough. You talked things through and worked out your issues, and as a result, things were better than before. I said I hoped my marriage would be as resilient, as strong, and as full of enduring love as yours. Your marriage is all of those things, Mom, and I hope my marriage will be too."

Sarah did not know what to say. Overwhelmed with relief

and gratitude, her eyes filling with tears, she embraced her daughter, who had grown up wiser than Sarah had ever known.

The storm broke overnight, and in the morning the sun rose golden over the Elm Creek Valley in a clear, cloudless, ocean blue sky. Sarah had slept well, with Matt's arm around her, and she woke feeling calm and content.

After breakfast, Sarah gathered a group of teenagers and sent them out to the north gardens with armfuls of towels, instructing them to dry off the chairs and pick up any that had toppled over from the high winds. When Matt went out later to inspect the area around the gazebo, he returned with the good news that aside from a few fallen twigs and scattered leaves, which he had easily swept away, the gardens had not suffered any ill effects from the storm. Even most of the rainwater had dried, leaving only a few small puddles that would surely evaporate by the time the ceremony began. The white gingerbread of the gazebo amid the autumn blooms and evergreen foliage would be as lovely and picturesque a setting for a wedding as Caroline had hoped.

Later that morning, while Caroline spent time with her bridesmaids, Sarah and the Elm Creek Quilters gathered in the library for mimosas and reminiscing. Each of Sarah's friends had a favorite memory of Caroline to share, and soon Sarah was laughing and crying. "Don't make me cry now," Sarah begged, laughing as she wiped away tears. "If I'm crying already, just think what a mess I'll be at the ceremony."

"On the other hand," offered Summer, smiling sympathetically, "if you cry all your tears out now, you might not have any left by then."

Sarah didn't want to test that theory, for she suspected she had a limitless supply. But at least her tears were tears of joy.

As the Elm Creek Quilters chatted, they also organized the signed and unsigned blocks for the bride and groom's Memory Album quilt, reading off the names, sharing the heartfelt messages, and checking off guests on their master list. Despite the numerous false starts, mishaps, and distractions, they had collected signatures from all but a handful of the guests who were staying in the manor. All that remained were a few who had somehow unwittingly eluded them, and those friends and family members who lived close enough that they were coming in only for the day. Sarah was confident that with the help of the Elm Creek Quilters, she would be able to collect their signatures discreetly at the reception. Sarah couldn't imagine a lovelier first Christmas gift as a married couple than the Memory Album quilt would be. It wouldn't be the wedding quilt that Caroline had wished, too late, that she had made herself, but Sarah hoped it would forever remind the newlyweds of the joy and love they had felt on their wedding day.

At eleven Sarah met Caroline, Leo's mother, and the bridesmaids in the kitchen for an early lunch, but although the roasted autumn vegetable salads and goat cheese biscuits smelled delicious, Sarah could hardly eat a bite, and she observed that Caroline only nibbled at her biscuit and sampled a few bites of her salad. She seemed in good spirits, animated and lively, but her cheeks were flushed and her eyes bright, and every so often Sarah caught her pressing a hand to her waist as if to calm the nervous fluttering in her stomach. Sarah knew exactly how she felt, and she stayed close in case Caroline needed her.

After lunch the women climbed aboard the Elm Creek

Quilts shuttle for a trip to Sarah's favorite salon to have their hair, nails, and makeup done. The attentive staff played soothing music and served them iced fruit juices, sparkling water with lime, and hot herbal tea, and Sarah was pleased and relieved to see her daughter visibly relaxing. Caroline's friends amused and encouraged her with jokes and cheerful conversation, reminding Sarah of the Elm Creek Quilters, who never failed to support Sarah in times of need.

"Such a beautiful bride," Leo's mother murmured to Sarah as they watched the stylist brush out Caroline's soft golden curls. She choked up and dug in her purse for a tissue.

"You can't cry now," said Sarah, with alarm that was only partially feigned. "You'll mess up your makeup, and you'll make me cry too!"

They laughed together and managed to compose themselves, admiring Caroline and her lovely, vibrant, affectionate friends. Sarah couldn't imagine that a prettier or more charming group of bridesmaids had ever been assembled in the history of matrimony, but she was a bit biased.

Afterward, they climbed carefully back into the shuttle, determined not to tousle their hair or chip their manicures. Halfway home, with Gina at the wheel and bridesmaids chattering happily all around them, Caroline took Sarah's hand and offered her a small, tremulous smile. Sarah squeezed her hand—it felt small and cold in hers—and smiled encouragingly. "It'll be fine," she murmured as Caroline rested her head upon her shoulder. "Don't worry. Everything's going to be wonderful."

"But not perfect?"

Sarah laughed softly. "No, I can't promise you that, and you wouldn't believe me if I did."

At that Caroline's laugh rang out, pure and sweet and true.

Back at Elm Creek Manor, the bridesmaids went off to dress, promising Caroline they would meet her in the library as soon as they were ready. Sarah accompanied Caroline to her room and helped her into her wedding dress, a strapless, ivory silk organza gown with a draped tulle bodice, an embellished silver antique belt worn at the natural waist, and a swirling ballgown skirt. Caroline's eyes shone with gratitude and happiness as Sarah fastened Sylvia's beautiful pearls around her neck. The precious Bergstrom family heirloom provided the last, perfect touch to her wedding finery, and Sarah knew that Sylvia would have been pleased.

Matt knocked on the door and entered just as Sarah was making a last few adjustments to Caroline's headpiece. He had to clear his throat twice before he could speak. "You look beautiful, sweetheart," he managed to say.

She embraced him. "Thanks, Dad."

After Matt checked the hallway and assured them Leo was nowhere in sight, Caroline and Sarah hurried down the hall to the library, where the bridesmaids were to gather before the ceremony. The musicians had arrived and were setting up their instruments on the gazebo, Matt reported as they closed the French doors behind them. Guests were mingling on the verandah and making their way to the north gardens, Grandma Carol among them, reveling in the company of friends and family she had not seen in years—and Sarah knew that in her handbag she carried the remaining unsigned Memory Album blocks and several fabric pens. Anna had the dinner preparations well in hand, and although Gina had fussed with the wedding cake up until the last moment before she had to hurry off to change into her bridesmaid's gown, Anna had assured Matt that all would be ready in time. James was helping her.

Caroline laughed. "James is helping her? James, with no training as a pastry chef whatsoever?"

"I think he's mostly offering moral support," said Matt, "although he offered to carry the cake to the banquet hall too."

"It's good of him to help, but I wanted him to meet us here before the bridesmaids arrived," said Sarah, glancing at the clock.

Just then, one of the French doors opened and James entered, right on time. His eyes went to his sister, and he beamed proudly. "You look amazing," he said, crossing the room and kissing her cheek. "Leo's going to pass out when he sees you."

Caroline feigned offense. "You mean I look so bad on an ordinary day that he's going to collapse from shock to see me like this?"

James nodded solemnly. "That's exactly what I mean." He snorted, struggling to keep a straight face, and the twins burst out laughing.

"I don't know how Gina puts up with you." Caroline flung her arms around her brother and kissed him on the cheek. "Even so, I know your wedding day is going to be as happy as mine."

James let out a sigh of mild exasperation. "Caroline—"

"Oops." Caroline released her brother and covered her mouth with her fingertips. "I'm sorry, James, I'm sorry."

Sarah and Matt exchanged a startled glance. "What's this?" asked Matt. "Caroline, you're speaking theoretically, right?"

Caroline raised her palms to fend off any more questions. "I'm not saying another word."

Sarah whirled upon her son. "James, are you and Gina—" She gasped as James nodded. "You're engaged? Oh, James, that's wonderful!"

She embraced him, and James said, "We wanted to keep it a secret until after Caroline and Leo's honeymoon."

"I'm sorry," Caroline said again, with uncharacteristic meekness.

"Congratulations, son," said Matt, hugging him. "Gina's a lovely girl."

"Thanks, Dad." James looked from Matt to Sarah. "Please don't say anything to anyone. Anna and Jeremy don't know yet."

"Actually, they do," said Caroline. "Gina slipped up yesterday when Anna was helping her balance the layers of the wedding cake. She was thinking aloud about what she would do differently for her own cake, and Anna pounced and dragged the truth out of her."

"I knew something was going on." Sarah slapped James lightly on the shoulder. "Why didn't you tell me when I asked? Why the secrecy?"

"We didn't want to steal Caroline and Leo's thunder," explained James.

"That wasn't our idea," Caroline declared, looking from her mother to her father and back. "Leo and I told them it would be fine with us if they announced their good news, but they insisted on keeping quiet."

"We had another good reason," said James, smiling at Sarah. "We also didn't want you to have to think about another wedding so soon."

Sarah clapped a hand to her forehead. "Oh, no, let's not do that. Not yet." Her thoughts were in a whirl—Caroline, about to marry, and James, newly engaged—it was indeed an occasion for rejoicing, and if Sylvia were there, Sarah knew she would agree.

"Kids, would you please have a seat for a moment?" Sarah asked, gesturing toward the sofa. "I want a few minutes alone with you two before the bridesmaids arrive."

"Uh-oh," said James, shooting his twin sister a sidelong glance as they sat down, and for a brief instant they both seemed very young. "Whatever it was, I didn't do it."

"No, it's nothing like that," said Sarah. From behind the desk she retrieved the old department store shopping bag that she had brought down from Emily's studio earlier that morning. "I think you'll find this is a good surprise."

She handed Caroline the larger ribbon-tied gift, and James the smaller. "This is Sylvia's handwriting," said James in surprise as he examined the tag.

Sarah nodded. "These gifts are from Sylvia. She loved you two very much."

"And we loved her," said Caroline, and James nodded. "I wish she could be here to share this day with us."

"She wished that too." Sarah bit her lip to keep from tearing up again. "But since she couldn't, she chose these special gifts and hid them away with instructions to give them to you on the wedding day of the first of you to marry, or your thirtieth birthday, whichever came first."

"I bet you wish it had been the latter," said Caroline wryly.

"As it happens, you're wrong," Sarah countered. It was true. For the first time, Sarah felt as if everything was unfolding precisely as it should, and at the perfect time. "I'm happy that I don't have to wait another day. You don't know how many times I was tempted to unwrap these gifts, satisfy my curiosity, and wrap them up again."

"Mom," the twins admonished in unison.

"You never would have known," Sarah pointed out, laughing. "But now the time has come, and you can open them yourselves. That's what Sylvia wanted."

The twins needed no further inducement. Caroline carefully untied her ribbon as if planning to save it, but James snapped his in two with a firm tug and tore off the paper. "It's a book," he said thoughtfully, turning over a small leather-bound volume in his hands. Sarah glimpsed neither a title nor the author's name on the cover or spine.

Forgetting her own gift for the moment, Caroline leaned closer to her brother as he opened the cover. "It's Sylvia's writing, all of it," she exclaimed as he flipped through the pages. Suddenly a folded piece of white paper fluttered from the book to the floor. Quicker than her brother, Caroline snatched it up. "I bet it's a letter."

"Caroline," said Sarah mildly.

With a contrite smile, Caroline handed the note to James. He unfolded it and read it through silently once before reading it aloud. "'Dear James,'" he began. "'I wish I could be there to enjoy this special day with you, but since I cannot, I hope this small token of my love will help you to remember me fondly. I remember when you were in second grade, and you begged me to let you read my great-great-aunt's memoir, which you had heard your mother and me discuss many times. I granted your request, but I made you promise to take very good care of it. You may recall that I required you to wash your hands carefully before you held the book, and I allowed you to read it only in the library and to take it nowhere else. I still smile when I think of you sitting at my father's old oak desk, your legs dangling off the edge of the chair with your feet several inches above the ground.'" James paused, smiling. "I remember Sylvia's clean-hands inspections very well."

"I remember being amazed that a second-grade boy would be willing to scrub his hands so well just to read a book," Matt remarked.

"That wasn't just any book," James reminded him, returning his gaze to the letter. "Sylvia then says, 'Seeing how captivated you were by Gerda's memoir, it occurred to me that you might also be interested in my story. Thus I began writing my own memoir, from my earliest childhood memories through the present day. I won't claim that my tale is as exciting as Gerda's, but I think it is nonetheless a significant part of the history of the Bergstrom family and of Elm Creek Manor, and I know that both are very important to you. I'm entrusting my chronicle to you, my dear James. One day, I believe, your mother will entrust the future of Elm Creek Manor to you. It is only fitting that you should also be the steward of its rich history. Be a good boy. Yours most affectionately, Sylvia Bergstrom Compson Cooper.'"

"Sylvia wrote a memoir," breathed Sarah. She could only imagine what riches it would offer—untold stories of the Bergstrom children, Sylvia's parents, her time in exile from Elm Creek Manor, and her impressions of the manor's transformation into a world-renowned artist's retreat. What a treasure Sylvia had given her son!

"It would seem so." James smiled, and his eyes shone. "I promise I'll let you read it when I've finished."

"If you wash your hands first," Caroline added, and they all laughed, and for a moment it seemed as if Sylvia were among them, laughing along and enjoying their happiness. Then Caroline started, as if she had only just remembered the unwrapped box resting on her lap. She lifted the white cardboard lid, brushed aside layers of tissue paper, and gasped. "It's a quilt." She took the soft, folded bundle from the box and stood, and Sarah quickly stepped forward to help her unfold it.

Then Sarah, too, gasped as recognition struck her. Sylvia's gift was a Double Wedding Ring quilt in a gradation of pink and green hues, embellished with floral appliqués—the reproduction of the beautiful, long-lost quilt the women of the Bergstrom family had made for Sylvia's beloved cousin Elizabeth.

The letter Sylvia included with the quilt explained everything, how Elizabeth had taken the original quilt with her when she moved to California as a new bride, how it had been mysteriously lost, and how a photograph of the quilt had been discovered in a book. When the original quilt could not be found, Sylvia and Melissa decided to collaborate on two versions of the quilt, one for each of them, but over time Melissa had lost interest in the project, so Sylvia had finished hers alone. "You may not remember this, my darling Caroline," Sylvia had written, "but when you were young, you often watched me as I worked upon this quilt, and I knew how much you admired it. One day you asked me, very sweetly, if I would please make a quilt just like it for you when you became a bride like Elizabeth. I told you I would try my very best to do so, but even then my fingers were failing me, and I soon realized that this would be my last quilt. And so it is, and so, my dear, it is yours. I hope your marriage is blessed with love and happiness, and when you and your new husband sleep beneath this quilt, I pray it brings you good, peaceful dreams."

Caroline's eyes brimmed with tears as she reached the last lines. A hush fell over the library, and after a long moment, Caroline folded the letter and returned it to the envelope. They all admired the quilt, Sylvia's last masterpiece, knowing that every stitch had been sewn with love.

"Leo will appreciate this very much," Caroline said at last, softly. "I wish he had known Sylvia."

"He'll know her," said James. "He'll know her through the stories of her you'll tell."

Caroline nodded, and she seemed cheered by the thought. Just then, there was a clamoring of laughter and voices in the hall outside the library, and then the French doors swung open and the bridesmaids burst in, lovely in their burgundy silk sheath gowns. Gina led them inside, her eyes bright and happy, her smile deepening as her gaze fell upon James. Soon there would be another wedding at Elm Creek Manor, Sarah thought, and she almost laughed aloud thinking of how much fun she and Anna would have planning it together.

James greeted Gina with a kiss, and then he and Matt had to hurry off for the north gardens to prepare for the ceremony. Caroline's friends immediately surrounded her, showering her with praise and admiration, assurances and embraces. Sarah wished, for a moment, that she could be alone with her daughter one last time, so she could tell her that her wedding day didn't mark a happily ever after, a still life frozen in time at a moment of perfect happiness. Instead it would mark the day she and Leo began to create something new and potentially wonderful together, piecing together love and promises and mistakes and laughter and tears and little things like cooking breakfast together and life-changing moments like the birth of their children—sickness and health, good times and bad, all stitched together with hope and commitment, forgiveness and love. The union of their shared lives could be a masterpiece, even if the colors of one piece clashed with another, even if uneven stitches showed, even if, from time to time, they had to pick out seams, realign the pieces, and sew them back together again. It would not be perfect, but it could be beautiful, if they worked together and persevered. Sarah longed to tell Caroline all this, but she could not find the words for all she wanted her daughter to know. And yet she knew, too, that Caroline had already learned all Sarah could possibly teach her, by watching her, day by day, from the time she was a very young child. She had learned from her mother's mistakes as well as her triumphs, and Sarah was content, knowing the confident, brave, loving young woman her daughter had become. For as long as she lived, Sarah would always be there whenever her daughter needed a compassionate listener or a shoulder to cry on, but now she must have faith and let her daughter go on without her, her husband by her side.

Soon the appointed hour arrived. Sarah and the bridesmaids escorted Caroline from the manor to the edge of the north gardens, where, through the evergreens, they glimpsed the rows of white chairs—sufficiently dry, or so Sarah hoped—filling with guests as the ushers led them to their seats. The minister stood in the gazebo, clasping his prayer book and smiling broadly as he faced the gathering of friends and family. Seated behind him, the string quartet played "Simple Gifts," which made Sarah think fondly of Bonnie, who had loved the traditional Shaker tune. So many dear friends would have wanted to be there that day, to celebrate and to share in their happiness, but although Sarah missed them all, she knew they were with her in spirit, blessing her with their love, blessing the day.

"It's a good thing we didn't ask the musicians to come to yesterday's rehearsal," Caroline murmured in her ear. "We don't have an umbrella big enough for that cello."

Sarah muffled a laugh and squeezed her daughter's hand. Then James appeared, and she had only time enough for one last hug and a quick, whispered, "I love you, Caroline," before James escorted her to her chair in the front row, where her mother already waited, beaming proudly. Everyone murmured expectantly at the sight of the mother of the bride taking her seat, the signal that the ceremony was about to begin.

As the string quartet struck up Beethoven's "Ode to Joy," Sarah smiled up at Leo, who stood in the gazebo between the minister and his brother, his gaze eager as he looked for his bride. One by one the groomsmen escorted the bridesmaids down the aisle, the couples parting when they reached the gazebo and taking their places on opposite sides.

Then the music swelled, and everyone rose, and through a glimmer of happy tears, Sarah watched her daughter enter on her father's arm, as radiant and happy, as excited and nervous, as sure to find joy and hope, laughter and tears with the man she loved as any bride had ever been.

As she drew closer, Caroline's eyes met Sarah's, and she smiled.

ACKNOWLEDGMENTS

It is a privilege and a pleasure to work with Denise Roy, Maria Massie, Ava Kavyani, Christine Ball, and everyone at Dutton, and I'm grateful for their contributions to *The Wedding Quilt* and the Elm Creek Quilts series.

I wish to thank my friends and family for their support as I wrote this book, especially Geraldine Neidenbach, Heather Neidenbach, Marty Chiaverini, and Brian Grover, who read early drafts and provided useful feedback. Many thanks to Nic Neidenbach for his informed predictions regarding the future of gaming and to James Antony for his thorough explanation of the university tenure process.

Most of all, I thank my wonderful husband, Marty, for his love and encouragement, and my sons, Nicholas and Michael, for filling my life with laughter, hope, love, and joy. You have enriched my life beyond measure, and I am forever thankful.

Jennifer Chiaverini

Coming from Plume in February 2013

ISBN 978-0-452-29899-6

Turn the page for a sneak peek...

www.elmcreek.net

Plume
A member of Penguin Group (USA) Inc.
www.penguin.com

Chapter One

Clad in the faded apron she had sewn from a cotton feed sack, Rosa sat at the foot of the kitchen table sipping a cup of coffee and planning her day while her husband bolted down his bacon and eggs. Sitting quietly side by side on her left, twelve-year-old Marta, and Lupita, almost five, ate their oatmeal in silence, sneaking furtive glances at each other or at Rosa but avoiding John. Rosa couldn't blame them. She didn't like to draw his attention either.

John wiped his mouth, pushed back his chair, and stood. "I'm going out."

"When will you be back?" She knew as soon as she spoke that the question was a mistake.

"Why?" he asked, immediately suspicious. "Are you planning to have company?"

"Not unless someone comes for their mail." John was the postmaster for the entire Arboles Valley and ran the post office out of their front room. Residents from the small town a few miles to the west and neighbors from nearby farms might stop by at any time throughout the day to post letters or pick up the bundles of envelopes and catalogues Rosa tied up with twine for them. "I only wanted to know when I should have your lunch ready."

"I won't be back for lunch."

The girls incautiously brightened, but John had already left the kitchen and didn't glimpse their sudden smiles. The front door squeaked open and banged shut, and a few moments later, Rosa heard John's roadster roar to life in the garage. She listened for the sound of gravel churning beneath the new tires as he pulled out, and for the sound of the engine fading as he sped away. Only then could she take a deep breath and feel the tension leave her face and neck and shoulders. Even the kitchen windows seemed to let in more of the warm California sunshine in her husband's absence, and the breeze that had felt clammy and oppressive as she served him his breakfast seemed newly refreshing as it carried ocean mists over the Santa Monica Mountains to the small adobe farmhouse on the mesa where Rosa had lived since her wedding day. Even after thirteen years of marriage and eight children, four of whom still lived, the adobe felt more like John's home than theirs together.

As soon as only birdsong and the wind drifted through the open windows, Marta and Lupita began planning their Saturday adventures in earnest. "Mamá, do you think Ana will feel good enough to play today?" asked Lupita.

Rosa glanced down the hallway toward the bedroom where her middle daughter slept fitfully in the bedroom with Miguel, who at two years old was still her baby. "I don't know, *mija*. I hope so."

She hoped so every morning, but far too often, Ana could do little more than sit on the front step and smile as she watched her sisters play beneath the orange trees. She had become so accustomed to her illness that she had long ago forgotten to be jealous.

Rosa's anger rose, sharp and sudden. John insisted he had no money to spare to search for a better doctor for Ana and Miguel, one wise and skilled enough to cure them of the terrible affliction that had already taken the lives of four of their brothers and sisters, and yet he had enough to waste on that ridiculous roadster, a lavish, impractical, and frivolous expense for a rye farmer in the rural Arboles Valley. When John first brought it home, beaming proudly through the open top, he demanded that Rosa go for a ride with him. "I will never set foot in that machine," Rosa declared, "unless it's to take Ana and Miguel to Oxnard or Los Angeles to see a new doctor."

"I've told you," said John, his dark blue eyes narrowing. "We can't afford it."

"We can't afford it now," she retorted, gesturing to the car angrily—and then she reeled as he struck her across the face.

In the weeks that followed, Rosa decided that the only good to come of John's extravagance was that the roadster took him away from home, and kept him away for hours at a time on errands he did not bother to explain. As the harvest approached, the rye fields lay forgotten beneath the September sun, except when Lars Jorgensen—her childhood sweetheart and dearest friend until she married John—tended them for Rosa and the children's sake. They would not starve, thanks to Lars's kindness, but if John had mortgaged the farm to pay for that roadster, what would become of them when the bill came due?

As much as Rosa despised the roadster, sometimes she was tempted to lift the keys from John's coat pocket while he slept, steal out into the night with the children, help them into the car, and speed away, far, far away where John would never find them. But there the dream came to an abrupt halt, because she knew that escape alone was not enough to ensure the children's safety. Where would they go? How would they live? What could she do to keep a roof over their heads, clothes on their backs, and food in their tummies? The litany of questions always led to the same bleak conclusion: She had nowhere to go, no money, no means to provide for her children. And she was certain John would pursue them no matter how great a distance separated them. He would not relent. If Rosa ran off with the children, she could never stop running. John would want her back, even though he no longer loved her. He would want the children back, even those he surely suspected were not his.

Ana and Miguel woke by mid-morning to a day that had turned overcast and breezy, with a metallic taste in the air that hinted at coming rain. While Marta and Lupita played outside, Rosa tried to entice Ana and Miguel to eat by drizzling honey on their biscuits and promising them a story if they each ate a little. Miguel turned his head away every time she brought the fork close to his mouth, but Ana bravely took a few bites and glowed when Rosa praised her. Rosa had saved the best of the milk for them, but no sooner had they drained their cups than it all came back up again—milk, biscuits, honey, everything. After Rosa cleaned them up and helped Ana change into a fresh blouse, she asked Ana to mind her little brother while she cleaned the floor. Tearfully Ana apologized for the mess, wiping her eyes with her sleeve as she held a restless Miguel on her lap.

"It's all right, *mija*," Rosa assured her, on her hands and knees with the rag and bucket of soapy water. "It's not your fault."

Drawn by the sound of Ana's sobs, Marta darted into the

adobe with Lupita close behind. "What's wrong?" asked Marta, eyeing the scene from the doorway before hurrying to take Miguel from Ana.

"Breakfast didn't agree with them," replied Rosa as calmly as she could manage, but Marta caught her eye, and she saw her own worry reflected in her eldest daughter's face. At twelve, Marta had seen two younger brothers and two sisters waste away, and she knew as well as Rosa did that not one of them had reached their sixth birthday. At eight years old, Ana had endured the affliction longer than any of her siblings. Sometimes Ana's refusal to succumb gave Rosa hope that Ana might yet survive to adulthood. More often, Rosa feared that each passing day brought Ana closer to the end. Miguel, who had fallen ill shortly after his second birthday, was much weaker than his sister and probably would not reach his third birthday.

Quickly Rosa turned her head away and closed her eyes to hold back her tears. If she gave in to her grief and anger, she might never stop weeping. She must not let the children know how close she had come to despair.

While Rosa finished cleaning the floor, Marta took charge of her younger siblings, carrying Miguel on her hip as she led her sisters outside. When Rosa went to empty the bucket, she spotted the children in the shade of the barn playing school—Ana's favorite game, one she could play while seated and without tiring herself. Although her sisters preferred to run and dance, they indulged her, knowing Ana longed to attend the Arboles School with them. She had for a single year, but when she began missing too many days, the teacher suggested that it would be best if Rosa kept her home.

"But Ana is so bright," Rosa had protested. "She loves to learn. Her heart would break if we didn't let her go to school."

"The long day exhausts her," the teacher had gently replied. "And some of the other parents are . . . concerned."

She didn't need to elaborate. Rosa had already lost three children by then, and the Barclay children's mysterious illnesses had become the source of much speculation and suspicion throughout the valley. Rosa was well aware of the rumors, the whispered conversations that fell silent when she approached neighbors and former friends in the grocery store. She knew some parents warned their children not to play with her girls, and entire families changed pews if the Barclays sat next to them in church. There had even been talk of moving the Arboles Valley Post Office from the Barclays' front room, but since John was postmaster and no one wanted to spend the money to build a new post office, the grumblings eventually faded. Rosa told herself that her neighbors did not mean to be unkind, that it would be difficult not to be suspicious, even fearful, when so much misfortune had beset their family. But understanding her neighbors' fears did not mean giving in to them, especially when her daughter's happiness was at stake.

"The other students are in no danger," Rosa had replied tightly. "Marta and Lupita are with Ana every day, and they haven't fallen ill."

"I'm not agreeing that their fears are reasonable, but either way, Ana would be far better off at home with you. And for your sake—" The teacher hesitated. "In the years to come, won't you regret every moment you didn't spend with the poor dear?"

Rosa's throat closed around a retort, and without another word, she gathered up her girls and took them home. She taught Ana herself after that, going over Marta's old lessons in reading, math, and spelling at the kitchen table. Some days Ana was too weary to study, but when she was strong enough, she absorbed every lesson with quiet, solemn purposefulness, as if she were determined to learn as much as possible in the brief time fate would grant her.

She rarely studied anymore, and when she was too tired to hold up a book, Marta read to her. "If I grow up, I want to be a librarian," she told Rosa dreamily one evening as Rosa tucked her in. "Think of all those books. Think of reading all day long, every day."

"I think there's more to being a librarian than reading all day," said Rosa, with a catch in her throat. She longed to assure Ana that of course she would grow up, that it was nonsense to think she might not, but Rosa wouldn't lie, and Ana wouldn't believe her if she did.

While the children played outside, Rosa made the beds, brought in the laundry from the line, and tended her garden. Gray clouds filled the sky from west to east, so she worked quickly, spurred on by the threat of rain. At noon she called the children in for lunch—corn tortillas and rice with fresh tomatoes and mild peppers, with water to drink, since they had no more milk. Miraculously, Ana and Miguel kept the food down, but the nourishment failed to invigorate them, so Rosa put them down for a nap while Marta and Lupita played with dolls in the front room.

She was tidying the kitchen when she heard an automobile approaching—not the smooth purr of John's roadster but the rattle and growl of an older and far more welcome vehicle.

Quickly she smoothed her hair back from her face and snatched off her soiled apron. When a knock sounded on the door, she hastened to answer it only to find Elizabeth Nelson standing on the doorstep, a tan cloche with a jaunty upturned brim upon her bobbed blonde curls. Behind her, Rosa glimpsed the Jorgensens' car parked near the garage, but Lars was nowhere to be seen.

Rosa quickly quashed her disappointment. Elizabeth, a newcomer to the Arboles Valley, had flouted local custom by befriending her, undeterred by her children's strange sickness and John's sarcastic malice. She and her husband, Henry, had moved to the Arboles Valley a few months before, carrying with them the photographs and maps of the thriving cattle ranch they believed they had purchased from a land agent back in Pennsylvania. When they came to the post office to pick up the deed of trust, they discovered that they had been swindled. Triumph Ranch did not exist—or rather, it had once, but Rosa's great-grandparents had sold it to the Jorgensen family long ago and the old Spanish name had all but faded into memory. Suddenly penniless, the Nelsons found work as hired hands on the Jorgensen ranch, and ever since, John had never missed an opportunity to mock Elizabeth when she came to the post office to collect letters addressed to Mrs. Henry Nelson of Triumph Ranch. Apparently Elizabeth would rather endure his jeers than admit to her family back in Pennsylvania that she and Henry had been cheated out of their life savings.

Before Rosa could greet her, Elizabeth's pretty features drew together in concern. "What's wrong?"

"Nothing." When Elizabeth looked dubious, Rosa quickly amended, "Nothing new. Nothing that hasn't been wrong for a very long time." She opened the door wider and beckoned Elizabeth inside. "Please come in while I get your letters."

Marta and Lupita glanced up warily when Rosa led Elizabeth into the front room, but they quickly recognized the pretty young farmwife with the blonde bob, so after returning her bright smile with bashful grins, they returned to their play.

Rosa left them and went to retrieve the Nelsons' and Jorgensens' mail from the kitchen. Although John bore the title of postmaster and collected the paycheck, Rosa sorted the mail and was most often the one who met the valley's residents at the door when they came to collect their letters and parcels. Since purchasing the roadster, John had been too busy touring the countryside to pay any more attention to the daily mail than he did the ripening crops. The work had fallen entirely to Rosa, and as she sorted envelopes and boxes on the kitchen table in between tending children and folding laundry and preparing meals, she wished that she could claim John's wages for herself. She couldn't help tallying his income in her mind and calculating how many months he would have had to work, saving every dime, in order to purchase that loathsome automobile. How could he have amassed enough money unless he had mortgaged the farm?

Rosa had to know.

As soon as Elizabeth left, she would search John's desk for bank documents. She had already checked the strongbox where they kept the deed to the farm and other important papers safe from brush fires and earthquakes, but of course he had not put any mortgage papers there, where she could easily find them. He would have put them somewhere out of sight, someplace where she wouldn't accidentally discover them while dusting or putting away clothes.

Rosa brought the bundles of letters back to the front room and gave them to Elizabeth, who thanked her and added, "I found something in the cabin that belongs to you."

The ramshackle cabin on the Jorgensen ranch? Rosa had visited it many times, long before the Nelsons had made it their home, but she had always been careful to leave nothing behind.

Bewildered, Rosa waited while Elizabeth took the mail out to Lars's car and returned with two folded quilts—but Rosa knew she had never left any quilts at the cabin.

While Rosa, Marta, and Lupita looked on, Elizabeth set one quilt on the sofa and began to unfold the other. Rosa glimpsed homespun plaids and wools in deep blues and dark barn reds and forest greens, sturdy and warm—and suddenly she recognized the pattern. With an eager gasp, she reached out to take the bottom corners of the quilt, lifting them so the quilt unfurled between her hands and Elizabeth's. The quilt was comprised not of square blocks but of hexagons, each composed of twelve triangular wedges with a smaller hexagon appliquéd in the center where the points met. The quilt had been well used and well loved, with tiny quilting stitches outlining each piece and many more arranged in concentric curves so the hexagons resembled wagon wheels in motion. The slight shrinkage of the wool and batting in the wash throughout the years had created a patina of wrinkles all over the quilt, and Rosa could almost imagine she knew each one by heart.

"*Dios mío,*" she murmured.

"It is your great-grandmother's, isn't it?" prompted Elizabeth. "I recognized it from the photograph you showed me."

"Without a doubt, it is hers." As Rosa's gaze traveled over the quilt, long-forgotten memories came alive—her grandmother in a rocking chair, the quilt tucked around her lap. Rosa and her younger brother, Carlos, draping the quilt over a table and pretending it was a tent high in the Santa Monica Mountains. Climbing beneath it and snuggling up to her mother after fleeing to her parents' bedroom in the dark hours of the night, frightened awake by nightmares. Yes, she knew the quilt intimately. "It is just as I remember it."

"Almost but not exactly," said Elizabeth. "It needed some mending. I matched the fabric as best as I could when I replaced worn pieces."

Rosa smiled, touched by her friend's thoughtfulness, pained by the realization that it had been a long time since anyone had shown her such kindness. "Then it is even lovelier than I remember." She sat down in a rocking chair, draped the quilt across her lap, and ran her hands over it. The fabric had softened with age, the colors mellowed, but it was no less beautiful. "I remember my mother cuddling me in this quilt when I was a little girl no bigger than Lupita. My great-grandmother made it when she was a young bride-to-be in Texas. Her parents had arranged for her to marry my great-grandfather through a cousin who lived in Los Angeles. The first time she saw him was the day he came to San Antonio to bring her back to El Rancho Triunfo."

"Triumph Ranch," said Elizabeth.

"Yes, and for many years the name rang true." Rosa could almost hear her grandmother's voice as she remembered her stories of days gone by, so full of happiness and sorrow, joy and disappointment. "They raised barley and rye. One hundred head of cattle grazed where the sheep pasture and the apricot orchard stand today. But my family lost everything in a terrible drought, the worst ever to strike the Arboles Valley. Every farm in the valley suffered. Some families sold their land after the first summer without rain, but by the time my great-grandparents decided to put El Rancho Triunfo up for sale the following year, there were no buyers. My great-grandparents sold all the cattle to slaughterhouses rather than let them starve. They were thankful and relieved when Mrs. Jorgensen's grandfather bought the ranch and permitted them to remain on the land in exchange for their labor. The rains fell two months later. My great-grandparents never forgave themselves for not holding out a little while longer, for giving up too soon and accepting less than the land was truly worth."

"They never forgave the Jorgensens either," said Elizabeth carefully, "or so I've heard."

"That is also true." The elder Rodriguezes had passed their anger on to their children, who had passed it on to Rosa's mother, Isabel. Isabel had mourned the loss of the land all her life, and she had resented the Jorgensens from the time she was a young woman until she took her last breath. Her enmity extended even to the Jorgensen descendants, who had nothing to do with the sale of El Rancho Triunfo.

Rosa stroked her great-grandmother's quilt in wonder while Elizabeth unfolded the second quilt and held it up high by the corners so that only the bottom edge touched the floor. "It's lovely," Rosa said, wondering why Elizabeth believed the wrinkled, faded quilt belonged to her. Instead of the dark homespun plaids and wools of the hexagon quilt, it had been pieced from a variety of cottons, satins, and other fabrics that looked to be decades more recent. Rosa admired it politely, but she soon felt her gaze drawn back to her great-grandmother's quilt. She could hardly believe she held it once more, and she could not imagine how it had come to be in the dilapidated old cabin on the Jorgensen ranch, especially knowing how her mother had felt about the Jorgensens. The last time Rosa had seen the quilt, it had been spread upon her parents' bed in her childhood home.

"I call this quilt the Arboles Valley Star." Elizabeth folded the second quilt in half with the pieced top showing and draped it over the sofa. "I found it with your great-grandmother's. Don't you recognize it?"

Although Rosa didn't, she examined it more carefully for

Elizabeth's sake. The complex, intricate pattern resembled the traditional Blazing Star in that each segment of the eight-pointed stars was comprised of four congruent diamonds, but the smaller diamonds fanned out in a half star in the four corner squares of each block, giving the quilt the illusion of brilliance and fire. Great care must have gone into the making of each block for the divided stars to fit the corners exactly so. Few quilters had the patience for such painstaking work, and she knew only one personally—her late mother. But Rosa had never seen this quilt among her mother's collection.

"I've never seen it before," she finally admitted, reluctant to disappoint Elizabeth. "I suppose I could look through the album and see if it appears in any of my family's photographs, but I've looked at them so many times. I think I would have recognized this quilt if it were in any of them. It seems too new for my great-grandmother's handiwork."

"I thought you had made it."

"Me?" Rosa shook her head. "Why would you think that?"

"Because of this."

Elizabeth turned over the quilt and showed Rosa a square of lace-trimmed satin appliquéd to the back. Upon the square, a wreath of needlepoint rosebuds surrounded a pair of intertwined initials embroidered in silk—R. D. and L. J.

For a moment, Rosa could only stare in stunned amazement at the letters, but then she tentatively touched her fingertips to the embroidered monograms. R. D. for Rosa Diaz, her maiden name. And L. J. could refer only to—

"What is it?" Elizabeth asked, concerned. "Do you remember the quilt now?"

"No," Rosa replied, bewildered. "I've never seen this quilt, but I—I do know this embroidery. This is my mother's work.

She made these stitches. And this satin and lace. It came from Ana's baptismal cap."

Ana's baptism, an occasion that should have been full of joy, had been shrouded in grief, following soon after the death of Rosa's firstborn son. Though John had banished Isabel from the Barclay farm, he was unaware that she had come to the church to share in her granddaughter's holy day. But Rosa had known her mother would attend, just as she had attended her other grandchildren's christenings.

After the ceremony, Rosa had spotted her mother at the back of the church, standing in a darkened alcove and disguised by a heavy black veil, and she felt a pang of gratitude and shame. Her mother shouldn't have to lurk in the back of the church at her granddaughter's baptism; she should have sat proudly in the first pew, as John's mother had done, as was a grandmother's privilege. Trailing behind the others as they left the church, Rosa drew the quilt over Ana's head to protect her from the cold November rain, and as she did, she gently swept off Ana's soft satin cap, trimmed in lace to match her baptismal gown, and let it fall to the floor of the vestibule behind them. Rosa knew her mother would keep it, recognizing it not only as a memento of the blessed occasion but also an apology for all that Isabel had been denied that day—and had been in days past, and would be in years yet to come.

"But—why? And—when?" How had the pure white satin of Ana's christening cap come to appear in this unfamiliar quilt embroidered with Rosa's initials and Lars's—Lars, the man whose family Isabel had despised, the man Isabel had forbidden her to marry? Rosa swiftly turned the quilt over and studied the pieced stars, running her hands over the patches until her fingers came to rest on a piece of ivory sateen that was wondrously, painfully familiar. "This was from her wedding gown. I know it. And this—" She touched a triangle of pink floral calico. She could never forget the soft cotton print she herself had sewn so lovingly. "This was from the dress Marta wore on her first day of school. But how did my mother come to have it? I don't understand. Where did you find this quilt?"

"Both quilts were in an old steamer trunk in the cabin," said Elizabeth. "On the Jorgensen farm, where your family once lived. I assumed your grandmother had forgotten the older quilt there when they moved out, but as for the newer—"

"Oh, no, no. They left nothing behind. The homespun-and-wool quilt was in my mother's home all my life. It never left her bed. But this star quilt—" Rosa looked from one quilt to the other, thinking. "My mother must have taken the quilts to the cabin and left them there. But I don't understand—" Suddenly Rosa grew very still, and all at once, she knew. "She wanted me to have them. And she could not bring them to me here."

"Why not?"

"My husband would not allow my parents on his property, not even to visit their grandchildren. When I wanted to see my mother, we had to meet on the mesa. Once a week, when John went to pick up the mail from the train station, I would take the children to see her. You know the place." Everyone knew the story; everyone knew the place her mother had dearly loved, the place where she had slipped and fallen to her death. The authorities had declared it a suicide, but Rosa knew it must have been a terrible accident. Isabel never would have desecrated the place where they and the children had enjoyed brief moments of happiness.

"Rosa," said Elizabeth warily. "The day your mother died—were you supposed to meet her on the mesa?"